MARVEL-VERSE
DOCTOR STRANGE

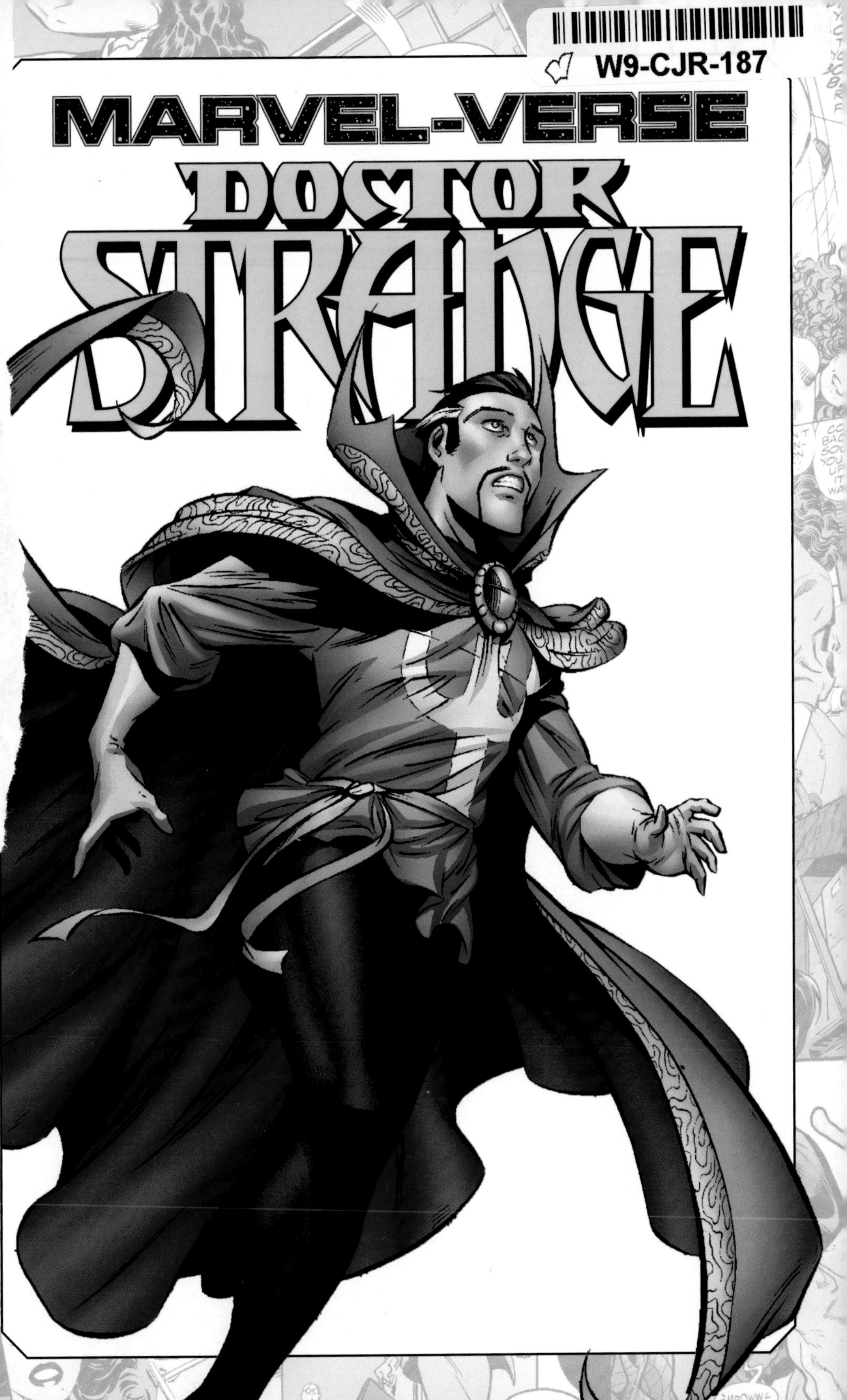

MARVEL-VERSE
DOCTOR STRANGE

UNCANNY ORIGINS #12

WRITER: **LEN WEIN**
ARTIST: **MARC CAMPOS**
COLORIST: **BOB SHAREN**
LETTERER: **JACK MORELLI**
EDITOR: **JOE ANDREANI**

STRANGE TALES #126-127

WRITER & EDITOR: **STAN LEE**
ARTIST: **STEVE DITKO**
LETTERERS: **ART SIMEK** & **SAM ROSEN**

MARVEL-VERSE: DOCTOR STRANGE. Contains material originally published in magazine form as UNCANNY ORIGINS (1996) #12, DOCTOR STRANGE (1974) #55, MARVEL ADVENTURES HULK (2007) #5, MARVEL ADVENTURES SUPER HEROES (2008) #5 and STRANGE TALES (1951) #126-127. First printing 2021. ISBN 978-1-302-93081-3. Published by MARVEL WORLDWIDE, INC., a subsidiary of MARVEL ENTERTAINMENT, LLC. OFFICE OF PUBLICATION: 1290 Avenue of the Americas, New York, NY 10104. © 2021 MARVEL No similarity between any of the names, characters, persons, and/or institutions in this magazine with those of any living or dead person or institution is intended, and any such similarity which may exist is purely coincidental. **Printed in Canada.** KEVIN FEIGE, Chief Creative Officer; DAN BUCKLEY, President, Marvel Entertainment; JOE QUESADA, EVP & Creative Director; DAVID BOGART, Associate Publisher & SVP of Talent Affairs; TOM BREVOORT, VP, Executive Editor; NICK LOWE, Executive Editor, VP of Content, Digital Publishing; DAVID GABRIEL, VP of Print & Digital Publishing; JEFF YOUNGQUIST, VP of Production & Special Projects; ALEX MORALES, Director of Publishing Operations; DAN EDINGTON, Managing Editor; RICKEY PURDIN, Director of Talent Relations; JENNIFER GRÜNWALD, Senior Editor, Special Projects; SUSAN CRESPI, Production Manager; STAN LEE, Chairman Emeritus. For information regarding advertising in Marvel Comics or on Marvel.com, please contact Vit DeBellis, Custom Solutions & Integrated Advertising Manager, at vdebellis@marvel.com. For Marvel subscription inquiries, please call 888-511-5480. **Manufactured between 6/25/2021 and 7/27/2021 by SOLISCO PRINTERS, SCOTT, QC, CANADA.**

10 9 8 7 6 5 4 3 2 1

DOCTOR STRANGE #55

WRITER: **ROGER STERN**
PENCILER: **MICHAEL GOLDEN**
INKER: **TERRY AUSTIN**
COLORIST: **GLYNIS WEIN**
LETTERER: **JIM NOVAK**
ASSISTANT EDITOR: **ANN NOCENTI**
EDITOR: **AL MILGROM**

MARVEL ADVENTURES HULK #5

WRITER: **PAUL BENJAMIN**
PENCILER: **DAVID NAKAYAMA**
INKER: **GARY MARTIN**
COLORIST: **MICHELLE MADSEN**
LETTERER: **DAVE SHARPE**
COVER ART: **JUAN SANTACRUZ** & **CHRIS SOTOMAYOR**
ASSISTANT EDITOR: **JORDAN D. WHITE**
EDITOR: **MARK PANICCIA**

MARVEL ADVENTURES SUPER HEROES #5

WRITER: **PAUL TOBIN**
PENCILER: **JACOPO CAMAGNI**
INKER: **NORMAN LEE**
COLORIST: **GURU-EFX**
LETTERER: **DAVE SHARPE**
COVER ART: **ROGER CRUZ** & **WIL QUINTANA**
CONSULTING EDITORS: **MARK PANICCIA** & **RALPH MACCHIO**
EDITOR: **NATHAN COSBY**

DOCTOR STRANGE CREATED BY **STAN LEE** & **STEVE DITKO**

COLLECTION EDITOR: **JENNIFER GRÜNWALD** ASSISTANT EDITOR: **DANIEL KIRCHHOFFER** ASSISTANT MANAGING EDITOR: **MAIA LOY**
ASSISTANT MANAGING EDITOR: **LISA MONTALBANO** ASSOCIATE MANAGER, DIGITAL ASSETS: **JOE HOCHSTEIN**
MASTERWORKS EDITOR: **CORY SEDLMEIER** VP PRODUCTION & SPECIAL PROJECTS: **JEFF YOUNGQUIST**
RESEARCH: **JESS HARROLD** BOOK DESIGNERS: **STACIE ZUCKER** & **ADAM DEL RE** WITH **JAY BOWEN**
SVP PRINT, SALES & MARKETING: **DAVID GABRIEL** EDITOR IN CHIEF: **C.B. CEBULSKI**

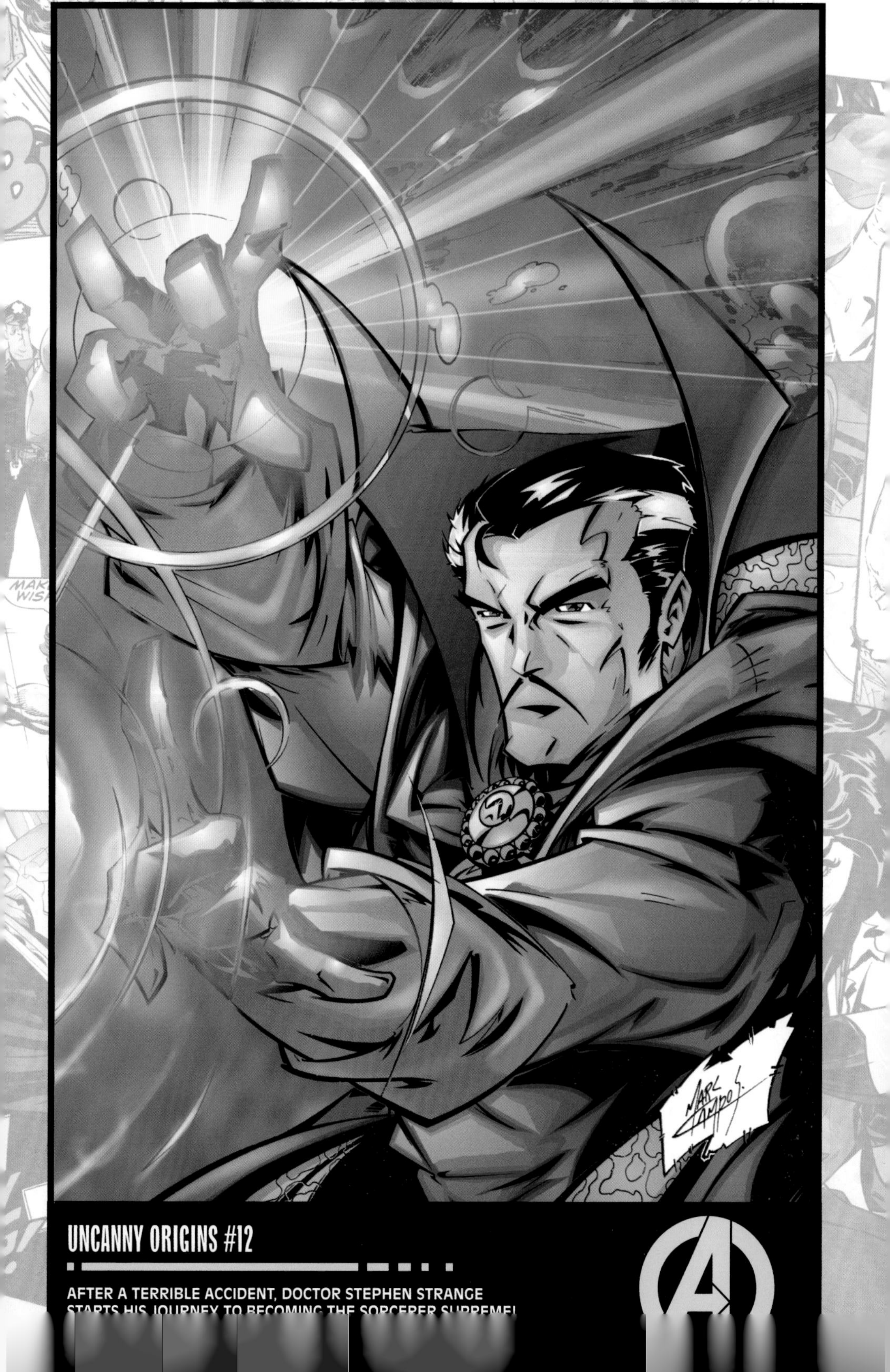

UNCANNY ORIGINS #12

AFTER A TERRIBLE ACCIDENT, DOCTOR STEPHEN STRANGE STARTS HIS JOURNEY TO BECOMING THE SORCERER SUPREME!

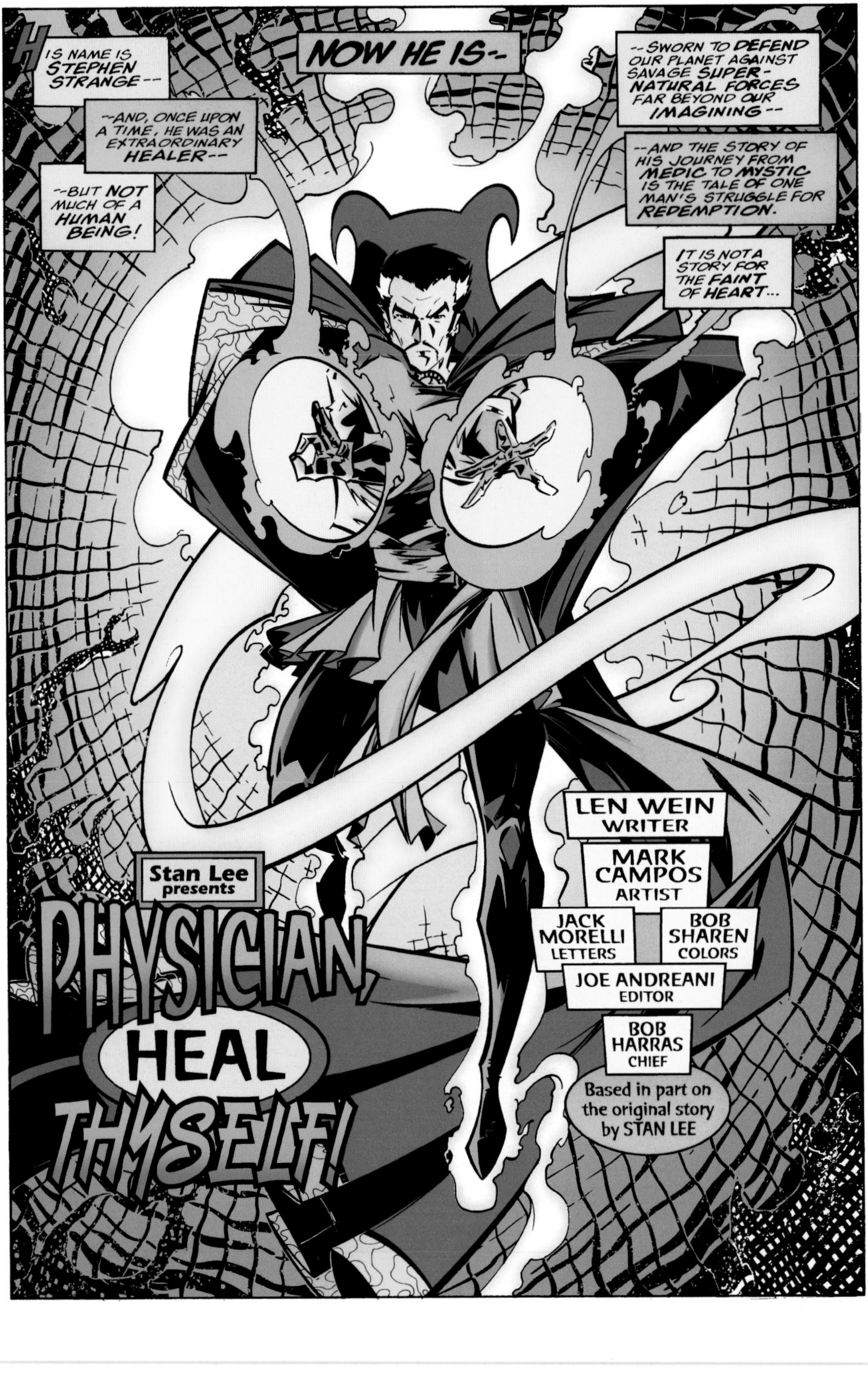
HIS NAME IS STEPHEN STRANGE--
--AND, ONCE UPON A TIME, HE WAS AN EXTRAORDINARY HEALER--
--BUT NOT MUCH OF A HUMAN BEING!
NOW HE IS--
--SWORN TO DEFEND OUR PLANET AGAINST SAVAGE SUPER-NATURAL FORCES FAR BEYOND OUR IMAGINING--
--AND THE STORY OF HIS JOURNEY FROM MEDIC TO MYSTIC IS THE TALE OF ONE MAN'S STRUGGLE FOR REDEMPTION.
IT IS NOT A STORY FOR THE FAINT OF HEART...
Stan Lee presents
PHYSICIAN, HEAL THYSELF!
LEN WEIN WRITER
MARK CAMPOS ARTIST
JACK MORELLI LETTERS
BOB SHAREN COLORS
JOE ANDREANI EDITOR
BOB HARRAS CHIEF
Based in part on the original story by STAN LEE

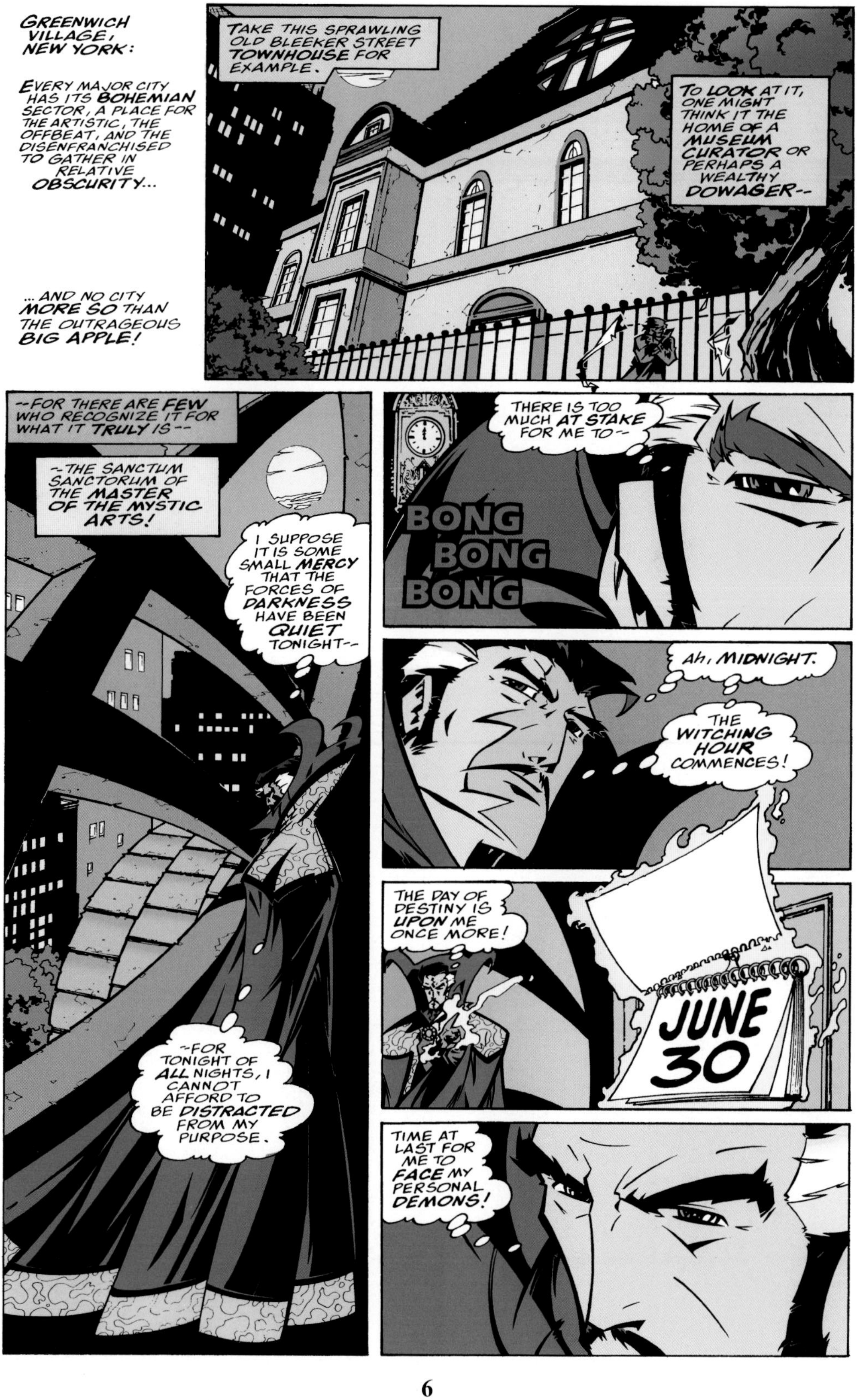
GREENWICH VILLAGE, NEW YORK:
EVERY MAJOR CITY HAS ITS BOHEMIAN SECTOR, A PLACE FOR THE ARTISTIC, THE OFFBEAT, AND THE DISENFRANCHISED TO GATHER IN RELATIVE OBSCURITY...
TAKE THIS SPRAWLING OLD BLEEKER STREET TOWNHOUSE FOR EXAMPLE.
TO LOOK AT IT, ONE MIGHT THINK IT THE HOME OF A MUSEUM CURATOR OR PERHAPS A WEALTHY DOWAGER--
...AND NO CITY MORE SO THAN THE OUTRAGEOUS BIG APPLE!
--FOR THERE ARE FEW WHO RECOGNIZE IT FOR WHAT IT TRULY IS--
--THE SANCTUM SANCTORUM OF THE MASTER OF THE MYSTIC ARTS!
I SUPPOSE IT IS SOME SMALL MERCY THAT THE FORCES OF DARKNESS HAVE BEEN QUIET TONIGHT--
--FOR TONIGHT OF ALL NIGHTS, I CANNOT AFFORD TO BE DISTRACTED FROM MY PURPOSE.
THERE IS TOO MUCH AT STAKE FOR ME TO--
BONG BONG BONG
Ah, MIDNIGHT.
THE WITCHING HOUR COMMENCES!
THE DAY OF DESTINY IS UPON ME ONCE MORE!
JUNE 30
TIME AT LAST FOR ME TO FACE MY PERSONAL DEMONS!

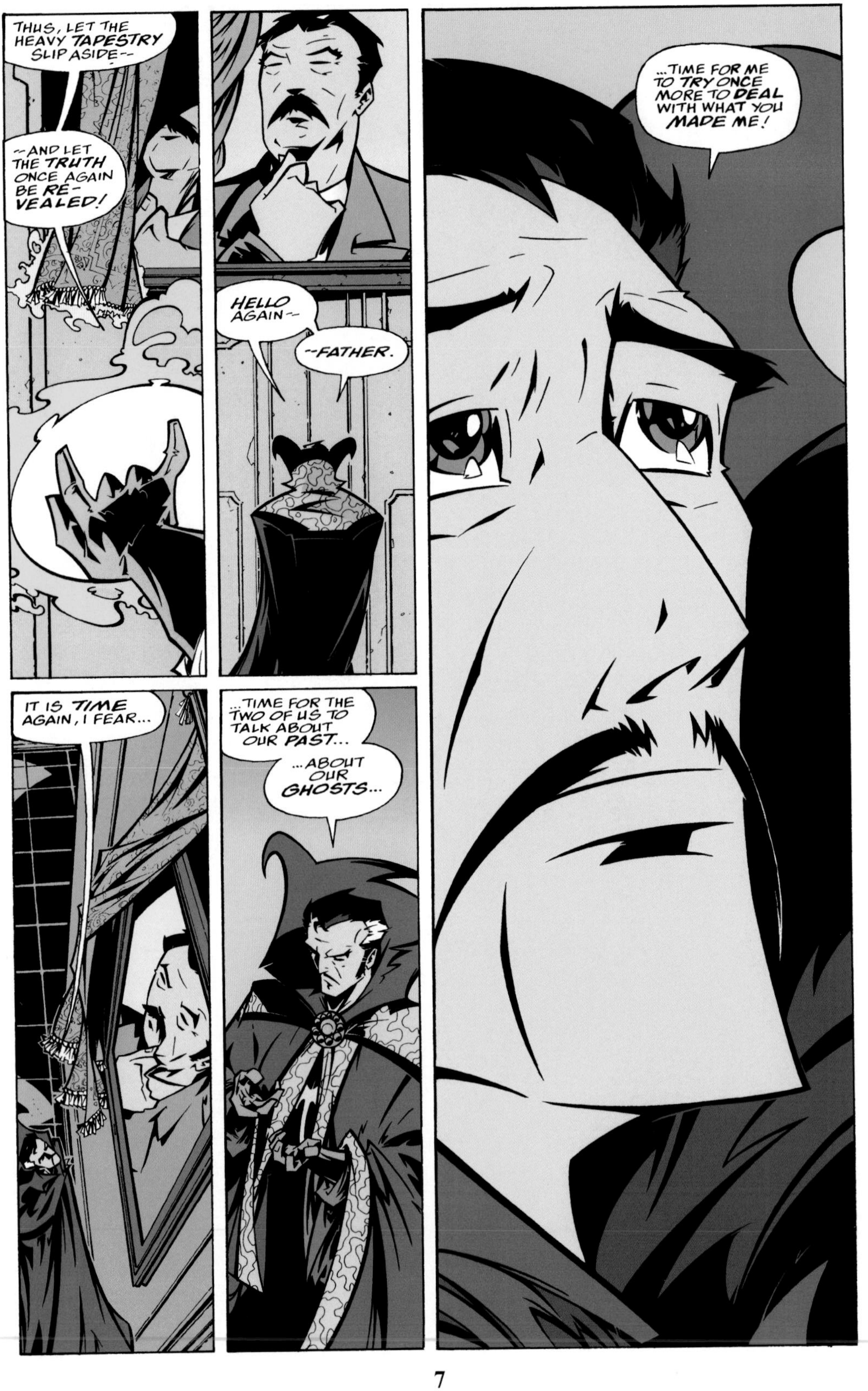
THUS, LET THE HEAVY TAPESTRY SLIP ASIDE--
--AND LET THE TRUTH ONCE AGAIN BE RE-VEALED!
HELLO AGAIN--
--FATHER.
IT IS TIME AGAIN, I FEAR...
...TIME FOR THE TWO OF US TO TALK ABOUT OUR PAST...
...ABOUT OUR GHOSTS...
...TIME FOR ME TO TRY ONCE MORE TO DEAL WITH WHAT YOU MADE ME!

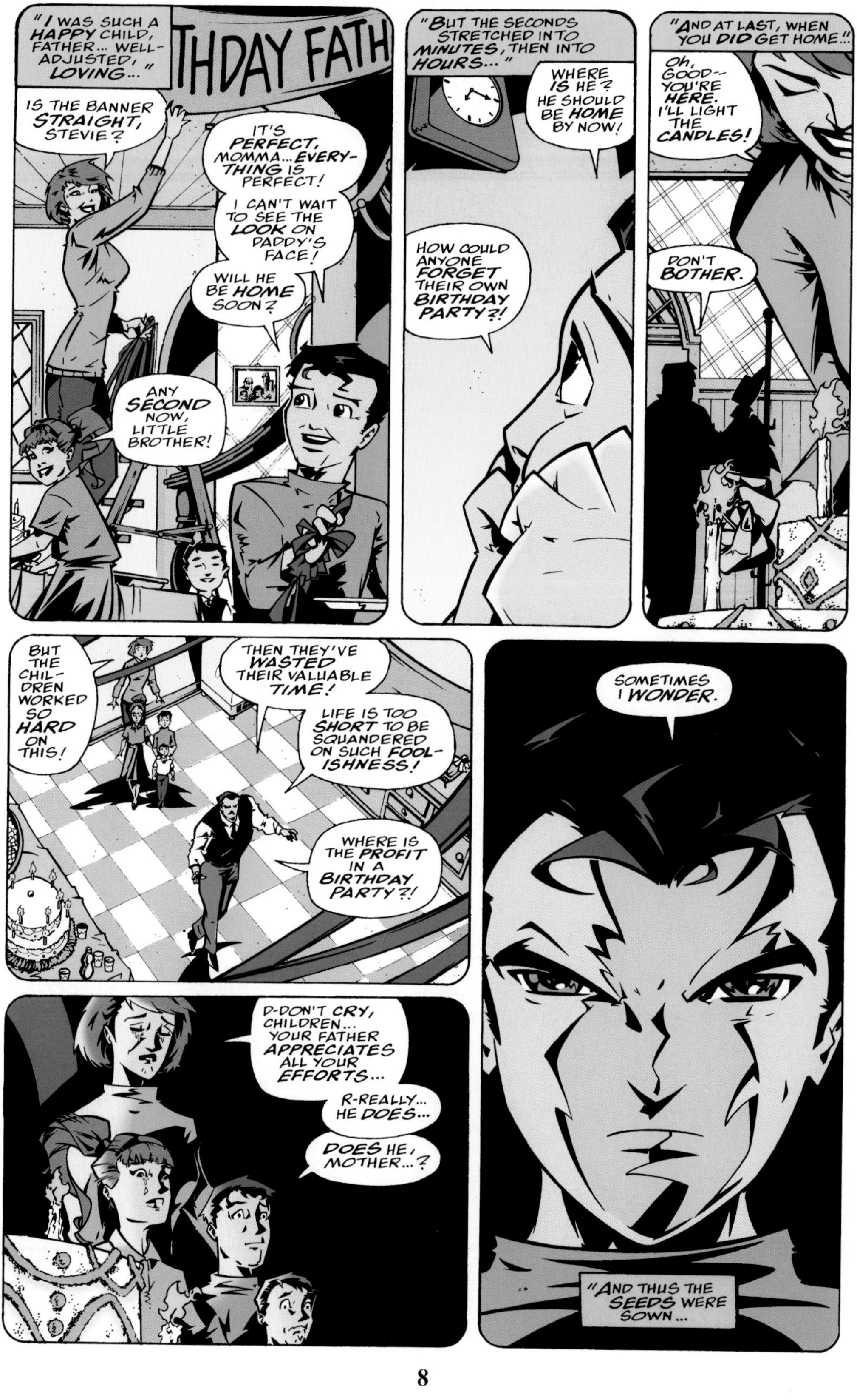

"I WAS SUCH A HAPPY CHILD, FATHER... WELL-ADJUSTED, LOVING..."
THDAY FATH
IS THE BANNER STRAIGHT, STEVIE?
IT'S PERFECT, MOMMA... EVERYTHING IS PERFECT!
I CAN'T WAIT TO SEE THE LOOK ON DADDY'S FACE!
WILL HE BE HOME SOON?
ANY SECOND NOW, LITTLE BROTHER!
"BUT THE SECONDS STRETCHED INTO MINUTES, THEN INTO HOURS..."
WHERE IS HE? HE SHOULD BE HOME BY NOW!
HOW COULD ANYONE FORGET THEIR OWN BIRTHDAY PARTY?!
"AND AT LAST, WHEN YOU DID GET HOME..."
Oh, GOOD-- YOU'RE HERE. I'LL LIGHT THE CANDLES!
DON'T BOTHER.
BUT THE CHILDREN WORKED SO HARD ON THIS!
THEN THEY'VE WASTED THEIR VALUABLE TIME!
LIFE IS TOO SHORT TO BE SQUANDERED ON SUCH FOOLISHNESS!
WHERE IS THE PROFIT IN A BIRTHDAY PARTY?!
D-DON'T CRY, CHILDREN... YOUR FATHER APPRECIATES ALL YOUR EFFORTS...
R-REALLY... HE DOES...
DOES HE, MOTHER...?
SOMETIMES I WONDER.
"AND THUS THE SEEDS WERE SOWN...

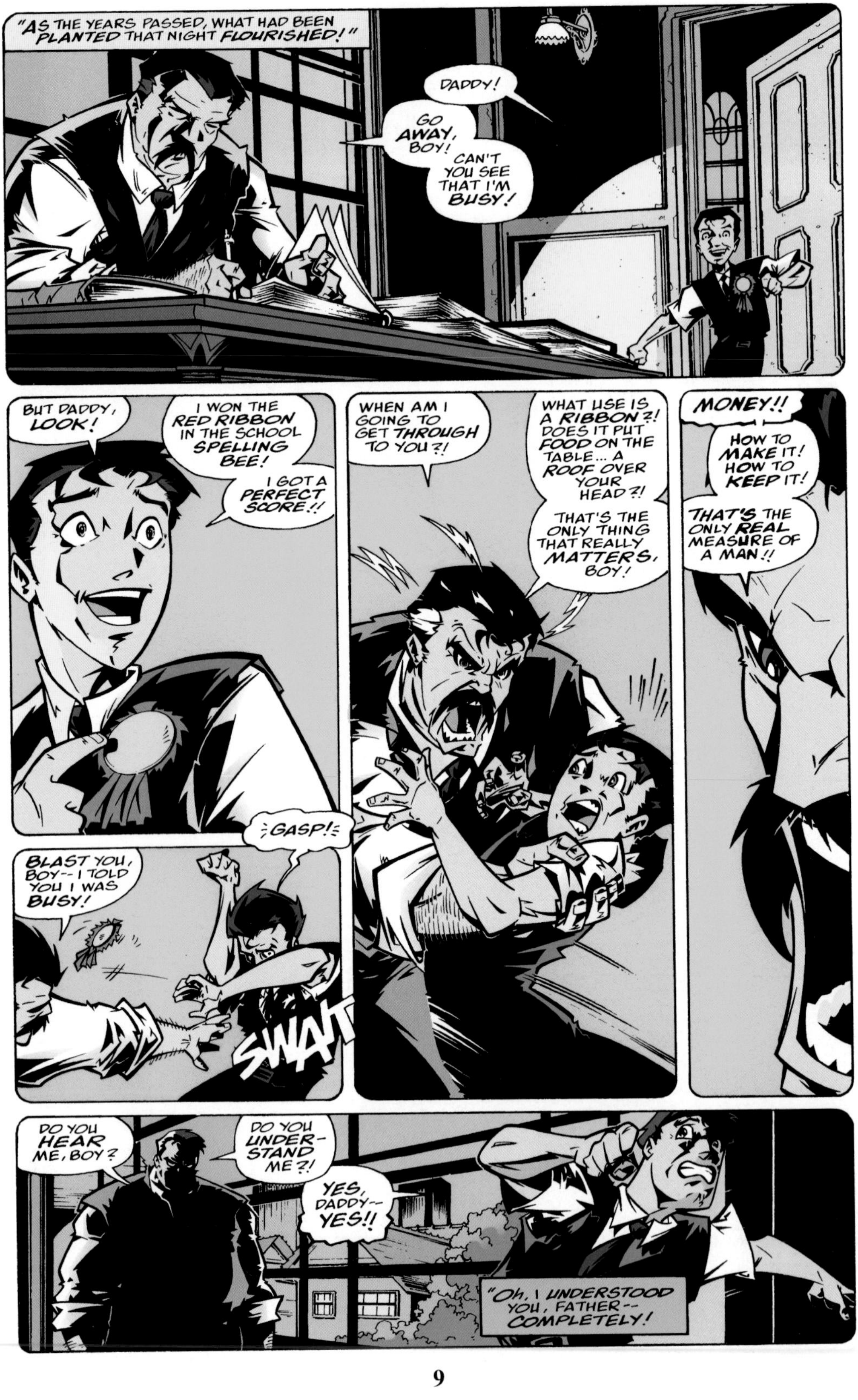
"AS THE YEARS PASSED, WHAT HAD BEEN PLANTED THAT NIGHT FLOURISHED!"
DADDY!
GO AWAY, BOY! CAN'T YOU SEE THAT I'M BUSY!
BUT DADDY, LOOK!
I WON THE RED RIBBON IN THE SCHOOL SPELLING BEE!
I GOT A PERFECT SCORE!!
BLAST YOU, BOY-- I TOLD YOU I WAS BUSY!
GASP!
SWAT
WHEN AM I GOING TO GET THROUGH TO YOU?!
WHAT USE IS A RIBBON?! DOES IT PUT FOOD ON THE TABLE... A ROOF OVER YOUR HEAD?!
THAT'S THE ONLY THING THAT REALLY MATTERS, BOY!
MONEY!!
HOW TO MAKE IT! HOW TO KEEP IT!
THAT'S THE ONLY REAL MEASURE OF A MAN!!
DO YOU HEAR ME, BOY?
DO YOU UNDER-STAND ME?!
YES, DADDY-- YES!!
"Oh, I UNDERSTOOD YOU, FATHER-- COMPLETELY!

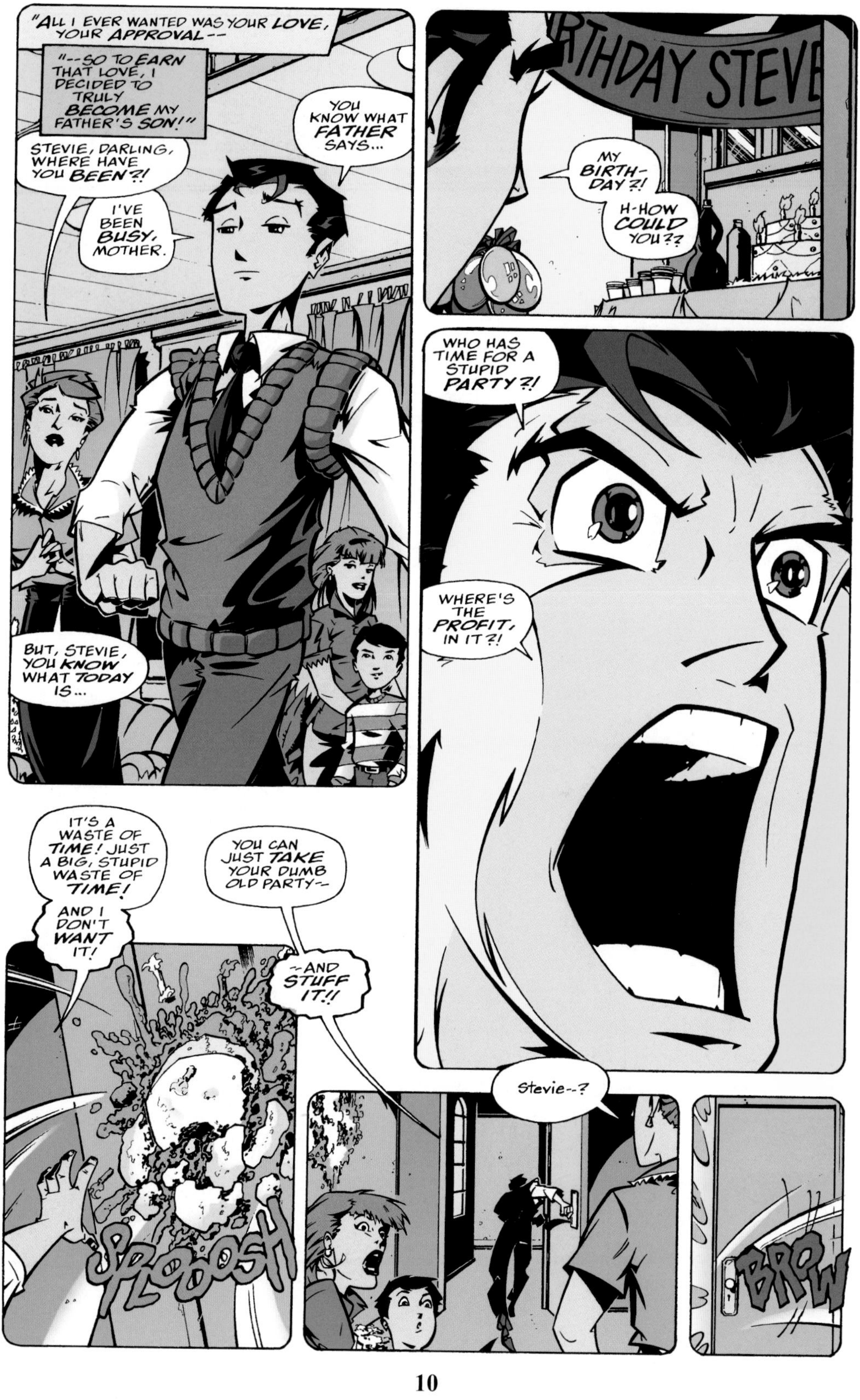

"ALL I EVER WANTED WAS YOUR LOVE, YOUR APPROVAL--
"--SO TO EARN THAT LOVE, I DECIDED TO TRULY BECOME MY FATHER'S SON!"
STEVIE, DARLING, WHERE HAVE YOU BEEN?!
I'VE BEEN BUSY, MOTHER.
YOU KNOW WHAT FATHER SAYS...
BUT, STEVIE, YOU KNOW WHAT TODAY IS...
RTHDAY STEVE
MY BIRTHDAY?!
H-HOW COULD YOU??
WHO HAS TIME FOR A STUPID PARTY?!
WHERE'S THE PROFIT, IN IT?!
IT'S A WASTE OF TIME! JUST A BIG, STUPID WASTE OF TIME!
AND I DON'T WANT IT!
YOU CAN JUST TAKE YOUR DUMB OLD PARTY--
--AND STUFF IT!!
SPLOOSH
Stevie--?
BROW

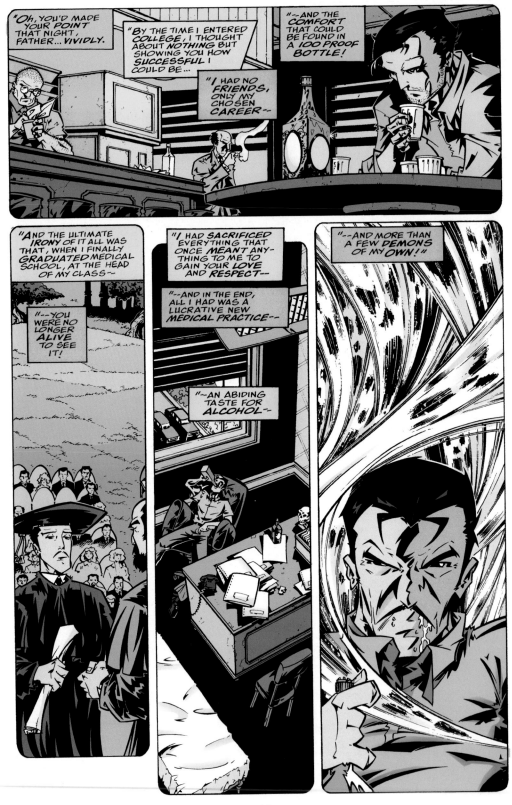

"Oh, YOU'D MADE YOUR POINT THAT NIGHT, FATHER... VIVIDLY."

"BY THE TIME I ENTERED COLLEGE, I THOUGHT ABOUT NOTHING BUT SHOWING YOU HOW SUCCESSFUL I COULD BE..."

"I HAD NO FRIENDS, ONLY MY CHOSEN CAREER--"

"--AND THE COMFORT THAT COULD BE FOUND IN A 100 PROOF BOTTLE!"

"AND THE ULTIMATE IRONY OF IT ALL WAS THAT, WHEN I FINALLY GRADUATED MEDICAL SCHOOL, AT THE HEAD OF MY CLASS--"

"--YOU WERE NO LONGER ALIVE TO SEE IT!"

"I HAD SACRIFICED EVERYTHING THAT ONCE MEANT ANY-THING TO ME TO GAIN YOUR LOVE AND RESPECT--"

"--AND IN THE END, ALL I HAD WAS A LUCRATIVE NEW MEDICAL PRACTICE--"

"--AN ABIDING TASTE FOR ALCOHOL--"

"--AND MORE THAN A FEW DEMONS OF MY OWN!"

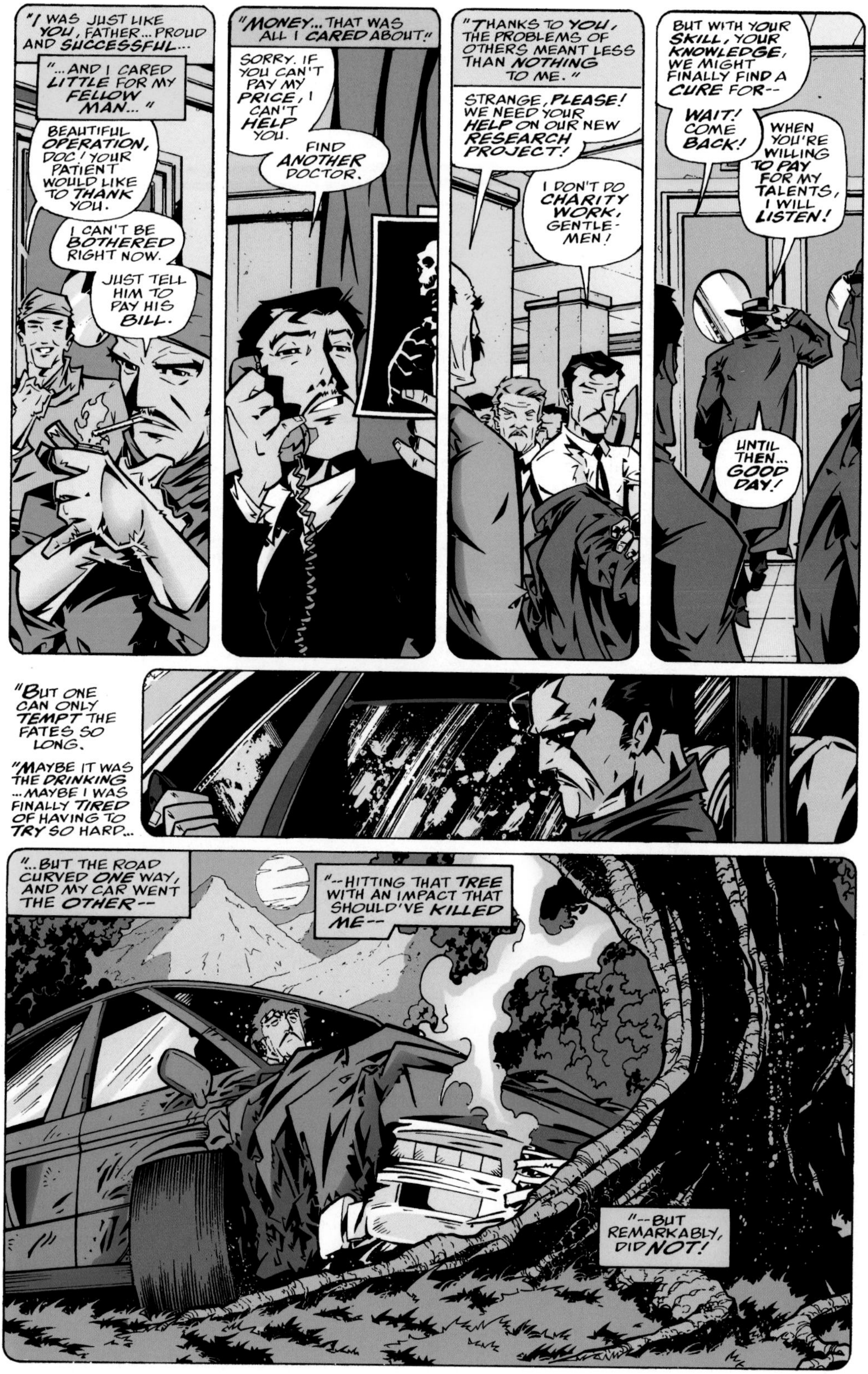
"I WAS JUST LIKE YOU, FATHER... PROUD AND SUCCESSFUL...
"...AND I CARED LITTLE FOR MY FELLOW MAN..."
BEAUTIFUL OPERATION, DOC! YOUR PATIENT WOULD LIKE TO THANK YOU.
I CAN'T BE BOTHERED RIGHT NOW.
JUST TELL HIM TO PAY HIS BILL.
"MONEY... THAT WAS ALL I CARED ABOUT!"
SORRY. IF YOU CAN'T PAY MY PRICE, I CAN'T HELP YOU.
FIND ANOTHER DOCTOR.
"THANKS TO YOU, THE PROBLEMS OF OTHERS MEANT LESS THAN NOTHING TO ME."
STRANGE, PLEASE! WE NEED YOUR HELP ON OUR NEW RESEARCH PROJECT!
I DON'T DO CHARITY WORK, GENTLEMEN!
BUT WITH YOUR SKILL, YOUR KNOWLEDGE, WE MIGHT FINALLY FIND A CURE FOR--
WAIT! COME BACK!
WHEN YOU'RE WILLING TO PAY FOR MY TALENTS, I WILL LISTEN!
UNTIL THEN... GOOD DAY!
"BUT ONE CAN ONLY TEMPT THE FATES SO LONG.
"MAYBE IT WAS THE DRINKING ...MAYBE I WAS FINALLY TIRED OF HAVING TO TRY SO HARD...
"...BUT THE ROAD CURVED ONE WAY, AND MY CAR WENT THE OTHER--
"--HITTING THAT TREE WITH AN IMPACT THAT SHOULD'VE KILLED ME--
"--BUT REMARKABLY, DID NOT!

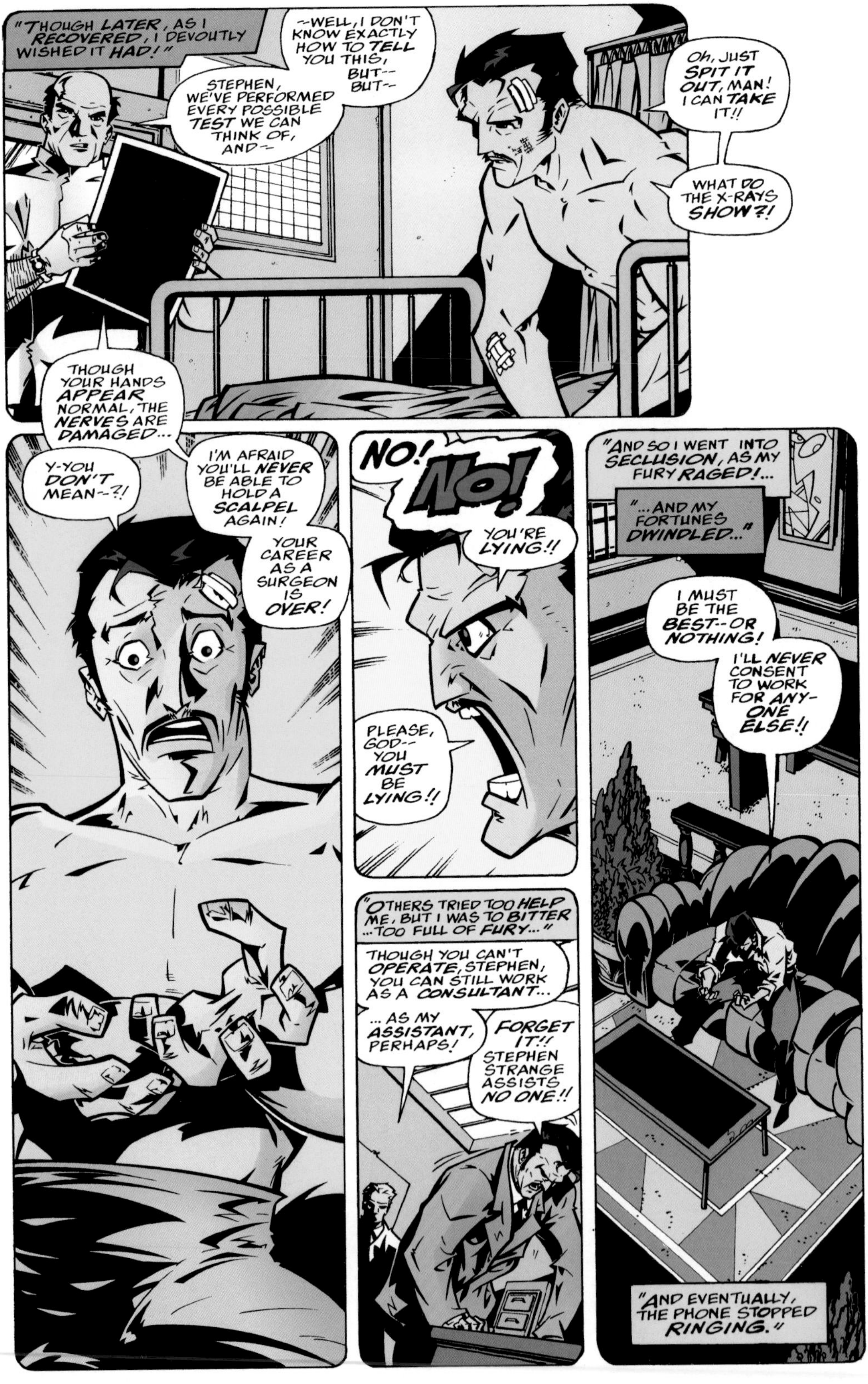
"THOUGH LATER, AS I RECOVERED, I DEVOUTLY WISHED IT HAD!"
STEPHEN, WE'VE PERFORMED EVERY POSSIBLE TEST WE CAN THINK OF, AND--
--WELL, I DON'T KNOW EXACTLY HOW TO TELL YOU THIS, BUT-- BUT--
Oh, JUST SPIT IT OUT, MAN! I CAN TAKE IT!!
WHAT DO THE X-RAYS SHOW?!
THOUGH YOUR HANDS APPEAR NORMAL, THE NERVES ARE DAMAGED...
Y-YOU DON'T MEAN--?!
I'M AFRAID YOU'LL NEVER BE ABLE TO HOLD A SCALPEL AGAIN!
YOUR CAREER AS A SURGEON IS OVER!
NO! NO!
YOU'RE LYING!!
PLEASE, GOD-- YOU MUST BE LYING!!
"OTHERS TRIED TOO HELP ME, BUT I WAS TO BITTER ...TOO FULL OF FURY..."
THOUGH YOU CAN'T OPERATE, STEPHEN, YOU CAN STILL WORK AS A CONSULTANT...
... AS MY ASSISTANT, PERHAPS!
FORGET IT!! STEPHEN STRANGE ASSISTS NO ONE!!
"AND SO I WENT INTO SECLUSION, AS MY FURY RAGED!...
"...AND MY FORTUNES DWINDLED..."
I MUST BE THE BEST--OR NOTHING!
I'LL NEVER CONSENT TO WORK FOR ANY-ONE ELSE!!
"AND EVENTUALLY, THE PHONE STOPPED RINGING."

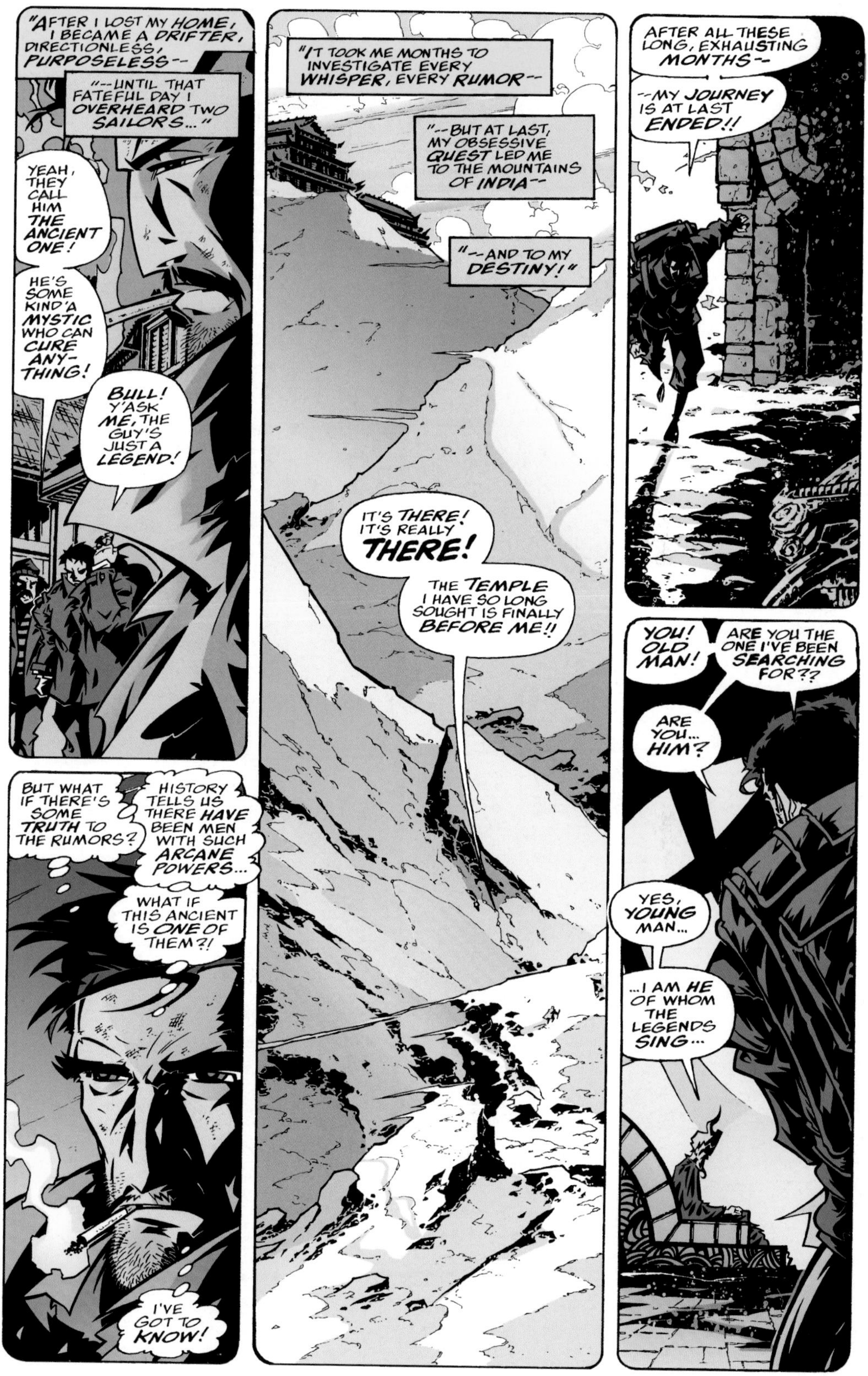
"AFTER I LOST MY HOME, I BECAME A DRIFTER, DIRECTIONLESS, PURPOSELESS--
"--UNTIL THAT FATEFUL DAY I OVERHEARD TWO SAILORS..."
YEAH, THEY CALL HIM THE ANCIENT ONE!
HE'S SOME KIND'A MYSTIC WHO CAN CURE ANY-THING!
BULL! Y'ASK ME, THE GUY'S JUST A LEGEND!
BUT WHAT IF THERE'S SOME TRUTH TO THE RUMORS?
HISTORY TELLS US THERE HAVE BEEN MEN WITH SUCH ARCANE POWERS...
WHAT IF THIS ANCIENT IS ONE OF THEM?!
I'VE GOT TO KNOW!
"IT TOOK ME MONTHS TO INVESTIGATE EVERY WHISPER, EVERY RUMOR--
"--BUT AT LAST, MY OBSESSIVE QUEST LED ME TO THE MOUNTAINS OF INDIA--
"--AND TO MY DESTINY!"
IT'S THERE! IT'S REALLY THERE!
THE TEMPLE I HAVE SO LONG SOUGHT IS FINALLY BEFORE ME!!
AFTER ALL THESE LONG, EXHAUSTING MONTHS--
--MY JOURNEY IS AT LAST ENDED!!
YOU! OLD MAN!
ARE YOU THE ONE I'VE BEEN SEARCHING FOR??
ARE YOU... HIM?
YES, YOUNG MAN...
...I AM HE OF WHOM THE LEGENDS SING...

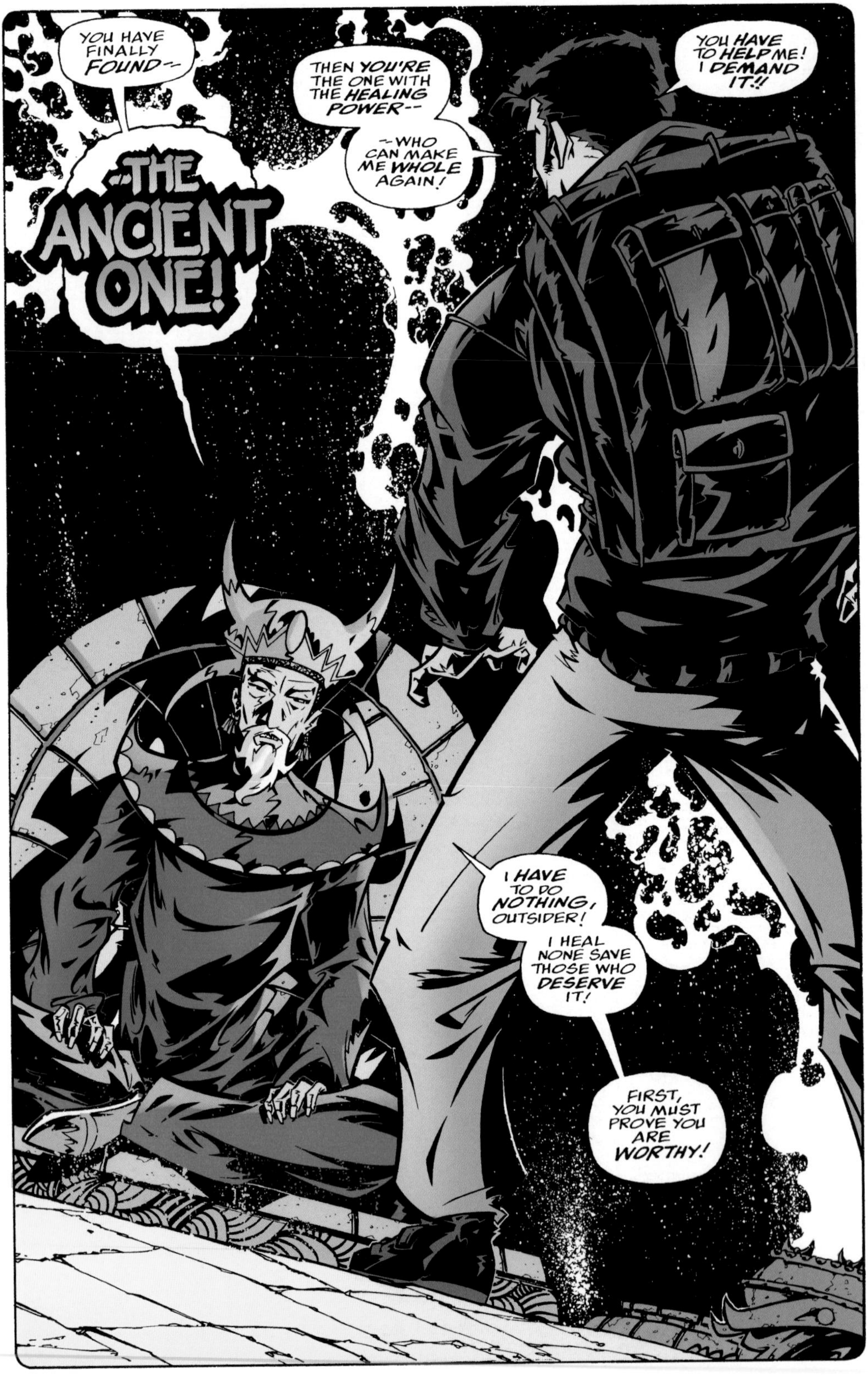
YOU HAVE FINALLY FOUND--
--THE ANCIENT ONE!
THEN YOU'RE THE ONE WITH THE HEALING POWER--
--WHO CAN MAKE ME WHOLE AGAIN!
YOU HAVE TO HELP ME! I DEMAND IT!!
I HAVE TO DO NOTHING, OUTSIDER!
I HEAL NONE SAVE THOSE WHO DESERVE IT!
FIRST, YOU MUST PROVE YOU ARE WORTHY!

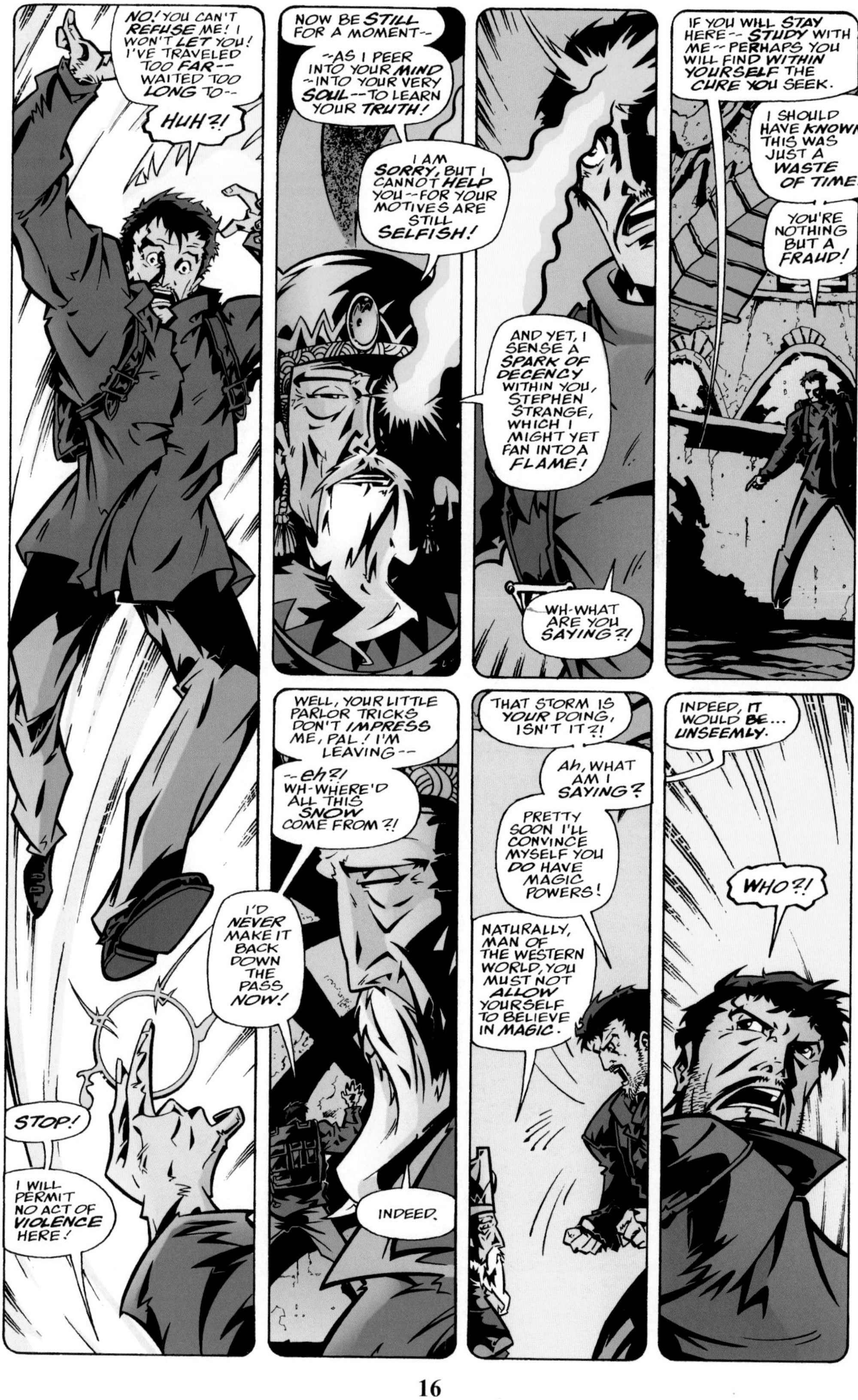

NO! YOU CAN'T REFUSE ME! I WON'T LET YOU! I'VE TRAVELED TOO FAR-- WAITED TOO LONG TO--
HUH?!
STOP!
I WILL PERMIT NO ACT OF VIOLENCE HERE!
NOW BE STILL FOR A MOMENT--
--AS I PEER INTO YOUR MIND --INTO YOUR VERY SOUL--TO LEARN YOUR TRUTH!
I AM SORRY, BUT I CANNOT HELP YOU--FOR YOUR MOTIVES ARE STILL SELFISH!
AND YET, I SENSE A SPARK OF DECENCY WITHIN YOU, STEPHEN STRANGE, WHICH I MIGHT YET FAN INTO A FLAME!
WH-WHAT ARE YOU SAYING?!
IF YOU WILL STAY HERE-- STUDY WITH ME--PERHAPS YOU WILL FIND WITHIN YOURSELF THE CURE YOU SEEK.
I SHOULD HAVE KNOWN! THIS WAS JUST A WASTE OF TIME!
YOU'RE NOTHING BUT A FRAUD!
WELL, YOUR LITTLE PARLOR TRICKS DON'T IMPRESS ME, PAL! I'M LEAVING--
--eh?! WH-WHERE'D ALL THIS SNOW COME FROM?!
I'D NEVER MAKE IT BACK DOWN THE PASS NOW!
INDEED.
THAT STORM IS YOUR DOING, ISN'T IT?!
Ah, WHAT AM I SAYING?
PRETTY SOON I'LL CONVINCE MYSELF YOU DO HAVE MAGIC POWERS!
NATURALLY, MAN OF THE WESTERN WORLD, YOU MUST NOT ALLOW YOURSELF TO BELIEVE IN MAGIC.
INDEED, IT WOULD BE... UNSEEMLY.
WHO?!

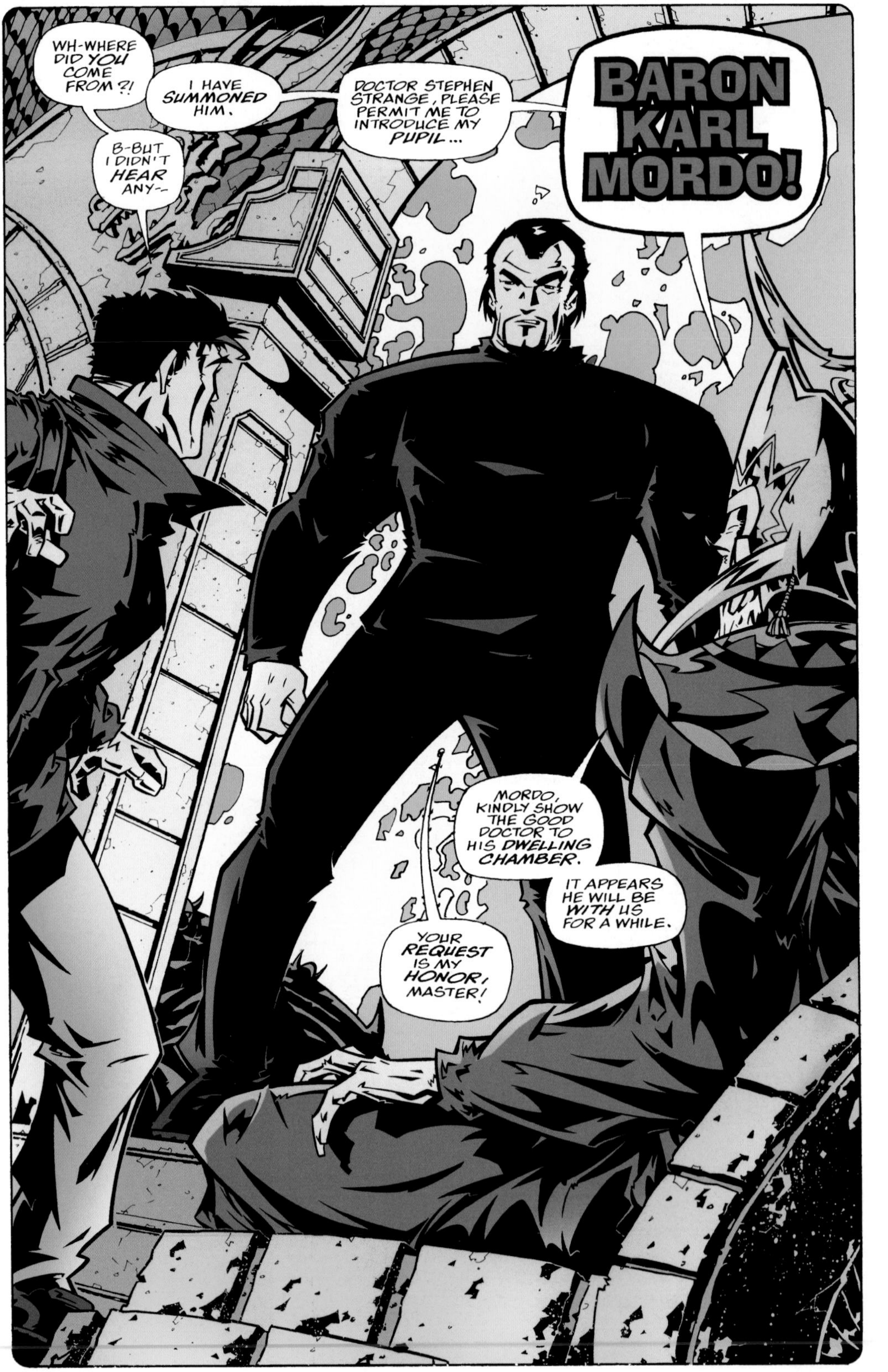
WH-WHERE DID YOU COME FROM ?!
I HAVE SUMMONED HIM.
B-BUT I DIDN'T HEAR ANY--
DOCTOR STEPHEN STRANGE, PLEASE PERMIT ME TO INTRODUCE MY PUPIL...
BARON KARL MORDO!
MORDO, KINDLY SHOW THE GOOD DOCTOR TO HIS DWELLING CHAMBER.
IT APPEARS HE WILL BE WITH US FOR A WHILE.
YOUR REQUEST IS MY HONOR, MASTER!

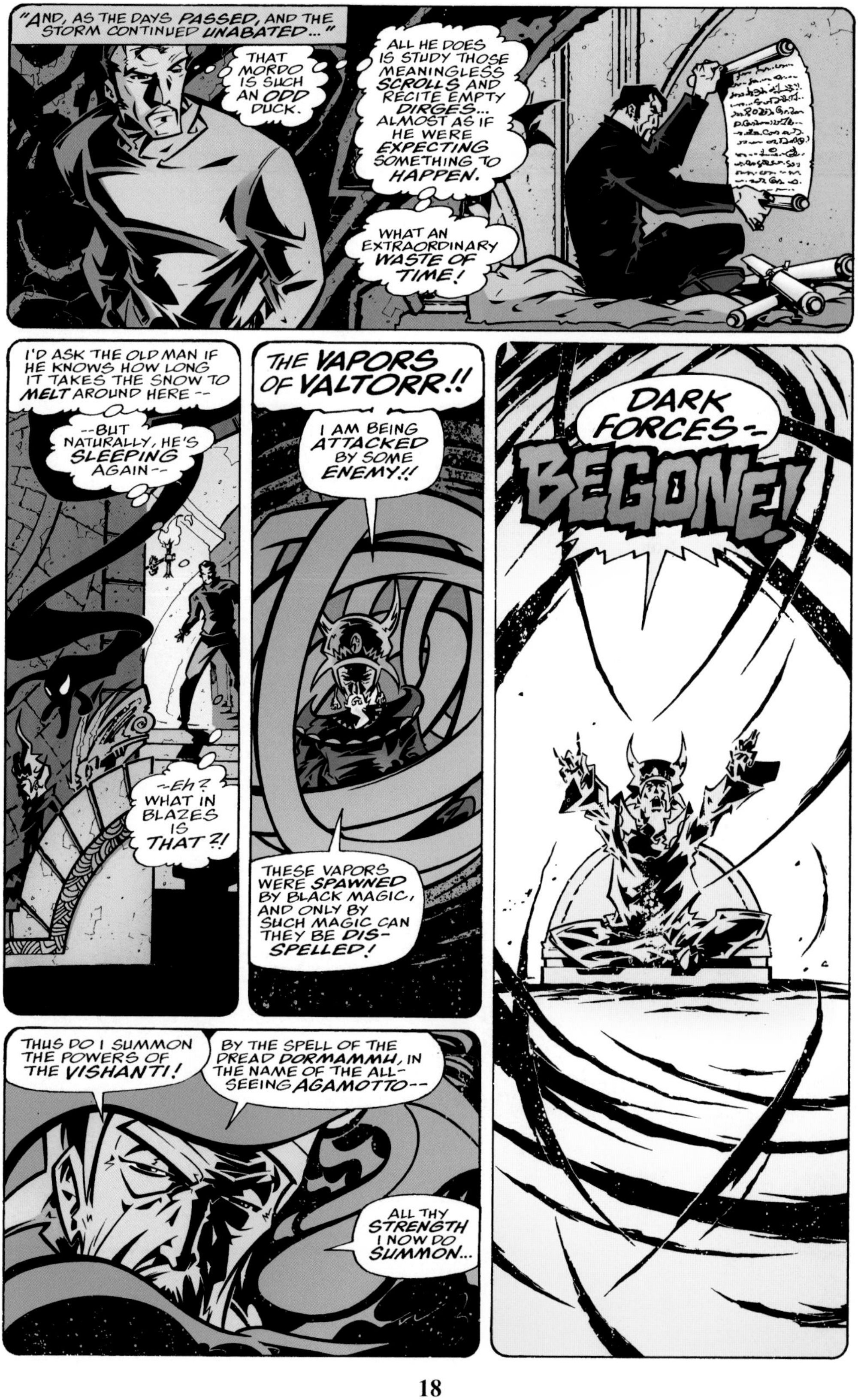
"AND, AS THE DAYS PASSED, AND THE STORM CONTINUED UNABATED..."
THAT MORDO IS SUCH AN ODD DUCK.
ALL HE DOES IS STUDY THOSE MEANINGLESS SCROLLS AND RECITE EMPTY DIRGES... ALMOST AS IF HE WERE EXPECTING SOMETHING TO HAPPEN.
WHAT AN EXTRAORDINARY WASTE OF TIME!
I'D ASK THE OLD MAN IF HE KNOWS HOW LONG IT TAKES THE SNOW TO MELT AROUND HERE --
--BUT NATURALLY, HE'S SLEEPING AGAIN--
--Eh? WHAT IN BLAZES IS THAT?!
THE VAPORS OF VALTORR!!
I AM BEING ATTACKED BY SOME ENEMY!!
THESE VAPORS WERE SPAWNED BY BLACK MAGIC, AND ONLY BY SUCH MAGIC CAN THEY BE DIS-SPELLED!
THUS DO I SUMMON THE POWERS OF THE VISHANTI!
BY THE SPELL OF THE DREAD DORMAMMU, IN THE NAME OF THE ALL-SEEING AGAMOTTO--
ALL THY STRENGTH I NOW DO SUMMON...
DARK FORCES-- BEGONE!

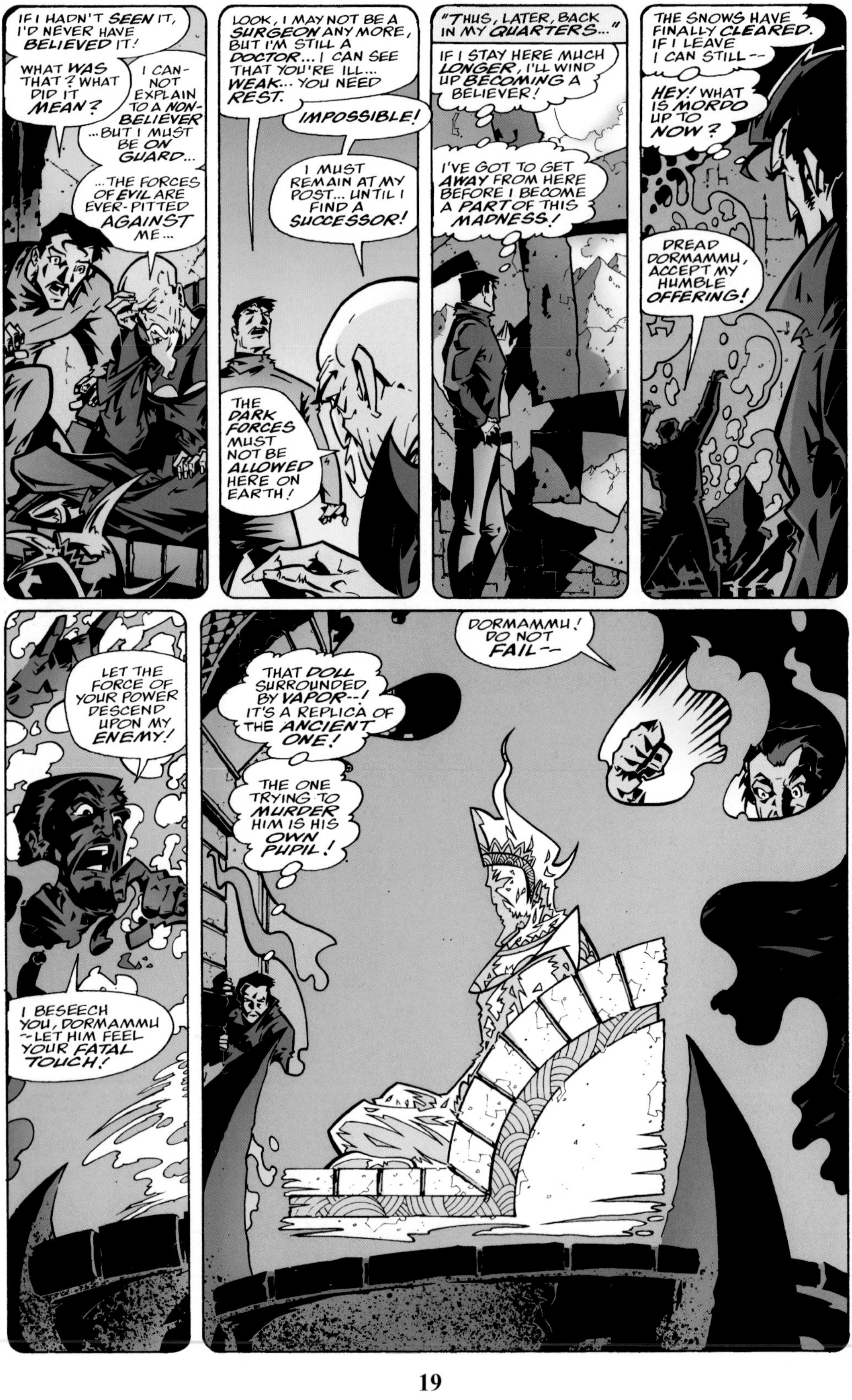
IF I HADN'T SEEN IT, I'D NEVER HAVE BELIEVED IT!
WHAT WAS THAT? WHAT DID IT MEAN?
I CAN-NOT EXPLAIN TO A NON-BELIEVER ...BUT I MUST BE ON GUARD...
...THE FORCES OF EVIL ARE EVER-PITTED AGAINST ME...
LOOK, I MAY NOT BE A SURGEON ANY MORE, BUT I'M STILL A DOCTOR... I CAN SEE THAT YOU'RE ILL... WEAK... YOU NEED REST.
IMPOSSIBLE!
I MUST REMAIN AT MY POST... UNTIL I FIND A SUCCESSOR!
THE DARK FORCES MUST NOT BE ALLOWED HERE ON EARTH!
"THUS, LATER, BACK IN MY QUARTERS..."
IF I STAY HERE MUCH LONGER, I'LL WIND UP BECOMING A BELIEVER!
I'VE GOT TO GET AWAY FROM HERE BEFORE I BECOME A PART OF THIS MADNESS!
THE SNOWS HAVE FINALLY CLEARED. IF I LEAVE I CAN STILL--
HEY! WHAT IS MORDO UP TO NOW?
DREAD DORMAMMU, ACCEPT MY HUMBLE OFFERING!
LET THE FORCE OF YOUR POWER DESCEND UPON MY ENEMY!
I BESEECH YOU, DORMAMMU --LET HIM FEEL YOUR FATAL TOUCH!
DORMAMMU! DO NOT FAIL--
THAT DOLL SURROUNDED BY VAPOR--! IT'S A REPLICA OF THE ANCIENT ONE!
THE ONE TRYING TO MURDER HIM IS HIS OWN PUPIL!

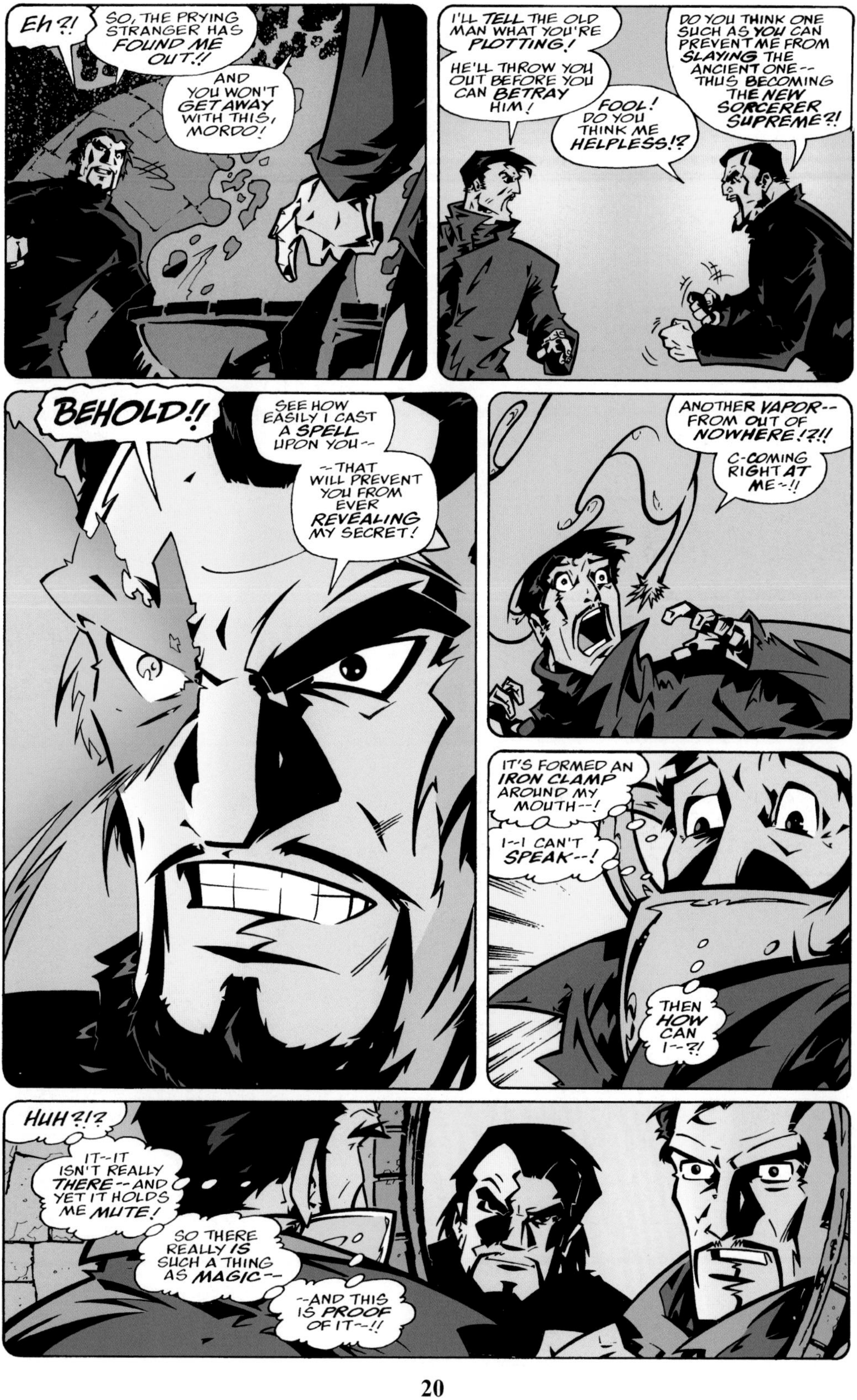
Eh?!
SO, THE PRYING STRANGER HAS FOUND ME OUT!!
AND YOU WON'T GET AWAY WITH THIS, MORDO!
I'LL TELL THE OLD MAN WHAT YOU'RE PLOTTING!
HE'LL THROW YOU OUT BEFORE YOU CAN BETRAY HIM!
FOOL! DO YOU THINK ME HELPLESS!?
DO YOU THINK ONE SUCH AS YOU CAN PREVENT ME FROM SLAYING THE ANCIENT ONE -- THUS BECOMING THE NEW SORCERER SUPREME?!
BEHOLD!!
SEE HOW EASILY I CAST A SPELL UPON YOU--
--THAT WILL PREVENT YOU FROM EVER REVEALING MY SECRET!
ANOTHER VAPOR-- FROM OUT OF NOWHERE!?!!
C-COMING RIGHT AT ME--!!
IT'S FORMED AN IRON CLAMP AROUND MY MOUTH--!
I--I CAN'T SPEAK--!
THEN HOW CAN I--?!
HUH?!?
IT--IT ISN'T REALLY THERE--AND YET IT HOLDS ME MUTE!
SO THERE REALLY IS SUCH A THING AS MAGIC--
--AND THIS IS PROOF OF IT--!!

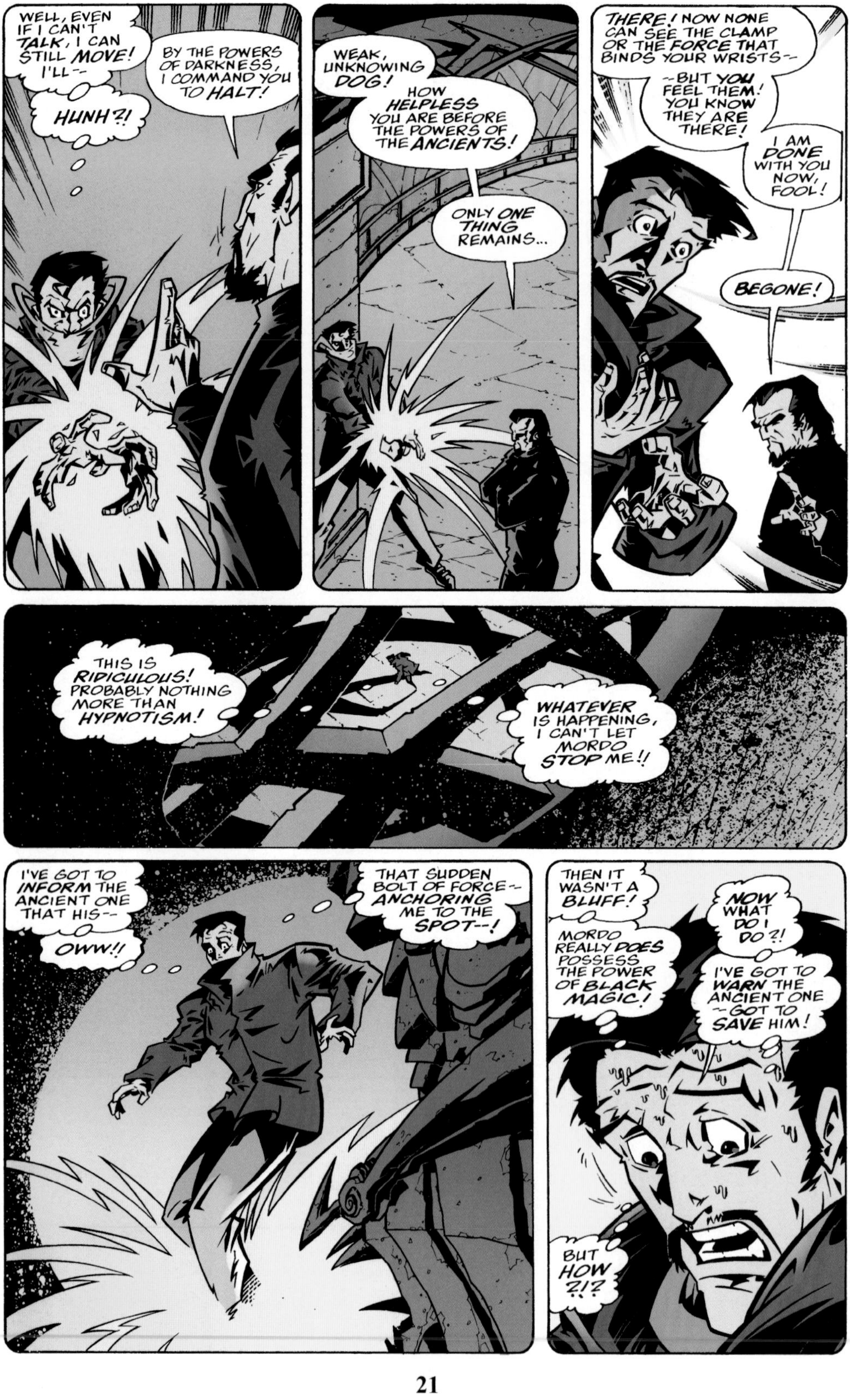
WELL, EVEN IF I CAN'T TALK, I CAN STILL MOVE! I'LL--
HUNH?!
BY THE POWERS OF DARKNESS, I COMMAND YOU TO HALT!
WEAK, UNKNOWING DOG!
HOW HELPLESS YOU ARE BEFORE THE POWERS OF THE ANCIENTS!
ONLY ONE THING REMAINS...
THERE! NOW NONE CAN SEE THE CLAMP OR THE FORCE THAT BINDS YOUR WRISTS--
--BUT YOU FEEL THEM! YOU KNOW THEY ARE THERE!
I AM DONE WITH YOU NOW, FOOL!
BEGONE!
THIS IS RIDICULOUS! PROBABLY NOTHING MORE THAN HYPNOTISM!
WHATEVER IS HAPPENING, I CAN'T LET MORDO STOP ME!!
I'VE GOT TO INFORM THE ANCIENT ONE THAT HIS--
OWW!!
THAT SUDDEN BOLT OF FORCE-- ANCHORING ME TO THE SPOT--!
THEN IT WASN'T A BLUFF!
MORDO REALLY DOES POSSESS THE POWER OF BLACK MAGIC!
NOW WHAT DO I DO?!
I'VE GOT TO WARN THE ANCIENT ONE --GOT TO SAVE HIM!
BUT HOW?!?

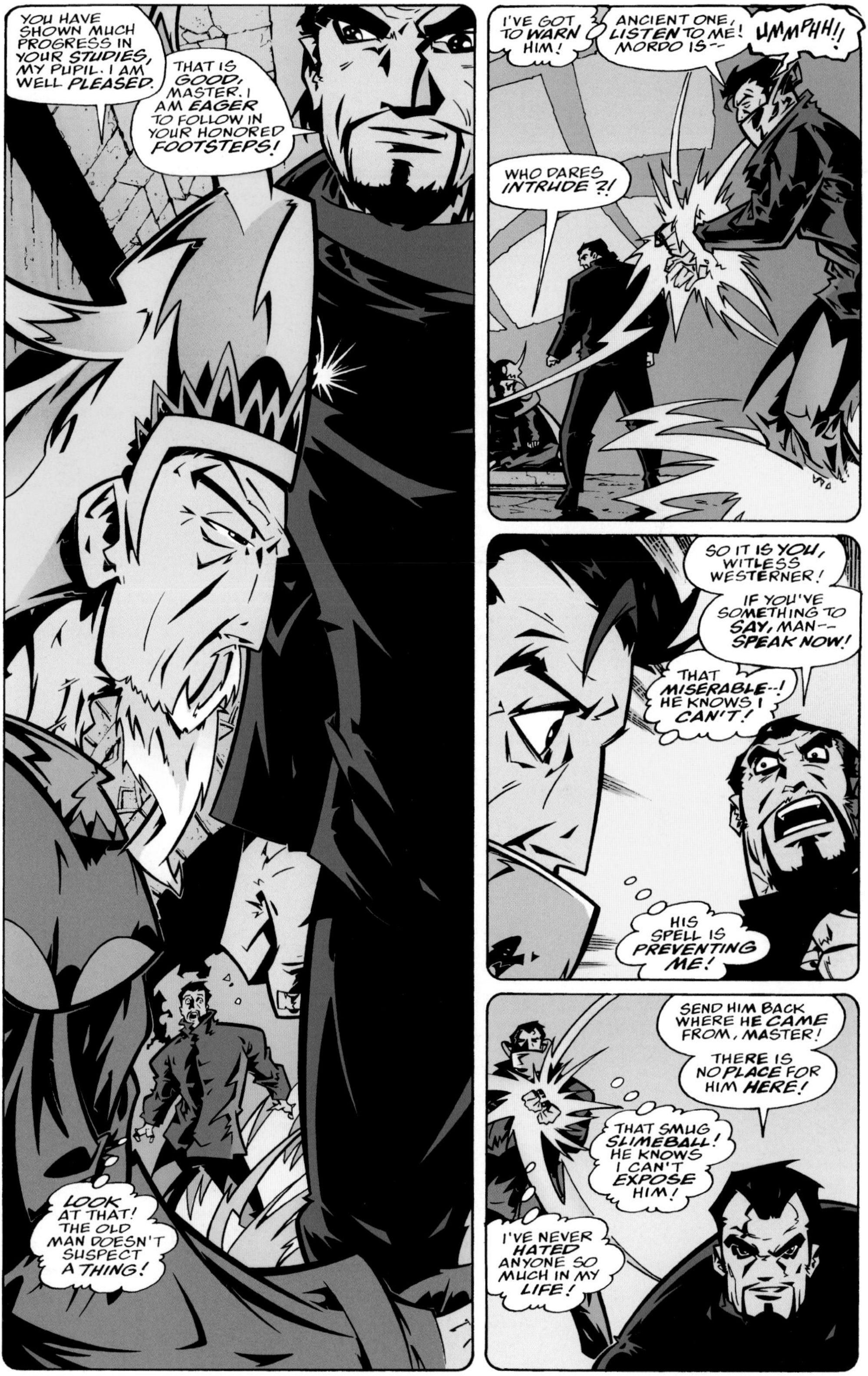
YOU HAVE SHOWN MUCH PROGRESS IN YOUR STUDIES, MY PUPIL. I AM WELL PLEASED.
THAT IS GOOD, MASTER. I AM EAGER TO FOLLOW IN YOUR HONORED FOOTSTEPS!
LOOK AT THAT! THE OLD MAN DOESN'T SUSPECT A THING!
I'VE GOT TO WARN HIM!
ANCIENT ONE, LISTEN TO ME! MORDO IS--
UMMPHH!!
WHO DARES INTRUDE ?!
SO IT IS YOU, WITLESS WESTERNER!
IF YOU'VE SOMETHING TO SAY, MAN-- SPEAK NOW!
THAT MISERABLE--! HE KNOWS I CAN'T!
HIS SPELL IS PREVENTING ME!
SEND HIM BACK WHERE HE CAME FROM, MASTER!
THERE IS NO PLACE FOR HIM HERE!
THAT SMUG SLIMEBALL! HE KNOWS I CAN'T EXPOSE HIM!
I'VE NEVER HATED ANYONE SO MUCH IN MY LIFE!

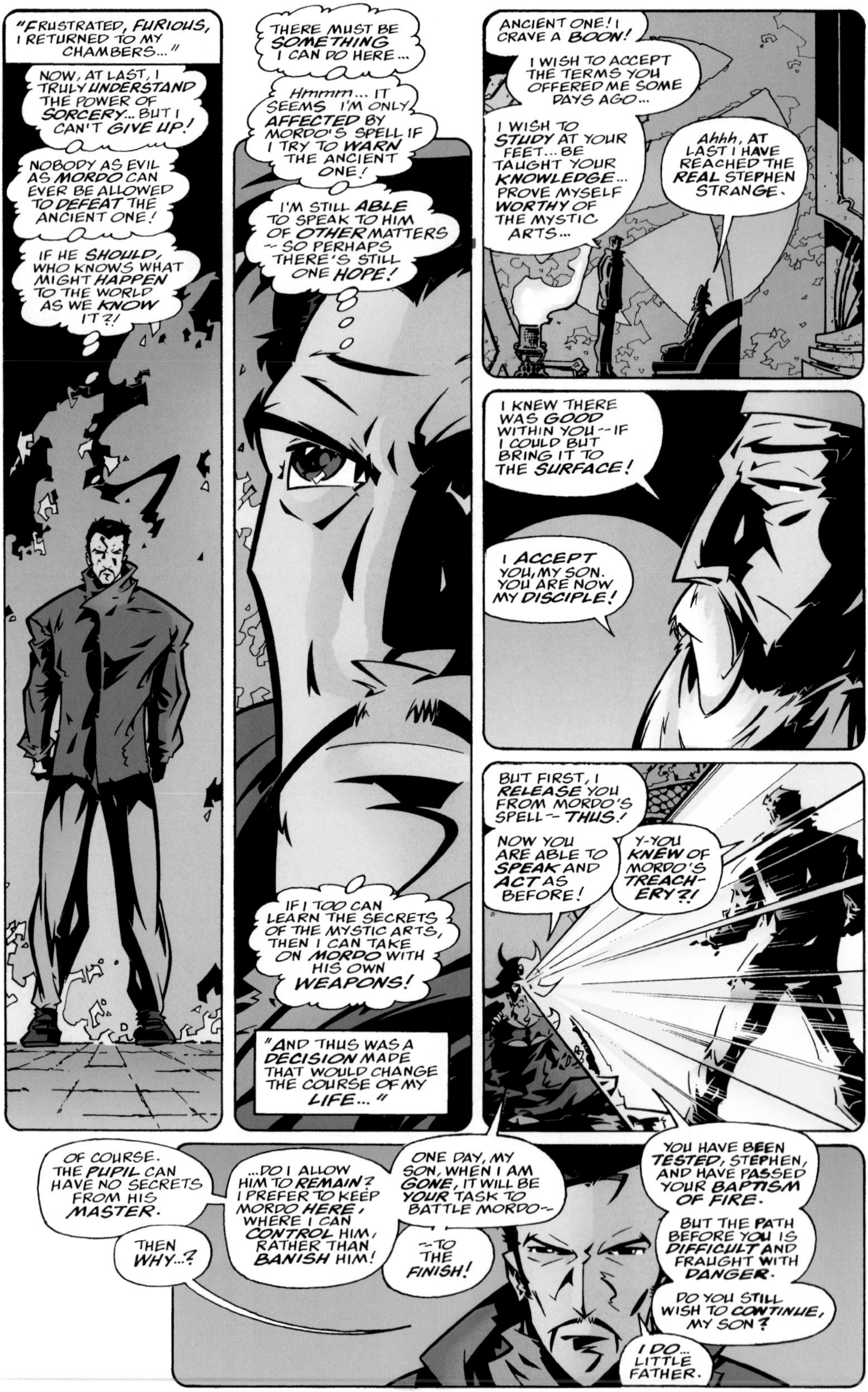
"FRUSTRATED, FURIOUS, I RETURNED TO MY CHAMBERS..."
NOW, AT LAST, I TRULY UNDERSTAND THE POWER OF SORCERY... BUT I CAN'T GIVE UP!
NOBODY AS EVIL AS MORDO CAN EVER BE ALLOWED TO DEFEAT THE ANCIENT ONE!
IF HE SHOULD, WHO KNOWS WHAT MIGHT HAPPEN TO THE WORLD AS WE KNOW IT?!
THERE MUST BE SOMETHING I CAN DO HERE...
Hmmm... IT SEEMS I'M ONLY AFFECTED BY MORDO'S SPELL IF I TRY TO WARN THE ANCIENT ONE!
I'M STILL ABLE TO SPEAK TO HIM OF OTHER MATTERS -- SO PERHAPS THERE'S STILL ONE HOPE!
IF I TOO CAN LEARN THE SECRETS OF THE MYSTIC ARTS, THEN I CAN TAKE ON MORDO WITH HIS OWN WEAPONS!
"AND THUS WAS A DECISION MADE THAT WOULD CHANGE THE COURSE OF MY LIFE..."
ANCIENT ONE! I CRAVE A BOON!
I WISH TO ACCEPT THE TERMS YOU OFFERED ME SOME DAYS AGO...
I WISH TO STUDY AT YOUR FEET... BE TAUGHT YOUR KNOWLEDGE... PROVE MYSELF WORTHY OF THE MYSTIC ARTS...
Ahhh, AT LAST I HAVE REACHED THE REAL STEPHEN STRANGE.
I KNEW THERE WAS GOOD WITHIN YOU -- IF I COULD BUT BRING IT TO THE SURFACE!
I ACCEPT YOU, MY SON. YOU ARE NOW MY DISCIPLE!
BUT FIRST, I RELEASE YOU FROM MORDO'S SPELL -- THUS!
NOW YOU ARE ABLE TO SPEAK AND ACT AS BEFORE!
Y-YOU KNEW OF MORDO'S TREACH-ERY?!
OF COURSE. THE PUPIL CAN HAVE NO SECRETS FROM HIS MASTER.
THEN WHY...?
...DO I ALLOW HIM TO REMAIN? I PREFER TO KEEP MORDO HERE, WHERE I CAN CONTROL HIM, RATHER THAN BANISH HIM!
ONE DAY, MY SON, WHEN I AM GONE, IT WILL BE YOUR TASK TO BATTLE MORDO--
--TO THE FINISH!
YOU HAVE BEEN TESTED, STEPHEN, AND HAVE PASSED YOUR BAPTISM OF FIRE.
BUT THE PATH BEFORE YOU IS DIFFICULT AND FRAUGHT WITH DANGER.
DO YOU STILL WISH TO CONTINUE, MY SON?
I DO... LITTLE FATHER.

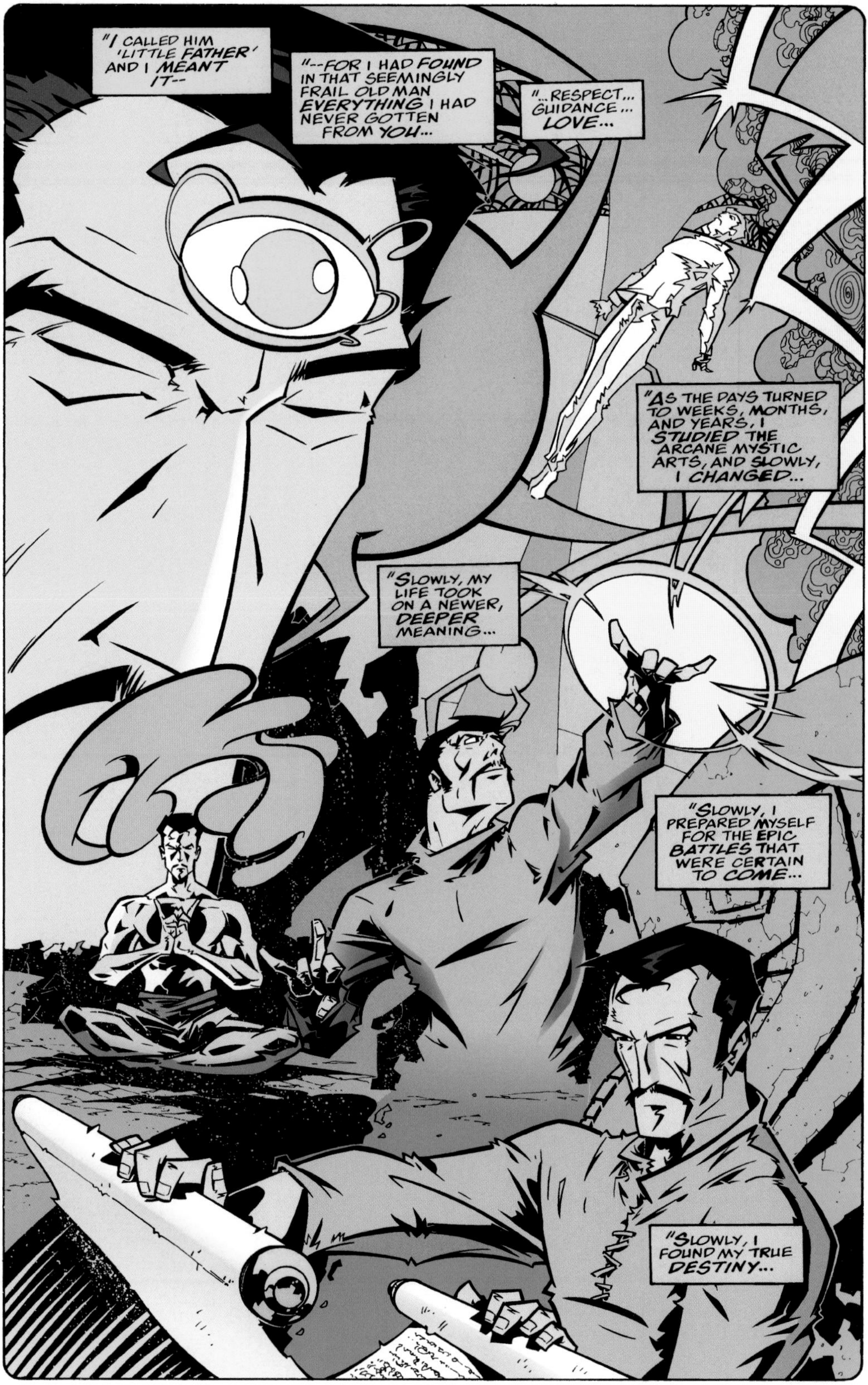
"I CALLED HIM 'LITTLE FATHER' AND I MEANT IT--
"--FOR I HAD FOUND IN THAT SEEMINGLY FRAIL OLD MAN EVERYTHING I HAD NEVER GOTTEN FROM YOU...
"...RESPECT... GUIDANCE... LOVE...
"AS THE DAYS TURNED TO WEEKS, MONTHS, AND YEARS, I STUDIED THE ARCANE MYSTIC ARTS, AND SLOWLY, I CHANGED...
"SLOWLY, MY LIFE TOOK ON A NEWER, DEEPER MEANING...
"SLOWLY, I PREPARED MYSELF FOR THE EPIC BATTLES THAT WERE CERTAIN TO COME...
"SLOWLY, I FOUND MY TRUE DESTINY...

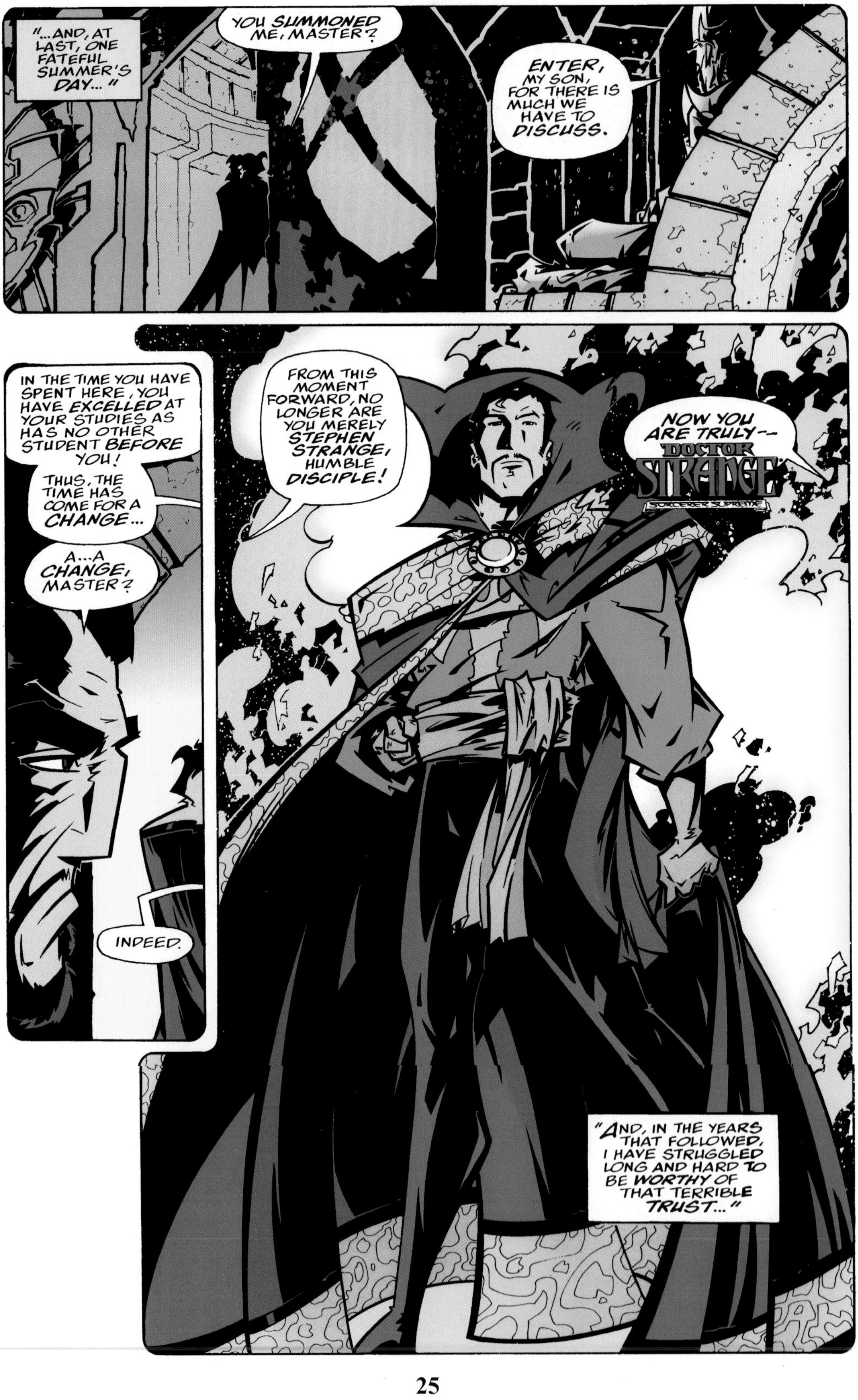
"...AND, AT LAST, ONE FATEFUL SUMMER'S DAY..."
YOU SUMMONED ME, MASTER?
ENTER, MY SON, FOR THERE IS MUCH WE HAVE TO DISCUSS.
IN THE TIME YOU HAVE SPENT HERE, YOU HAVE EXCELLED AT YOUR STUDIES AS HAS NO OTHER STUDENT BEFORE YOU!
THUS, THE TIME HAS COME FOR A CHANGE...
A...A CHANGE, MASTER?
INDEED.
FROM THIS MOMENT FORWARD, NO LONGER ARE YOU MERELY STEPHEN STRANGE, HUMBLE DISCIPLE!
NOW YOU ARE TRULY--
DOCTOR STRANGE
SORCERER SUPREME
"AND, IN THE YEARS THAT FOLLOWED, I HAVE STRUGGLED LONG AND HARD TO BE WORTHY OF THAT TERRIBLE TRUST..."

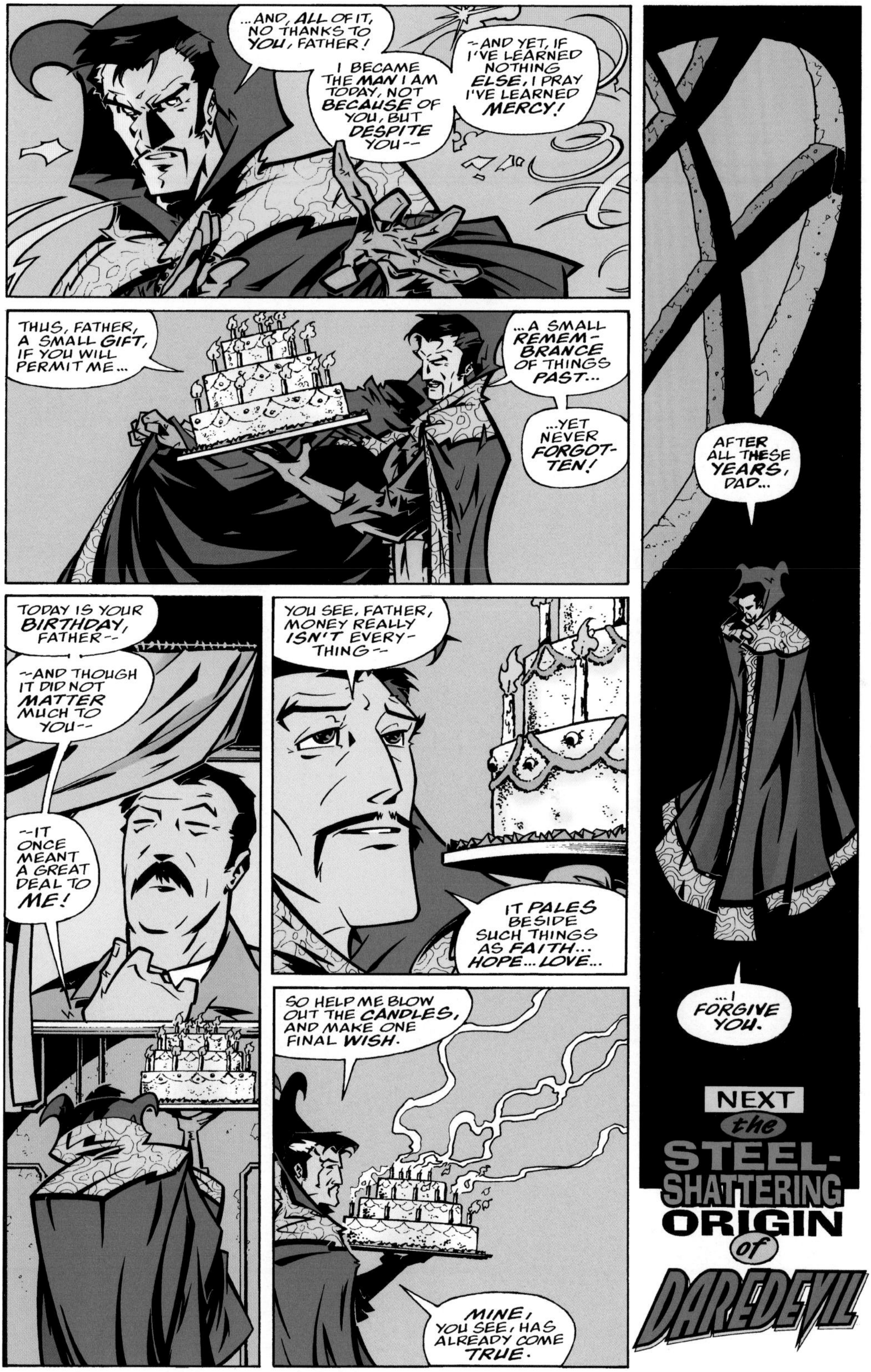
...AND, ALL OF IT, NO THANKS TO YOU, FATHER!
I BECAME THE MAN I AM TODAY, NOT BECAUSE OF YOU, BUT DESPITE YOU--
--AND YET, IF I'VE LEARNED NOTHING ELSE, I PRAY I'VE LEARNED MERCY!
THUS, FATHER, A SMALL GIFT, IF YOU WILL PERMIT ME...
...A SMALL REMEMBRANCE OF THINGS PAST...
...YET NEVER FORGOTTEN!
TODAY IS YOUR BIRTHDAY, FATHER--
--AND THOUGH IT DID NOT MATTER MUCH TO YOU--
--IT ONCE MEANT A GREAT DEAL TO ME!
YOU SEE, FATHER, MONEY REALLY ISN'T EVERYTHING--
IT PALES BESIDE SUCH THINGS AS FAITH... HOPE... LOVE...
SO HELP ME BLOW OUT THE CANDLES, AND MAKE ONE FINAL WISH.
MINE, YOU SEE, HAS ALREADY COME TRUE.
AFTER ALL THESE YEARS, DAD...
...I FORGIVE YOU.
NEXT
the
STEEL-SHATTERING
ORIGIN
of
DAREDEVIL

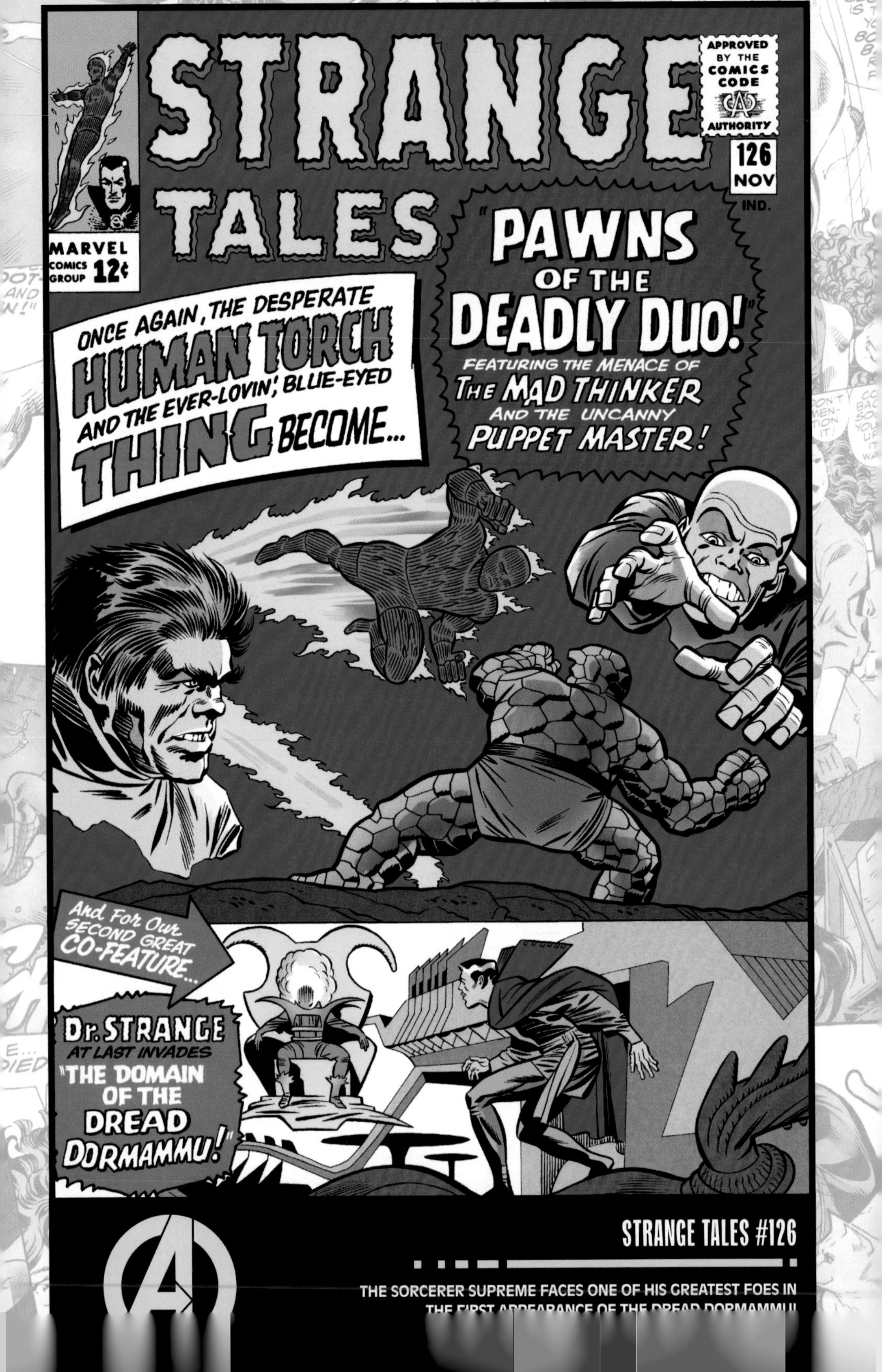
STRANGE TALES
APPROVED BY THE COMICS CODE AUTHORITY
126 NOV
IND.
MARVEL COMICS GROUP 12¢
"PAWNS OF THE DEADLY DUO!"
FEATURING THE MENACE OF THE MAD THINKER AND THE UNCANNY PUPPET MASTER!
ONCE AGAIN, THE DESPERATE HUMAN TORCH AND THE EVER-LOVIN', BLUE-EYED THING BECOME...
And For Our SECOND GREAT CO-FEATURE...
Dr. STRANGE AT LAST INVADES "THE DOMAIN OF THE DREAD DORMAMMU!"

STRANGE TALES #126

THE SORCERER SUPREME FACES ONE OF HIS GREATEST FOES IN THE FIRST APPEARANCE OF THE DREAD DORMAMMU!

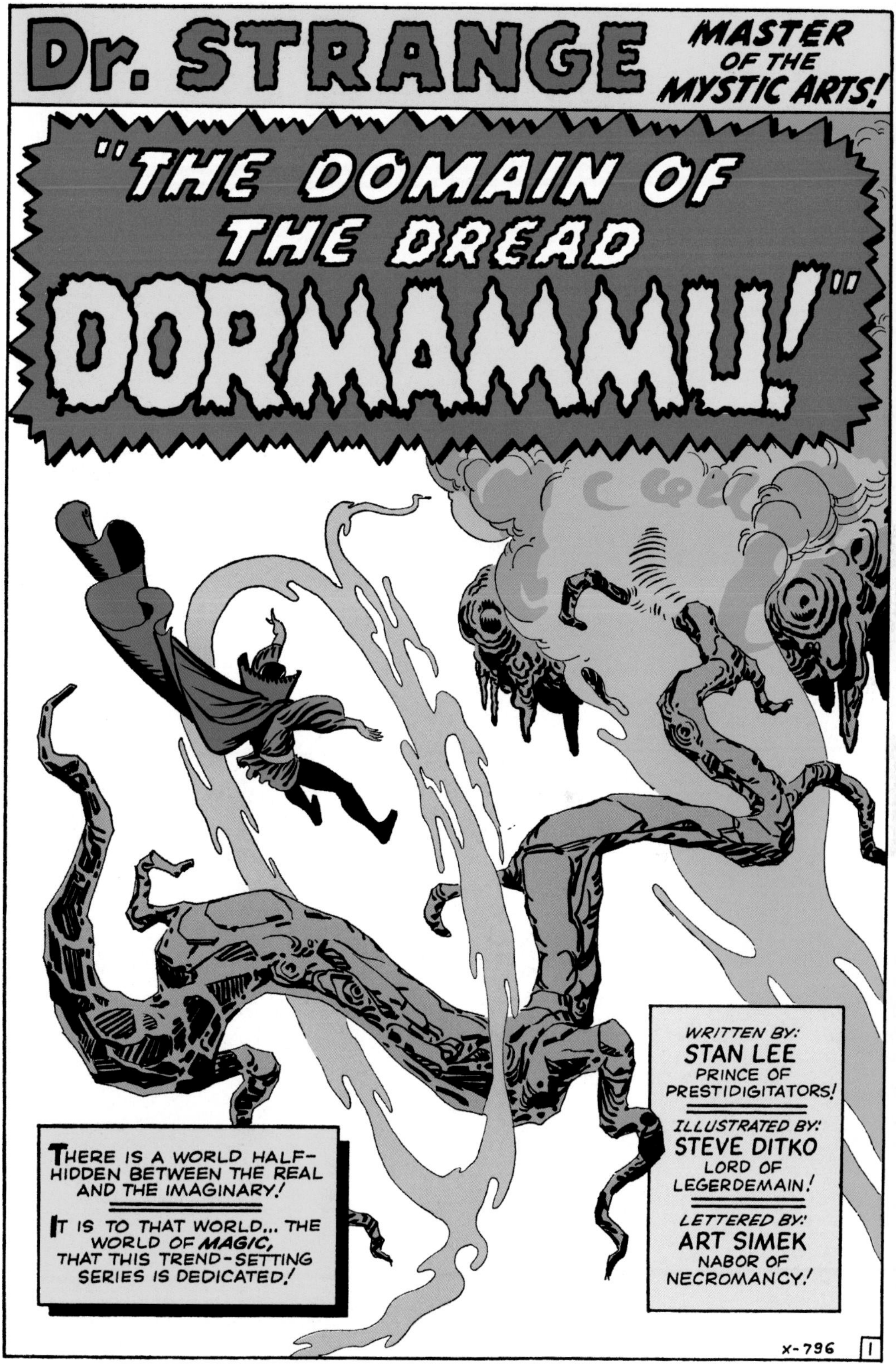
Dr. STRANGE
MASTER OF THE MYSTIC ARTS!
"THE DOMAIN OF THE DREAD DORMAMMU!"
WRITTEN BY: STAN LEE PRINCE OF PRESTIDIGITATORS!
ILLUSTRATED BY: STEVE DITKO LORD OF LEGERDEMAIN!
LETTERED BY: ART SIMEK NABOR OF NECROMANCY!
THERE IS A WORLD HALF-HIDDEN BETWEEN THE REAL AND THE IMAGINARY!
IT IS TO THAT WORLD... THE WORLD OF MAGIC, THAT THIS TREND-SETTING SERIES IS DEDICATED!
X-796
1

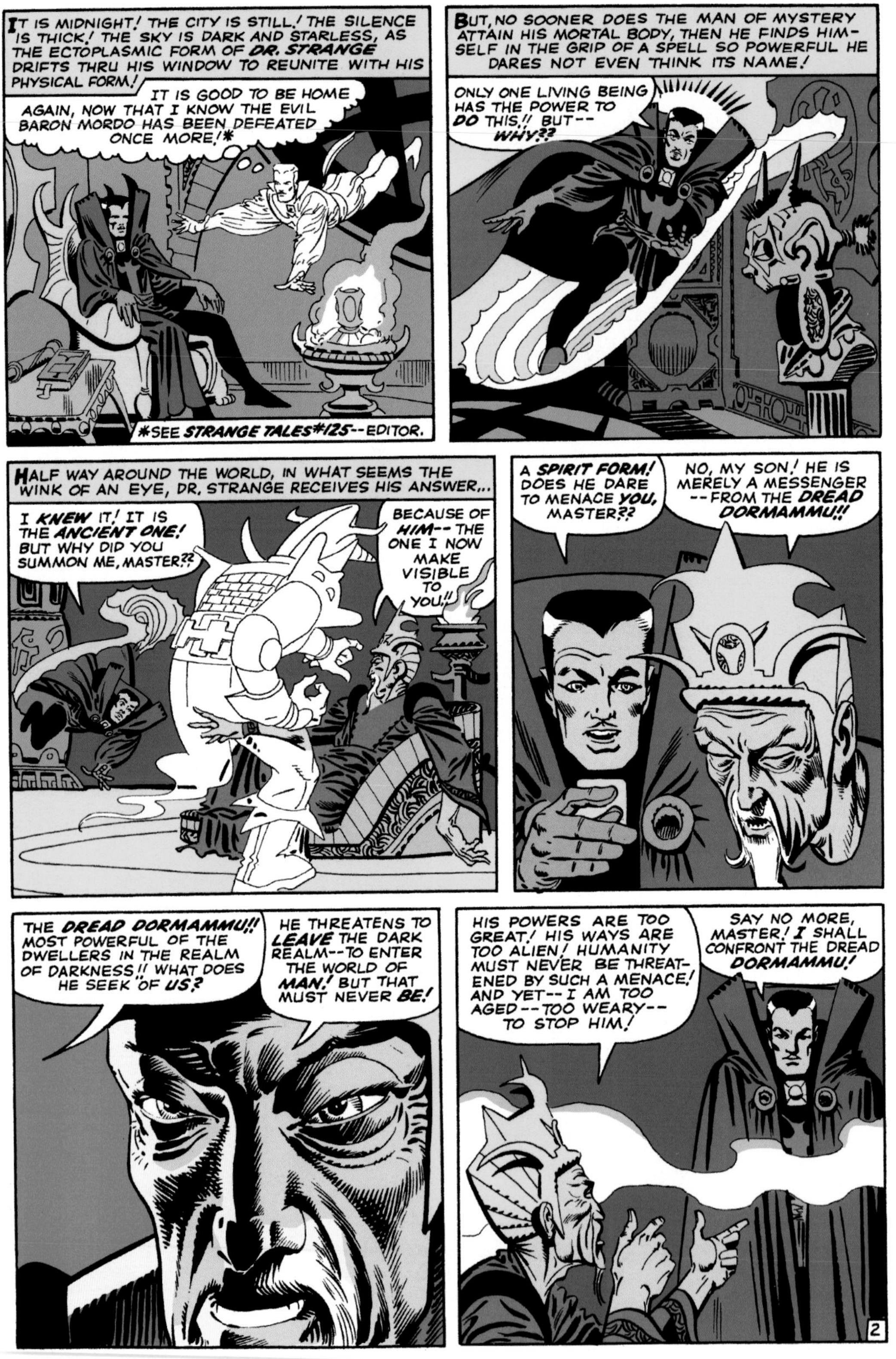
IT IS MIDNIGHT! THE CITY IS STILL! THE SILENCE IS THICK! THE SKY IS DARK AND STARLESS, AS THE ECTOPLASMIC FORM OF DR. STRANGE DRIFTS THRU HIS WINDOW TO REUNITE WITH HIS PHYSICAL FORM!
IT IS GOOD TO BE HOME AGAIN, NOW THAT I KNOW THE EVIL BARON MORDO HAS BEEN DEFEATED ONCE MORE!*
*SEE STRANGE TALES #125--EDITOR.
BUT, NO SOONER DOES THE MAN OF MYSTERY ATTAIN HIS MORTAL BODY, THEN HE FINDS HIMSELF IN THE GRIP OF A SPELL SO POWERFUL HE DARES NOT EVEN THINK ITS NAME!
ONLY ONE LIVING BEING HAS THE POWER TO DO THIS!! BUT-- WHY??
HALF WAY AROUND THE WORLD, IN WHAT SEEMS THE WINK OF AN EYE, DR. STRANGE RECEIVES HIS ANSWER...
I KNEW IT! IT IS THE ANCIENT ONE! BUT WHY DID YOU SUMMON ME, MASTER??
BECAUSE OF HIM-- THE ONE I NOW MAKE VISIBLE TO YOU!!
A SPIRIT FORM! DOES HE DARE TO MENACE YOU, MASTER??
NO, MY SON! HE IS MERELY A MESSENGER --FROM THE DREAD DORMAMMU!!
THE DREAD DORMAMMU!! MOST POWERFUL OF THE DWELLERS IN THE REALM OF DARKNESS!! WHAT DOES HE SEEK OF US?
HE THREATENS TO LEAVE THE DARK REALM--TO ENTER THE WORLD OF MAN! BUT THAT MUST NEVER BE!
HIS POWERS ARE TOO GREAT! HIS WAYS ARE TOO ALIEN! HUMANITY MUST NEVER BE THREATENED BY SUCH A MENACE! AND YET-- I AM TOO AGED--TOO WEARY-- TO STOP HIM!
SAY NO MORE, MASTER! I SHALL CONFRONT THE DREAD DORMAMMU!
2

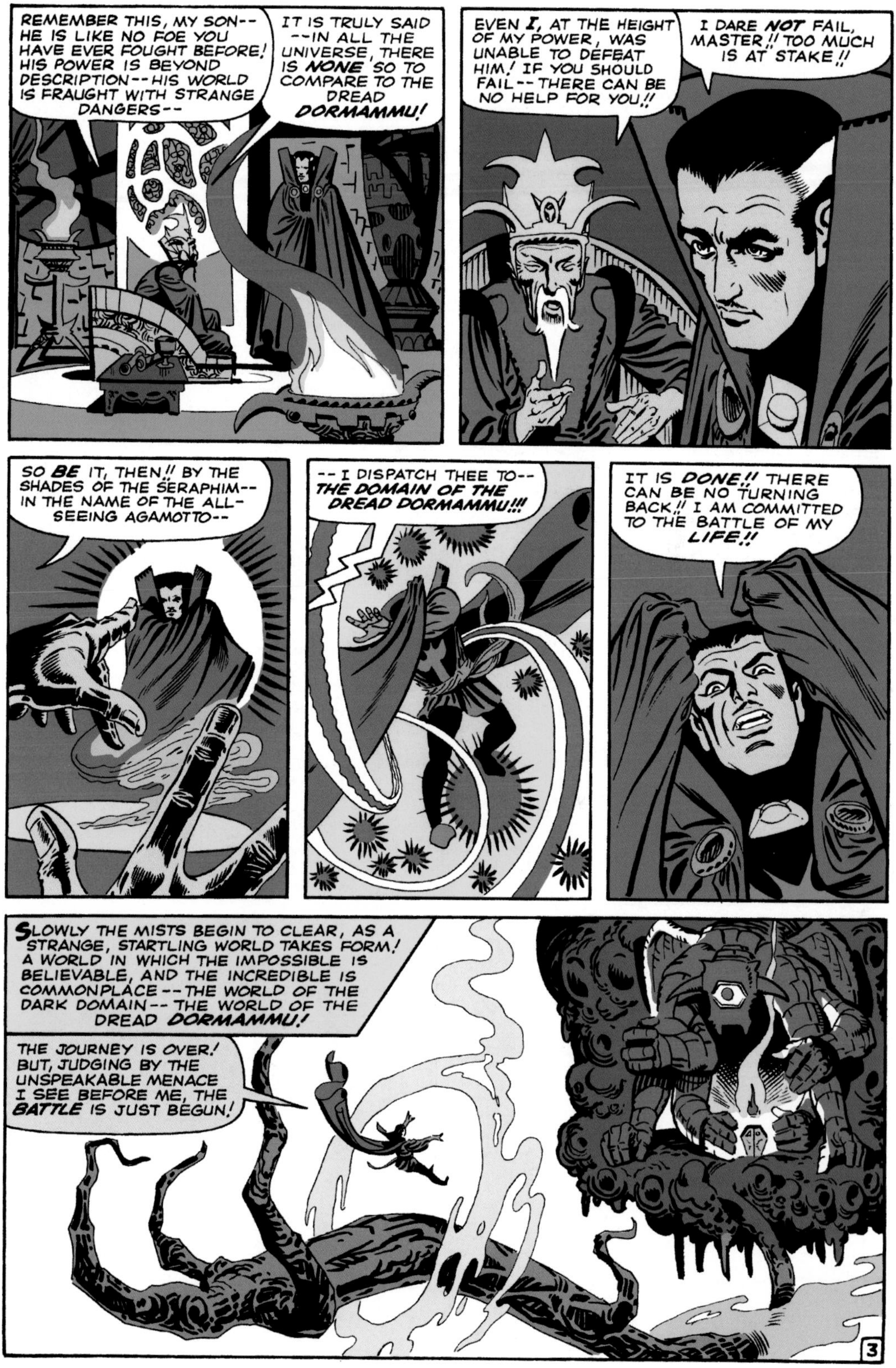
REMEMBER THIS, MY SON-- HE IS LIKE NO FOE YOU HAVE EVER FOUGHT BEFORE! HIS POWER IS BEYOND DESCRIPTION--HIS WORLD IS FRAUGHT WITH STRANGE DANGERS--
IT IS TRULY SAID --IN ALL THE UNIVERSE, THERE IS NONE SO TO COMPARE TO THE DREAD DORMAMMU!
EVEN I, AT THE HEIGHT OF MY POWER, WAS UNABLE TO DEFEAT HIM! IF YOU SHOULD FAIL--THERE CAN BE NO HELP FOR YOU!!
I DARE NOT FAIL, MASTER!! TOO MUCH IS AT STAKE!!
SO BE IT, THEN!! BY THE SHADES OF THE SERAPHIM-- IN THE NAME OF THE ALL-SEEING AGAMOTTO--
--I DISPATCH THEE TO-- THE DOMAIN OF THE DREAD DORMAMMU!!!
IT IS DONE!! THERE CAN BE NO TURNING BACK!! I AM COMMITTED TO THE BATTLE OF MY LIFE!!
SLOWLY THE MISTS BEGIN TO CLEAR, AS A STRANGE, STARTLING WORLD TAKES FORM! A WORLD IN WHICH THE IMPOSSIBLE IS BELIEVABLE, AND THE INCREDIBLE IS COMMONPLACE--THE WORLD OF THE DARK DOMAIN--THE WORLD OF THE DREAD DORMAMMU!
THE JOURNEY IS OVER! BUT, JUDGING BY THE UNSPEAKABLE MENACE I SEE BEFORE ME, THE BATTLE IS JUST BEGUN!
3

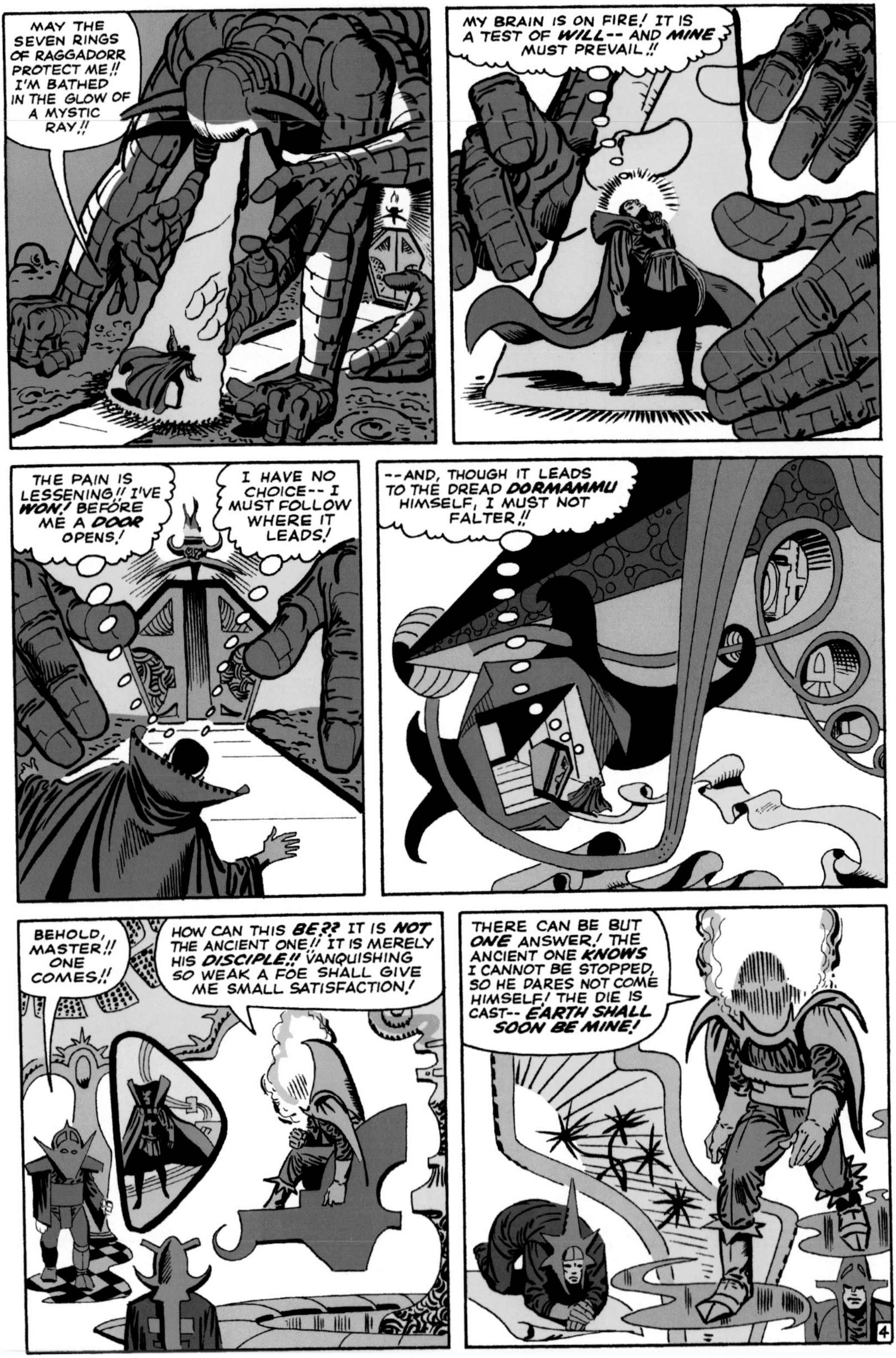
MAY THE SEVEN RINGS OF RAGGADORR PROTECT ME!! I'M BATHED IN THE GLOW OF A MYSTIC RAY!!
MY BRAIN IS ON FIRE! IT IS A TEST OF WILL-- AND MINE MUST PREVAIL!!
THE PAIN IS LESSENING!! I'VE WON! BEFORE ME A DOOR OPENS!
I HAVE NO CHOICE-- I MUST FOLLOW WHERE IT LEADS!
--AND, THOUGH IT LEADS TO THE DREAD DORMAMMU HIMSELF, I MUST NOT FALTER!!
BEHOLD, MASTER!! ONE COMES!!
HOW CAN THIS BE?? IT IS NOT THE ANCIENT ONE!! IT IS MERELY HIS DISCIPLE!! VANQUISHING SO WEAK A FOE SHALL GIVE ME SMALL SATISFACTION!
THERE CAN BE BUT ONE ANSWER! THE ANCIENT ONE KNOWS I CANNOT BE STOPPED, SO HE DARES NOT COME HIMSELF! THE DIE IS CAST-- EARTH SHALL SOON BE MINE!
4

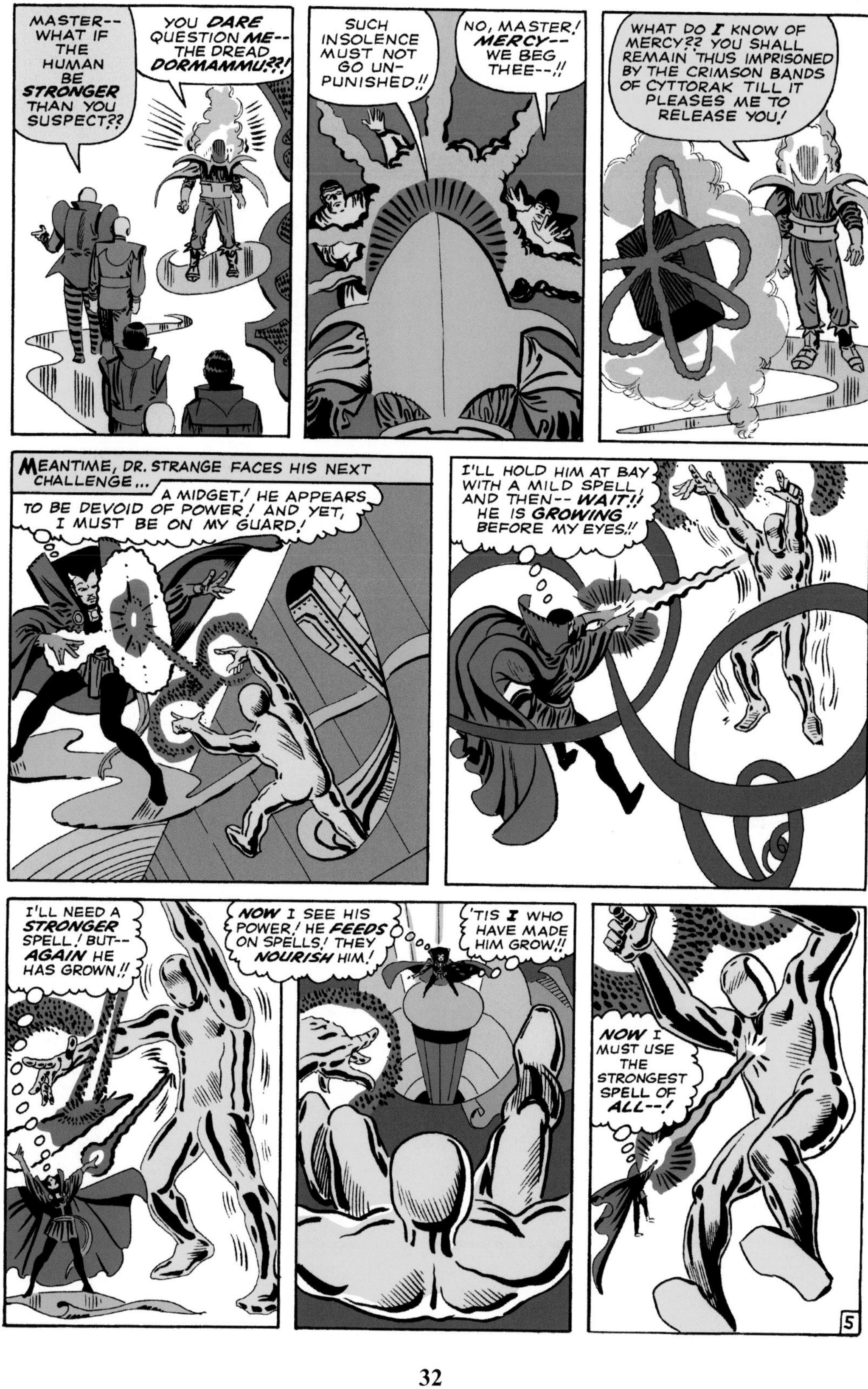
MASTER-- WHAT IF THE HUMAN BE STRONGER THAN YOU SUSPECT??
YOU DARE QUESTION ME-- THE DREAD DORMAMMU??!
SUCH INSOLENCE MUST NOT GO UN-PUNISHED!!
NO, MASTER! MERCY-- WE BEG THEE--!!
WHAT DO I KNOW OF MERCY?? YOU SHALL REMAIN THUS IMPRISONED BY THE CRIMSON BANDS OF CYTTORAK TILL IT PLEASES ME TO RELEASE YOU!
MEANTIME, DR. STRANGE FACES HIS NEXT CHALLENGE...
A MIDGET! HE APPEARS TO BE DEVOID OF POWER! AND YET, I MUST BE ON MY GUARD!
I'LL HOLD HIM AT BAY WITH A MILD SPELL, AND THEN-- WAIT!! HE IS GROWING BEFORE MY EYES!!
I'LL NEED A STRONGER SPELL! BUT-- AGAIN HE HAS GROWN!!
NOW I SEE HIS POWER! HE FEEDS ON SPELLS! THEY NOURISH HIM!
'TIS I WHO HAVE MADE HIM GROW!!
NOW I MUST USE THE STRONGEST SPELL OF ALL--!
5

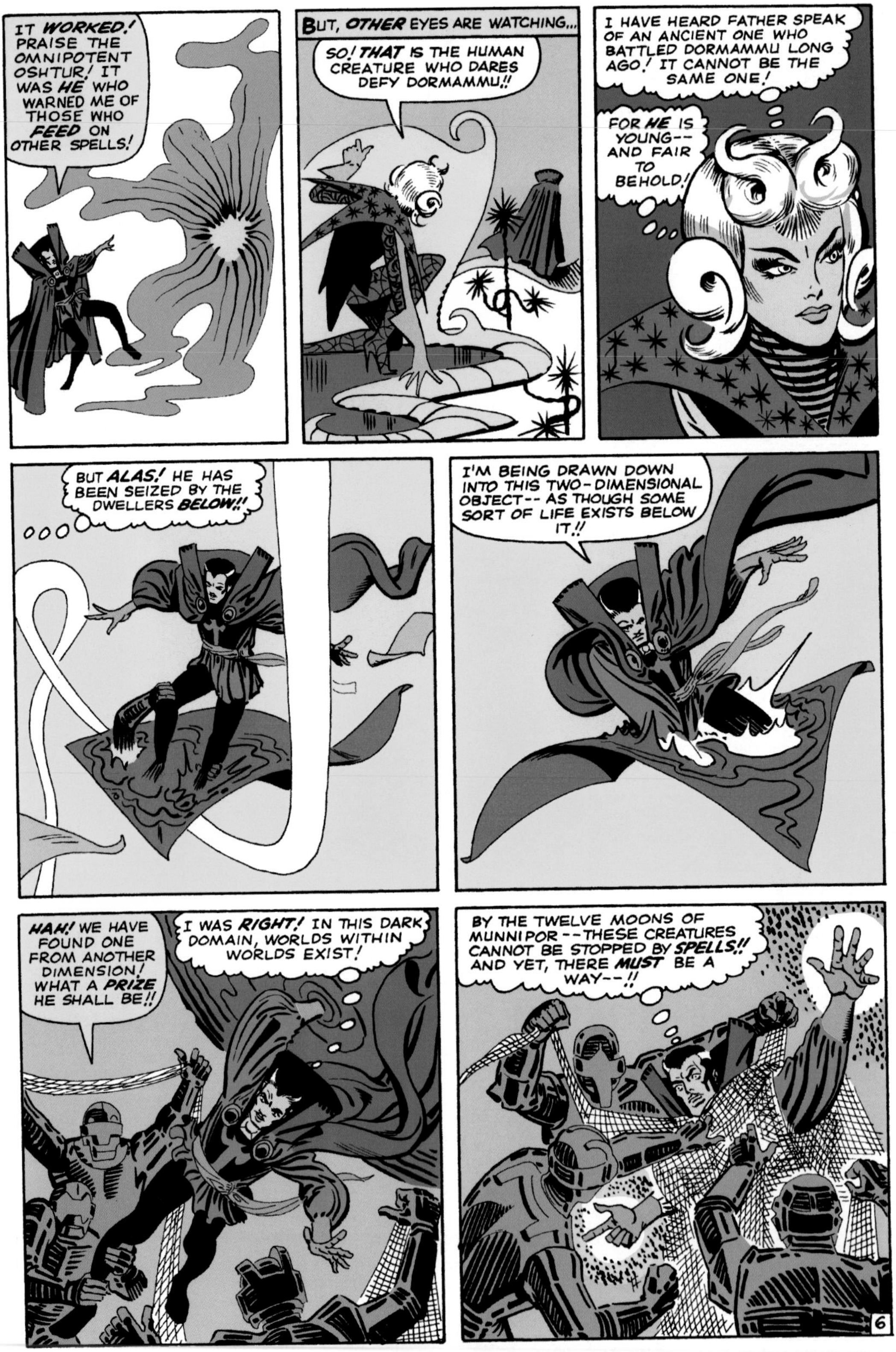
IT WORKED! PRAISE THE OMNIPOTENT OSHTUR! IT WAS HE WHO WARNED ME OF THOSE WHO FEED ON OTHER SPELLS!
BUT, OTHER EYES ARE WATCHING...
SO! THAT IS THE HUMAN CREATURE WHO DARES DEFY DORMAMMU!!
I HAVE HEARD FATHER SPEAK OF AN ANCIENT ONE WHO BATTLED DORMAMMU LONG AGO! IT CANNOT BE THE SAME ONE!
FOR HE IS YOUNG-- AND FAIR TO BEHOLD!
BUT ALAS! HE HAS BEEN SEIZED BY THE DWELLERS BELOW!!
I'M BEING DRAWN DOWN INTO THIS TWO-DIMENSIONAL OBJECT-- AS THOUGH SOME SORT OF LIFE EXISTS BELOW IT!!
HAH! WE HAVE FOUND ONE FROM ANOTHER DIMENSION! WHAT A PRIZE HE SHALL BE!!
I WAS RIGHT! IN THIS DARK DOMAIN, WORLDS WITHIN WORLDS EXIST!
BY THE TWELVE MOONS OF MUNNIPOR--THESE CREATURES CANNOT BE STOPPED BY SPELLS!! AND YET, THERE MUST BE A WAY--!!
6

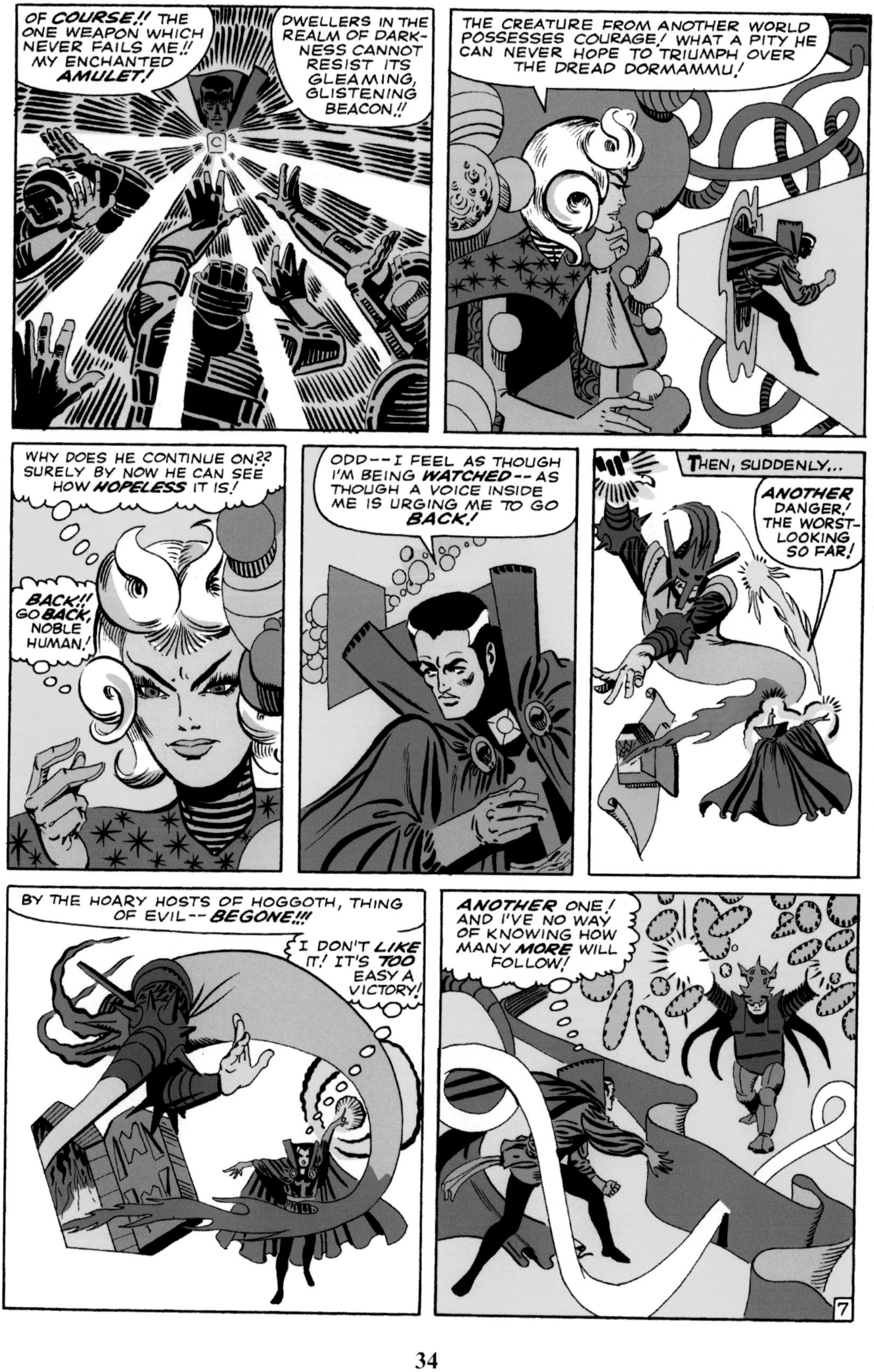

OF COURSE!! THE ONE WEAPON WHICH NEVER FAILS ME!! MY ENCHANTED AMULET!
DWELLERS IN THE REALM OF DARKNESS CANNOT RESIST ITS GLEAMING, GLISTENING BEACON!!
THE CREATURE FROM ANOTHER WORLD POSSESSES COURAGE! WHAT A PITY HE CAN NEVER HOPE TO TRIUMPH OVER THE DREAD DORMAMMU!
WHY DOES HE CONTINUE ON?? SURELY BY NOW HE CAN SEE HOW HOPELESS IT IS!
BACK!! GO BACK, NOBLE HUMAN!
ODD--I FEEL AS THOUGH I'M BEING WATCHED--AS THOUGH A VOICE INSIDE ME IS URGING ME TO GO BACK!
THEN, SUDDENLY...
ANOTHER DANGER! THE WORST-LOOKING SO FAR!
BY THE HOARY HOSTS OF HOGGOTH, THING OF EVIL--BEGONE!!!
I DON'T LIKE IT! IT'S TOO EASY A VICTORY!
ANOTHER ONE! AND I'VE NO WAY OF KNOWING HOW MANY MORE WILL FOLLOW!
7

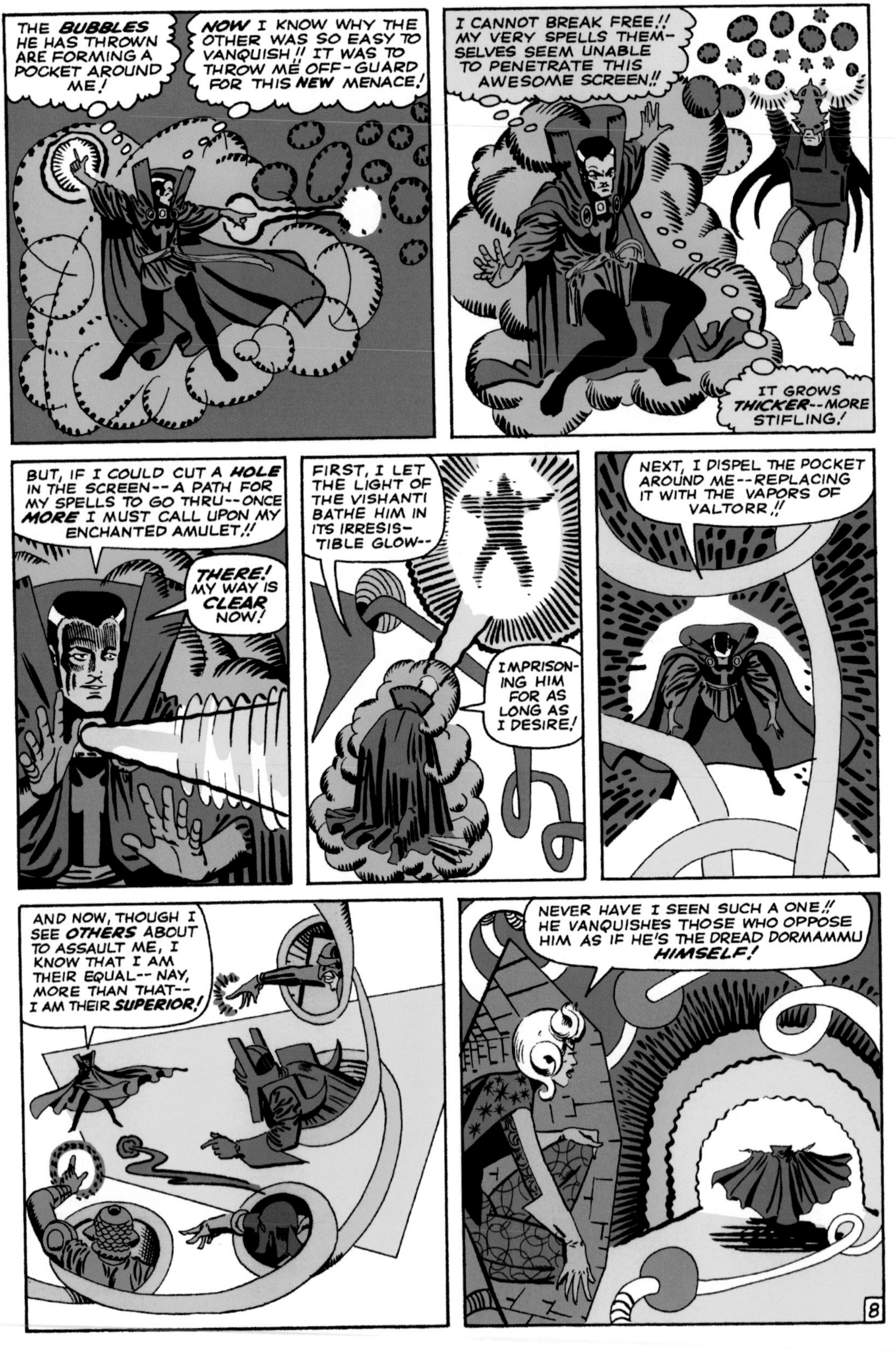

THE BUBBLES HE HAS THROWN ARE FORMING A POCKET AROUND ME!
NOW I KNOW WHY THE OTHER WAS SO EASY TO VANQUISH!! IT WAS TO THROW ME OFF-GUARD FOR THIS NEW MENACE!
I CANNOT BREAK FREE!! MY VERY SPELLS THEMSELVES SEEM UNABLE TO PENETRATE THIS AWESOME SCREEN!!
IT GROWS THICKER--MORE STIFLING!
BUT, IF I COULD CUT A HOLE IN THE SCREEN-- A PATH FOR MY SPELLS TO GO THRU--ONCE MORE I MUST CALL UPON MY ENCHANTED AMULET!!
THERE! MY WAY IS CLEAR NOW!
FIRST, I LET THE LIGHT OF THE VISHANTI BATHE HIM IN ITS IRRESISTIBLE GLOW--
IMPRISONING HIM FOR AS LONG AS I DESIRE!
NEXT, I DISPEL THE POCKET AROUND ME--REPLACING IT WITH THE VAPORS OF VALTORR!!
AND NOW, THOUGH I SEE OTHERS ABOUT TO ASSAULT ME, I KNOW THAT I AM THEIR EQUAL-- NAY, MORE THAN THAT-- I AM THEIR SUPERIOR!
NEVER HAVE I SEEN SUCH A ONE!! HE VANQUISHES THOSE WHO OPPOSE HIM AS IF HE'S THE DREAD DORMAMMU HIMSELF!
8

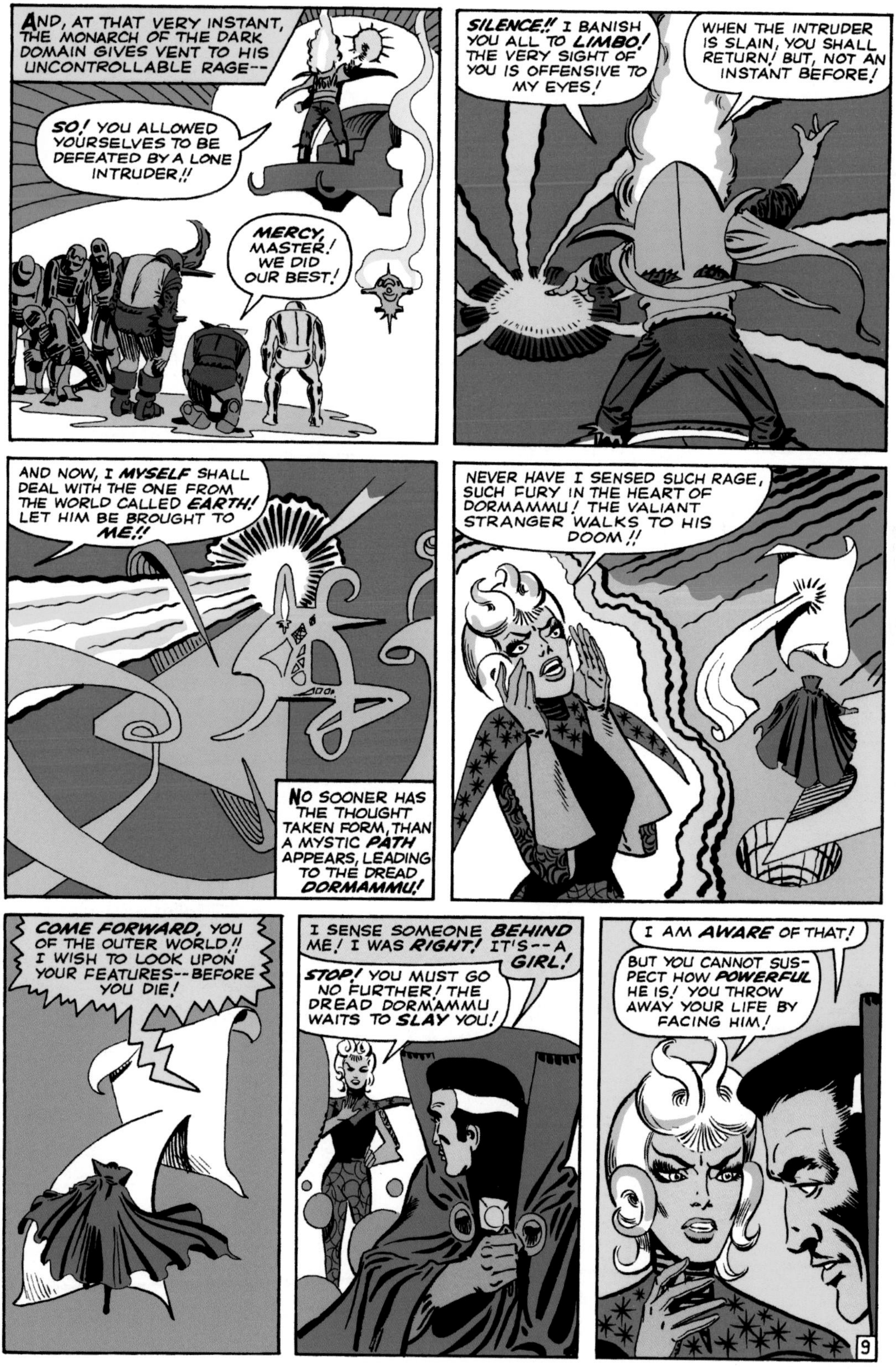
AND, AT THAT VERY INSTANT, THE MONARCH OF THE DARK DOMAIN GIVES VENT TO HIS UNCONTROLLABLE RAGE--
SO! YOU ALLOWED YOURSELVES TO BE DEFEATED BY A LONE INTRUDER!!
MERCY, MASTER! WE DID OUR BEST!
SILENCE!! I BANISH YOU ALL TO LIMBO! THE VERY SIGHT OF YOU IS OFFENSIVE TO MY EYES!
WHEN THE INTRUDER IS SLAIN, YOU SHALL RETURN! BUT, NOT AN INSTANT BEFORE!
AND NOW, I MYSELF SHALL DEAL WITH THE ONE FROM THE WORLD CALLED EARTH! LET HIM BE BROUGHT TO ME!!
NO SOONER HAS THE THOUGHT TAKEN FORM, THAN A MYSTIC PATH APPEARS, LEADING TO THE DREAD DORMAMMU!
NEVER HAVE I SENSED SUCH RAGE, SUCH FURY IN THE HEART OF DORMAMMU! THE VALIANT STRANGER WALKS TO HIS DOOM!!
COME FORWARD, YOU OF THE OUTER WORLD!! I WISH TO LOOK UPON YOUR FEATURES--BEFORE YOU DIE!
I SENSE SOMEONE BEHIND ME! I WAS RIGHT! IT'S--A GIRL!
STOP! YOU MUST GO NO FURTHER! THE DREAD DORMAMMU WAITS TO SLAY YOU!
I AM AWARE OF THAT!
BUT YOU CANNOT SUSPECT HOW POWERFUL HE IS! YOU THROW AWAY YOUR LIFE BY FACING HIM!
9

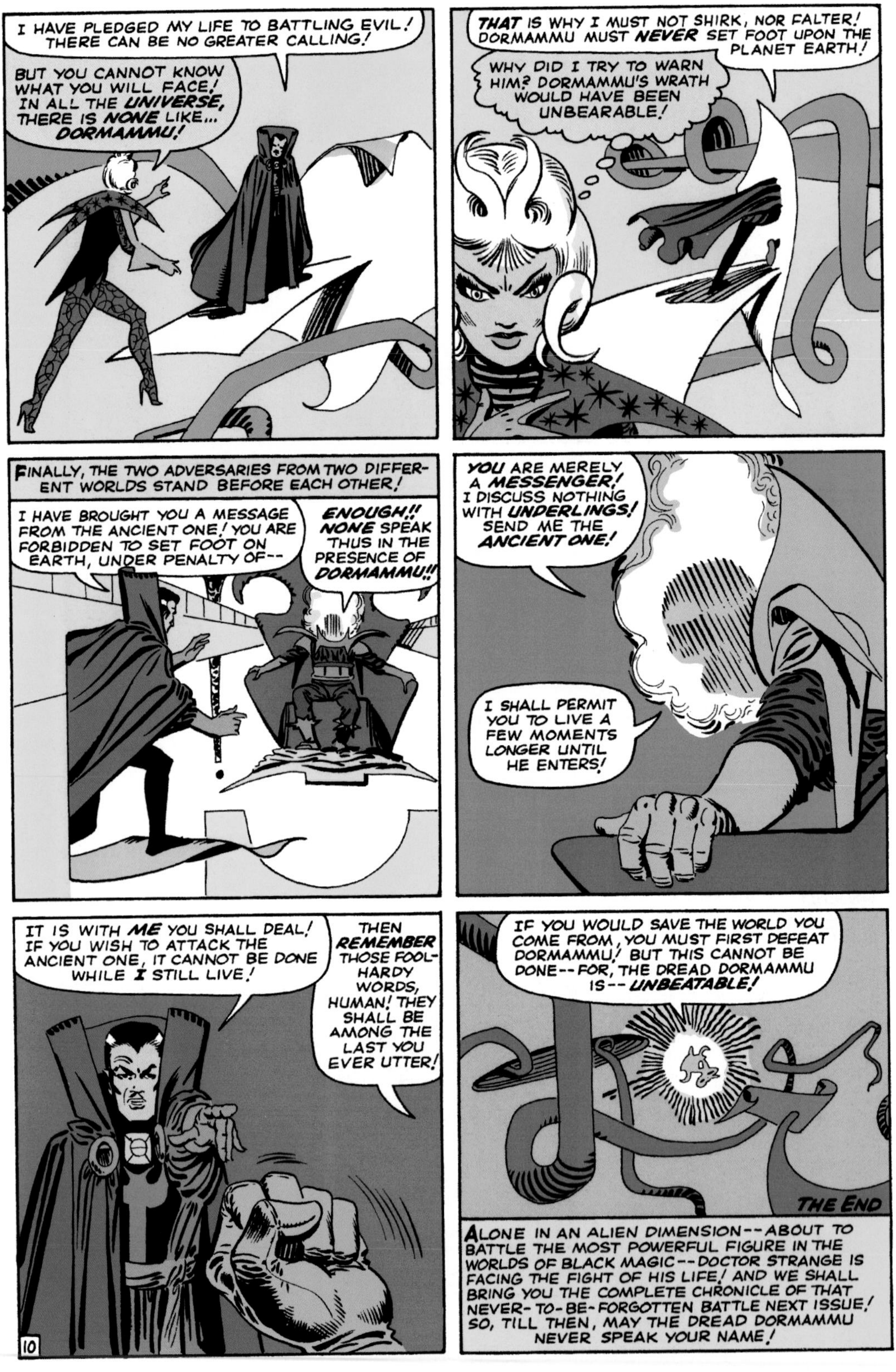
I HAVE PLEDGED MY LIFE TO BATTLING EVIL! THERE CAN BE NO GREATER CALLING!
BUT YOU CANNOT KNOW WHAT YOU WILL FACE! IN ALL THE UNIVERSE, THERE IS NONE LIKE... DORMAMMU!
THAT IS WHY I MUST NOT SHIRK, NOR FALTER! DORMAMMU MUST NEVER SET FOOT UPON THE PLANET EARTH!
WHY DID I TRY TO WARN HIM? DORMAMMU'S WRATH WOULD HAVE BEEN UNBEARABLE!
FINALLY, THE TWO ADVERSARIES FROM TWO DIFFERENT WORLDS STAND BEFORE EACH OTHER!
I HAVE BROUGHT YOU A MESSAGE FROM THE ANCIENT ONE! YOU ARE FORBIDDEN TO SET FOOT ON EARTH, UNDER PENALTY OF--
ENOUGH!! NONE SPEAK THUS IN THE PRESENCE OF DORMAMMU!!
YOU ARE MERELY A MESSENGER! I DISCUSS NOTHING WITH UNDERLINGS! SEND ME THE ANCIENT ONE!
I SHALL PERMIT YOU TO LIVE A FEW MOMENTS LONGER UNTIL HE ENTERS!
IT IS WITH ME YOU SHALL DEAL! IF YOU WISH TO ATTACK THE ANCIENT ONE, IT CANNOT BE DONE WHILE I STILL LIVE!
THEN REMEMBER THOSE FOOL-HARDY WORDS, HUMAN! THEY SHALL BE AMONG THE LAST YOU EVER UTTER!
10
IF YOU WOULD SAVE THE WORLD YOU COME FROM, YOU MUST FIRST DEFEAT DORMAMMU! BUT THIS CANNOT BE DONE--FOR, THE DREAD DORMAMMU IS--UNBEATABLE!
THE END
ALONE IN AN ALIEN DIMENSION--ABOUT TO BATTLE THE MOST POWERFUL FIGURE IN THE WORLDS OF BLACK MAGIC--DOCTOR STRANGE IS FACING THE FIGHT OF HIS LIFE! AND WE SHALL BRING YOU THE COMPLETE CHRONICLE OF THAT NEVER-TO-BE-FORGOTTEN BATTLE NEXT ISSUE! SO, TILL THEN, MAY THE DREAD DORMAMMU NEVER SPEAK YOUR NAME!

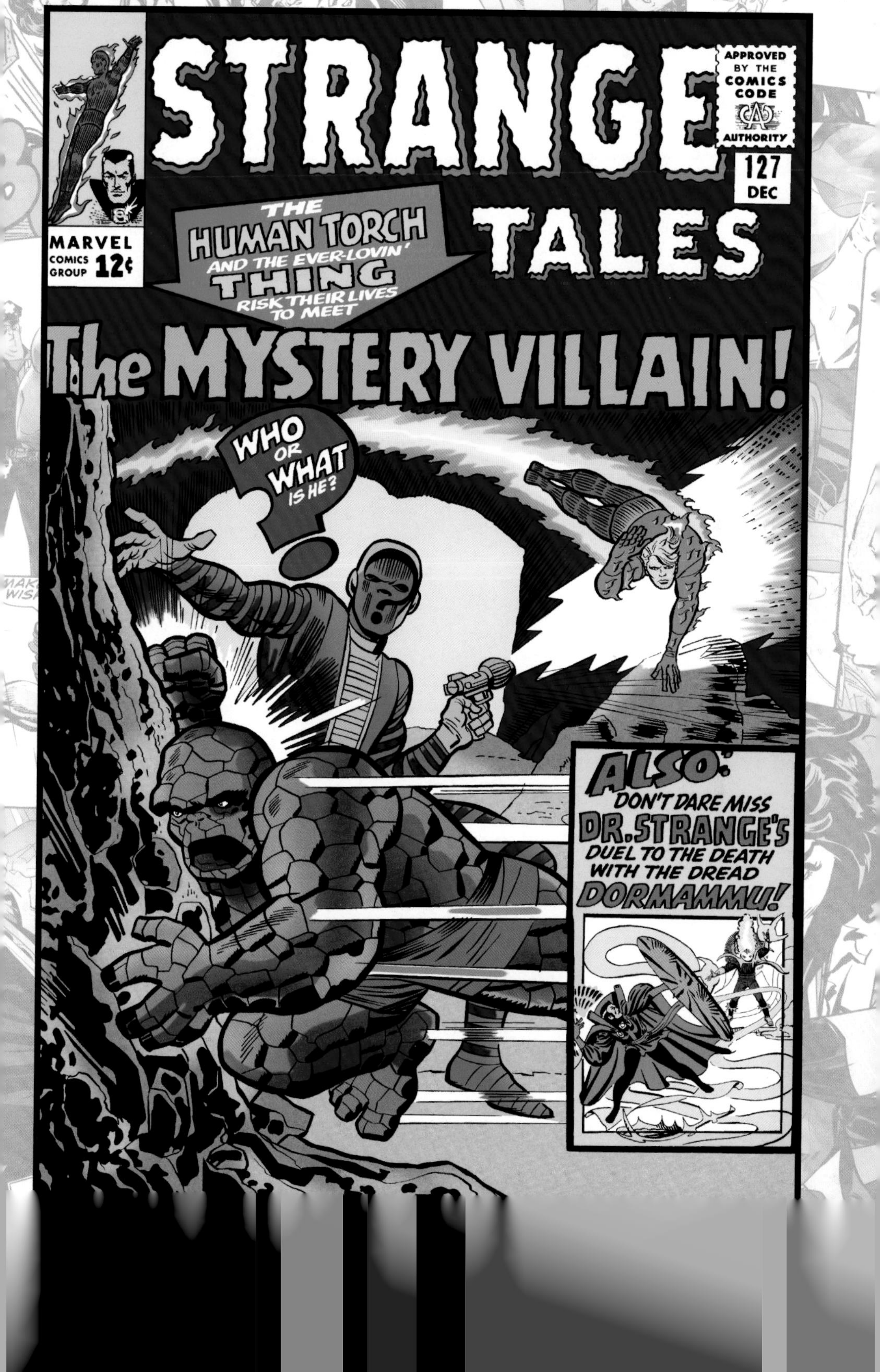
STRANGE TALES
APPROVED BY THE COMICS CODE AUTHORITY
127 DEC
MARVEL COMICS GROUP 12¢
THE HUMAN TORCH AND THE EVER-LOVIN' THING RISK THEIR LIVES TO MEET
The MYSTERY VILLAIN!
WHO OR WHAT IS HE?
ALSO: DON'T DARE MISS DR. STRANGE'S DUEL TO THE DEATH WITH THE DREAD DORMAMMU!

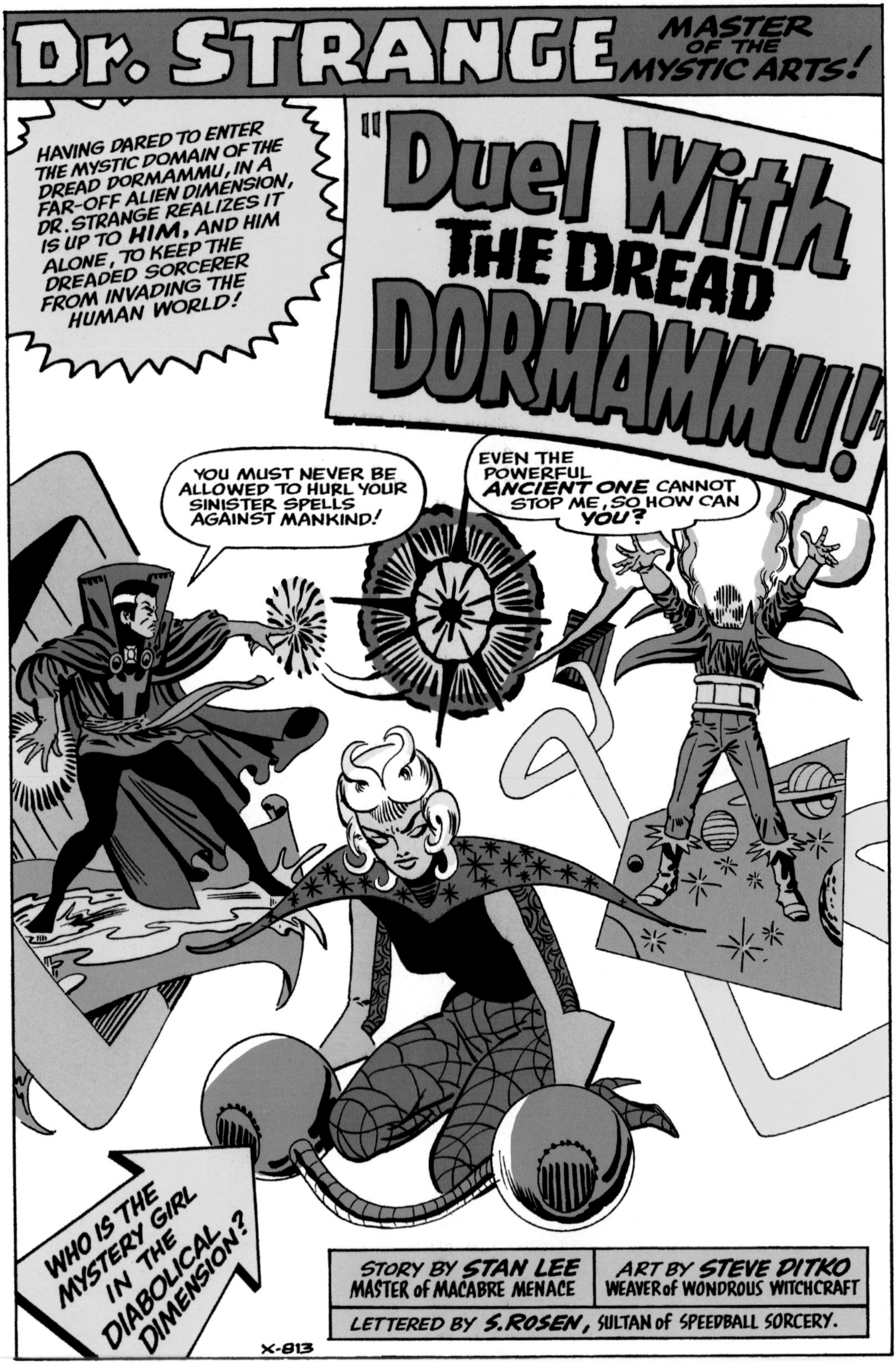
Dr. STRANGE MASTER OF THE MYSTIC ARTS!
HAVING DARED TO ENTER THE MYSTIC DOMAIN OF THE DREAD DORMAMMU, IN A FAR-OFF ALIEN DIMENSION, DR. STRANGE REALIZES IT IS UP TO HIM, AND HIM ALONE, TO KEEP THE DREADED SORCERER FROM INVADING THE HUMAN WORLD!
"Duel With THE DREAD DORMAMMU!"
YOU MUST NEVER BE ALLOWED TO HURL YOUR SINISTER SPELLS AGAINST MANKIND!
EVEN THE POWERFUL ANCIENT ONE CANNOT STOP ME, SO HOW CAN YOU?
WHO IS THE MYSTERY GIRL IN THE DIABOLICAL DIMENSION?
STORY BY STAN LEE MASTER of MACABRE MENACE
ART BY STEVE DITKO WEAVER of WONDROUS WITCHCRAFT
LETTERED BY S.ROSEN, SULTAN of SPEEDBALL SORCERY.
X-813

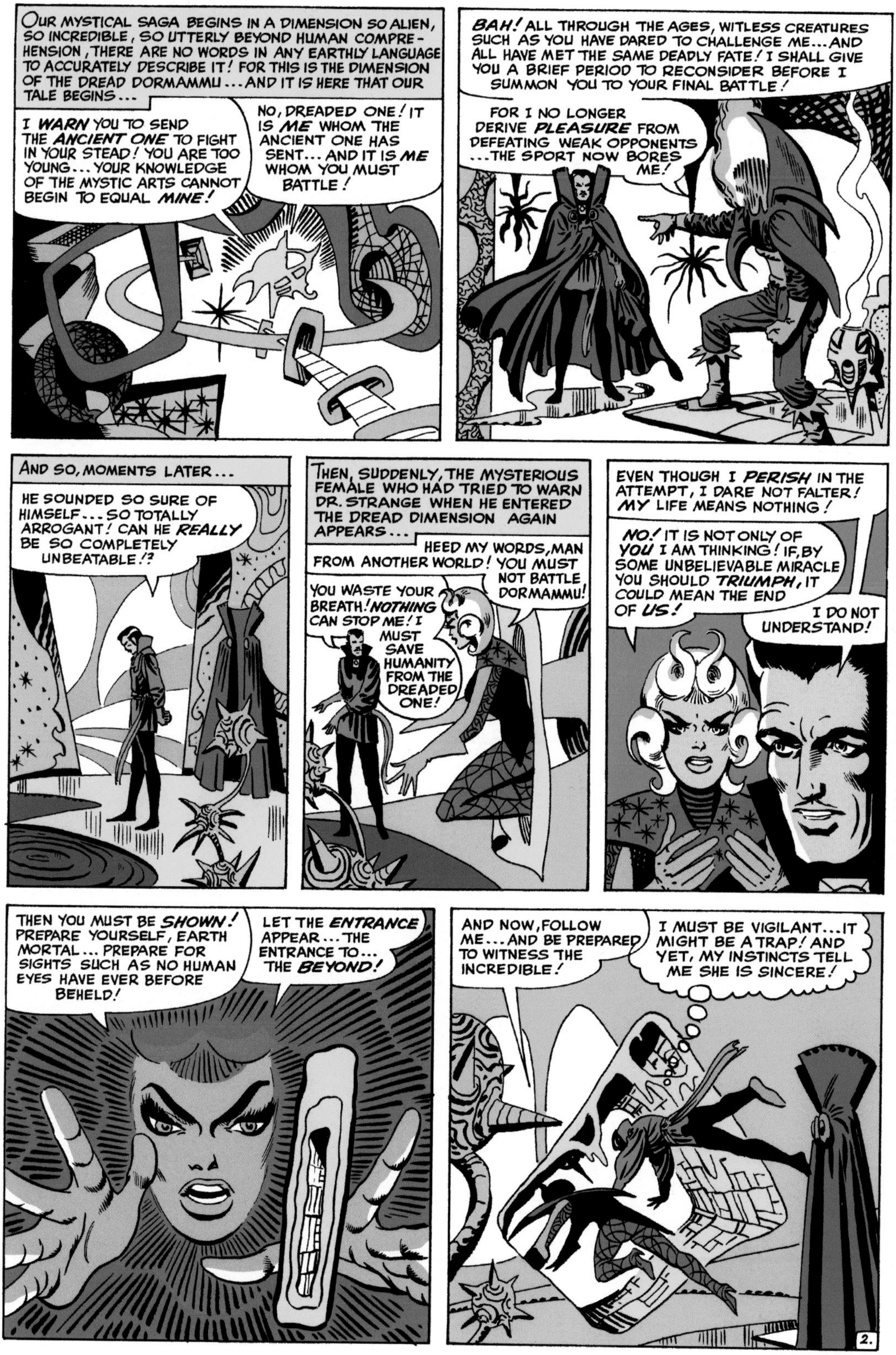

OUR MYSTICAL SAGA BEGINS IN A DIMENSION SO ALIEN, SO INCREDIBLE, SO UTTERLY BEYOND HUMAN COMPREHENSION, THERE ARE NO WORDS IN ANY EARTHLY LANGUAGE TO ACCURATELY DESCRIBE IT! FOR THIS IS THE DIMENSION OF THE DREAD DORMAMMU... AND IT IS HERE THAT OUR TALE BEGINS...
I WARN YOU TO SEND THE ANCIENT ONE TO FIGHT IN YOUR STEAD! YOU ARE TOO YOUNG... YOUR KNOWLEDGE OF THE MYSTIC ARTS CANNOT BEGIN TO EQUAL MINE!
NO, DREADED ONE! IT IS ME WHOM THE ANCIENT ONE HAS SENT... AND IT IS ME WHOM YOU MUST BATTLE!
BAH! ALL THROUGH THE AGES, WITLESS CREATURES SUCH AS YOU HAVE DARED TO CHALLENGE ME... AND ALL HAVE MET THE SAME DEADLY FATE! I SHALL GIVE YOU A BRIEF PERIOD TO RECONSIDER BEFORE I SUMMON YOU TO YOUR FINAL BATTLE!
FOR I NO LONGER DERIVE PLEASURE FROM DEFEATING WEAK OPPONENTS ...THE SPORT NOW BORES ME!
AND SO, MOMENTS LATER...
HE SOUNDED SO SURE OF HIMSELF... SO TOTALLY ARROGANT! CAN HE REALLY BE SO COMPLETELY UNBEATABLE!?
THEN, SUDDENLY, THE MYSTERIOUS FEMALE WHO HAD TRIED TO WARN DR. STRANGE WHEN HE ENTERED THE DREAD DIMENSION AGAIN APPEARS...
HEED MY WORDS, MAN FROM ANOTHER WORLD! YOU MUST NOT BATTLE DORMAMMU!
YOU WASTE YOUR BREATH! NOTHING CAN STOP ME! I MUST SAVE HUMANITY FROM THE DREADED ONE!
EVEN THOUGH I PERISH IN THE ATTEMPT, I DARE NOT FALTER! MY LIFE MEANS NOTHING!
NO! IT IS NOT ONLY OF YOU I AM THINKING! IF, BY SOME UNBELIEVABLE MIRACLE YOU SHOULD TRIUMPH, IT COULD MEAN THE END OF US!
I DO NOT UNDERSTAND!
THEN YOU MUST BE SHOWN! PREPARE YOURSELF, EARTH MORTAL... PREPARE FOR SIGHTS SUCH AS NO HUMAN EYES HAVE EVER BEFORE BEHELD!
LET THE ENTRANCE APPEAR... THE ENTRANCE TO... THE BEYOND!
AND NOW, FOLLOW ME... AND BE PREPARED TO WITNESS THE INCREDIBLE!
I MUST BE VIGILANT... IT MIGHT BE A TRAP! AND YET, MY INSTINCTS TELL ME SHE IS SINCERE!
2.

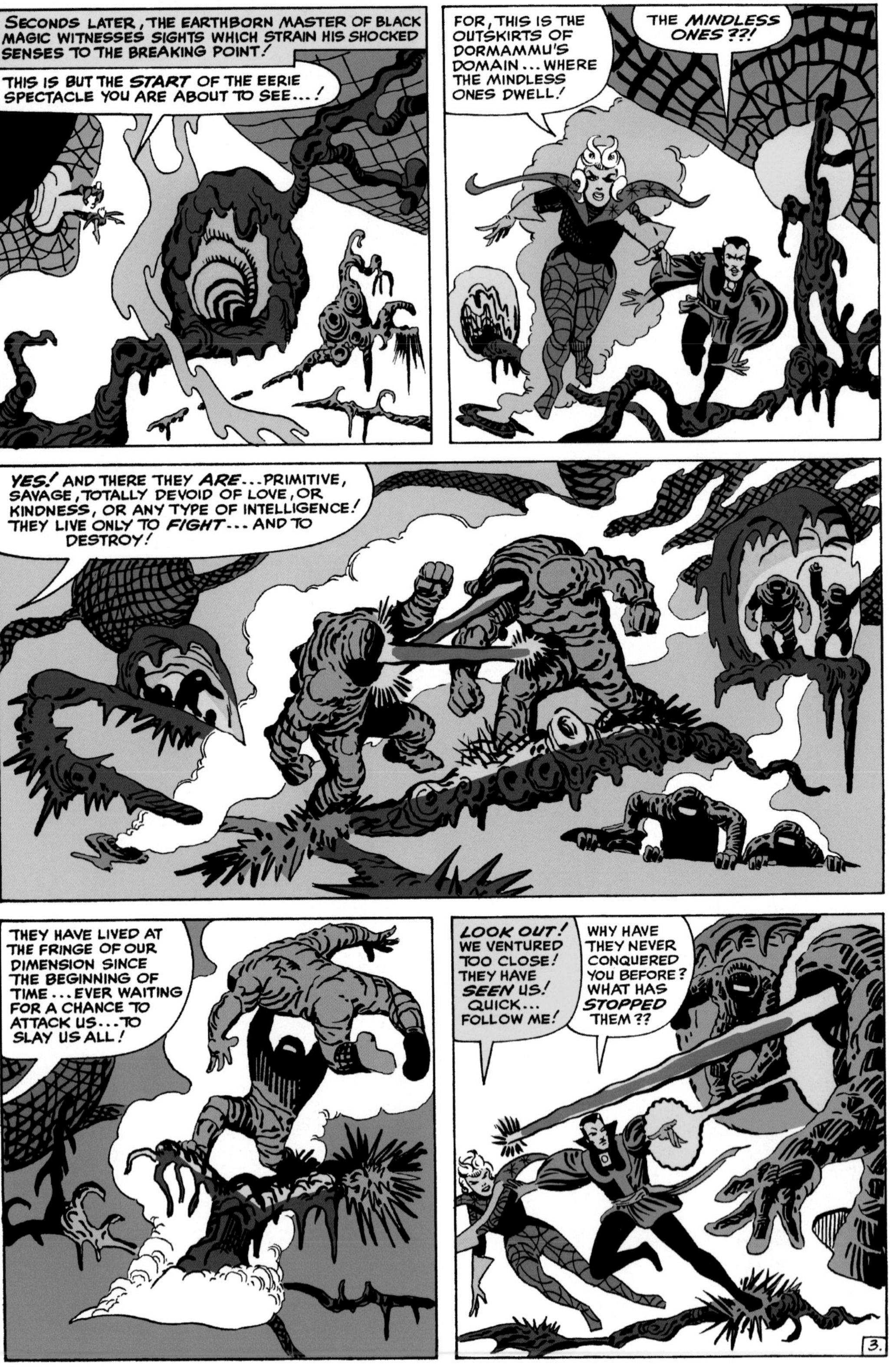

SECONDS LATER, THE EARTHBORN MASTER OF BLACK MAGIC WITNESSES SIGHTS WHICH STRAIN HIS SHOCKED SENSES TO THE BREAKING POINT!
THIS IS BUT THE START OF THE EERIE SPECTACLE YOU ARE ABOUT TO SEE...!
FOR, THIS IS THE OUTSKIRTS OF DORMAMMU'S DOMAIN... WHERE THE MINDLESS ONES DWELL!
THE MINDLESS ONES??!
YES! AND THERE THEY ARE... PRIMITIVE, SAVAGE, TOTALLY DEVOID OF LOVE, OR KINDNESS, OR ANY TYPE OF INTELLIGENCE! THEY LIVE ONLY TO FIGHT... AND TO DESTROY!
THEY HAVE LIVED AT THE FRINGE OF OUR DIMENSION SINCE THE BEGINNING OF TIME... EVER WAITING FOR A CHANCE TO ATTACK US... TO SLAY US ALL!
LOOK OUT! WE VENTURED TOO CLOSE! THEY HAVE SEEN US! QUICK... FOLLOW ME!
WHY HAVE THEY NEVER CONQUERED YOU BEFORE? WHAT HAS STOPPED THEM??
3.

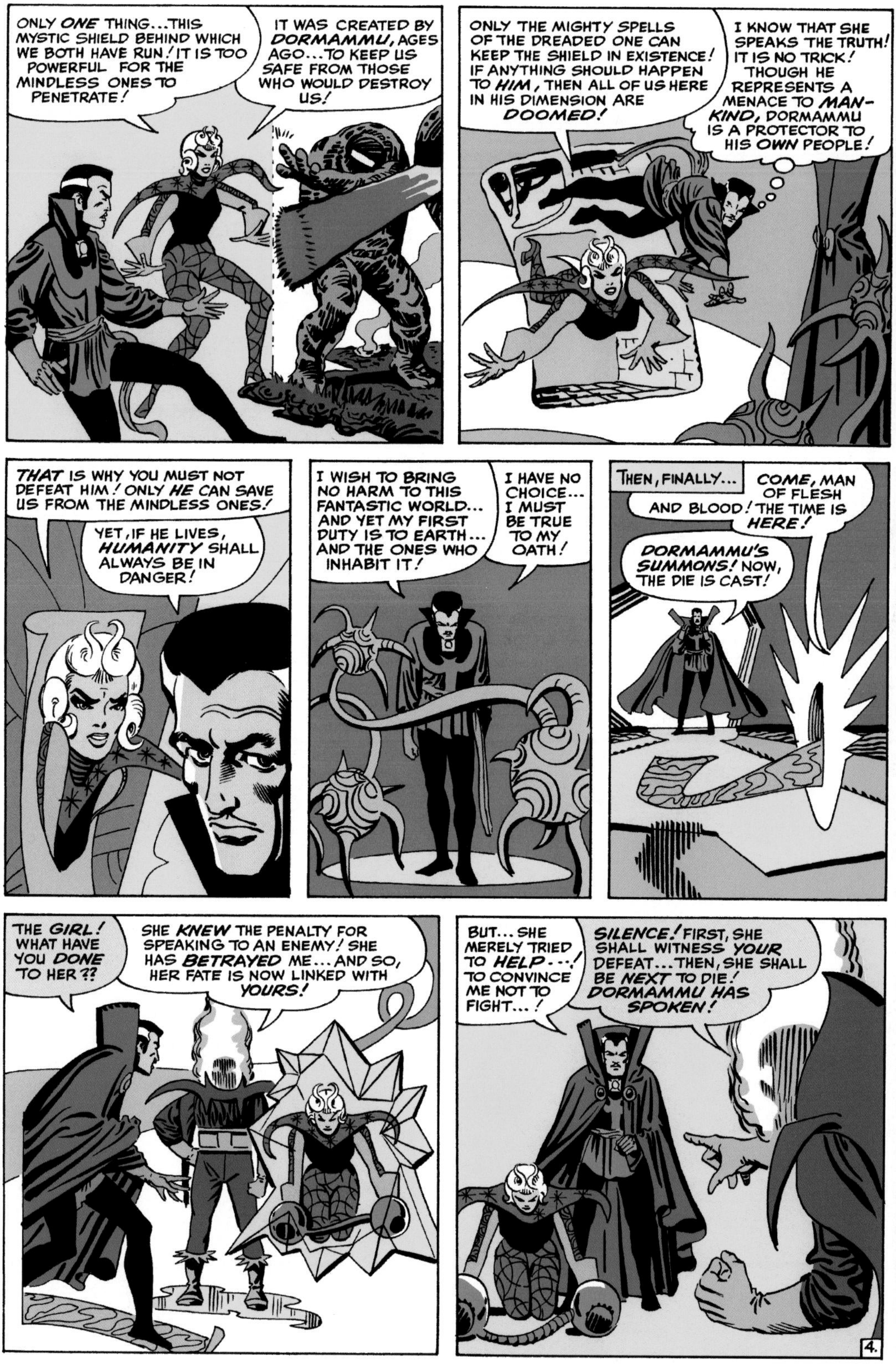
ONLY ONE THING...THIS MYSTIC SHIELD BEHIND WHICH WE BOTH HAVE RUN! IT IS TOO POWERFUL FOR THE MINDLESS ONES TO PENETRATE!
IT WAS CREATED BY DORMAMMU, AGES AGO...TO KEEP US SAFE FROM THOSE WHO WOULD DESTROY US!
ONLY THE MIGHTY SPELLS OF THE DREADED ONE CAN KEEP THE SHIELD IN EXISTENCE! IF ANYTHING SHOULD HAPPEN TO HIM, THEN ALL OF US HERE IN HIS DIMENSION ARE DOOMED!
I KNOW THAT SHE SPEAKS THE TRUTH! IT IS NO TRICK! THOUGH HE REPRESENTS A MENACE TO MAN-KIND, DORMAMMU IS A PROTECTOR TO HIS OWN PEOPLE!
THAT IS WHY YOU MUST NOT DEFEAT HIM! ONLY HE CAN SAVE US FROM THE MINDLESS ONES!
YET, IF HE LIVES, HUMANITY SHALL ALWAYS BE IN DANGER!
I WISH TO BRING NO HARM TO THIS FANTASTIC WORLD... AND YET MY FIRST DUTY IS TO EARTH... AND THE ONES WHO INHABIT IT!
I HAVE NO CHOICE... I MUST BE TRUE TO MY OATH!
THEN, FINALLY...
COME, MAN OF FLESH AND BLOOD! THE TIME IS HERE!
DORMAMMU'S SUMMONS! NOW, THE DIE IS CAST!
THE GIRL! WHAT HAVE YOU DONE TO HER??
SHE KNEW THE PENALTY FOR SPEAKING TO AN ENEMY! SHE HAS BETRAYED ME... AND SO, HER FATE IS NOW LINKED WITH YOURS!
BUT... SHE MERELY TRIED TO HELP...! TO CONVINCE ME NOT TO FIGHT...!
SILENCE! FIRST, SHE SHALL WITNESS YOUR DEFEAT... THEN, SHE SHALL BE NEXT TO DIE! DORMAMMU HAS SPOKEN!
4.

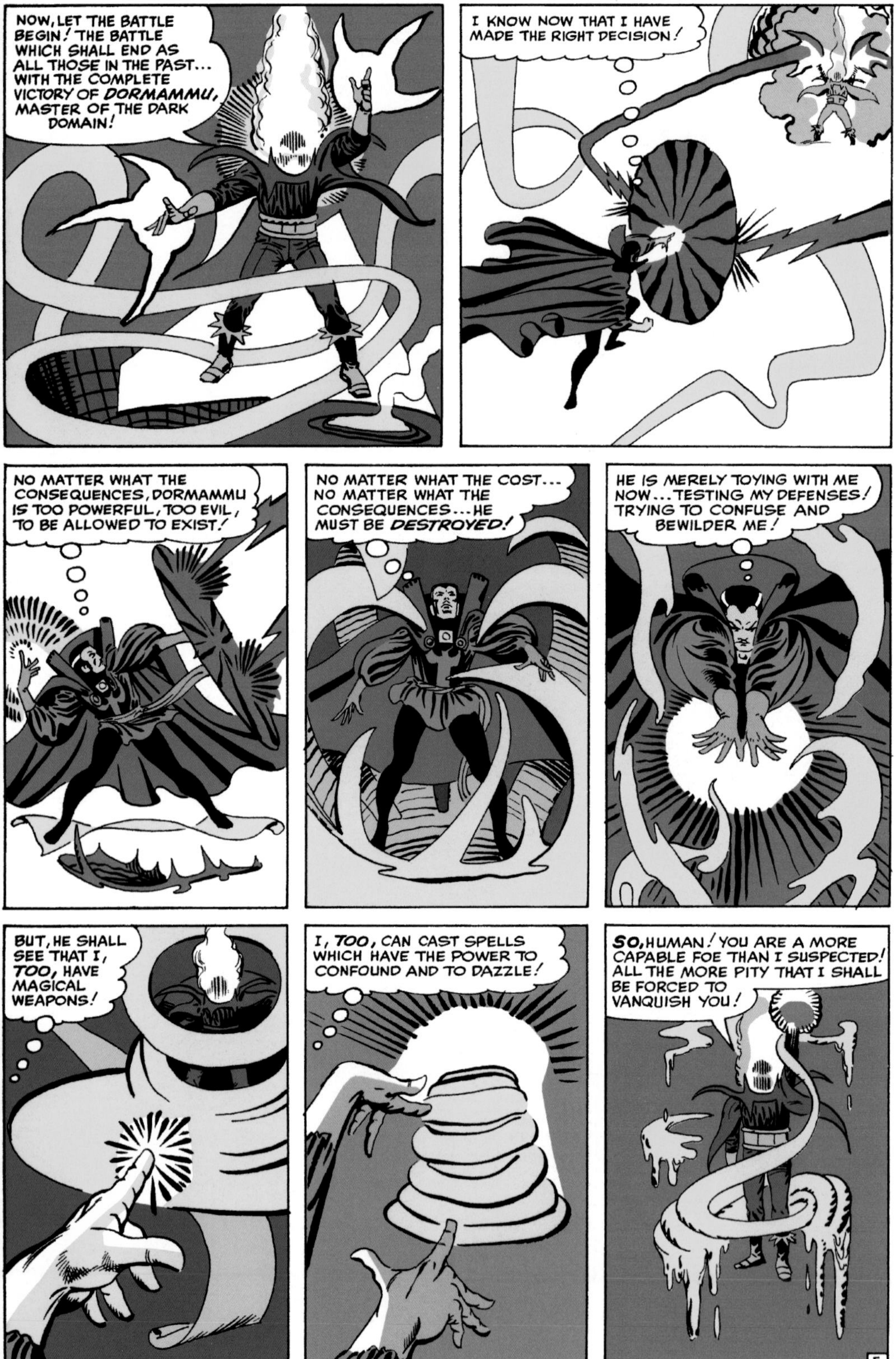
NOW, LET THE BATTLE BEGIN! THE BATTLE WHICH SHALL END AS ALL THOSE IN THE PAST... WITH THE COMPLETE VICTORY OF DORMAMMU, MASTER OF THE DARK DOMAIN!
I KNOW NOW THAT I HAVE MADE THE RIGHT DECISION!
NO MATTER WHAT THE CONSEQUENCES, DORMAMMU IS TOO POWERFUL, TOO EVIL, TO BE ALLOWED TO EXIST!
NO MATTER WHAT THE COST... NO MATTER WHAT THE CONSEQUENCES... HE MUST BE DESTROYED!
HE IS MERELY TOYING WITH ME NOW... TESTING MY DEFENSES! TRYING TO CONFUSE AND BEWILDER ME!
BUT, HE SHALL SEE THAT I, TOO, HAVE MAGICAL WEAPONS!
I, TOO, CAN CAST SPELLS WHICH HAVE THE POWER TO CONFOUND AND TO DAZZLE!
SO, HUMAN! YOU ARE A MORE CAPABLE FOE THAN I SUSPECTED! ALL THE MORE PITY THAT I SHALL BE FORCED TO VANQUISH YOU!
5.

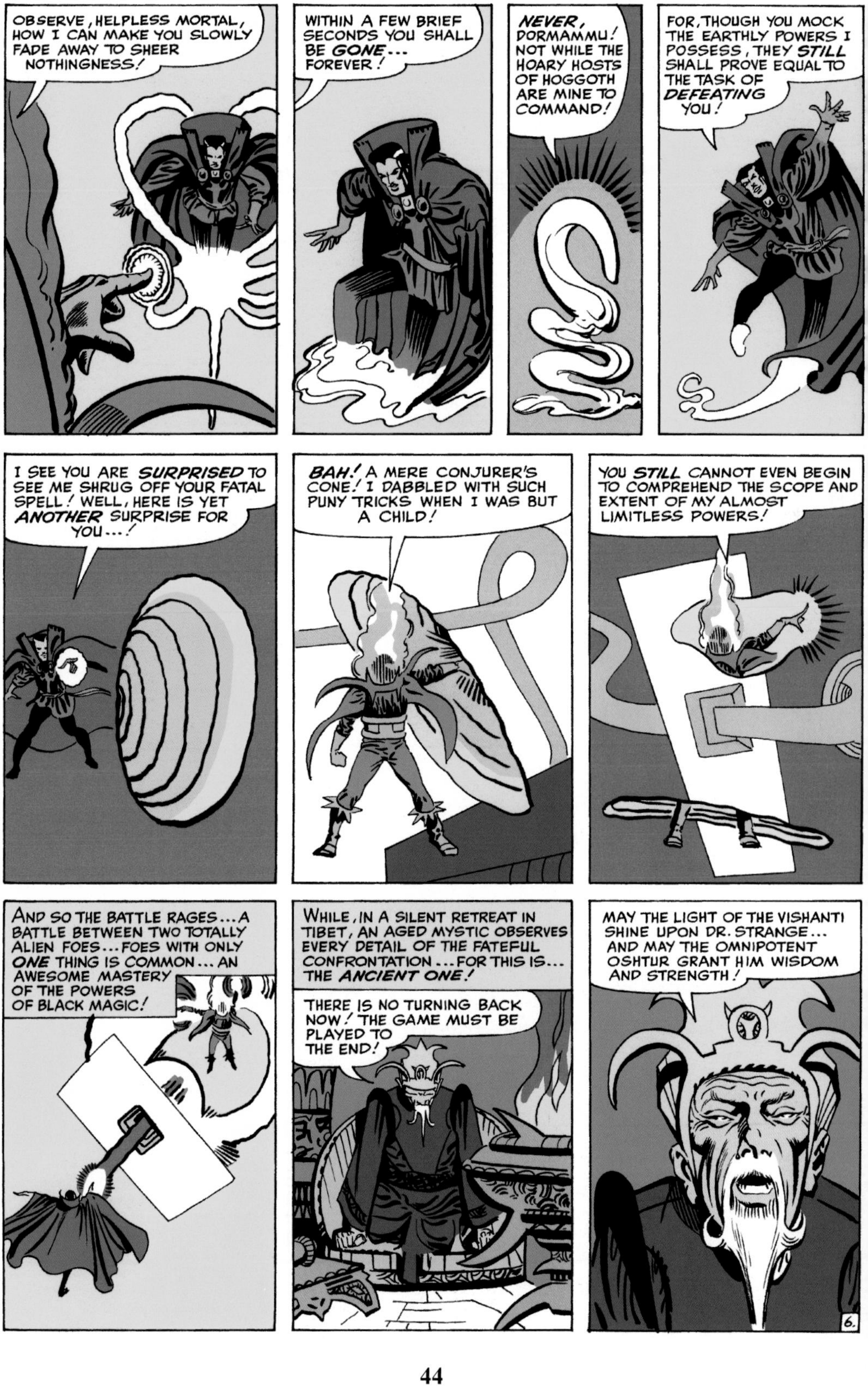

OBSERVE, HELPLESS MORTAL, HOW I CAN MAKE YOU SLOWLY FADE AWAY TO SHEER NOTHINGNESS!
WITHIN A FEW BRIEF SECONDS YOU SHALL BE GONE... FOREVER!
NEVER, DORMAMMU! NOT WHILE THE HOARY HOSTS OF HOGGOTH ARE MINE TO COMMAND!
FOR, THOUGH YOU MOCK THE EARTHLY POWERS I POSSESS, THEY STILL SHALL PROVE EQUAL TO THE TASK OF DEFEATING YOU!
I SEE YOU ARE SURPRISED TO SEE ME SHRUG OFF YOUR FATAL SPELL! WELL, HERE IS YET ANOTHER SURPRISE FOR YOU...!
BAH! A MERE CONJURER'S CONE! I DABBLED WITH SUCH PUNY TRICKS WHEN I WAS BUT A CHILD!
YOU STILL CANNOT EVEN BEGIN TO COMPREHEND THE SCOPE AND EXTENT OF MY ALMOST LIMITLESS POWERS!
AND SO THE BATTLE RAGES... A BATTLE BETWEEN TWO TOTALLY ALIEN FOES... FOES WITH ONLY ONE THING IS COMMON... AN AWESOME MASTERY OF THE POWERS OF BLACK MAGIC!
WHILE, IN A SILENT RETREAT IN TIBET, AN AGED MYSTIC OBSERVES EVERY DETAIL OF THE FATEFUL CONFRONTATION... FOR THIS IS... THE ANCIENT ONE!
THERE IS NO TURNING BACK NOW! THE GAME MUST BE PLAYED TO THE END!
MAY THE LIGHT OF THE VISHANTI SHINE UPON DR. STRANGE... AND MAY THE OMNIPOTENT OSHTUR GRANT HIM WISDOM AND STRENGTH!
6.

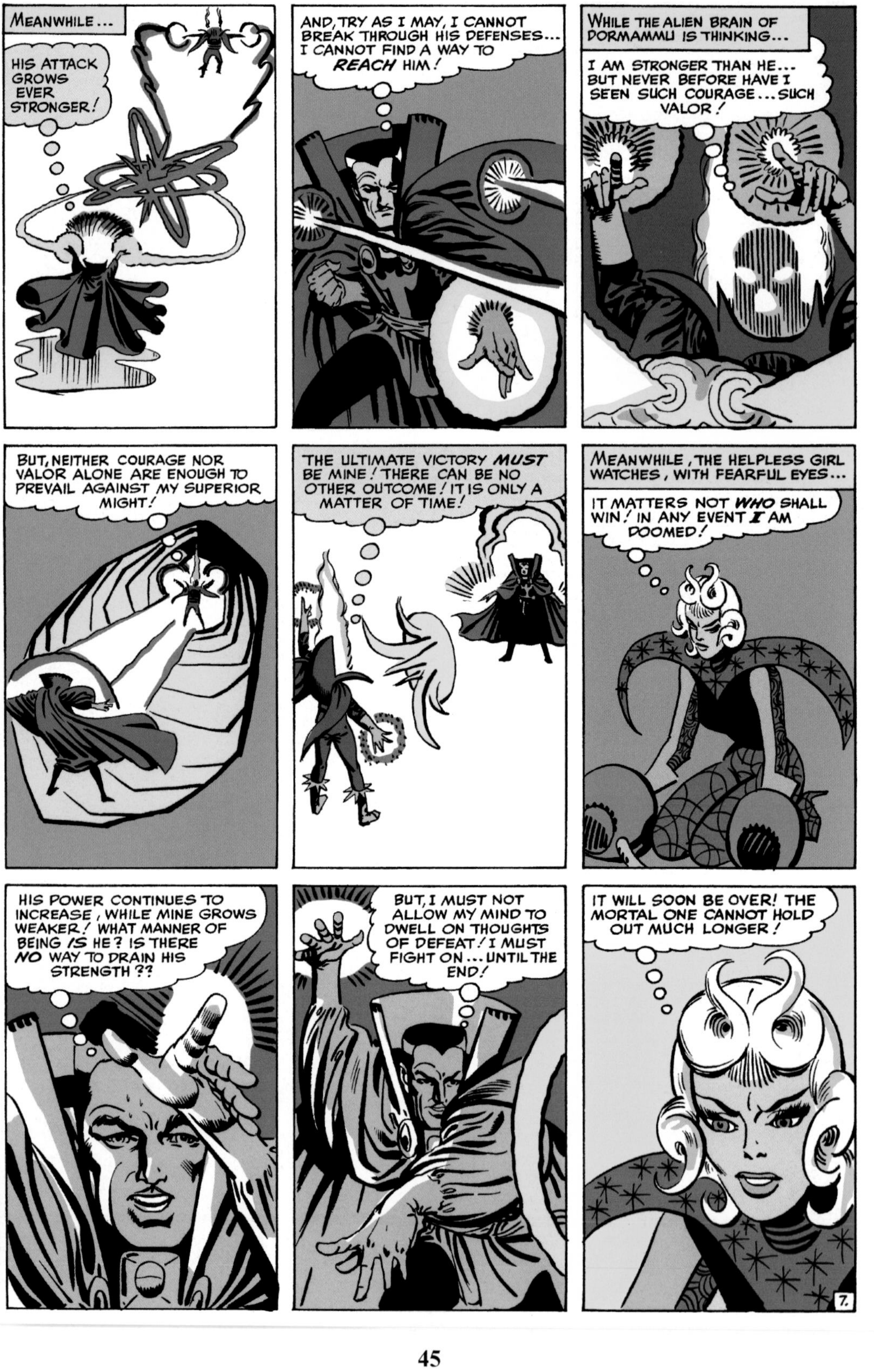
MEANWHILE...
HIS ATTACK GROWS EVER STRONGER!
AND, TRY AS I MAY, I CANNOT BREAK THROUGH HIS DEFENSES... I CANNOT FIND A WAY TO REACH HIM!
WHILE THE ALIEN BRAIN OF DORMAMMU IS THINKING...
I AM STRONGER THAN HE... BUT NEVER BEFORE HAVE I SEEN SUCH COURAGE... SUCH VALOR!
BUT, NEITHER COURAGE NOR VALOR ALONE ARE ENOUGH TO PREVAIL AGAINST MY SUPERIOR MIGHT!
THE ULTIMATE VICTORY MUST BE MINE! THERE CAN BE NO OTHER OUTCOME! IT IS ONLY A MATTER OF TIME!
MEANWHILE, THE HELPLESS GIRL WATCHES, WITH FEARFUL EYES...
IT MATTERS NOT WHO SHALL WIN! IN ANY EVENT I AM DOOMED!
HIS POWER CONTINUES TO INCREASE, WHILE MINE GROWS WEAKER! WHAT MANNER OF BEING IS HE? IS THERE NO WAY TO DRAIN HIS STRENGTH??
BUT, I MUST NOT ALLOW MY MIND TO DWELL ON THOUGHTS OF DEFEAT! I MUST FIGHT ON... UNTIL THE END!
IT WILL SOON BE OVER! THE MORTAL ONE CANNOT HOLD OUT MUCH LONGER!
7.

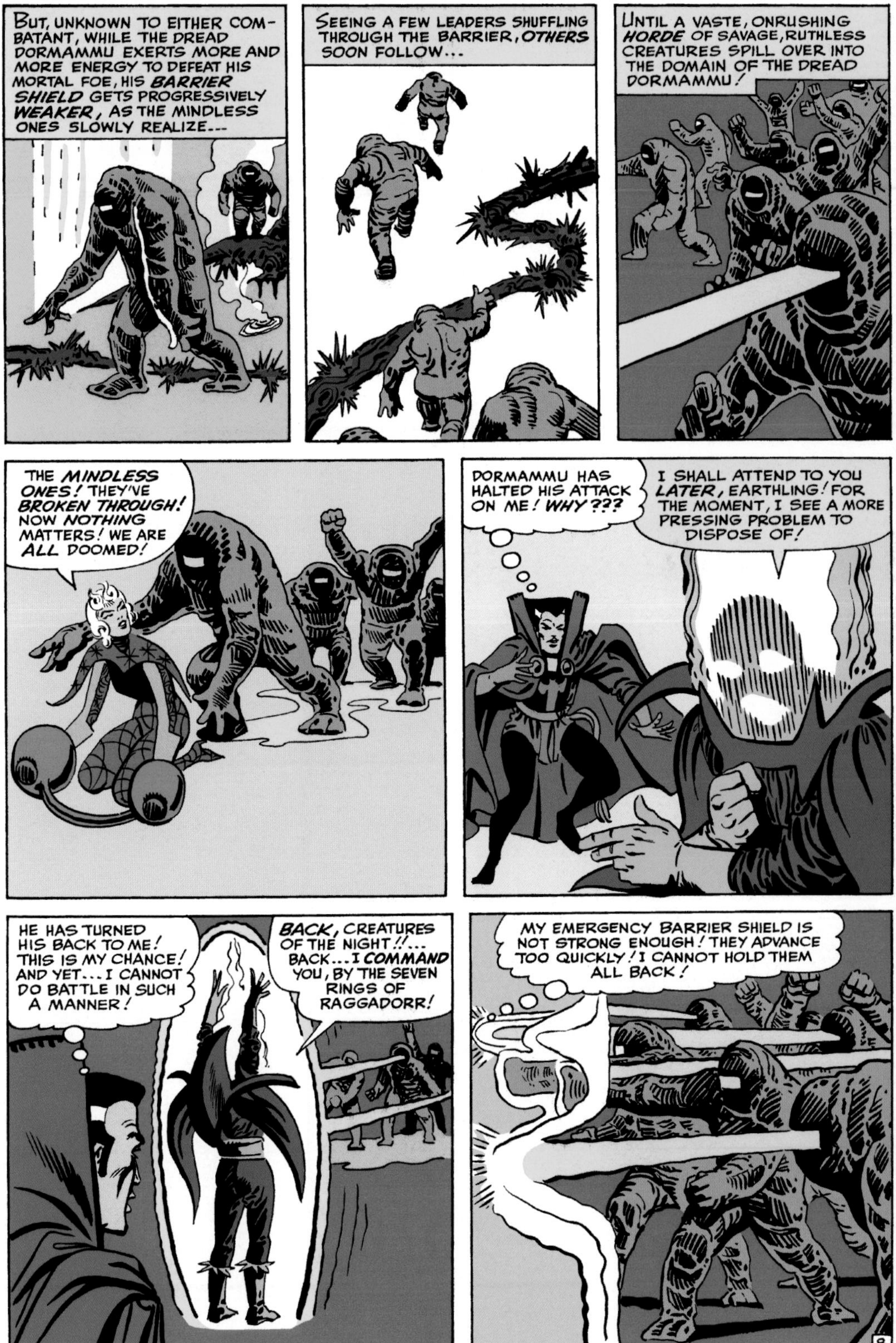

BUT, UNKNOWN TO EITHER COMBATANT, WHILE THE DREAD DORMAMMU EXERTS MORE AND MORE ENERGY TO DEFEAT HIS MORTAL FOE, HIS BARRIER SHIELD GETS PROGRESSIVELY WEAKER, AS THE MINDLESS ONES SLOWLY REALIZE---
SEEING A FEW LEADERS SHUFFLING THROUGH THE BARRIER, OTHERS SOON FOLLOW...
UNTIL A VASTE, ONRUSHING HORDE OF SAVAGE, RUTHLESS CREATURES SPILL OVER INTO THE DOMAIN OF THE DREAD DORMAMMU!
THE MINDLESS ONES! THEY'VE BROKEN THROUGH! NOW NOTHING MATTERS! WE ARE ALL DOOMED!
DORMAMMU HAS HALTED HIS ATTACK ON ME! WHY???
I SHALL ATTEND TO YOU LATER, EARTHLING! FOR THE MOMENT, I SEE A MORE PRESSING PROBLEM TO DISPOSE OF!
HE HAS TURNED HIS BACK TO ME! THIS IS MY CHANCE! AND YET... I CANNOT DO BATTLE IN SUCH A MANNER!
BACK, CREATURES OF THE NIGHT!!... BACK... I COMMAND YOU, BY THE SEVEN RINGS OF RAGGADORR!
MY EMERGENCY BARRIER SHIELD IS NOT STRONG ENOUGH! THEY ADVANCE TOO QUICKLY! I CANNOT HOLD THEM ALL BACK!
8.

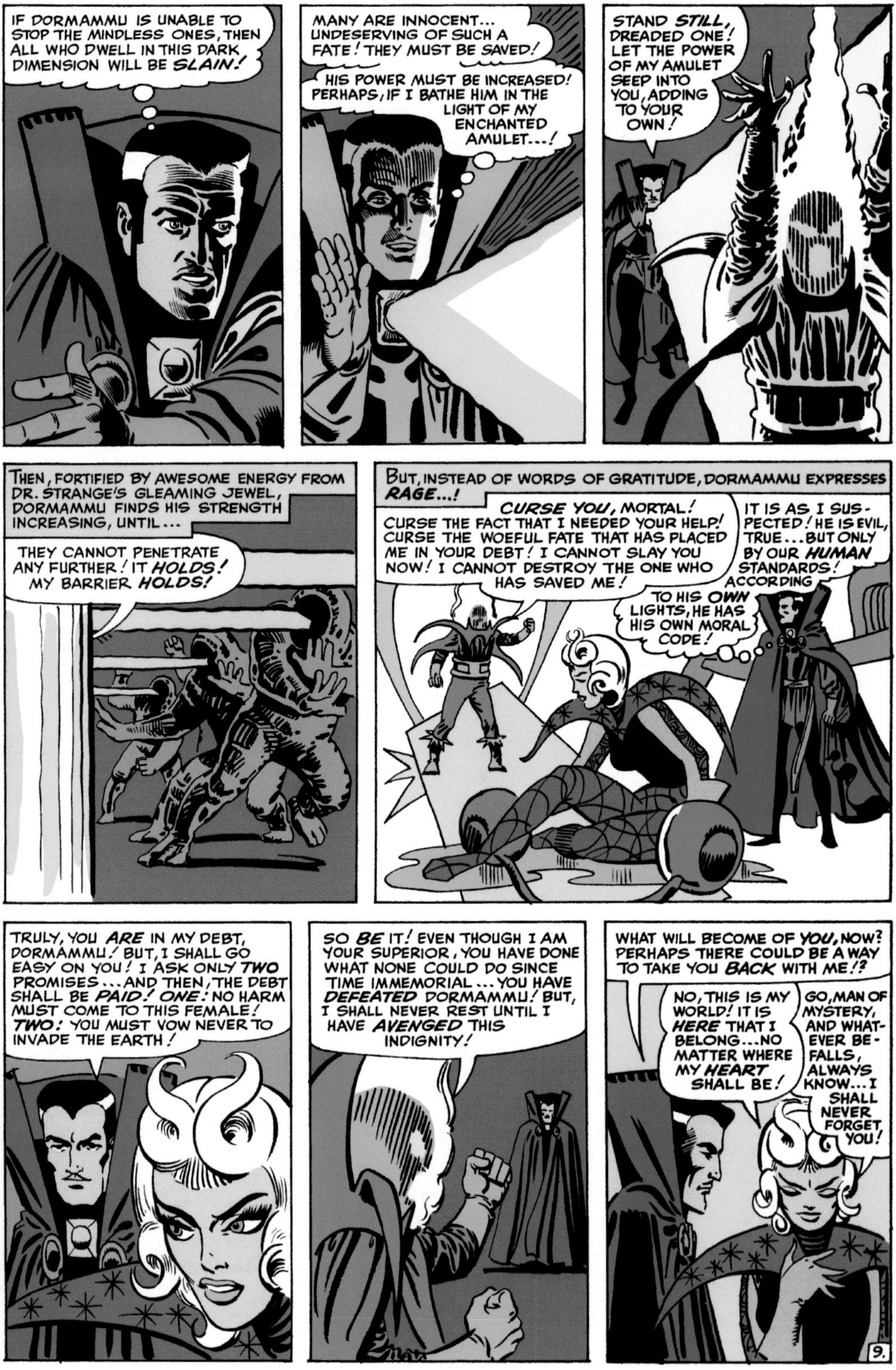
IF DORMAMMU IS UNABLE TO STOP THE MINDLESS ONES, THEN ALL WHO DWELL IN THIS DARK DIMENSION WILL BE SLAIN!
MANY ARE INNOCENT... UNDESERVING OF SUCH A FATE! THEY MUST BE SAVED!
HIS POWER MUST BE INCREASED! PERHAPS, IF I BATHE HIM IN THE LIGHT OF MY ENCHANTED AMULET...!
STAND STILL, DREADED ONE! LET THE POWER OF MY AMULET SEEP INTO YOU, ADDING TO YOUR OWN!
THEN, FORTIFIED BY AWESOME ENERGY FROM DR. STRANGE'S GLEAMING JEWEL, DORMAMMU FINDS HIS STRENGTH INCREASING, UNTIL...
THEY CANNOT PENETRATE ANY FURTHER! IT HOLDS! MY BARRIER HOLDS!
BUT, INSTEAD OF WORDS OF GRATITUDE, DORMAMMU EXPRESSES RAGE...!
CURSE YOU, MORTAL! CURSE THE FACT THAT I NEEDED YOUR HELP! CURSE THE WOEFUL FATE THAT HAS PLACED ME IN YOUR DEBT! I CANNOT SLAY YOU NOW! I CANNOT DESTROY THE ONE WHO HAS SAVED ME!
IT IS AS I SUSPECTED! HE IS EVIL, TRUE... BUT ONLY BY OUR HUMAN STANDARDS! ACCORDING TO HIS OWN LIGHTS, HE HAS HIS OWN MORAL CODE!
TRULY, YOU ARE IN MY DEBT, DORMAMMU! BUT, I SHALL GO EASY ON YOU! I ASK ONLY TWO PROMISES... AND THEN, THE DEBT SHALL BE PAID! ONE: NO HARM MUST COME TO THIS FEMALE! TWO: YOU MUST VOW NEVER TO INVADE THE EARTH!
SO BE IT! EVEN THOUGH I AM YOUR SUPERIOR, YOU HAVE DONE WHAT NONE COULD DO SINCE TIME IMMEMORIAL... YOU HAVE DEFEATED DORMAMMU! BUT, I SHALL NEVER REST UNTIL I HAVE AVENGED THIS INDIGNITY!
WHAT WILL BECOME OF YOU, NOW? PERHAPS THERE COULD BE A WAY TO TAKE YOU BACK WITH ME!?
NO, THIS IS MY WORLD! IT IS HERE THAT I BELONG... NO MATTER WHERE MY HEART SHALL BE!
GO, MAN OF MYSTERY, AND WHATEVER BEFALLS, ALWAYS KNOW... I SHALL NEVER FORGET YOU!
9.

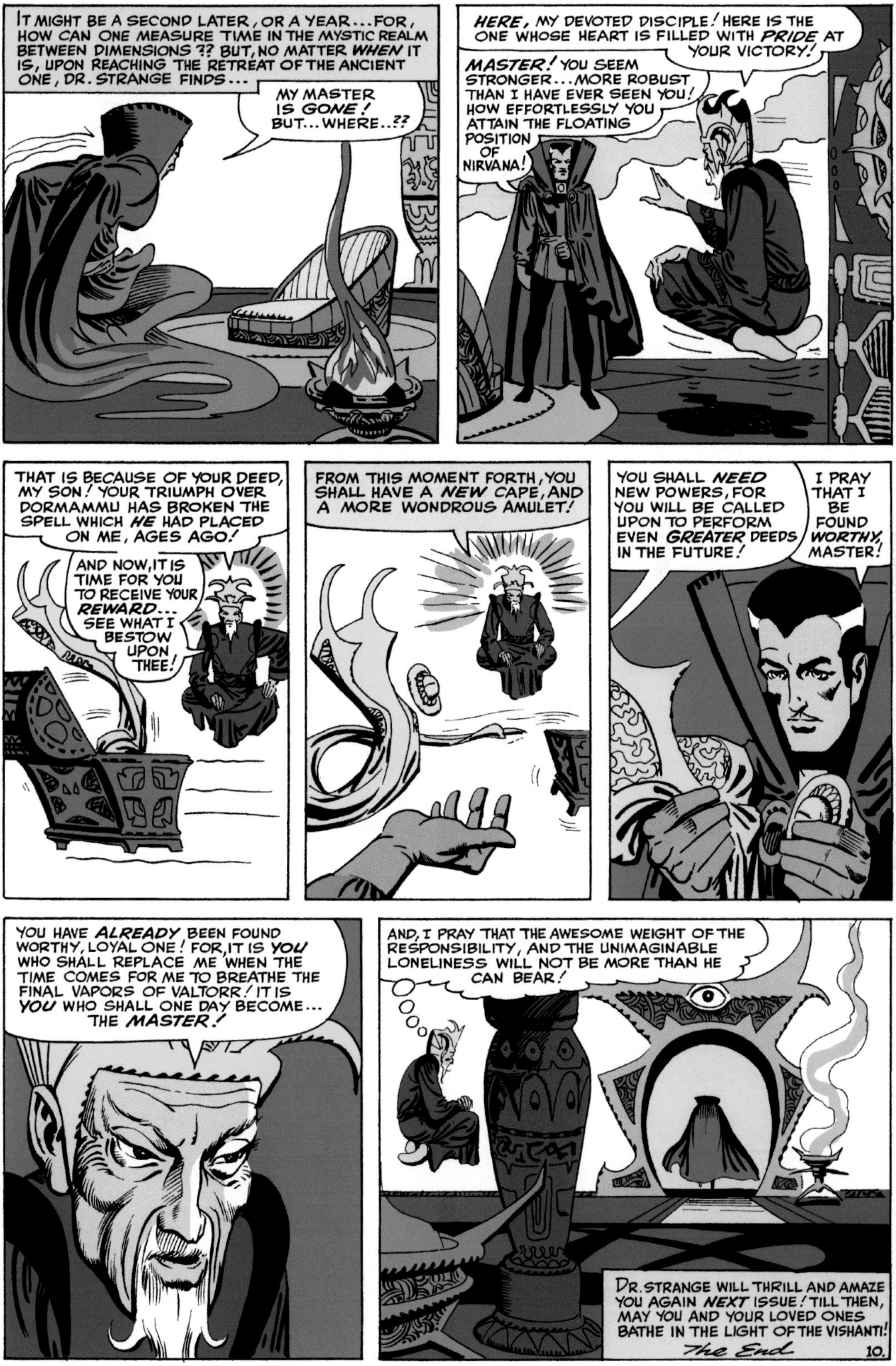

IT MIGHT BE A SECOND LATER, OR A YEAR... FOR, HOW CAN ONE MEASURE TIME IN THE MYSTIC REALM BETWEEN DIMENSIONS ?? BUT, NO MATTER WHEN IT IS, UPON REACHING THE RETREAT OF THE ANCIENT ONE, DR. STRANGE FINDS...
MY MASTER IS GONE! BUT... WHERE..??
HERE, MY DEVOTED DISCIPLE! HERE IS THE ONE WHOSE HEART IS FILLED WITH PRIDE AT YOUR VICTORY!
MASTER! YOU SEEM STRONGER... MORE ROBUST THAN I HAVE EVER SEEN YOU! HOW EFFORTLESSLY YOU ATTAIN THE FLOATING POSITION OF NIRVANA!
THAT IS BECAUSE OF YOUR DEED, MY SON! YOUR TRIUMPH OVER DORMAMMU HAS BROKEN THE SPELL WHICH HE HAD PLACED ON ME, AGES AGO!
AND NOW, IT IS TIME FOR YOU TO RECEIVE YOUR REWARD... SEE WHAT I BESTOW UPON THEE!
FROM THIS MOMENT FORTH, YOU SHALL HAVE A NEW CAPE, AND A MORE WONDROUS AMULET!
YOU SHALL NEED NEW POWERS, FOR YOU WILL BE CALLED UPON TO PERFORM EVEN GREATER DEEDS IN THE FUTURE!
I PRAY THAT I BE FOUND WORTHY, MASTER!
YOU HAVE ALREADY BEEN FOUND WORTHY, LOYAL ONE! FOR, IT IS YOU WHO SHALL REPLACE ME WHEN THE TIME COMES FOR ME TO BREATHE THE FINAL VAPORS OF VALTORR! IT IS YOU WHO SHALL ONE DAY BECOME... THE MASTER!
AND, I PRAY THAT THE AWESOME WEIGHT OF THE RESPONSIBILITY, AND THE UNIMAGINABLE LONELINESS WILL NOT BE MORE THAN HE CAN BEAR!
DR. STRANGE WILL THRILL AND AMAZE YOU AGAIN NEXT ISSUE! TILL THEN, MAY YOU AND YOUR LOVED ONES BATHE IN THE LIGHT OF THE VISHANTI!
The End
10.

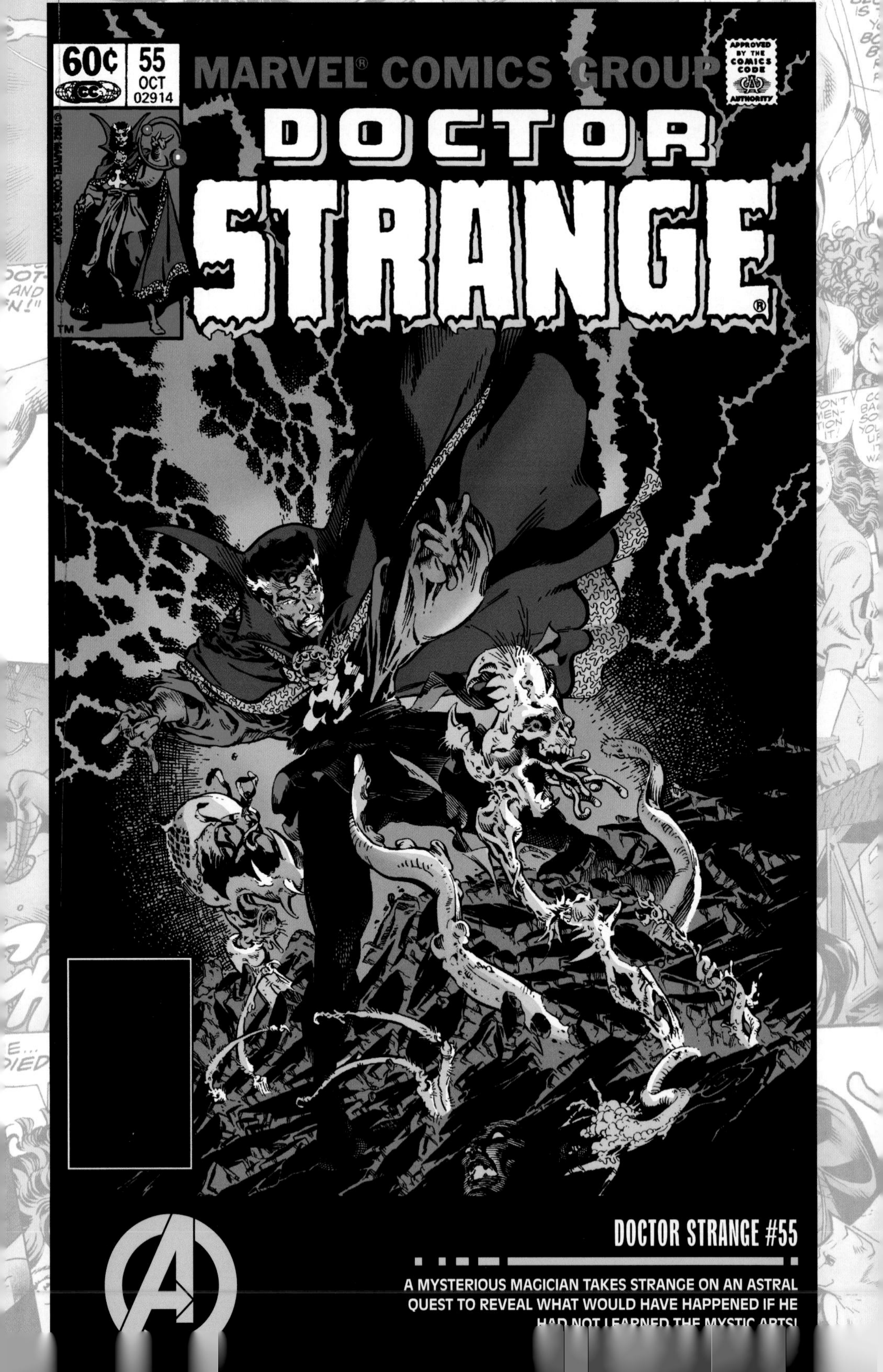
60¢
55
OCT
02914
MARVEL COMICS GROUP
APPROVED BY THE COMICS CODE AUTHORITY
DOCTOR STRANGE

DOCTOR STRANGE #55

A MYSTERIOUS MAGICIAN TAKES STRANGE ON AN ASTRAL QUEST TO REVEAL WHAT WOULD HAVE HAPPENED IF HE HAD NOT LEARNED THE MYSTIC ARTS!

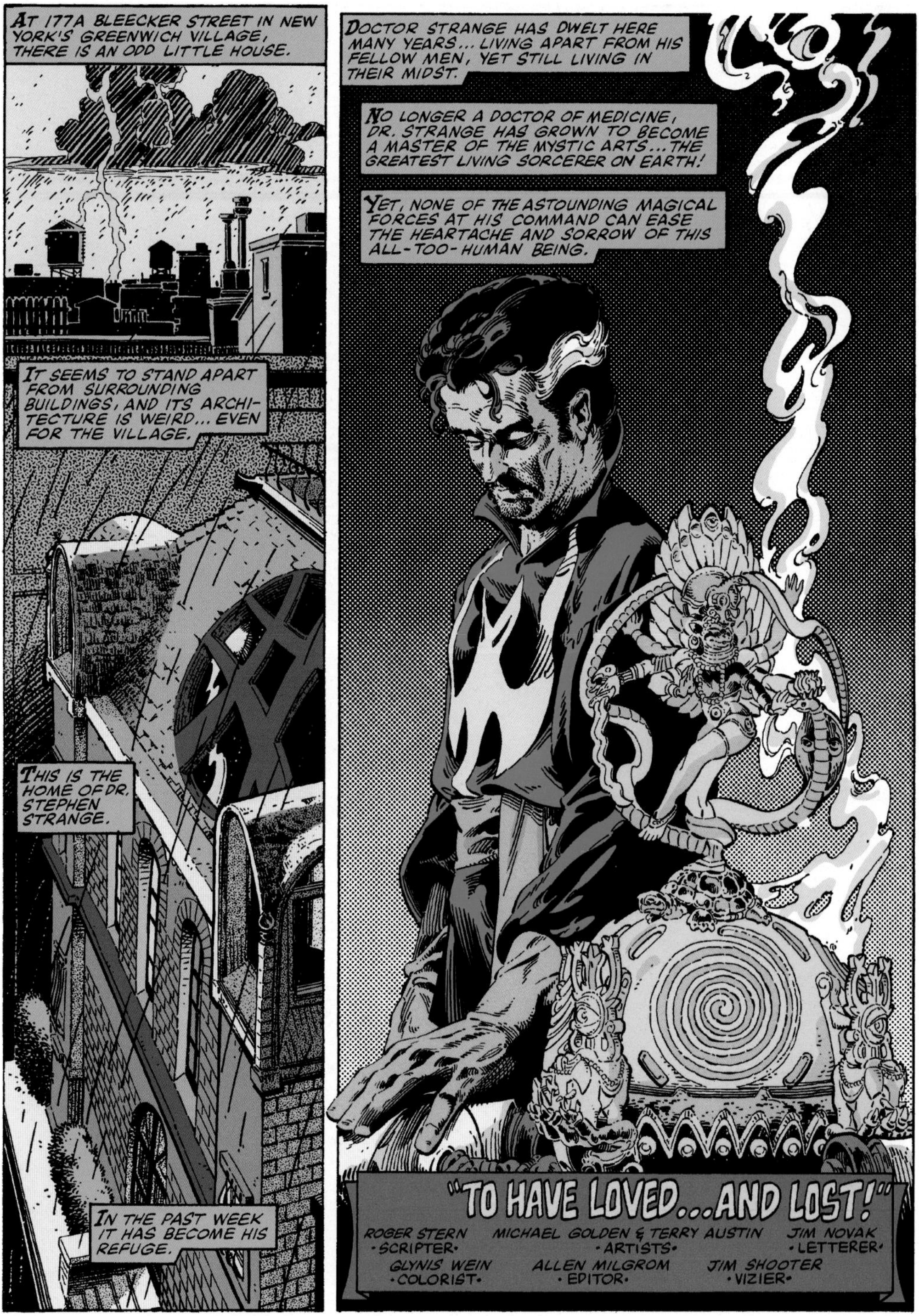
AT 177A BLEECKER STREET IN NEW YORK'S GREENWICH VILLAGE, THERE IS AN ODD LITTLE HOUSE.
IT SEEMS TO STAND APART FROM SURROUNDING BUILDINGS, AND ITS ARCHITECTURE IS WEIRD... EVEN FOR THE VILLAGE.
THIS IS THE HOME OF DR. STEPHEN STRANGE.
IN THE PAST WEEK IT HAS BECOME HIS REFUGE.
DOCTOR STRANGE HAS DWELT HERE MANY YEARS... LIVING APART FROM HIS FELLOW MEN, YET STILL LIVING IN THEIR MIDST.
NO LONGER A DOCTOR OF MEDICINE, DR. STRANGE HAS GROWN TO BECOME A MASTER OF THE MYSTIC ARTS... THE GREATEST LIVING SORCERER ON EARTH!
YET, NONE OF THE ASTOUNDING MAGICAL FORCES AT HIS COMMAND CAN EASE THE HEARTACHE AND SORROW OF THIS ALL-TOO-HUMAN BEING.
"TO HAVE LOVED...AND LOST!"
ROGER STERN ·SCRIPTER·
MICHAEL GOLDEN & TERRY AUSTIN ·ARTISTS·
JIM NOVAK ·LETTERER·
GLYNIS WEIN ·COLORIST·
ALLEN MILGROM ·EDITOR·
JIM SHOOTER ·VIZIER·

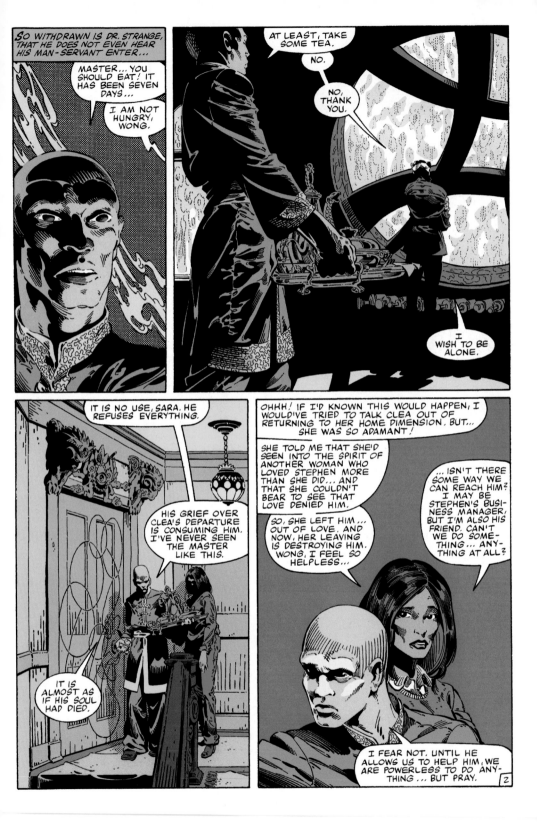

SO WITHDRAWN IS DR. STRANGE, THAT HE DOES NOT EVEN HEAR HIS MAN-SERVANT ENTER...

MASTER... YOU SHOULD EAT! IT HAS BEEN SEVEN DAYS...

I AM NOT HUNGRY, WONG.

AT LEAST, TAKE SOME TEA.

NO.

NO, THANK YOU.

I WISH TO BE ALONE.

IT IS NO USE, SARA. HE REFUSES EVERYTHING.

HIS GRIEF OVER CLEA'S DEPARTURE IS CONSUMING HIM. I'VE NEVER SEEN THE MASTER LIKE THIS.

IT IS ALMOST AS IF HIS SOUL HAD DIED.

OHHH! IF I'D KNOWN THIS WOULD HAPPEN, I WOULD'VE TRIED TO TALK CLEA OUT OF RETURNING TO HER HOME DIMENSION, BUT... SHE WAS SO ADAMANT!

SHE TOLD ME THAT SHE'D SEEN INTO THE SPIRIT OF ANOTHER WOMAN WHO LOVED STEPHEN MORE THAN SHE DID... AND THAT SHE COULDN'T BEAR TO SEE THAT LOVE DENIED HIM.

SO, SHE LEFT HIM... OUT OF LOVE. AND NOW, HER LEAVING IS DESTROYING HIM. WONG, I FEEL SO HELPLESS...

... ISN'T THERE SOME WAY WE CAN REACH HIM? I MAY BE STEPHEN'S BUSINESS MANAGER, BUT I'M ALSO HIS FRIEND. CAN'T WE DO SOMETHING... ANYTHING AT ALL?

I FEAR NOT. UNTIL HE ALLOWS US TO HELP HIM, WE ARE POWERLESS TO DO ANYTHING... BUT PRAY.

2

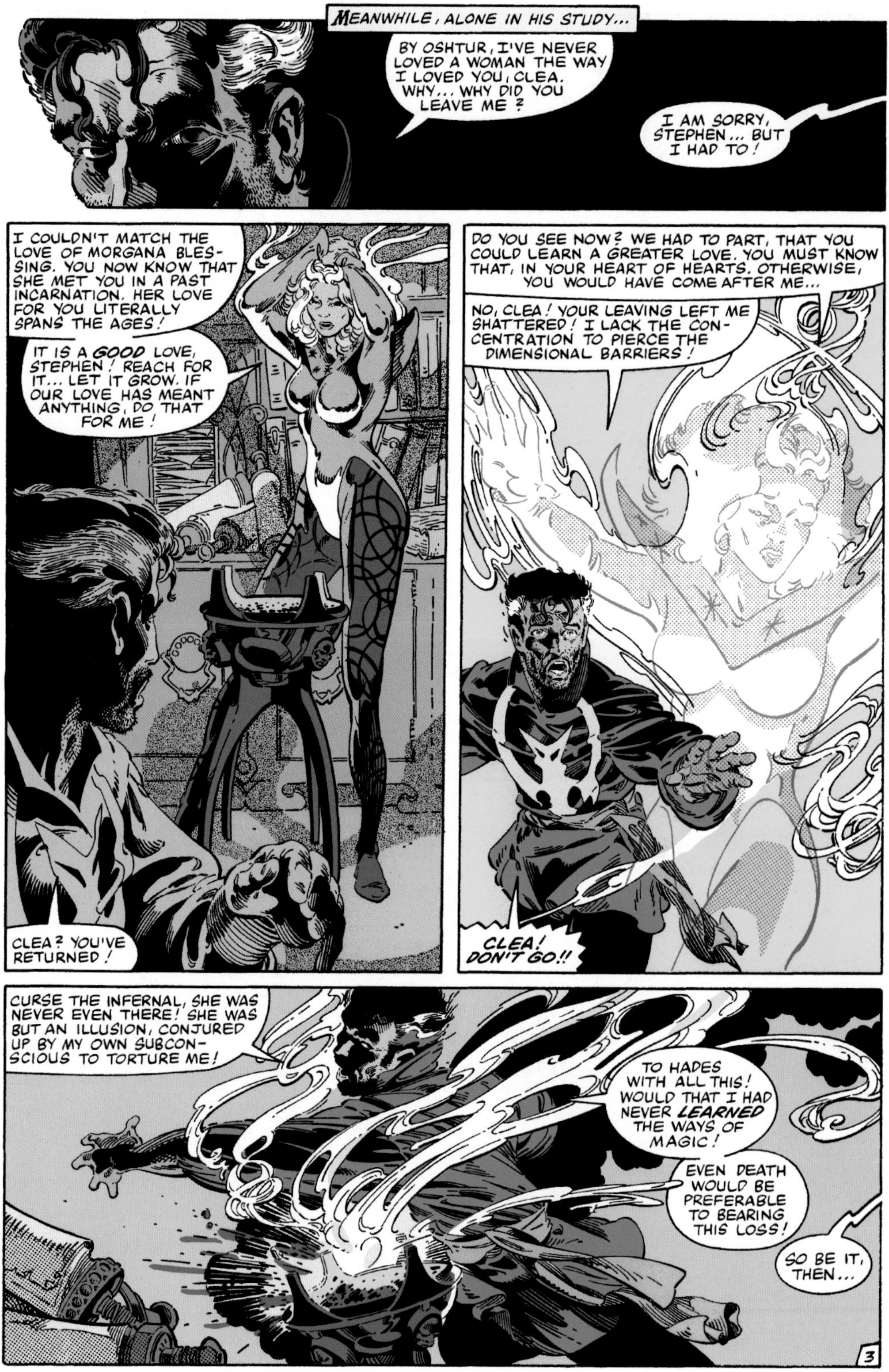
MEANWHILE, ALONE IN HIS STUDY...
BY OSHTUR, I'VE NEVER LOVED A WOMAN THE WAY I LOVED YOU, CLEA. WHY... WHY DID YOU LEAVE ME?
I AM SORRY, STEPHEN... BUT I HAD TO!
I COULDN'T MATCH THE LOVE OF MORGANA BLESSING. YOU NOW KNOW THAT SHE MET YOU IN A PAST INCARNATION. HER LOVE FOR YOU LITERALLY SPANS THE AGES!
IT IS A GOOD LOVE, STEPHEN! REACH FOR IT... LET IT GROW. IF OUR LOVE HAS MEANT ANYTHING, DO THAT FOR ME!
CLEA? YOU'VE RETURNED!
DO YOU SEE NOW? WE HAD TO PART, THAT YOU COULD LEARN A GREATER LOVE. YOU MUST KNOW THAT, IN YOUR HEART OF HEARTS. OTHERWISE, YOU WOULD HAVE COME AFTER ME...
NO, CLEA! YOUR LEAVING LEFT ME SHATTERED! I LACK THE CONCENTRATION TO PIERCE THE DIMENSIONAL BARRIERS!
CLEA! DON'T GO!!
CURSE THE INFERNAL, SHE WAS NEVER EVEN THERE! SHE WAS BUT AN ILLUSION, CONJURED UP BY MY OWN SUBCONSCIOUS TO TORTURE ME!
TO HADES WITH ALL THIS! WOULD THAT I HAD NEVER LEARNED THE WAYS OF MAGIC!
EVEN DEATH WOULD BE PREFERABLE TO BEARING THIS LOSS!
SO BE IT, THEN...
3

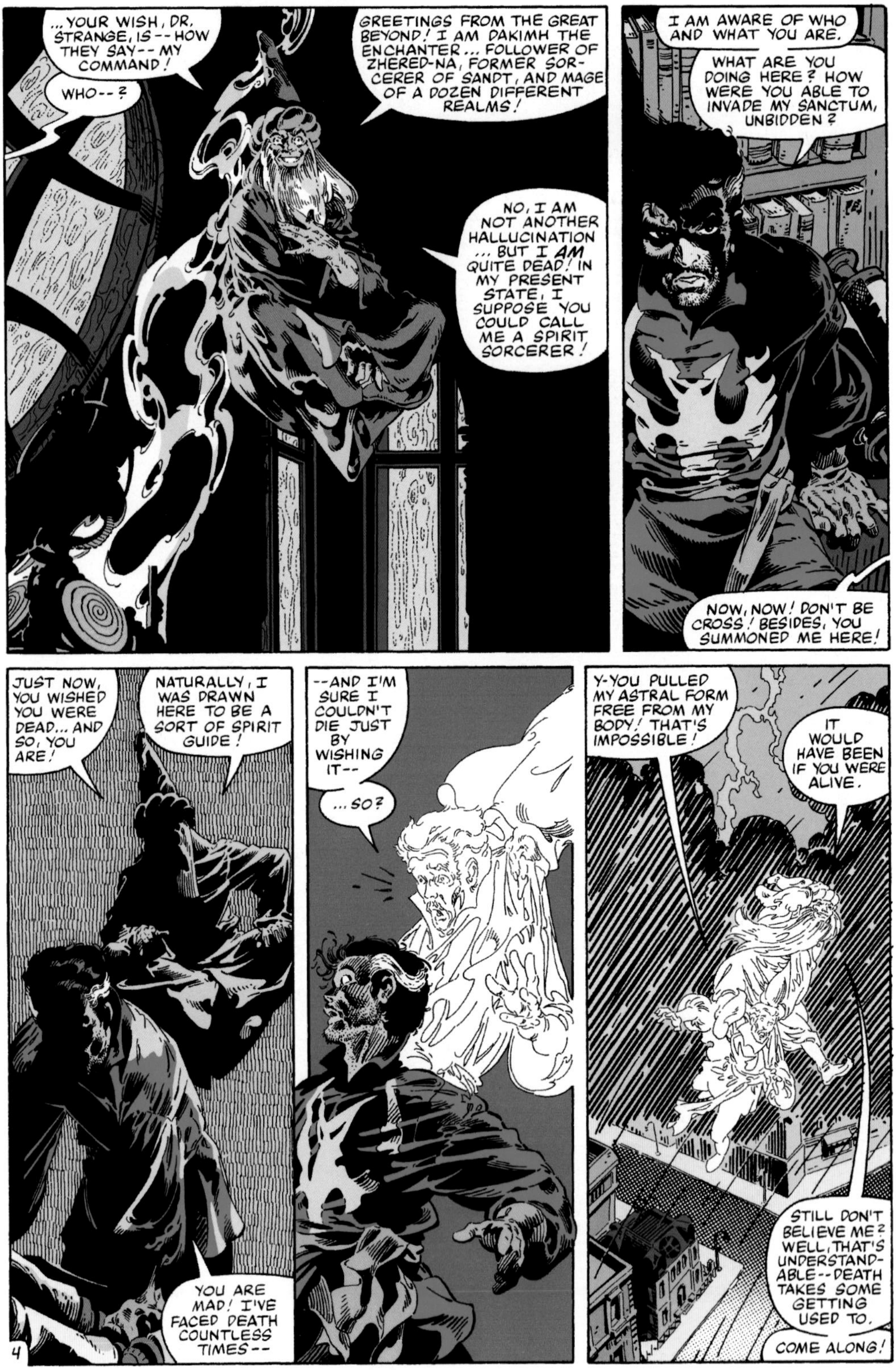
...YOUR WISH, DR. STRANGE, IS--HOW THEY SAY--MY COMMAND!
WHO--?
GREETINGS FROM THE GREAT BEYOND! I AM DAKIMH THE ENCHANTER... FOLLOWER OF ZHERED-NA, FORMER SORCERER OF SANDT, AND MAGE OF A DOZEN DIFFERENT REALMS!
NO, I AM NOT ANOTHER HALLUCINATION ...BUT I AM QUITE DEAD! IN MY PRESENT STATE, I SUPPOSE YOU COULD CALL ME A SPIRIT SORCERER!
I AM AWARE OF WHO AND WHAT YOU ARE.
WHAT ARE YOU DOING HERE? HOW WERE YOU ABLE TO INVADE MY SANCTUM, UNBIDDEN?
NOW, NOW! DON'T BE CROSS! BESIDES, YOU SUMMONED ME HERE!
JUST NOW, YOU WISHED YOU WERE DEAD... AND SO, YOU ARE!
NATURALLY, I WAS DRAWN HERE TO BE A SORT OF SPIRIT GUIDE!
YOU ARE MAD! I'VE FACED DEATH COUNTLESS TIMES--
4
--AND I'M SURE I COULDN'T DIE JUST BY WISHING IT--
...SO?
Y-YOU PULLED MY ASTRAL FORM FREE FROM MY BODY! THAT'S IMPOSSIBLE!
IT WOULD HAVE BEEN IF YOU WERE ALIVE.
STILL DON'T BELIEVE ME? WELL, THAT'S UNDERSTANDABLE--DEATH TAKES SOME GETTING USED TO.
COME ALONG!

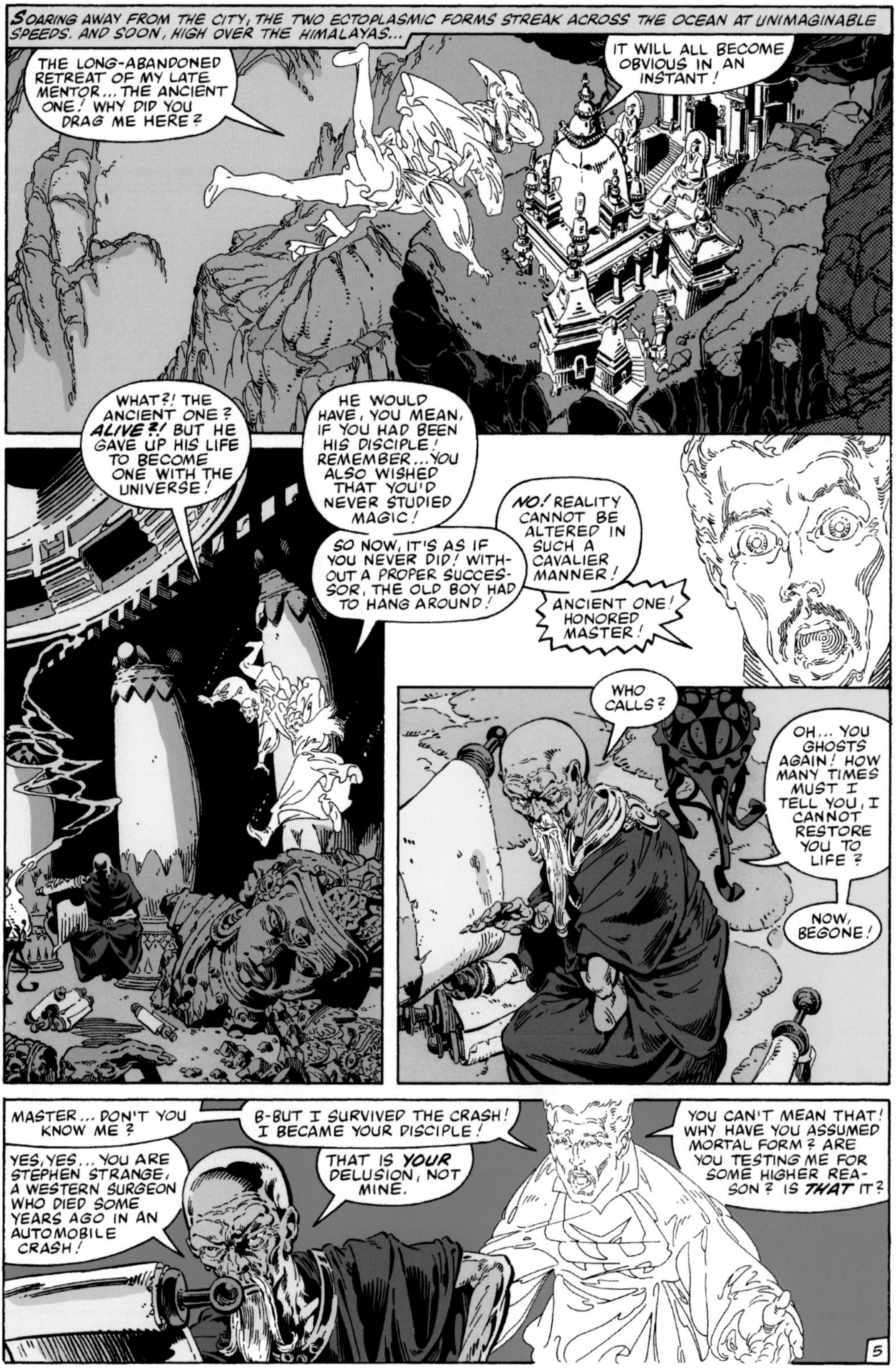
SOARING AWAY FROM THE CITY, THE TWO ECTOPLASMIC FORMS STREAK ACROSS THE OCEAN AT UNIMAGINABLE SPEEDS. AND SOON, HIGH OVER THE HIMALAYAS...
THE LONG-ABANDONED RETREAT OF MY LATE MENTOR... THE ANCIENT ONE! WHY DID YOU DRAG ME HERE?
IT WILL ALL BECOME OBVIOUS IN AN INSTANT!
WHAT?! THE ANCIENT ONE? ALIVE?! BUT HE GAVE UP HIS LIFE TO BECOME ONE WITH THE UNIVERSE!
HE WOULD HAVE, YOU MEAN, IF YOU HAD BEEN HIS DISCIPLE! REMEMBER... YOU ALSO WISHED THAT YOU'D NEVER STUDIED MAGIC!
SO NOW, IT'S AS IF YOU NEVER DID! WITHOUT A PROPER SUCCESSOR, THE OLD BOY HAD TO HANG AROUND!
NO! REALITY CANNOT BE ALTERED IN SUCH A CAVALIER MANNER!
ANCIENT ONE! HONORED MASTER!
WHO CALLS?
OH... YOU GHOSTS AGAIN! HOW MANY TIMES MUST I TELL YOU, I CANNOT RESTORE YOU TO LIFE?
NOW, BEGONE!
MASTER... DON'T YOU KNOW ME?
YES, YES... YOU ARE STEPHEN STRANGE, A WESTERN SURGEON WHO DIED SOME YEARS AGO IN AN AUTOMOBILE CRASH!
B-BUT I SURVIVED THE CRASH! I BECAME YOUR DISCIPLE!
THAT IS YOUR DELUSION, NOT MINE.
YOU CAN'T MEAN THAT! WHY HAVE YOU ASSUMED MORTAL FORM? ARE YOU TESTING ME FOR SOME HIGHER REASON? IS THAT IT?
5

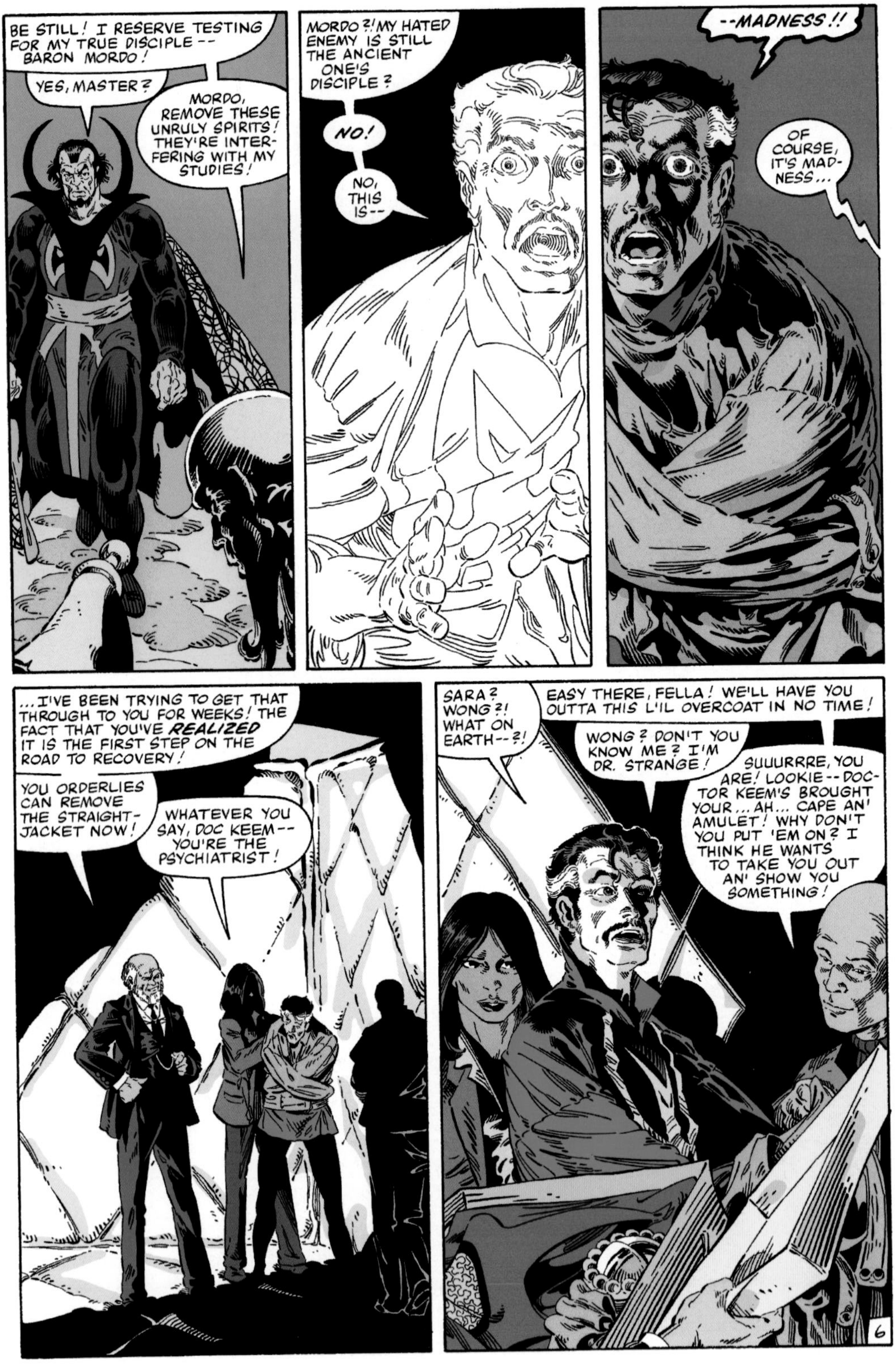
BE STILL! I RESERVE TESTING FOR MY TRUE DISCIPLE -- BARON MORDO!
YES, MASTER?
MORDO, REMOVE THESE UNRULY SPIRITS! THEY'RE INTERFERING WITH MY STUDIES!
MORDO?! MY HATED ENEMY IS STILL THE ANCIENT ONE'S DISCIPLE?
NO!
NO, THIS IS--
--MADNESS!!
OF COURSE, IT'S MADNESS...
...I'VE BEEN TRYING TO GET THAT THROUGH TO YOU FOR WEEKS! THE FACT THAT YOU'VE REALIZED IT IS THE FIRST STEP ON THE ROAD TO RECOVERY!
YOU ORDERLIES CAN REMOVE THE STRAIGHT-JACKET NOW!
WHATEVER YOU SAY, DOC KEEM-- YOU'RE THE PSYCHIATRIST!
SARA? WONG?! WHAT ON EARTH--?!
EASY THERE, FELLA! WE'LL HAVE YOU OUTTA THIS L'IL OVERCOAT IN NO TIME!
WONG? DON'T YOU KNOW ME? I'M DR. STRANGE!
SUUURRRE, YOU ARE! LOOKIE--DOCTOR KEEM'S BROUGHT YOUR... AH... CAPE AN' AMULET! WHY DON'T YOU PUT 'EM ON? I THINK HE WANTS TO TAKE YOU OUT AN' SHOW YOU SOMETHING!
6

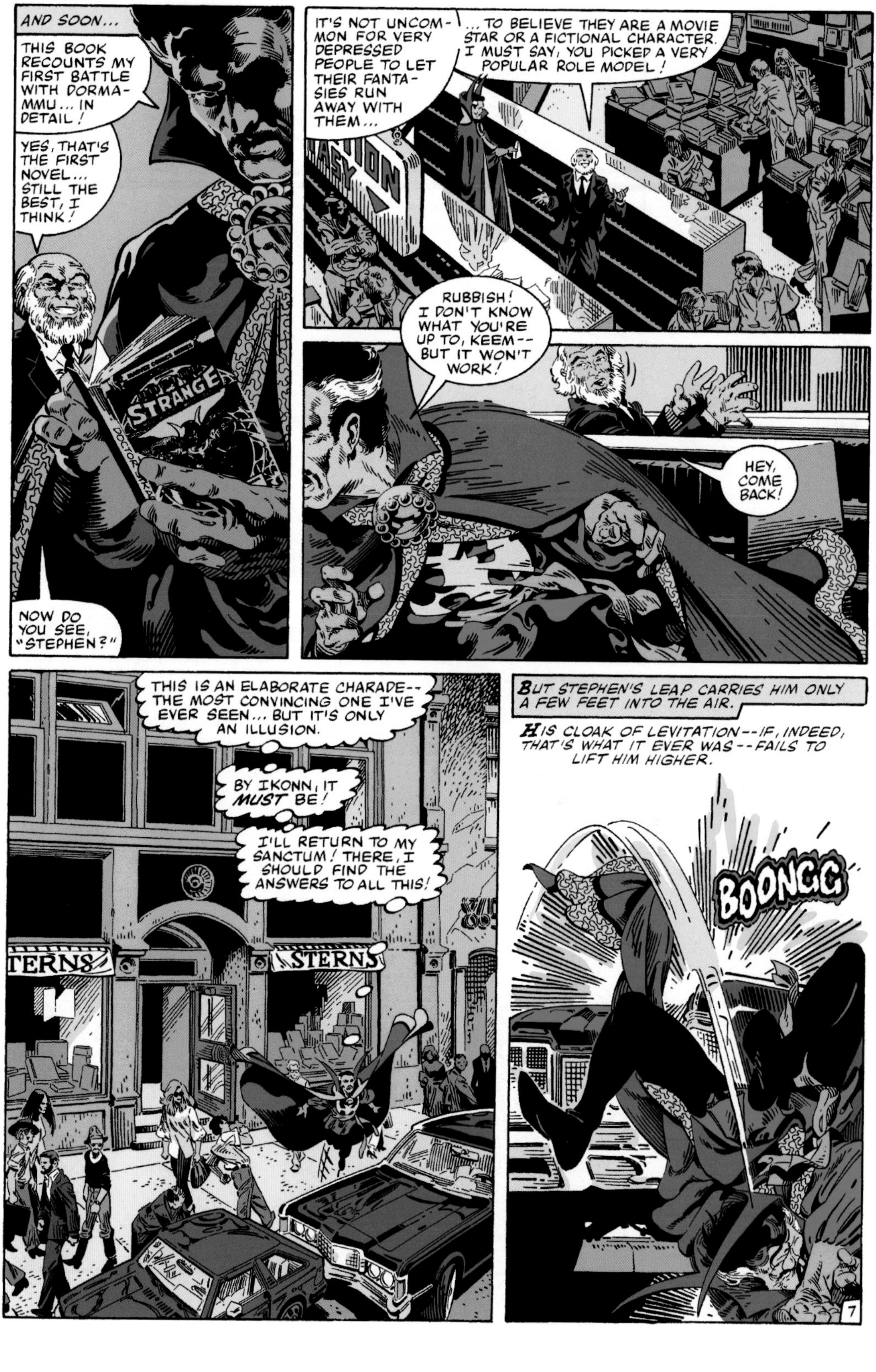
AND SOON...
THIS BOOK RECOUNTS MY FIRST BATTLE WITH DORMAMMU... IN DETAIL!
YES, THAT'S THE FIRST NOVEL... STILL THE BEST, I THINK!
STRANGE
NOW DO YOU SEE, "STEPHEN?"
IT'S NOT UNCOMMON FOR VERY DEPRESSED PEOPLE TO LET THEIR FANTASIES RUN AWAY WITH THEM...
...TO BELIEVE THEY ARE A MOVIE STAR OR A FICTIONAL CHARACTER. I MUST SAY, YOU PICKED A VERY POPULAR ROLE MODEL!
RUBBISH! I DON'T KNOW WHAT YOU'RE UP TO, KEEM-- BUT IT WON'T WORK!
HEY, COME BACK!
THIS IS AN ELABORATE CHARADE-- THE MOST CONVINCING ONE I'VE EVER SEEN... BUT IT'S ONLY AN ILLUSION.
BY IKONN, IT MUST BE!
I'LL RETURN TO MY SANCTUM! THERE, I SHOULD FIND THE ANSWERS TO ALL THIS!
TERNS
STERNS
BUT STEPHEN'S LEAP CARRIES HIM ONLY A FEW FEET INTO THE AIR.
HIS CLOAK OF LEVITATION--IF, INDEED, THAT'S WHAT IT EVER WAS--FAILS TO LIFT HIM HIGHER.
BOONGG
7

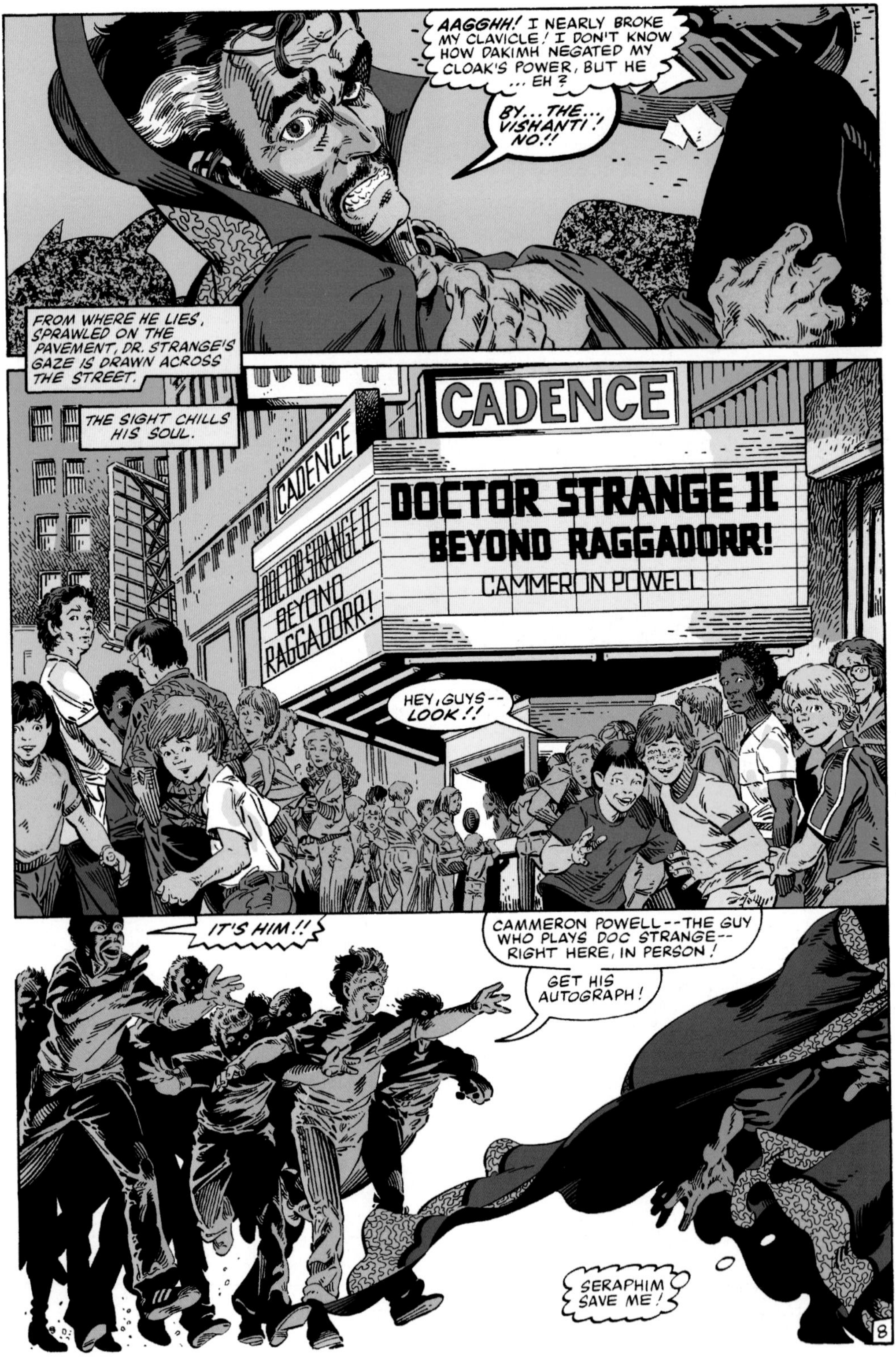
AAGGHH! I NEARLY BROKE MY CLAVICLE! I DON'T KNOW HOW DAKIMH NEGATED MY CLOAK'S POWER, BUT HE ... EH?
BY... THE... VISHANTI! NO!!
FROM WHERE HE LIES, SPRAWLED ON THE PAVEMENT, DR. STRANGE'S GAZE IS DRAWN ACROSS THE STREET.
THE SIGHT CHILLS HIS SOUL.
CADENCE
CADENCE
DOCTOR STRANGE II
BEYOND RAGGADORR!
CAMMERON POWELL
DOCTOR STRANGE II BEYOND RAGGADORR!
HEY, GUYS-- LOOK!!
IT'S HIM!!
CAMMERON POWELL--THE GUY WHO PLAYS DOC STRANGE-- RIGHT HERE, IN PERSON!
GET HIS AUTOGRAPH!
SERAPHIM SAVE ME!
8

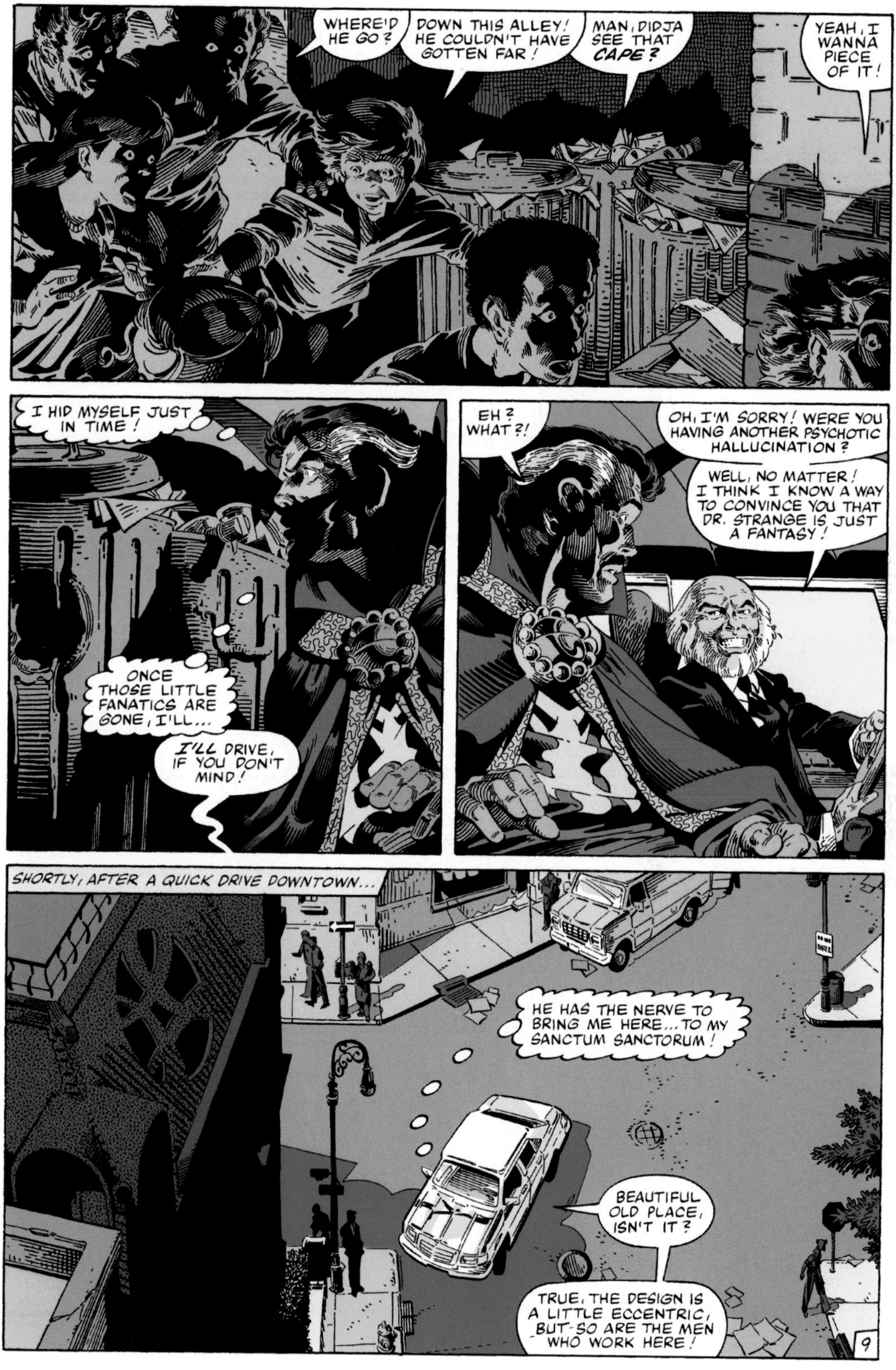
WHERE'D HE GO?
DOWN THIS ALLEY! HE COULDN'T HAVE GOTTEN FAR!
MAN, DIDJA SEE THAT CAPE?
YEAH, I WANNA PIECE OF IT!
I HID MYSELF JUST IN TIME!
ONCE THOSE LITTLE FANATICS ARE GONE, I'LL...
I'LL DRIVE, IF YOU DON'T MIND!
EH? WHAT?!
OH, I'M SORRY! WERE YOU HAVING ANOTHER PSYCHOTIC HALLUCINATION?
WELL, NO MATTER! I THINK I KNOW A WAY TO CONVINCE YOU THAT DR. STRANGE IS JUST A FANTASY!
SHORTLY, AFTER A QUICK DRIVE DOWNTOWN...
HE HAS THE NERVE TO BRING ME HERE... TO MY SANCTUM SANCTORUM!
BEAUTIFUL OLD PLACE, ISN'T IT?
TRUE, THE DESIGN IS A LITTLE ECCENTRIC, BUT-SO ARE THE MEN WHO WORK HERE!
9

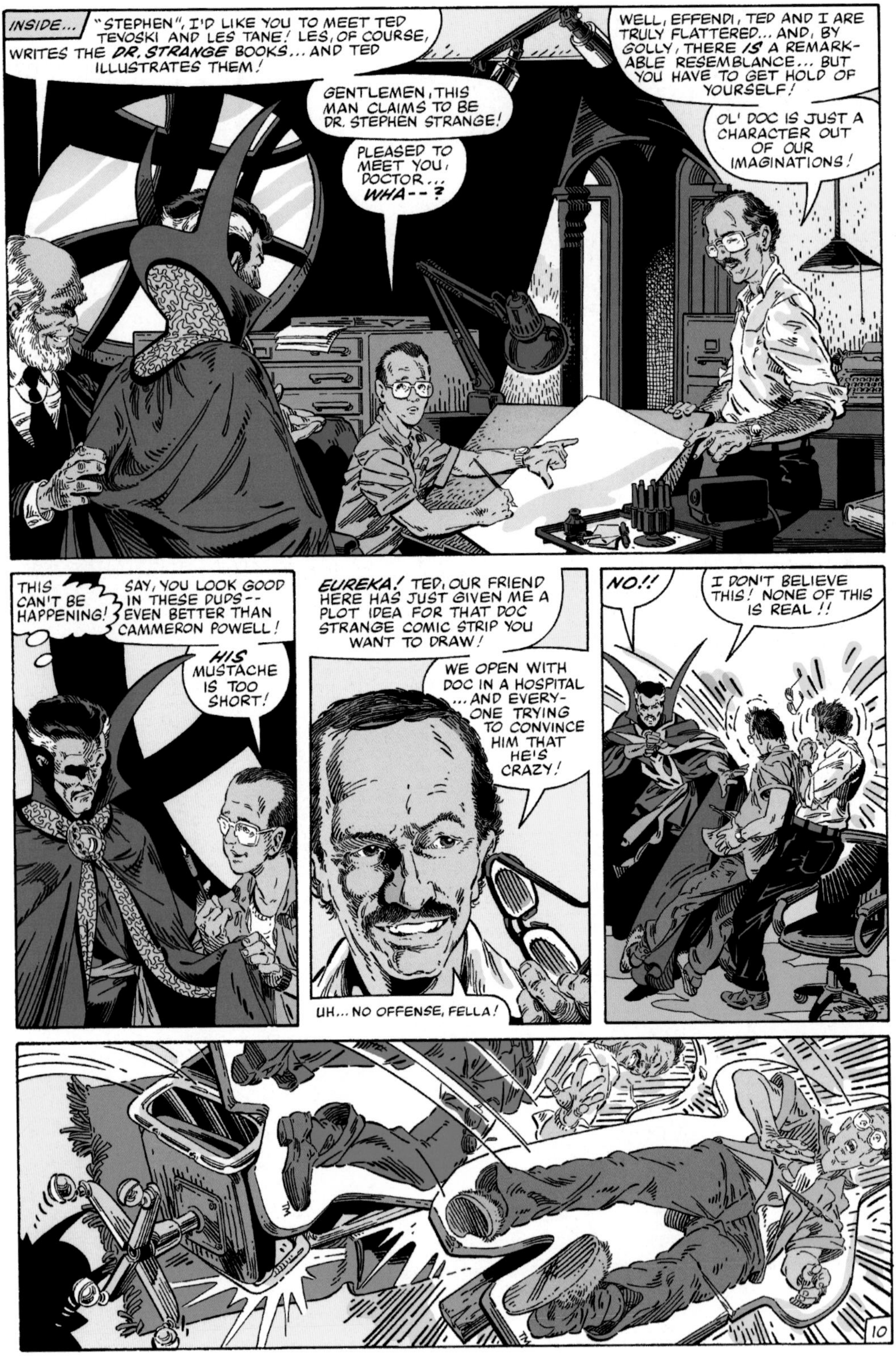
INSIDE...
"STEPHEN", I'D LIKE YOU TO MEET TED TEVOSKI AND LES TANE! LES, OF COURSE, WRITES THE DR. STRANGE BOOKS... AND TED ILLUSTRATES THEM!
GENTLEMEN, THIS MAN CLAIMS TO BE DR. STEPHEN STRANGE!
PLEASED TO MEET YOU, DOCTOR... WHA--?
WELL, EFFENDI, TED AND I ARE TRULY FLATTERED... AND, BY GOLLY, THERE IS A REMARKABLE RESEMBLANCE... BUT YOU HAVE TO GET HOLD OF YOURSELF!
OL' DOC IS JUST A CHARACTER OUT OF OUR IMAGINATIONS!
THIS CAN'T BE HAPPENING!
SAY, YOU LOOK GOOD IN THESE DUDS--EVEN BETTER THAN CAMMERON POWELL!
HIS MUSTACHE IS TOO SHORT!
EUREKA! TED, OUR FRIEND HERE HAS JUST GIVEN ME A PLOT IDEA FOR THAT DOC STRANGE COMIC STRIP YOU WANT TO DRAW!
WE OPEN WITH DOC IN A HOSPITAL... AND EVERYONE TRYING TO CONVINCE HIM THAT HE'S CRAZY!
UH... NO OFFENSE, FELLA!
NO!!
I DON'T BELIEVE THIS! NONE OF THIS IS REAL!!
10

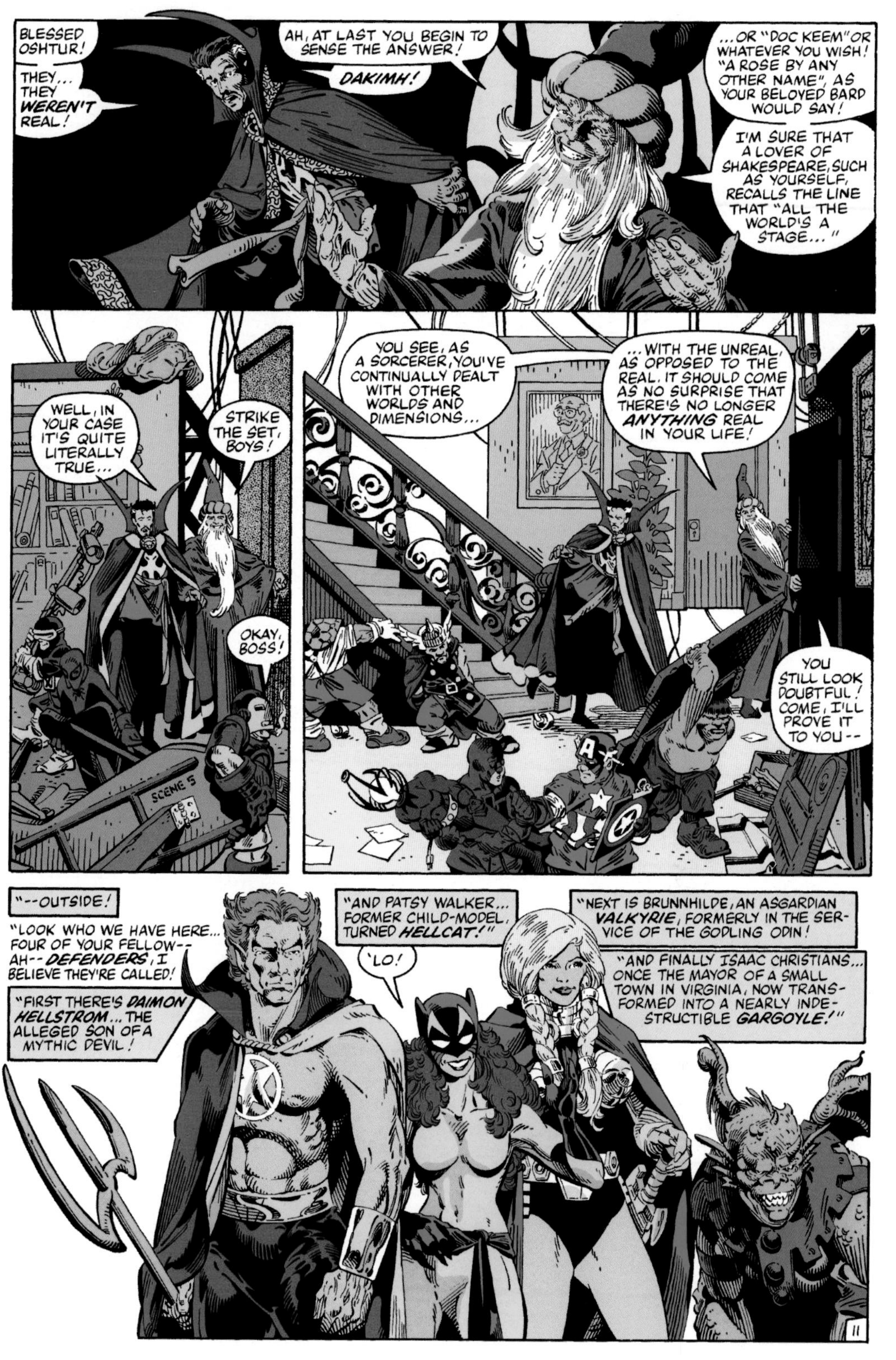
BLESSED OSHTUR!
THEY... THEY WEREN'T REAL!
AH, AT LAST YOU BEGIN TO SENSE THE ANSWER! DAKIMH!
...OR "DOC KEEM" OR WHATEVER YOU WISH! "A ROSE BY ANY OTHER NAME", AS YOUR BELOVED BARD WOULD SAY!
I'M SURE THAT A LOVER OF SHAKESPEARE, SUCH AS YOURSELF, RECALLS THE LINE THAT "ALL THE WORLD'S A STAGE..."
WELL, IN YOUR CASE IT'S QUITE LITERALLY TRUE...
STRIKE THE SET, BOYS!
OKAY, BOSS!
SCENE 5
YOU SEE, AS A SORCERER, YOU'VE CONTINUALLY DEALT WITH OTHER WORLDS AND DIMENSIONS...
...WITH THE UNREAL, AS OPPOSED TO THE REAL. IT SHOULD COME AS NO SURPRISE THAT THERE'S NO LONGER ANYTHING REAL IN YOUR LIFE!
YOU STILL LOOK DOUBTFUL! COME, I'LL PROVE IT TO YOU--
"--OUTSIDE!
"LOOK WHO WE HAVE HERE... FOUR OF YOUR FELLOW-- AH--DEFENDERS, I BELIEVE THEY'RE CALLED!
"FIRST THERE'S DAIMON HELLSTROM... THE ALLEGED SON OF A MYTHIC DEVIL!
"AND PATSY WALKER... FORMER CHILD-MODEL, TURNED HELLCAT!"
'LO!
"NEXT IS BRUNNHILDE, AN ASGARDIAN VALKYRIE, FORMERLY IN THE SERVICE OF THE GODLING ODIN!
"AND FINALLY ISAAC CHRISTIANS... ONCE THE MAYOR OF A SMALL TOWN IN VIRGINIA, NOW TRANSFORMED INTO A NEARLY INDESTRUCTIBLE GARGOYLE!"
11

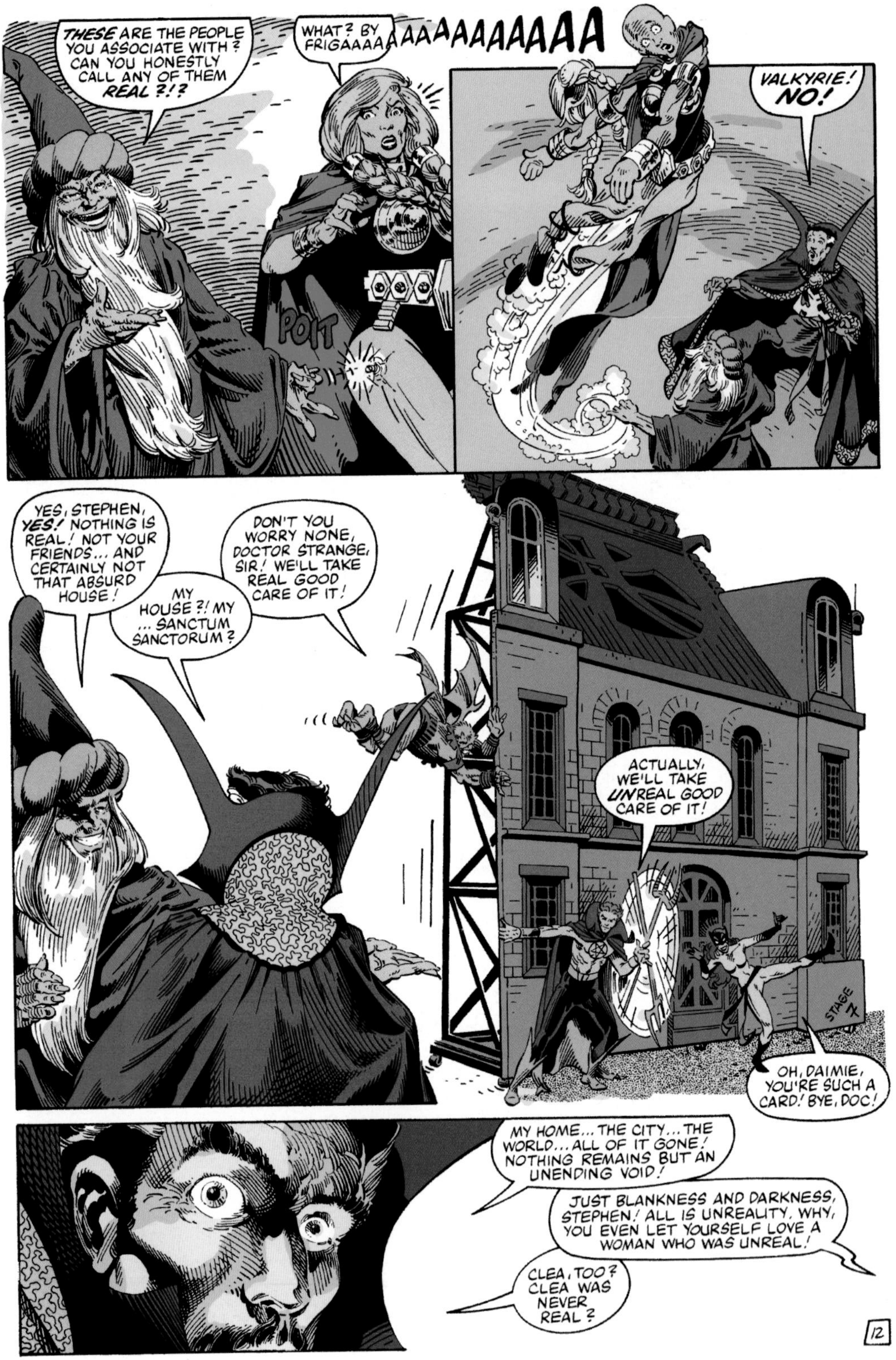
THESE ARE THE PEOPLE YOU ASSOCIATE WITH? CAN YOU HONESTLY CALL ANY OF THEM REAL?!?
WHAT? BY FRIGAAAAAAAAAAAAAAA
POIT
VALKYRIE! NO!
YES, STEPHEN, YES! NOTHING IS REAL! NOT YOUR FRIENDS... AND CERTAINLY NOT THAT ABSURD HOUSE!
MY HOUSE?! MY ... SANCTUM SANCTORUM?
DON'T YOU WORRY NONE, DOCTOR STRANGE, SIR! WE'LL TAKE REAL GOOD CARE OF IT!
ACTUALLY, WE'LL TAKE UNREAL GOOD CARE OF IT!
STAGE 7
OH, DAIMIE, YOU'RE SUCH A CARD! BYE, DOC!
MY HOME... THE CITY... THE WORLD... ALL OF IT GONE! NOTHING REMAINS BUT AN UNENDING VOID!
JUST BLANKNESS AND DARKNESS, STEPHEN! ALL IS UNREALITY. WHY, YOU EVEN LET YOURSELF LOVE A WOMAN WHO WAS UNREAL!
CLEA, TOO? CLEA WAS NEVER REAL?
12

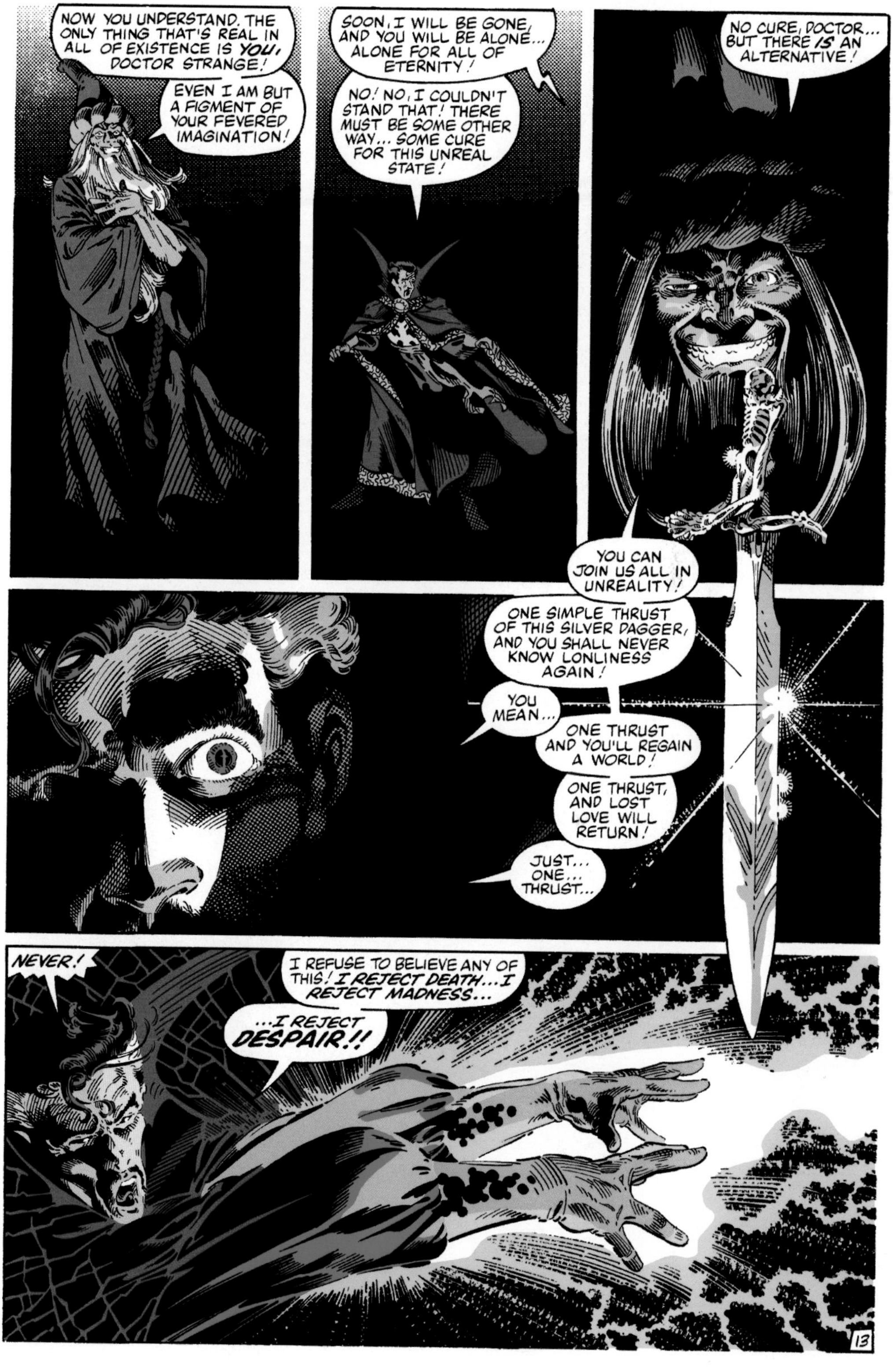
NOW YOU UNDERSTAND. THE ONLY THING THAT'S REAL IN ALL OF EXISTENCE IS YOU, DOCTOR STRANGE!
EVEN I AM BUT A FIGMENT OF YOUR FEVERED IMAGINATION!
SOON, I WILL BE GONE, AND YOU WILL BE ALONE... ALONE FOR ALL OF ETERNITY!
NO! NO, I COULDN'T STAND THAT! THERE MUST BE SOME OTHER WAY... SOME CURE FOR THIS UNREAL STATE!
NO CURE, DOCTOR... BUT THERE IS AN ALTERNATIVE!
YOU CAN JOIN US ALL IN UNREALITY!
ONE SIMPLE THRUST OF THIS SILVER DAGGER, AND YOU SHALL NEVER KNOW LONLINESS AGAIN!
YOU MEAN...
ONE THRUST AND YOU'LL REGAIN A WORLD!
ONE THRUST, AND LOST LOVE WILL RETURN!
JUST... ONE... THRUST...
NEVER!
I REFUSE TO BELIEVE ANY OF THIS! I REJECT DEATH... I REJECT MADNESS...
...I REJECT DESPAIR!!
13

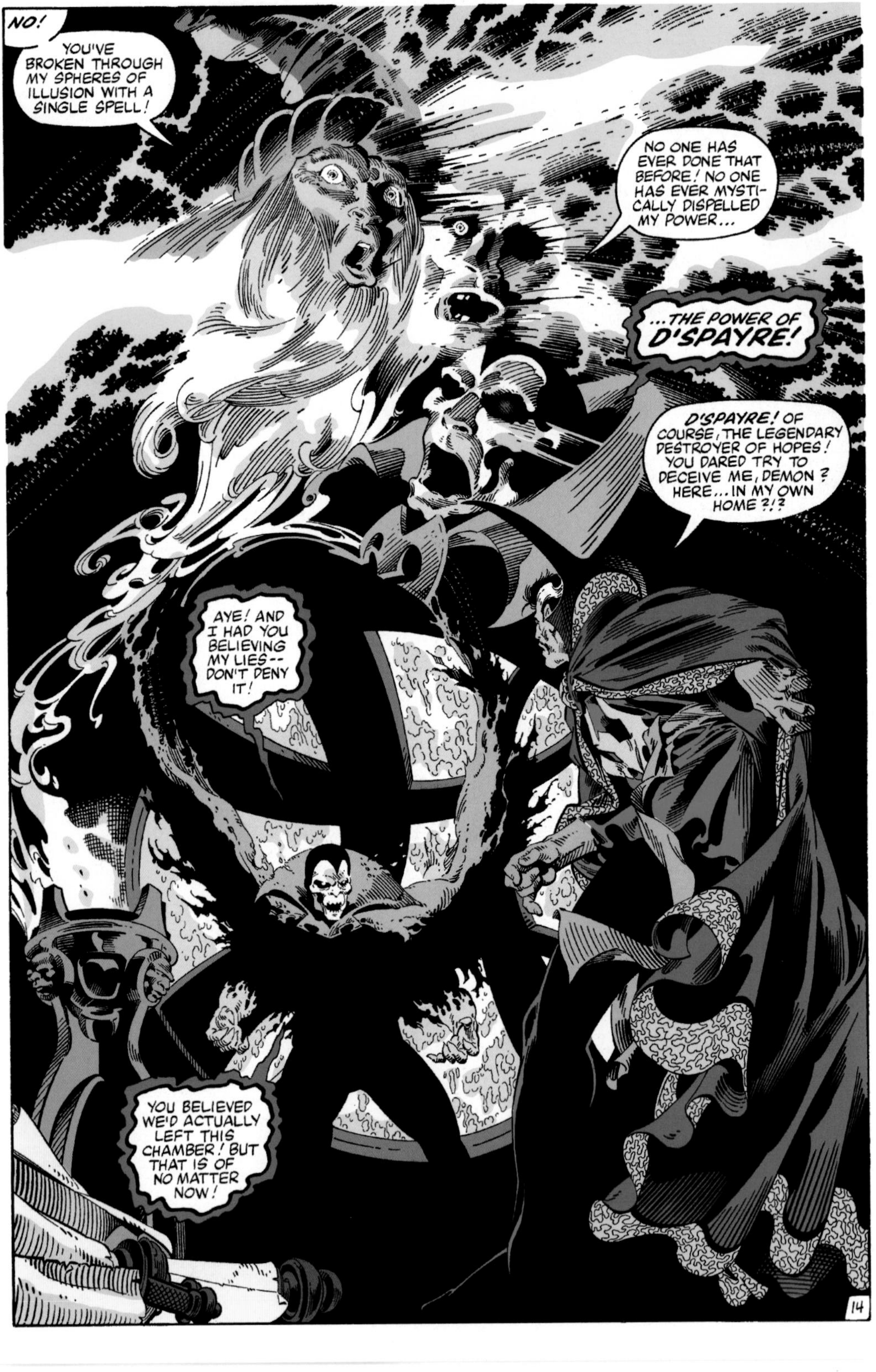
NO!
YOU'VE BROKEN THROUGH MY SPHERES OF ILLUSION WITH A SINGLE SPELL!
NO ONE HAS EVER DONE THAT BEFORE! NO ONE HAS EVER MYSTI-CALLY DISPELLED MY POWER...
...THE POWER OF D'SPAYRE!
D'SPAYRE! OF COURSE, THE LEGENDARY DESTROYER OF HOPES! YOU DARED TRY TO DECEIVE ME, DEMON? HERE... IN MY OWN HOME?!?
AYE! AND I HAD YOU BELIEVING MY LIES-- DON'T DENY IT!
YOU BELIEVED WE'D ACTUALLY LEFT THIS CHAMBER! BUT THAT IS OF NO MATTER NOW!
14

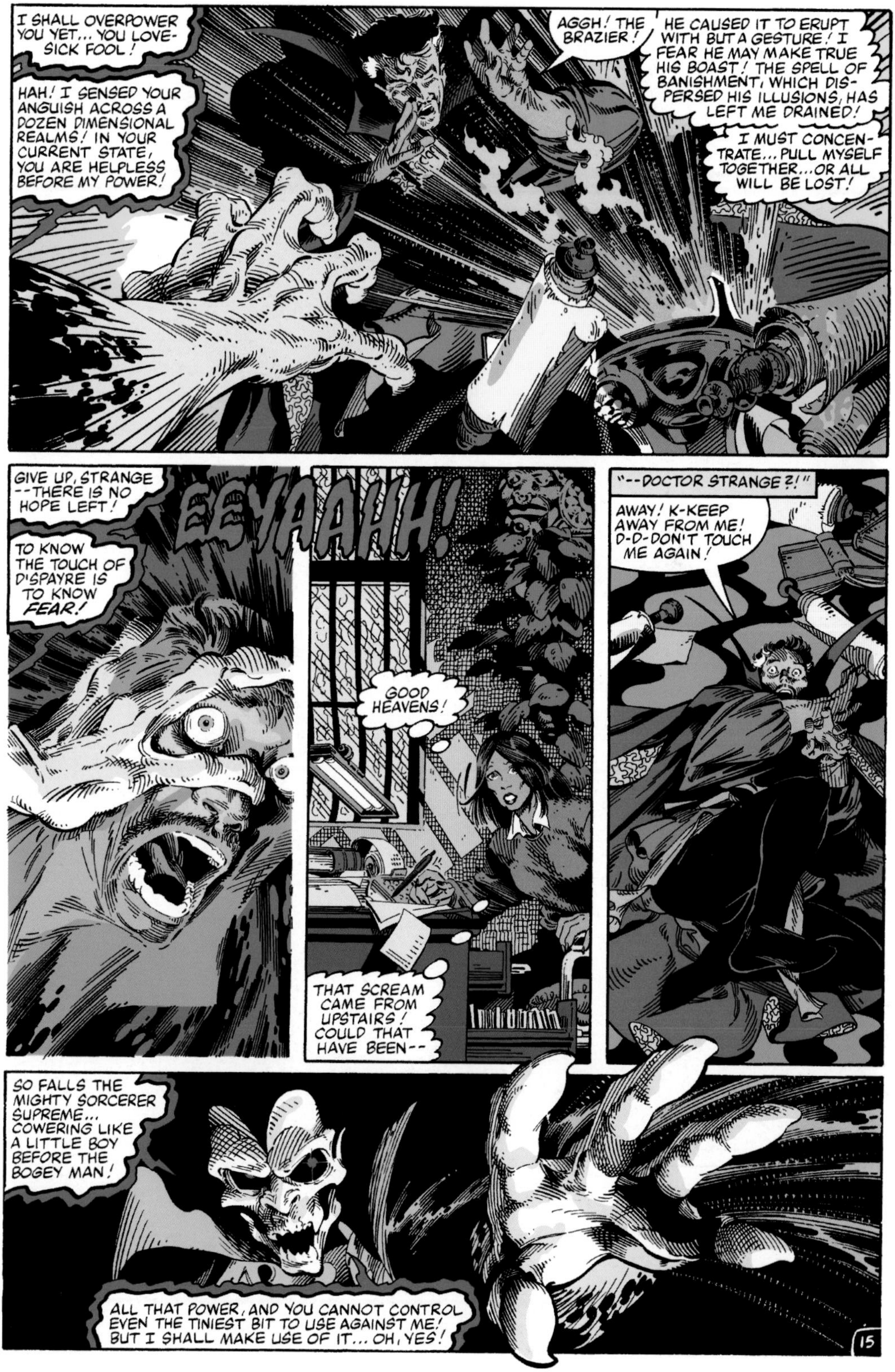
I SHALL OVERPOWER YOU YET... YOU LOVE-SICK FOOL!
HAH! I SENSED YOUR ANGUISH ACROSS A DOZEN DIMENSIONAL REALMS! IN YOUR CURRENT STATE, YOU ARE HELPLESS BEFORE MY POWER!
AGGH! THE BRAZIER!
HE CAUSED IT TO ERUPT WITH BUT A GESTURE! I FEAR HE MAY MAKE TRUE HIS BOAST! THE SPELL OF BANISHMENT, WHICH DISPERSED HIS ILLUSIONS, HAS LEFT ME DRAINED!
I MUST CONCENTRATE... PULL MYSELF TOGETHER... OR ALL WILL BE LOST!
GIVE UP, STRANGE --THERE IS NO HOPE LEFT!
TO KNOW THE TOUCH OF D'SPAYRE IS TO KNOW FEAR!
EEYAAHH!
GOOD HEAVENS!
THAT SCREAM CAME FROM UPSTAIRS! COULD THAT HAVE BEEN--
"--DOCTOR STRANGE?!"
AWAY! K-KEEP AWAY FROM ME! D-D-DON'T TOUCH ME AGAIN!
SO FALLS THE MIGHTY SORCERER SUPREME... COWERING LIKE A LITTLE BOY BEFORE THE BOGEY MAN!
ALL THAT POWER, AND YOU CANNOT CONTROL EVEN THE TINIEST BIT TO USE AGAINST ME! BUT I SHALL MAKE USE OF IT... OH, YES!
15

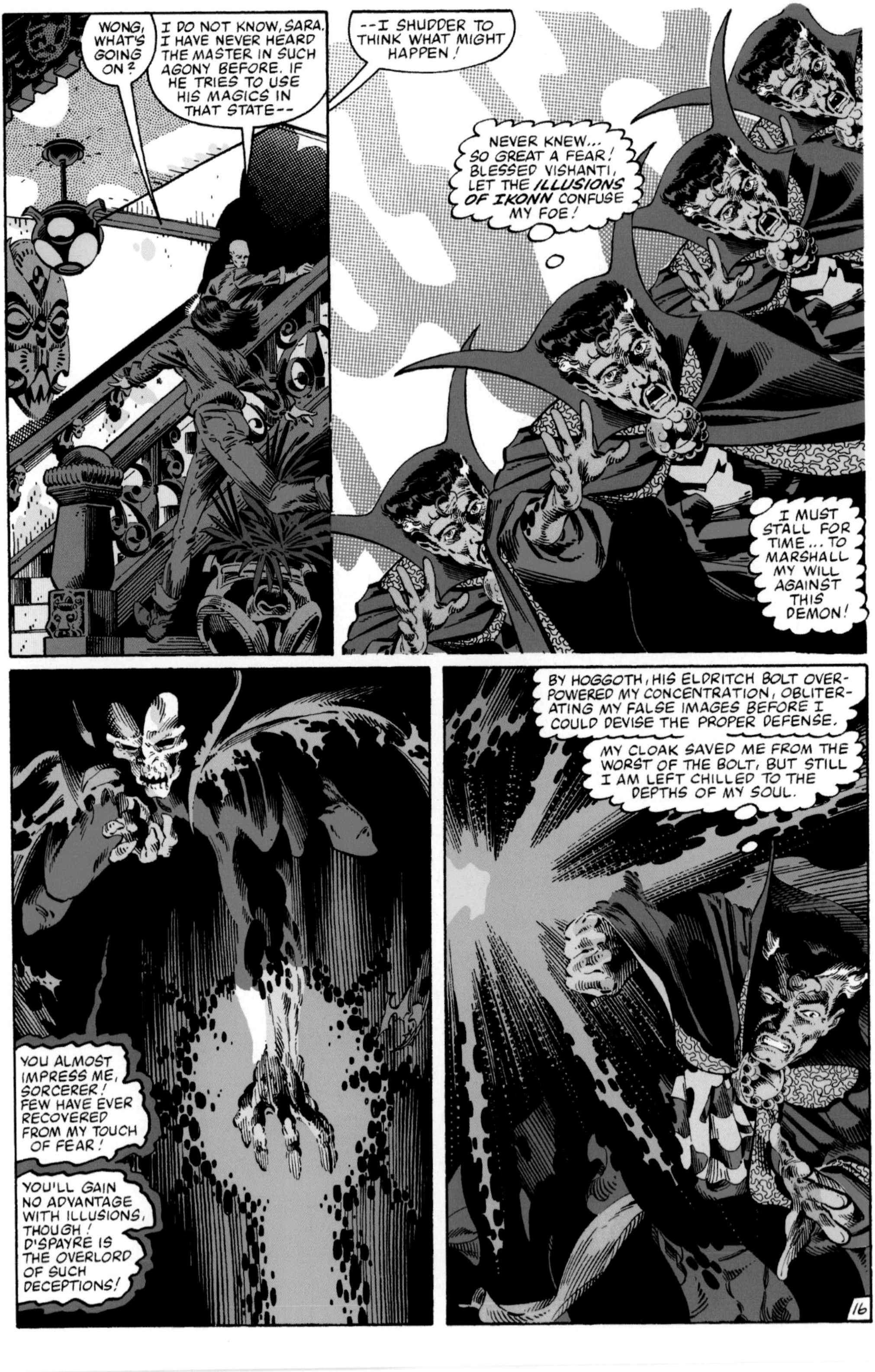
WONG, WHAT'S GOING ON?
I DO NOT KNOW, SARA. I HAVE NEVER HEARD THE MASTER IN SUCH AGONY BEFORE. IF HE TRIES TO USE HIS MAGICS IN THAT STATE--
--I SHUDDER TO THINK WHAT MIGHT HAPPEN!
NEVER KNEW... SO GREAT A FEAR! BLESSED VISHANTI, LET THE ILLUSIONS OF IKONN CONFUSE MY FOE!
I MUST STALL FOR TIME... TO MARSHALL MY WILL AGAINST THIS DEMON!
YOU ALMOST IMPRESS ME, SORCERER! FEW HAVE EVER RECOVERED FROM MY TOUCH OF FEAR!
YOU'LL GAIN NO ADVANTAGE WITH ILLUSIONS, THOUGH! D'SPAYRE IS THE OVERLORD OF SUCH DECEPTIONS!
BY HOGGOTH, HIS ELDRITCH BOLT OVERPOWERED MY CONCENTRATION, OBLITERATING MY FALSE IMAGES BEFORE I COULD DEVISE THE PROPER DEFENSE.
MY CLOAK SAVED ME FROM THE WORST OF THE BOLT, BUT STILL I AM LEFT CHILLED TO THE DEPTHS OF MY SOUL.
16

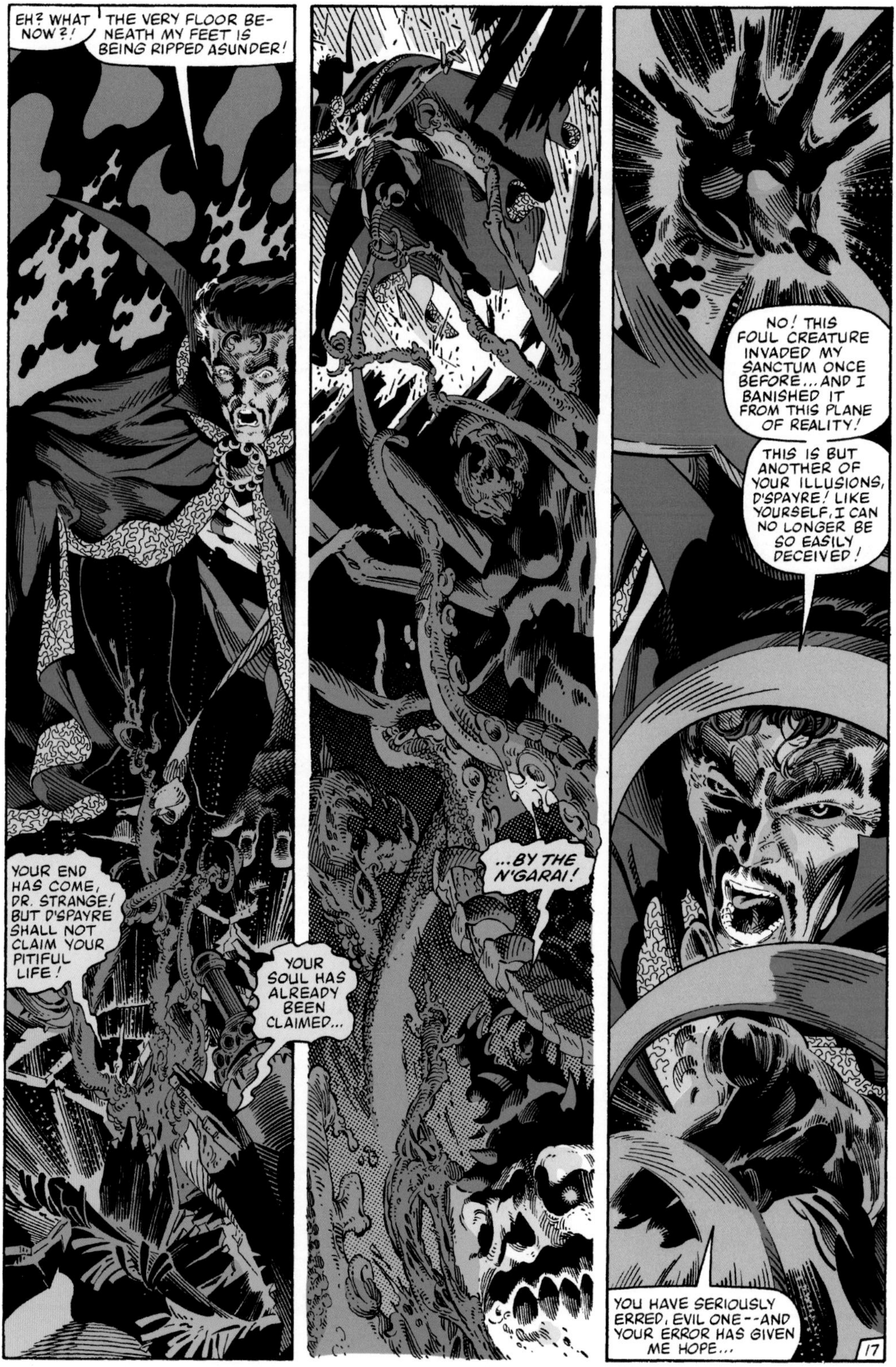
EH? WHAT NOW?!
THE VERY FLOOR BENEATH MY FEET IS BEING RIPPED ASUNDER!
YOUR END HAS COME, DR. STRANGE! BUT D'SPAYRE SHALL NOT CLAIM YOUR PITIFUL LIFE!
YOUR SOUL HAS ALREADY BEEN CLAIMED...
...BY THE N'GARAI!
NO! THIS FOUL CREATURE INVADED MY SANCTUM ONCE BEFORE... AND I BANISHED IT FROM THIS PLANE OF REALITY!
THIS IS BUT ANOTHER OF YOUR ILLUSIONS, D'SPAYRE! LIKE YOURSELF, I CAN NO LONGER BE SO EASILY DECEIVED!
YOU HAVE SERIOUSLY ERRED, EVIL ONE--AND YOUR ERROR HAS GIVEN ME HOPE...
17

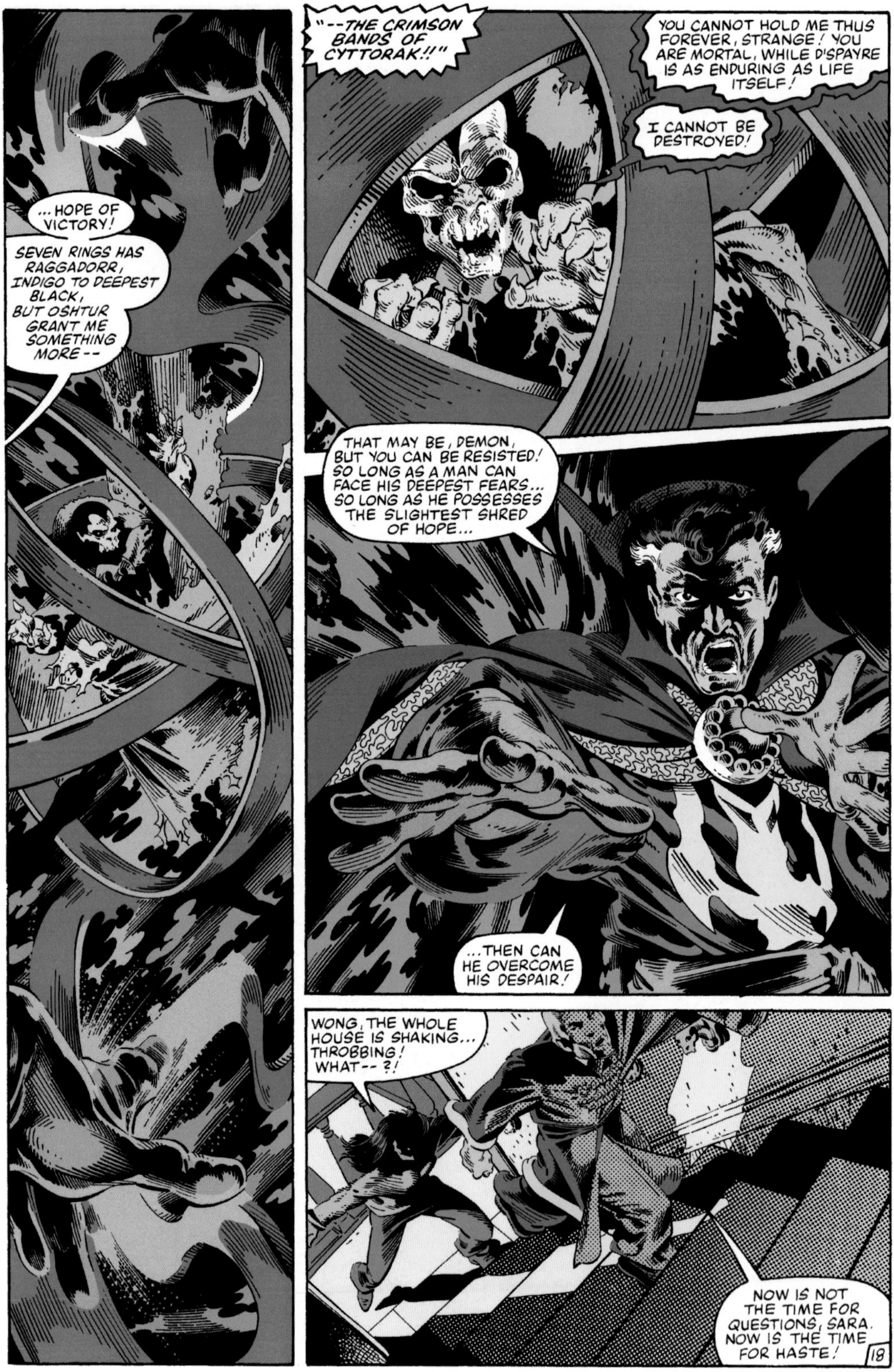
...HOPE OF VICTORY!
SEVEN RINGS HAS RAGGADORR, INDIGO TO DEEPEST BLACK, BUT OSHTUR GRANT ME SOMETHING MORE--
"--THE CRIMSON BANDS OF CYTTORAK!!"
YOU CANNOT HOLD ME THUS FOREVER, STRANGE! YOU ARE MORTAL, WHILE D'SPAYRE IS AS ENDURING AS LIFE ITSELF!
I CANNOT BE DESTROYED!
THAT MAY BE, DEMON, BUT YOU CAN BE RESISTED! SO LONG AS A MAN CAN FACE HIS DEEPEST FEARS... SO LONG AS HE POSSESSES THE SLIGHTEST SHRED OF HOPE...
...THEN CAN HE OVERCOME HIS DESPAIR!
WONG, THE WHOLE HOUSE IS SHAKING... THROBBING! WHAT-- ?!
NOW IS NOT THE TIME FOR QUESTIONS, SARA. NOW IS THE TIME FOR HASTE!
18

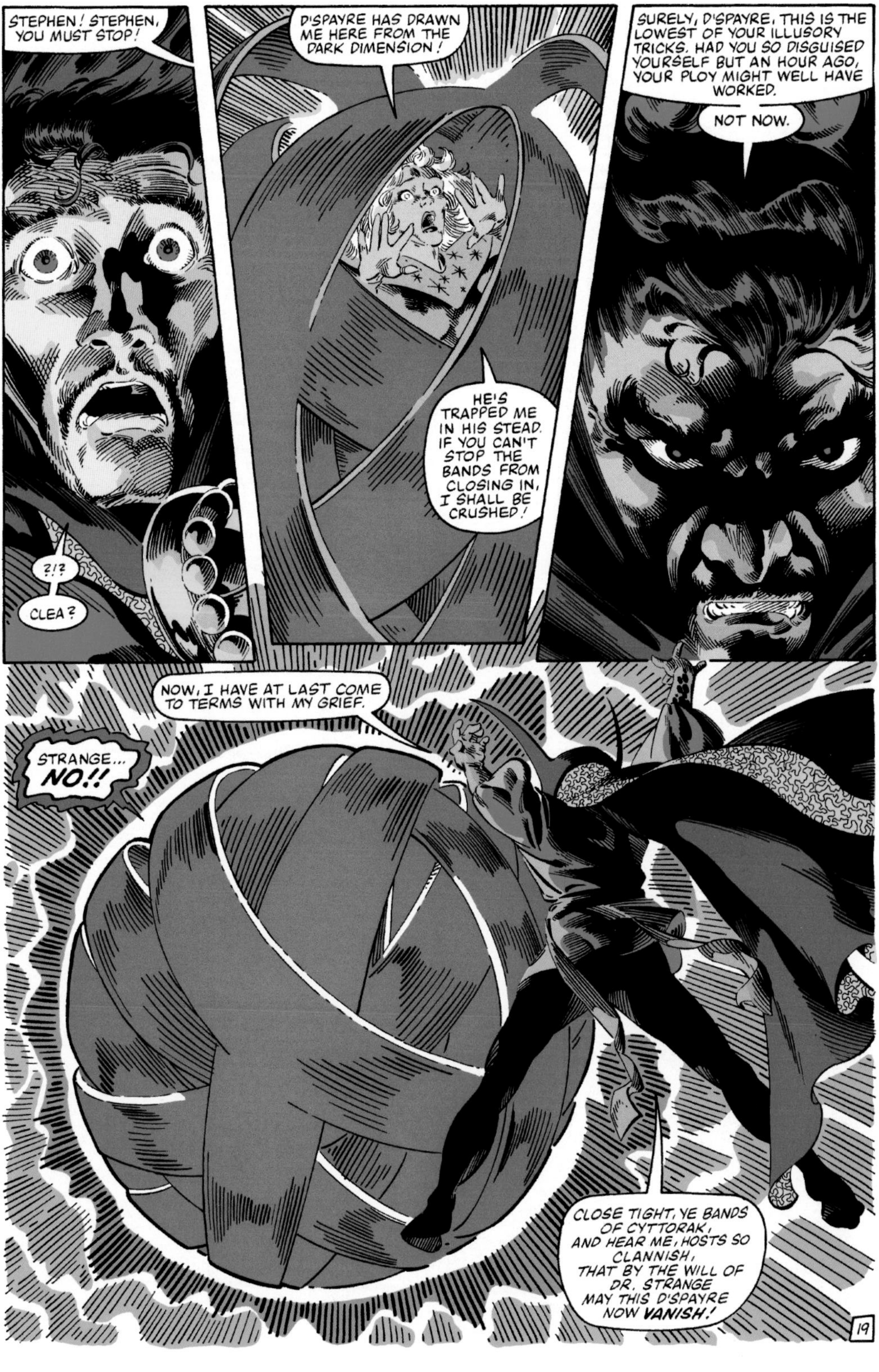

STEPHEN! STEPHEN, YOU MUST STOP!
?!?
CLEA?
D'SPAYRE HAS DRAWN ME HERE FROM THE DARK DIMENSION!
HE'S TRAPPED ME IN HIS STEAD. IF YOU CAN'T STOP THE BANDS FROM CLOSING IN, I SHALL BE CRUSHED!
SURELY, D'SPAYRE, THIS IS THE LOWEST OF YOUR ILLUSORY TRICKS. HAD YOU SO DISGUISED YOURSELF BUT AN HOUR AGO, YOUR PLOY MIGHT WELL HAVE WORKED.
NOT NOW.
NOW, I HAVE AT LAST COME TO TERMS WITH MY GRIEF.
STRANGE... NO!!
CLOSE TIGHT, YE BANDS OF CYTTORAK, AND HEAR ME, HOSTS SO CLANNISH, THAT BY THE WILL OF DR. STRANGE MAY THIS D'SPAYRE NOW VANISH!
19

KRA-KOOOM

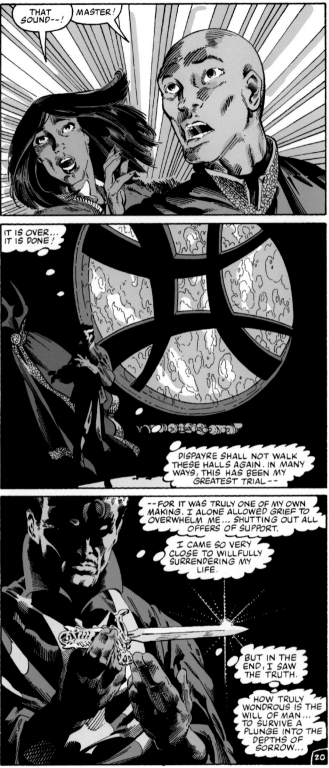

THAT SOUND--!

MASTER!

IT IS OVER... IT IS DONE!

DISPAYRE SHALL NOT WALK THESE HALLS AGAIN. IN MANY WAYS, THIS HAS BEEN MY GREATEST TRIAL--

--FOR IT WAS TRULY ONE OF MY OWN MAKING. I ALONE ALLOWED GRIEF TO OVERWHELM ME... SHUTTING OUT ALL OFFERS OF SUPPORT.

I CAME SO VERY CLOSE TO WILLFULLY SURRENDERING MY LIFE.

BUT IN THE END, I SAW THE TRUTH.

HOW TRULY WONDROUS IS THE WILL OF MAN... TO SURVIVE A PLUNGE INTO THE DEPTHS OF SORROW...

20

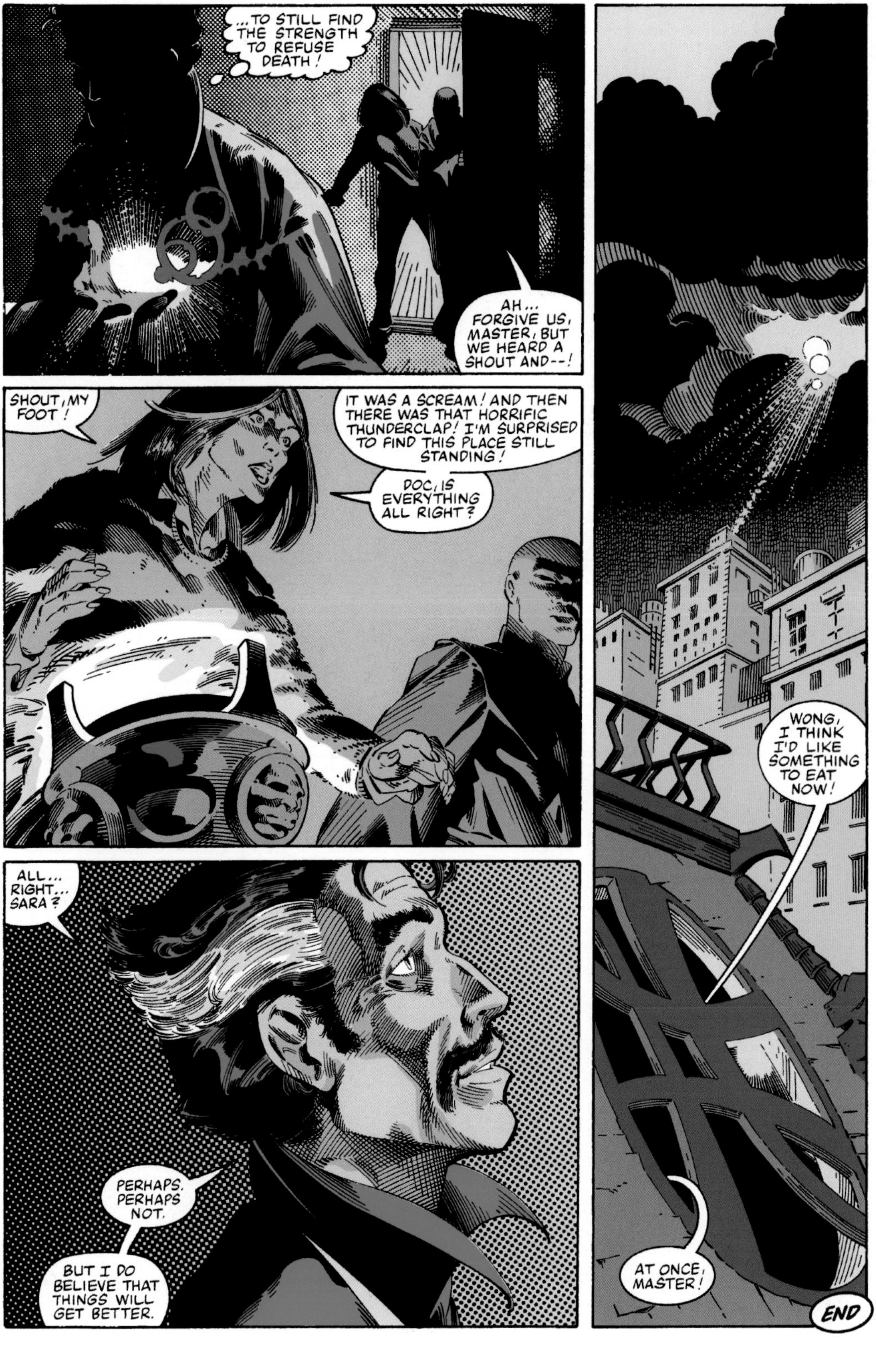
...TO STILL FIND THE STRENGTH TO REFUSE DEATH!
AH... FORGIVE US, MASTER, BUT WE HEARD A SHOUT AND--!
SHOUT, MY FOOT!
IT WAS A SCREAM! AND THEN THERE WAS THAT HORRIFIC THUNDERCLAP! I'M SURPRISED TO FIND THIS PLACE STILL STANDING!
DOC, IS EVERYTHING ALL RIGHT?
ALL... RIGHT... SARA?
PERHAPS. PERHAPS NOT.
BUT I DO BELIEVE THAT THINGS WILL GET BETTER.
WONG, I THINK I'D LIKE SOMETHING TO EAT NOW!
AT ONCE, MASTER!
END

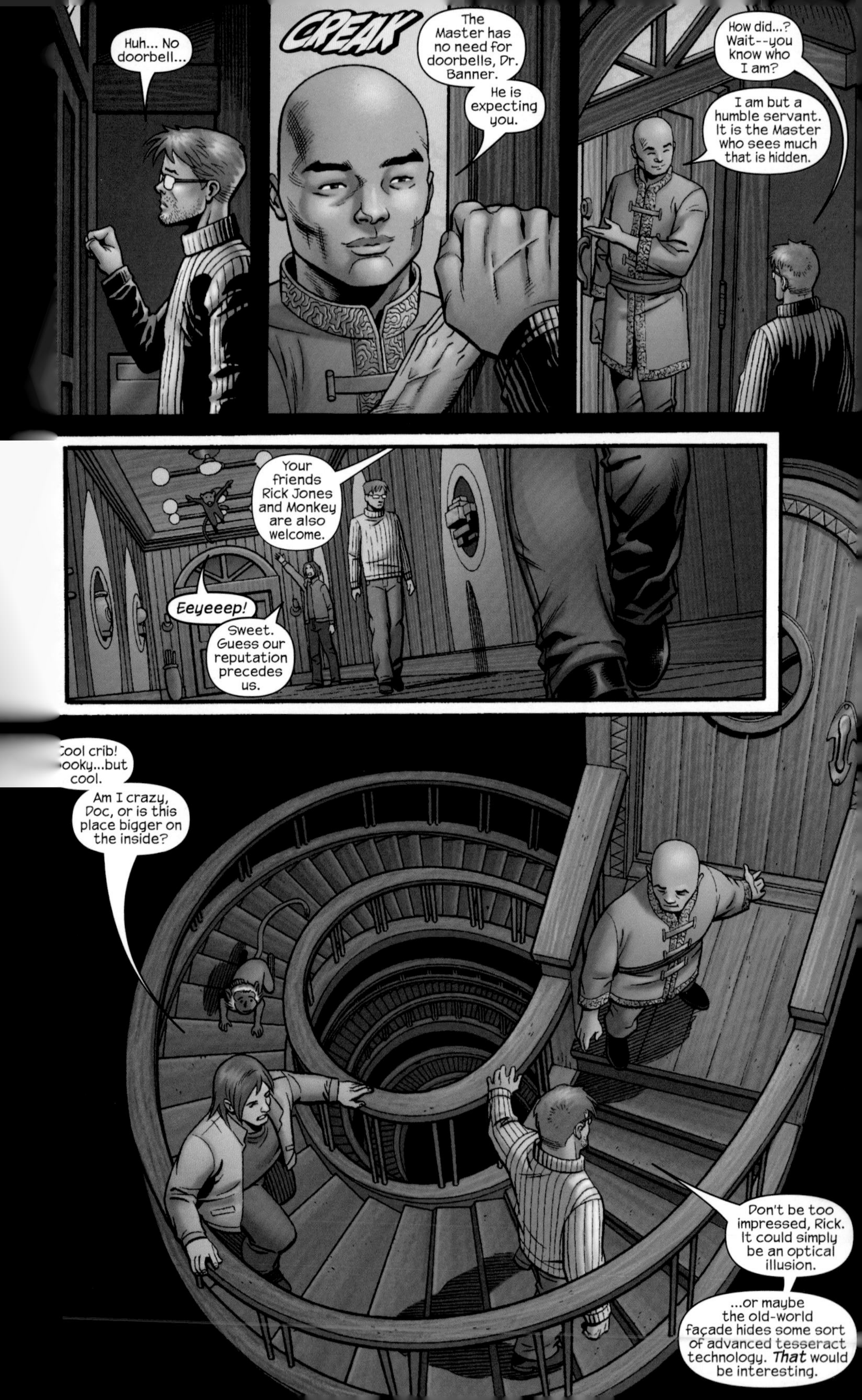
Huh... No doorbell...
CREAK
The Master has no need for doorbells, Dr. Banner.
He is expecting you.
How did...? Wait--you know who I am?
I am but a humble servant. It is the Master who sees much that is hidden.
Your friends Rick Jones and Monkey are also welcome.
Eeyeeep!
Sweet. Guess our reputation precedes us.
ool crib! ooky...but cool.
Am I crazy, Doc, or is this place bigger on the inside?
Don't be too impressed, Rick. It could simply be an optical illusion.
...or maybe the old-world façade hides some sort of advanced tesseract technology. *That* would be interesting.

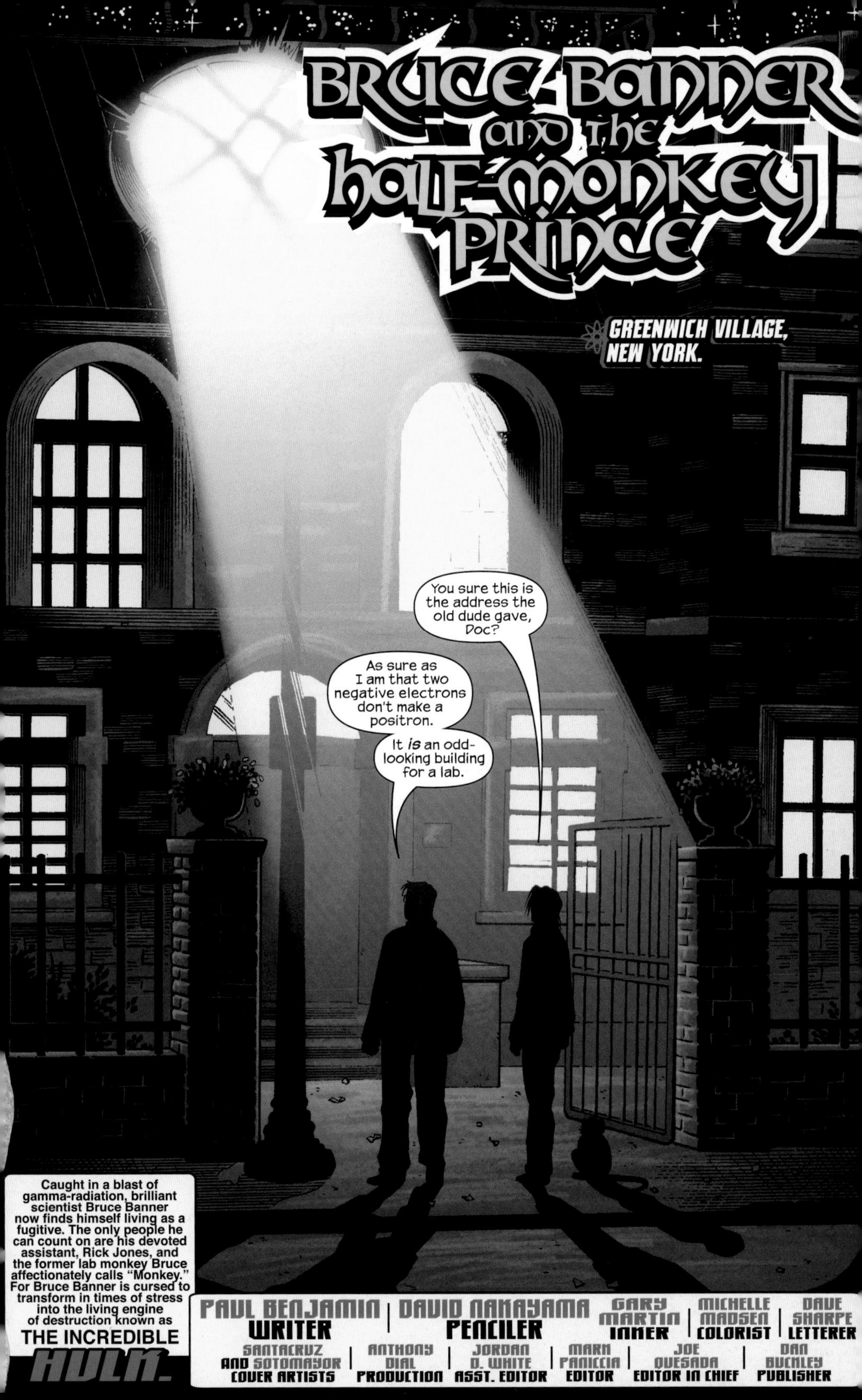

BRUCE BANNER AND THE HALF-MONKEY PRINCE
GREENWICH VILLAGE, NEW YORK.
You sure this is the address the old dude gave, Doc?
As sure as I am that two negative electrons don't make a positron.
It *is* an odd-looking building for a lab.
Caught in a blast of gamma-radiation, brilliant scientist Bruce Banner now finds himself living as a fugitive. The only people he can count on are his devoted assistant, Rick Jones, and the former lab monkey Bruce affectionately calls "Monkey." For Bruce Banner is cursed to transform in times of stress into the living engine of destruction known as THE INCREDIBLE HULK.
PAUL BENJAMIN WRITER
DAVID NAKAYAMA PENCILER
GARY MARTIN INKER
MICHELLE MADSEN COLORIST
DAVE SHARPE LETTERER
SANTACRUZ AND SOTOMAYOR COVER ARTISTS
ANTHONY DIAL PRODUCTION
JORDAN D. WHITE ASST. EDITOR
MARK PANICCIA EDITOR
JOE QUESADA EDITOR IN CHIEF
DAN BUCKLEY PUBLISHER

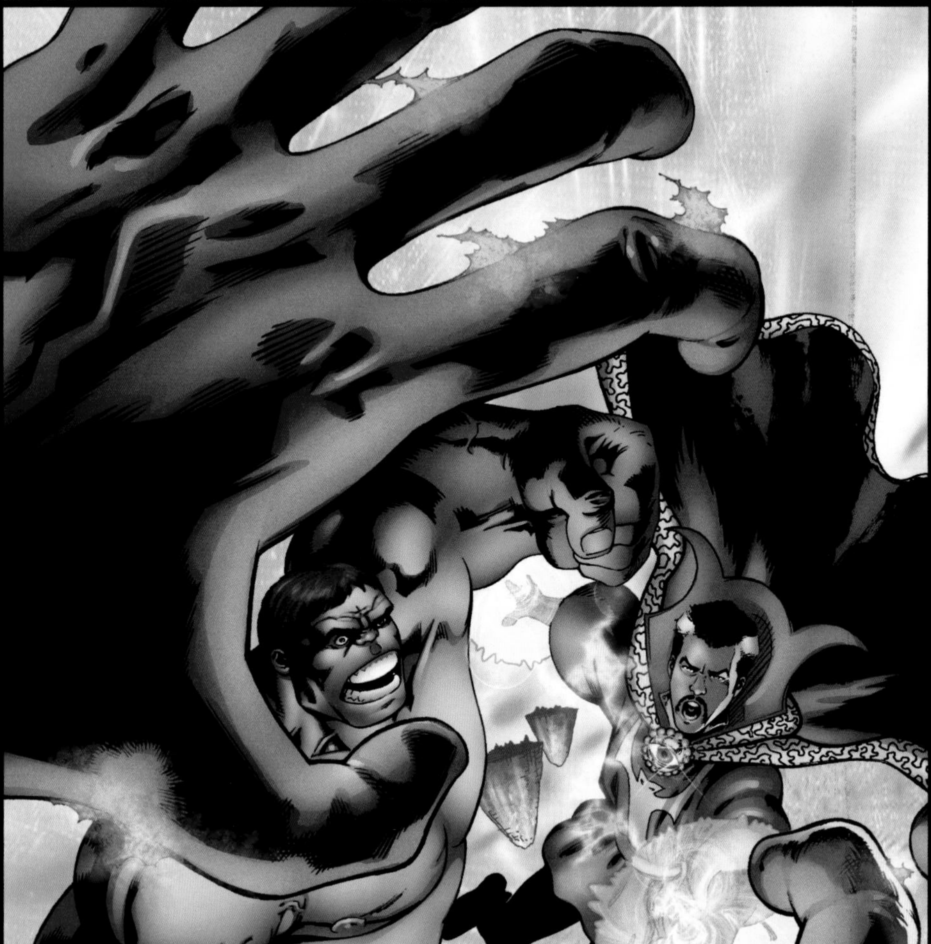
SANTACRUZ
07
¡SOTO!

MARVEL ADVENTURES HULK #5

BRUCE BANNER ASKS DOCTOR STRANGE TO HELP CAGE THE RAGE OF
THE HULK — BUT NOW, TWO OF MARVEL'S TITANS MUST DEAL WITH

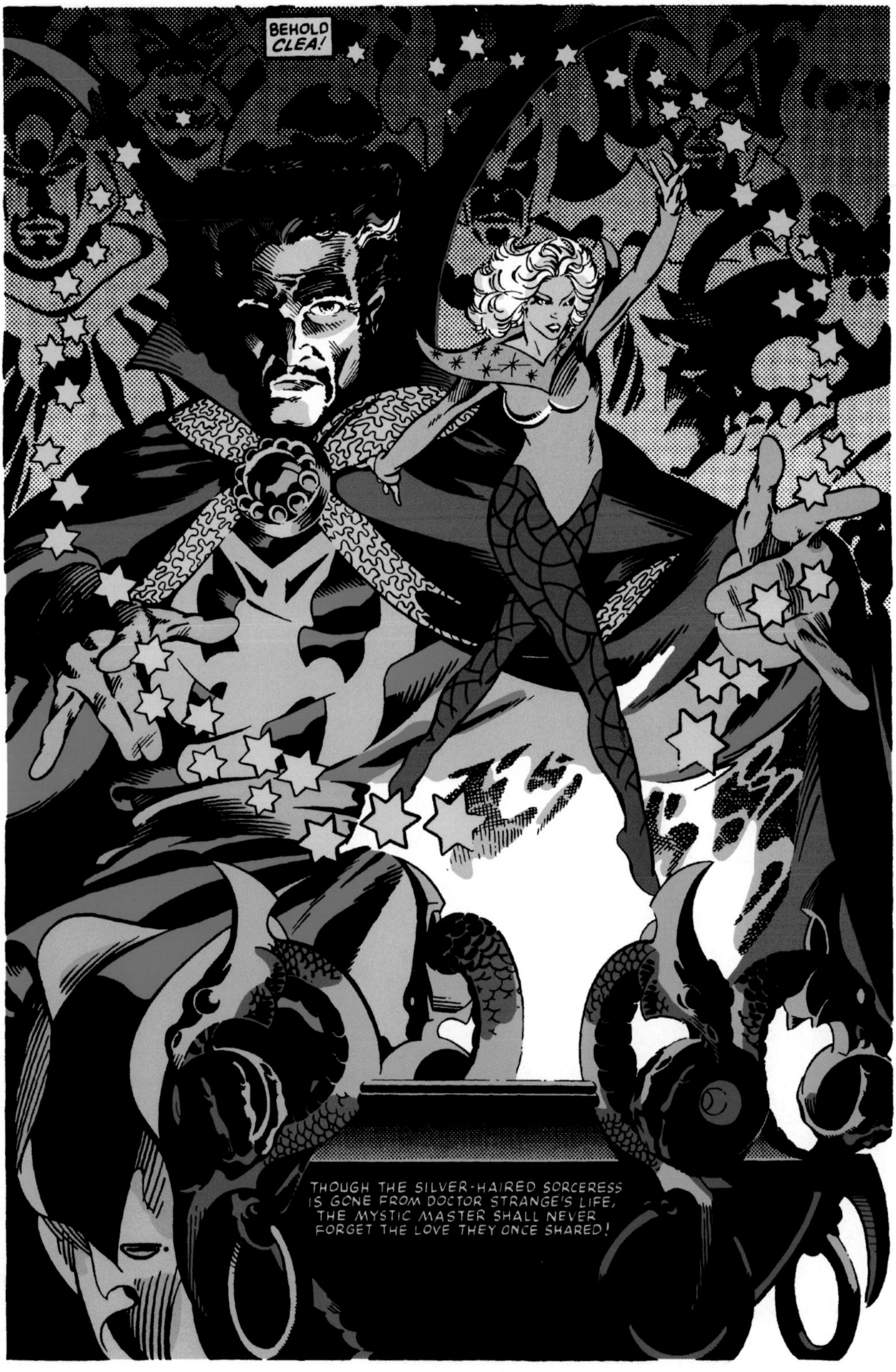
BEHOLD CLEA!
THOUGH THE SILVER-HAIRED SORCERESS IS GONE FROM DOCTOR STRANGE'S LIFE, THE MYSTIC MASTER SHALL NEVER FORGET THE LOVE THEY ONCE SHARED!

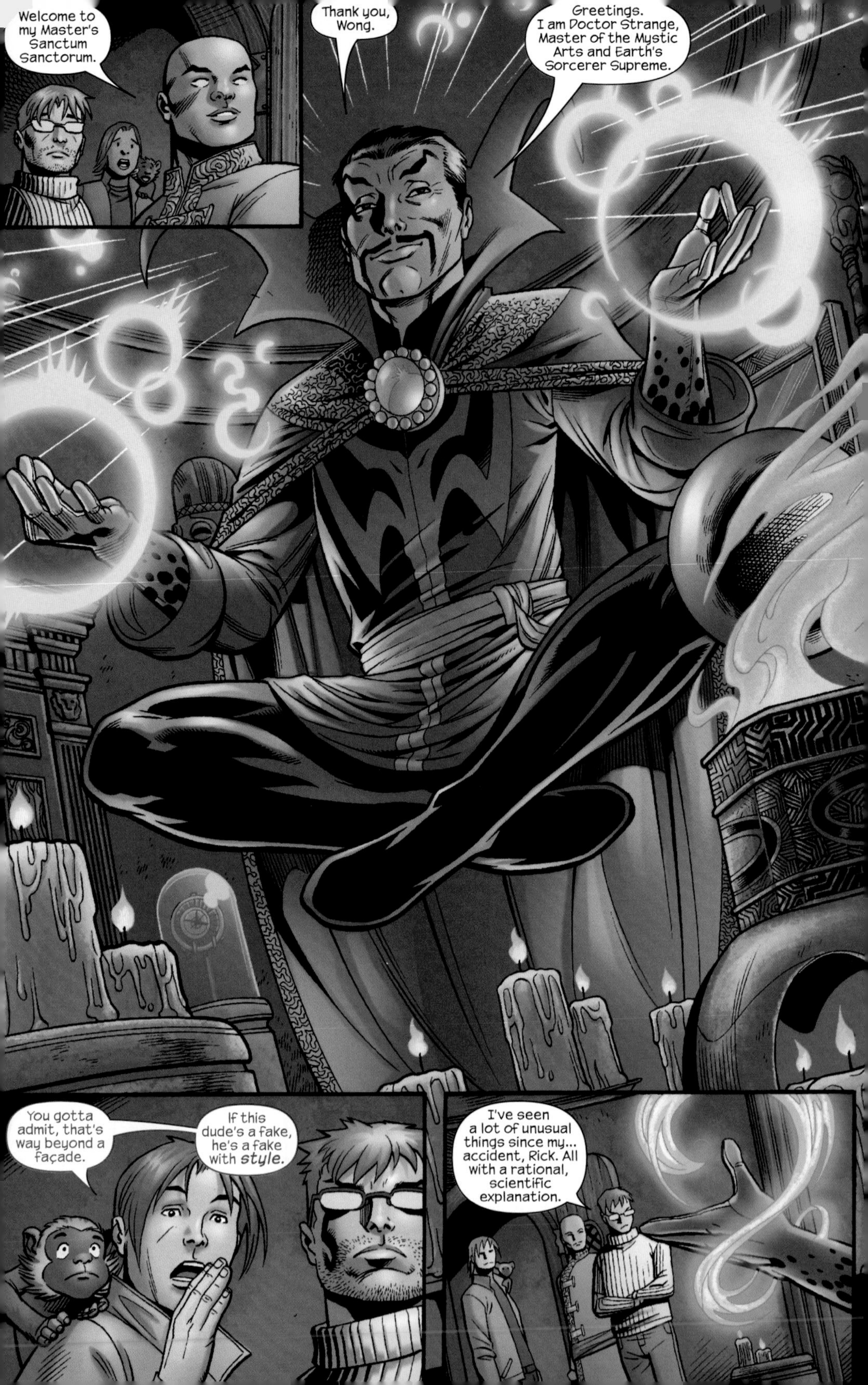

Welcome to my Master's Sanctum Sanctorum.
Thank you, Wong.
Greetings. I am Doctor Strange, Master of the Mystic Arts and Earth's Sorcerer Supreme.
You gotta admit, that's way beyond a façade.
If this dude's a fake, he's a fake with *style.*
I've seen a lot of unusual things since my... accident, Rick. All with a rational, scientific explanation.

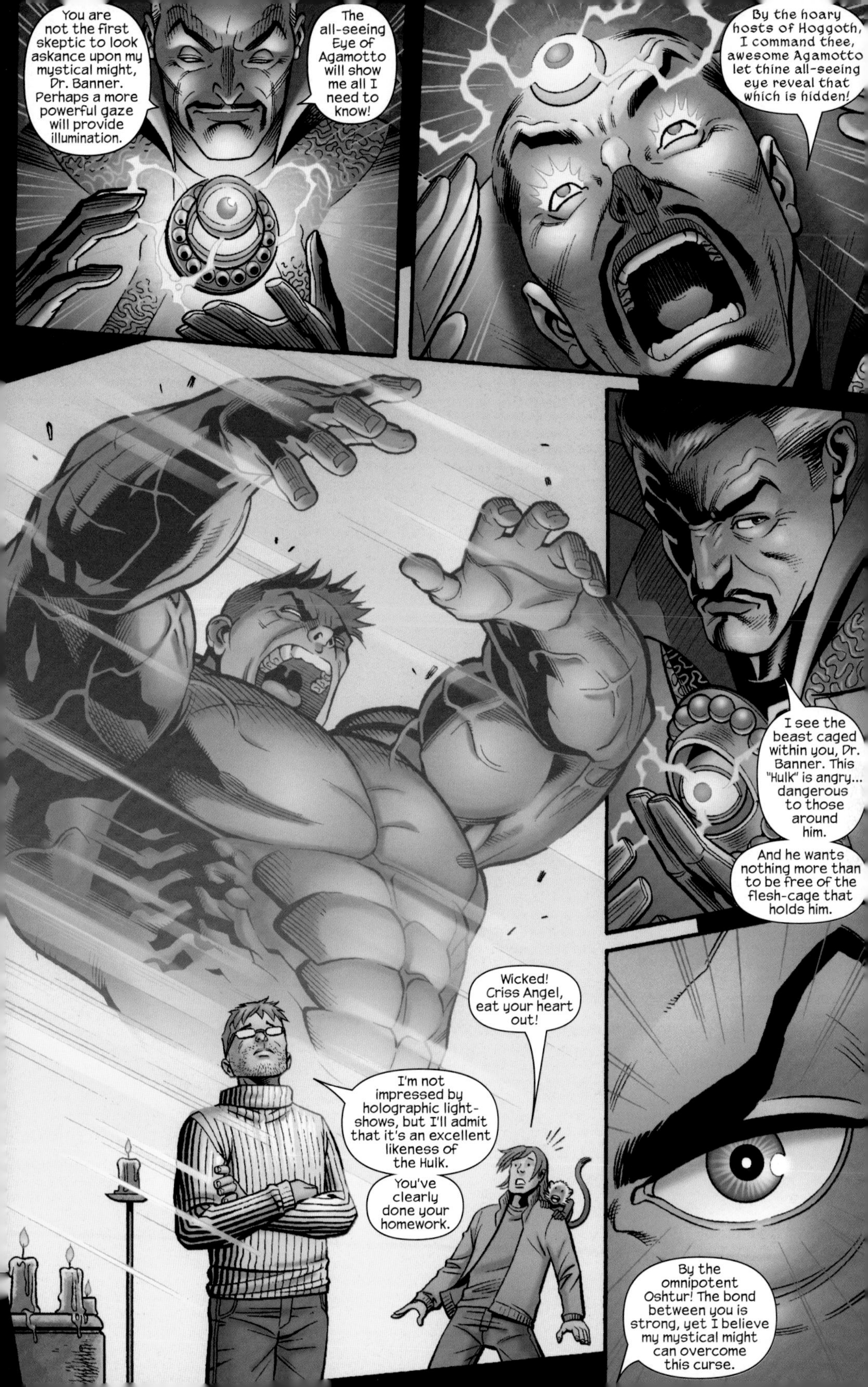
You are not the first skeptic to look askance upon my mystical might, Dr. Banner. Perhaps a more powerful gaze will provide illumination.
The all-seeing Eye of Agamotto will show me all I need to know!
By the hoary hosts of Hoggoth, I command thee, awesome Agamotto let thine all-seeing eye reveal that which is hidden!
I see the beast caged within you, Dr. Banner. This "Hulk" is angry... dangerous to those around him.
And he wants nothing more than to be free of the flesh-cage that holds him.
Wicked! Criss Angel, eat your heart out!
I'm not impressed by holographic light-shows, but I'll admit that it's an excellent likeness of the Hulk.
You've clearly done your homework.
By the omnipotent Oshtur! The bond between you is strong, yet I believe my mystical might can overcome this curse.

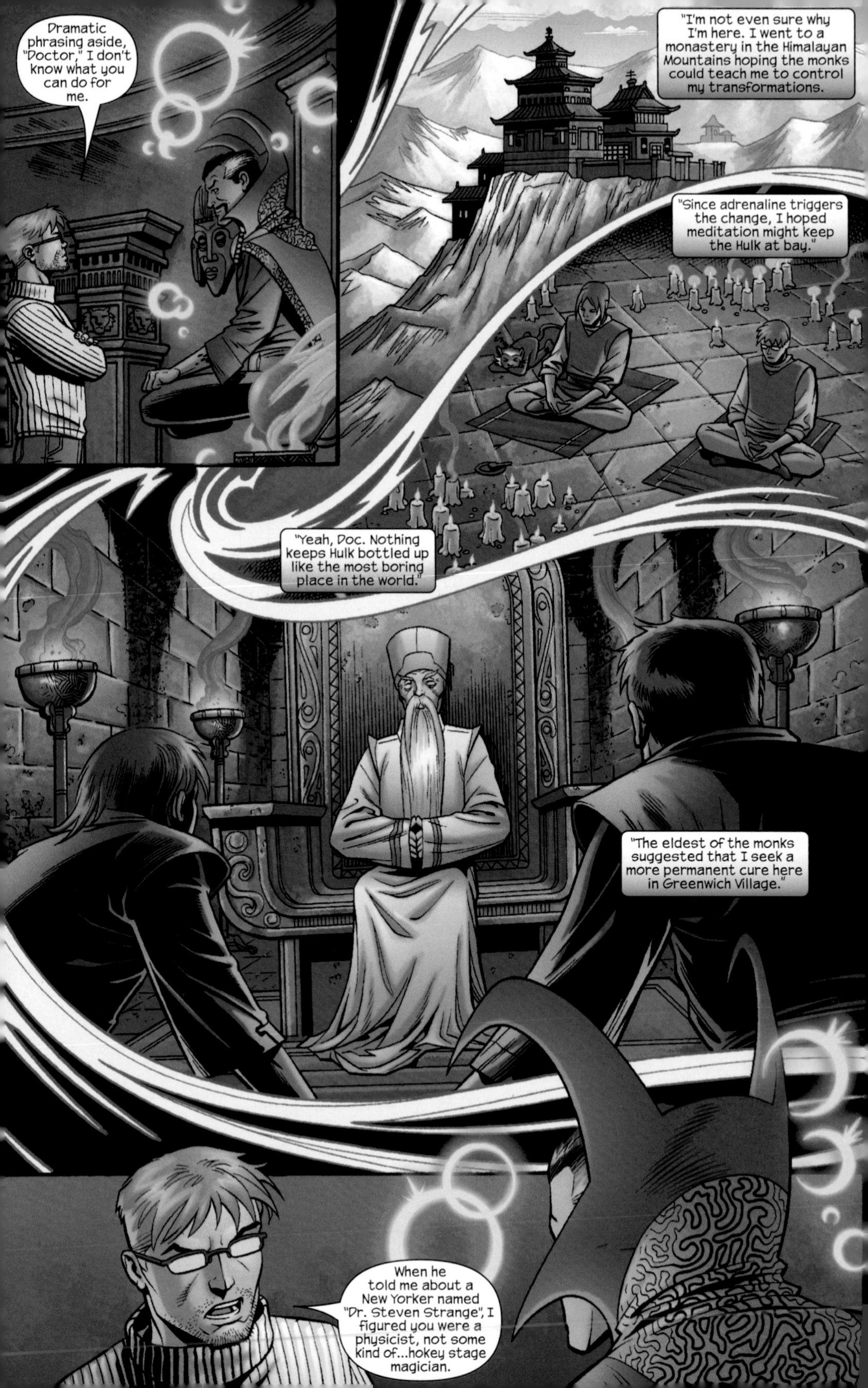

Dramatic phrasing aside, "Doctor," I don't know what you can do for me.
"I'm not even sure why I'm here. I went to a monastery in the Himalayan Mountains hoping the monks could teach me to control my transformations.
"Since adrenaline triggers the change, I hoped meditation might keep the Hulk at bay."
"Yeah, Doc. Nothing keeps Hulk bottled up like the most boring place in the world."
"The eldest of the monks suggested that I seek a more permanent cure here in Greenwich Village."
When he told me about a New Yorker named "Dr. Steven Strange", I figured you were a physicist, not some kind of...hokey stage magician.

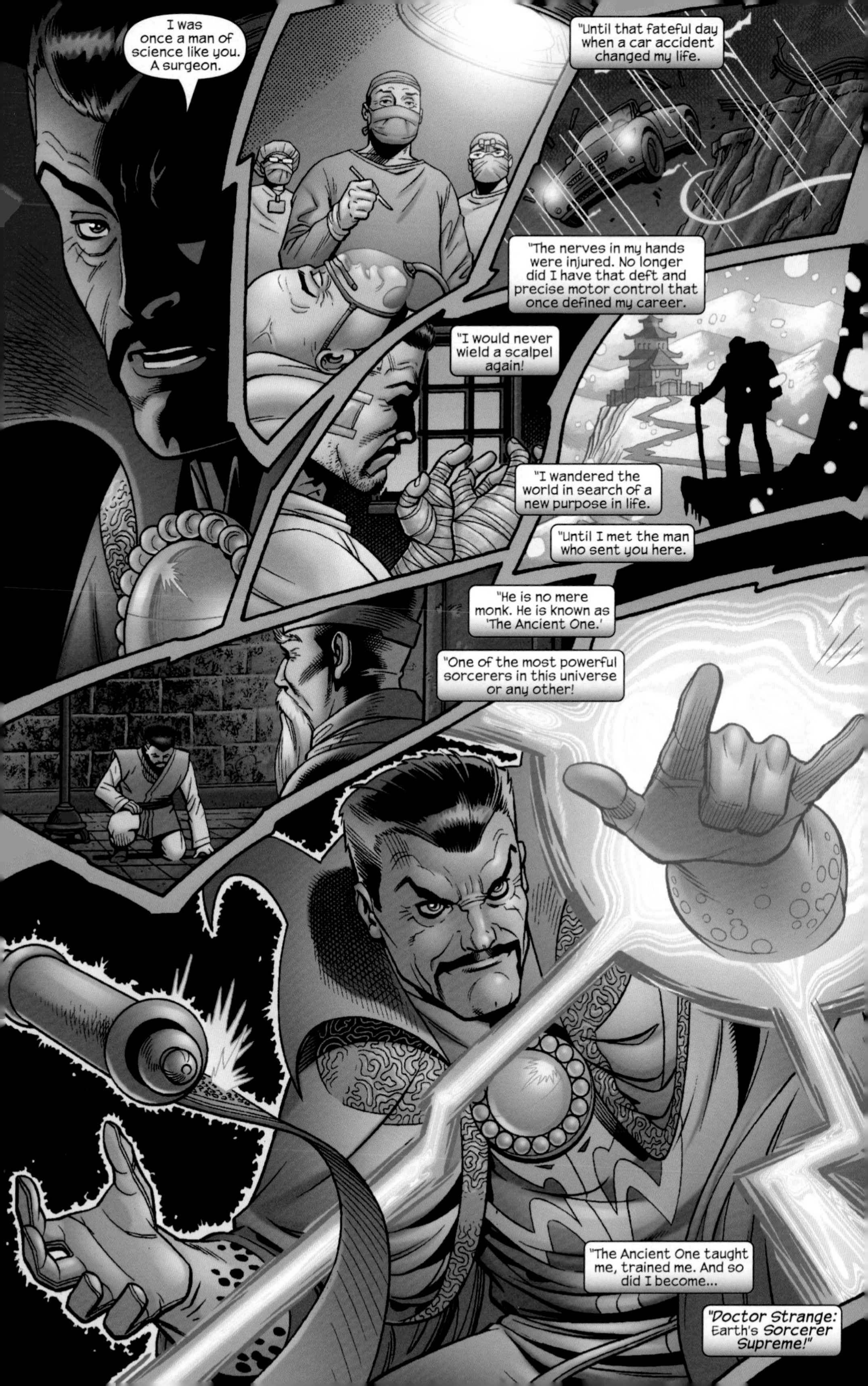
I was once a man of science like you. A surgeon.
"Until that fateful day when a car accident changed my life.
"The nerves in my hands were injured. No longer did I have that deft and precise motor control that once defined my career.
"I would never wield a scalpel again!
"I wandered the world in search of a new purpose in life.
"Until I met the man who sent you here.
"He is no mere monk. He is known as 'The Ancient One.'
"One of the most powerful sorcerers in this universe or any other!
"The Ancient One taught me, trained me. And so did I become...
"Doctor Strange: Earth's Sorcerer Supreme!"

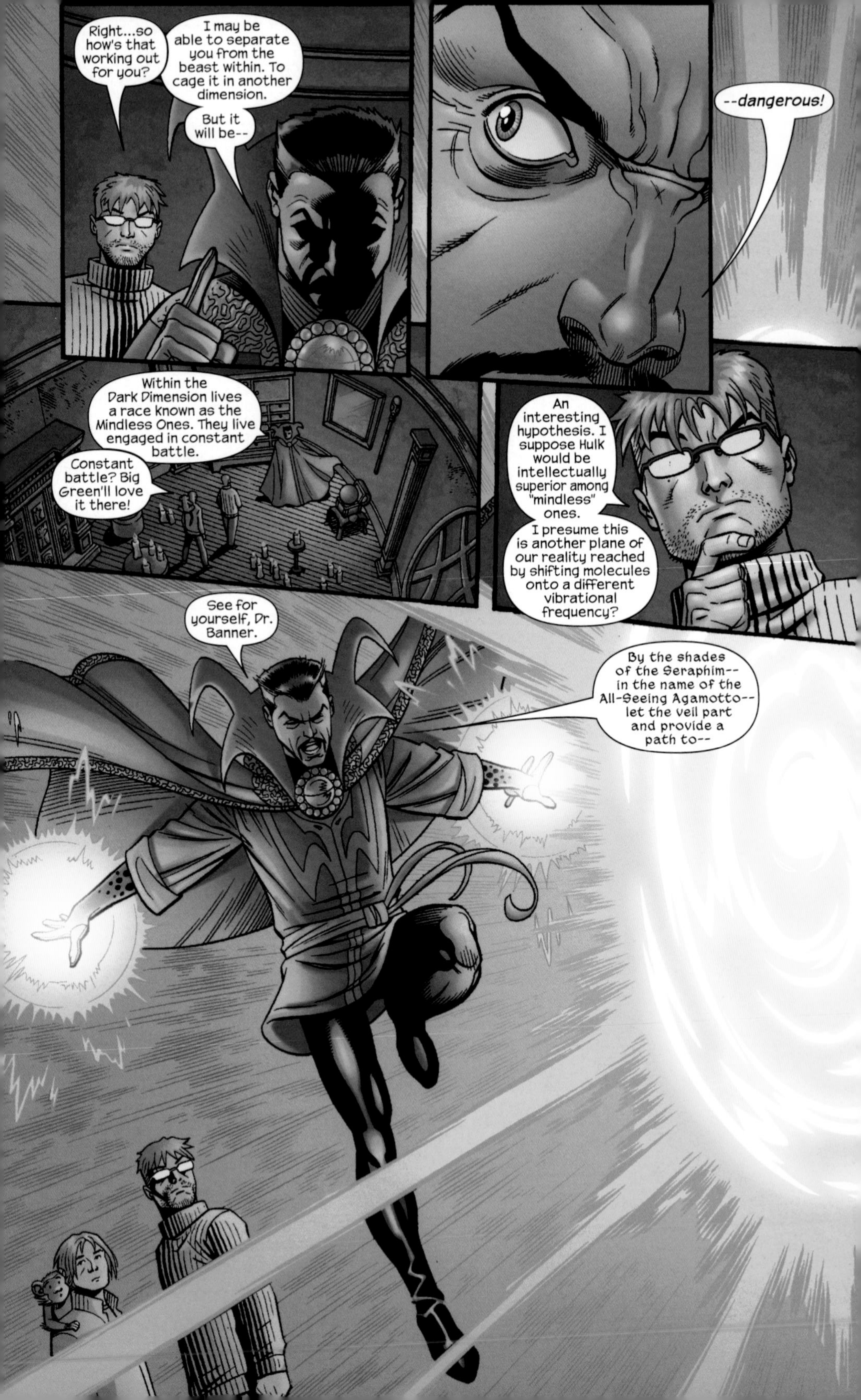
Right...so how's that working out for you?
I may be able to separate you from the beast within. To cage it in another dimension.
But it will be--
--dangerous!
Within the Dark Dimension lives a race known as the Mindless Ones. They live engaged in constant battle.
Constant battle? Big Green'll love it there!
An interesting hypothesis. I suppose Hulk would be intellectually superior among "mindless" ones.
I presume this is another plane of our reality reached by shifting molecules onto a different vibrational frequency?
See for yourself, Dr. Banner.
By the shades of the Seraphim-- in the name of the All-Seeing Agamotto-- let the veil part and provide a path to--

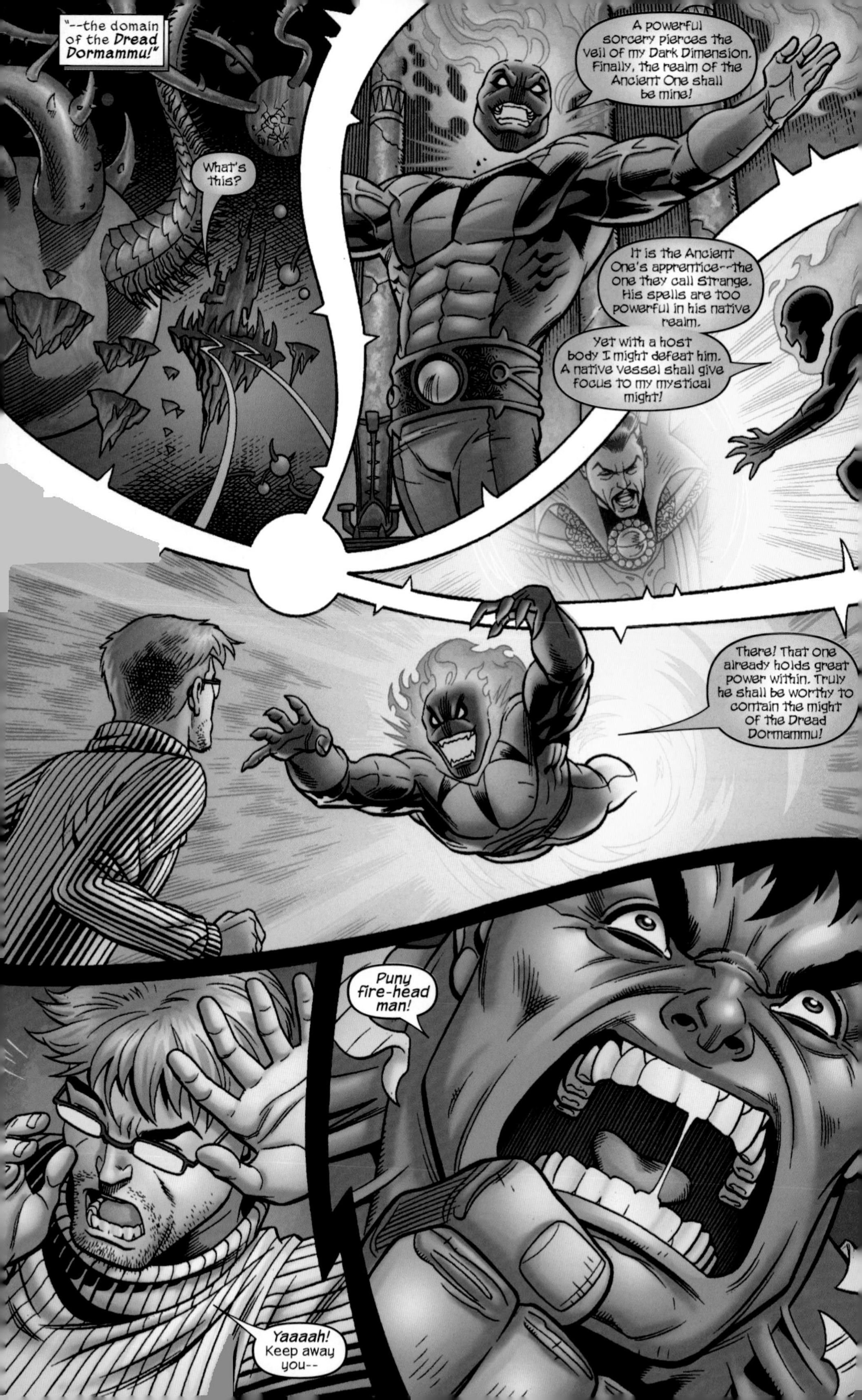
"--the domain of the Dread Dormammu!"
What's this?
A powerful sorcery pierces the veil of my Dark Dimension. Finally, the realm of the Ancient One shall be mine!
It is the Ancient One's apprentice--the one they call Strange. His spells are too powerful in his native realm.
Yet with a host body I might defeat him. A native vessel shall give focus to my mystical might!
There! That one already holds great power within. Truly he shall be worthy to contain the might of the Dread Dormammu!
Puny fire-head man!
Yaaaah! Keep away you--

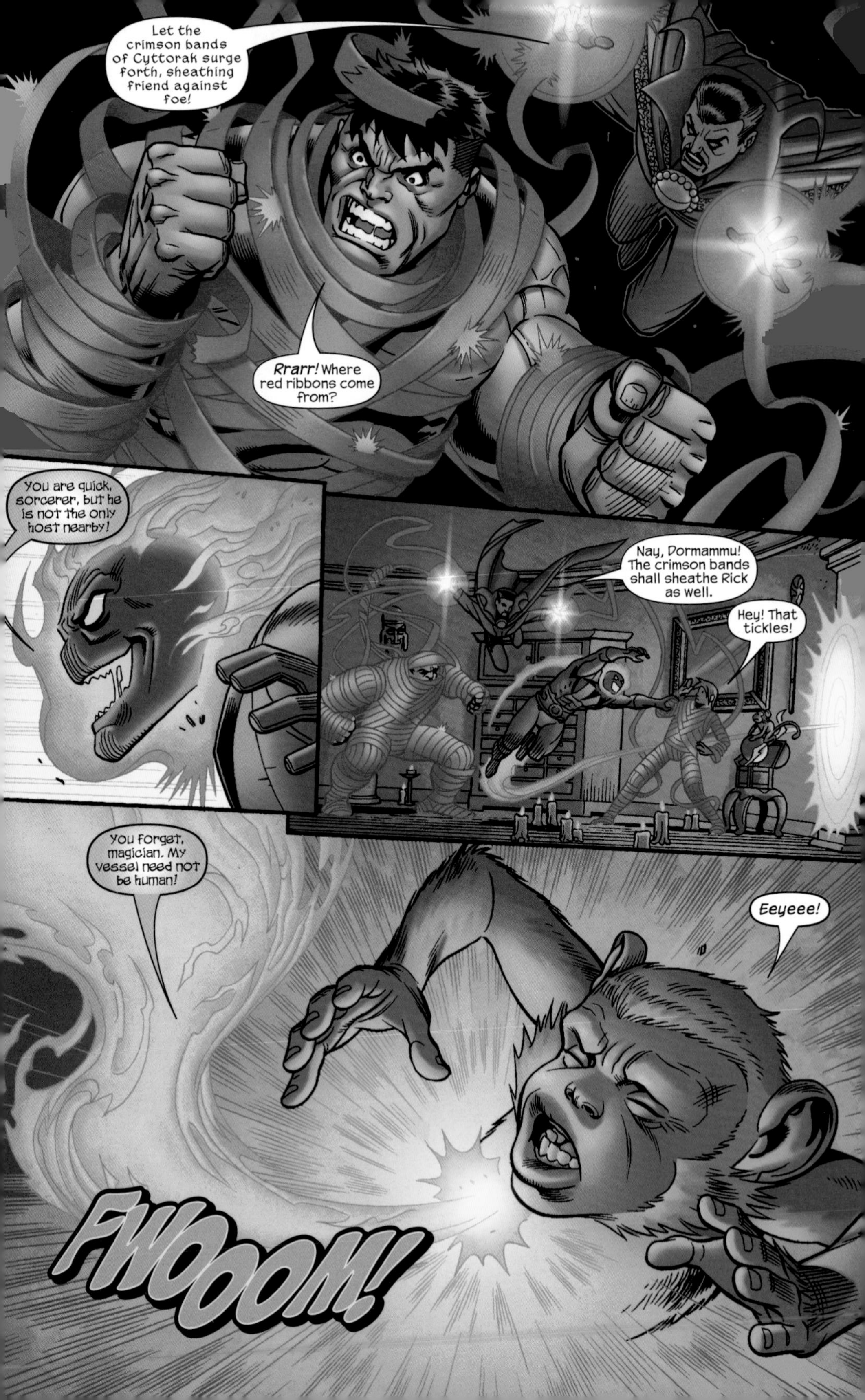
Let the crimson bands of Cyttorak surge forth, sheathing friend against foe!
Rrarr! Where red ribbons come from?
You are quick, sorcerer, but he is not the only host nearby!
Nay, Dormammu! The crimson bands shall sheathe Rick as well.
Hey! That tickles!
You forget, magician. My vessel need not be human!
Eeyeee!
FWOOOM!

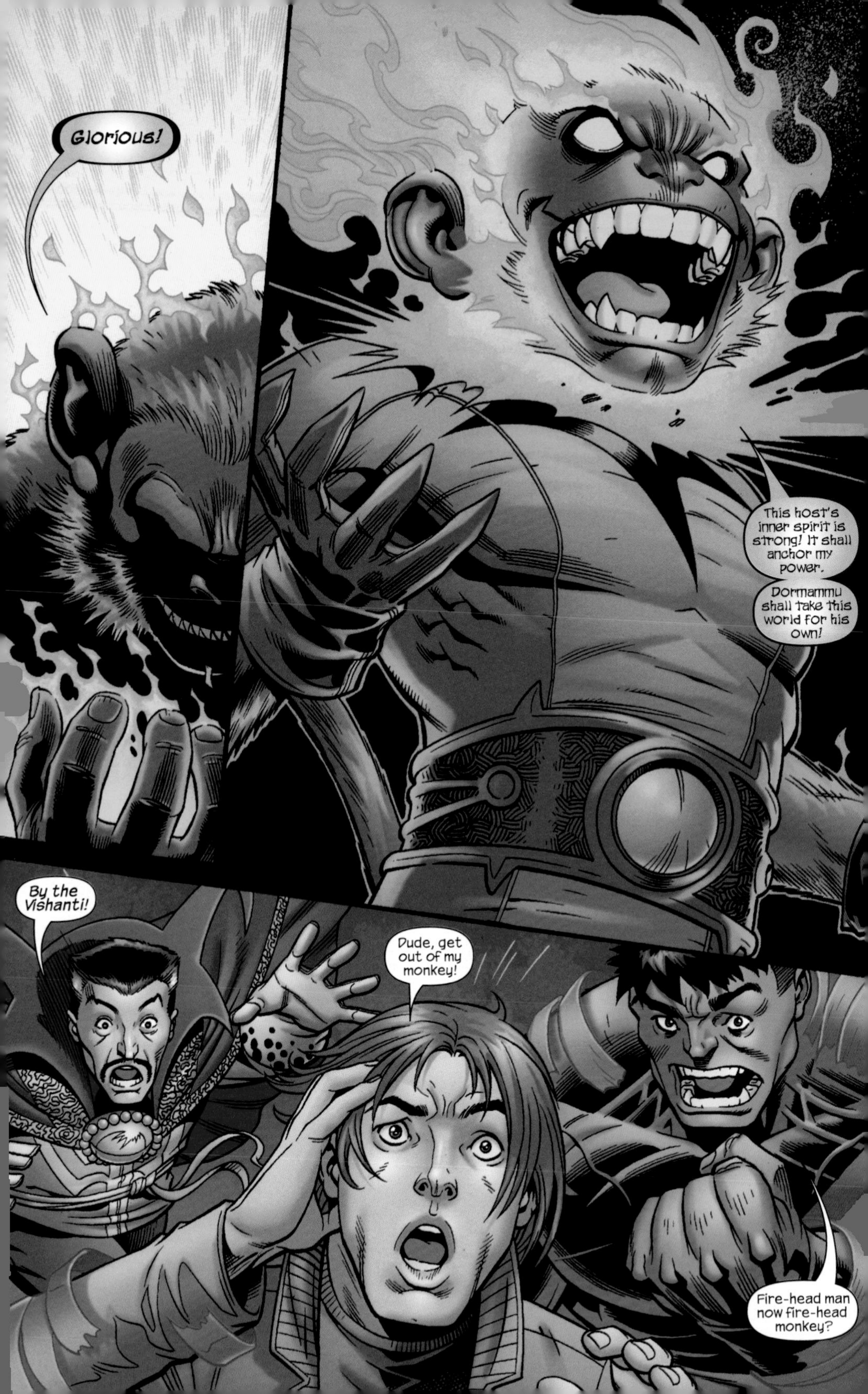
Glorious!
This host's inner spirit is strong! It shall anchor my power.
Dormammu shall take this world for his own!
By the Vishanti!
Dude, get out of my monkey!
Fire-head man now fire-head monkey?

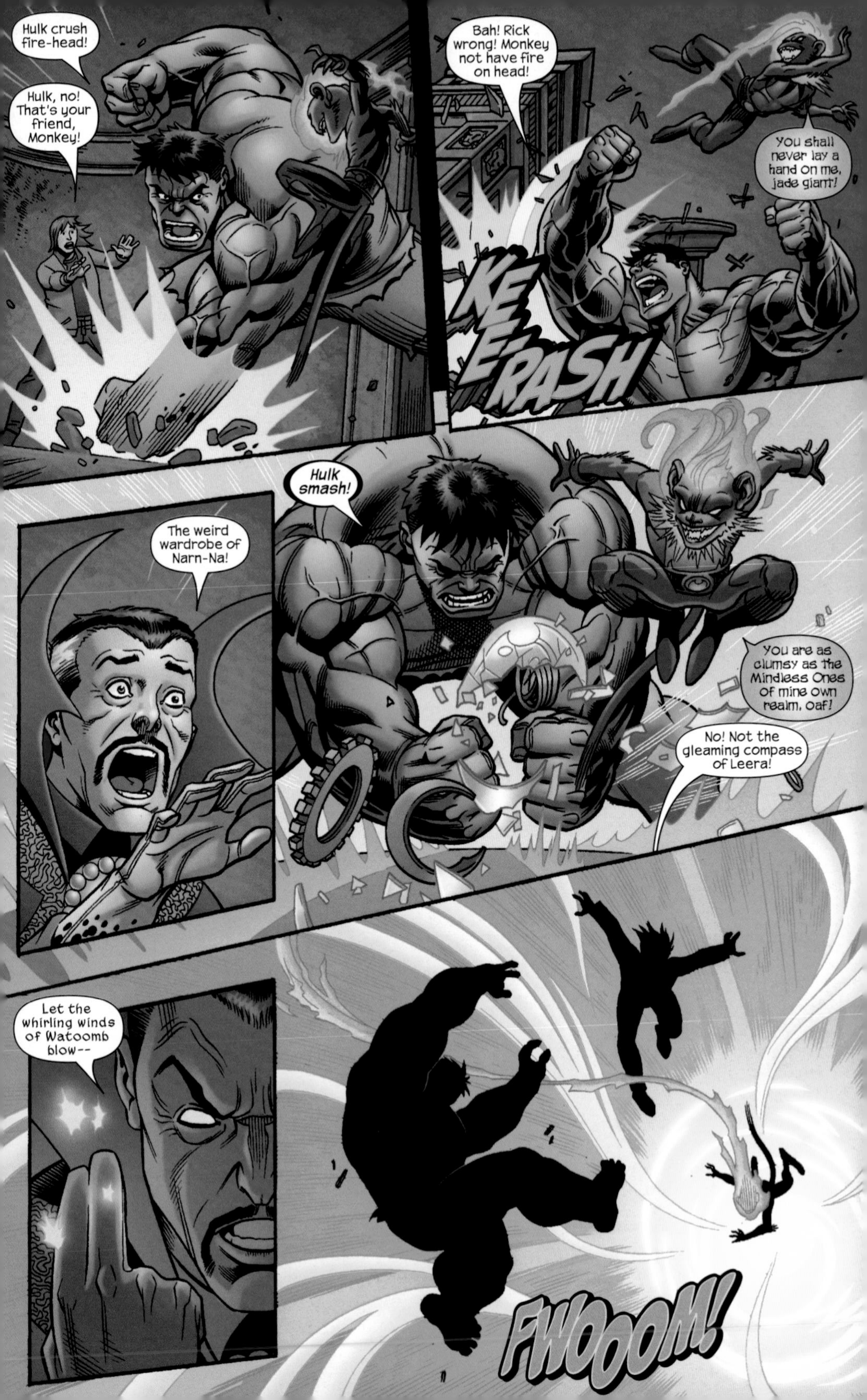
Hulk crush fire-head!
Hulk, no! That's your friend, Monkey!
Bah! Rick wrong! Monkey not have fire on head!
You shall never lay a hand on me, jade giant!
KE-E-RASH
Hulk smash!
The weird wardrobe of Narn-Na!
You are as clumsy as the Mindless Ones of mine own realm, oaf!
No! Not the gleaming compass of Leera!
Let the whirling winds of Watoomb blow--
FWOOOM!

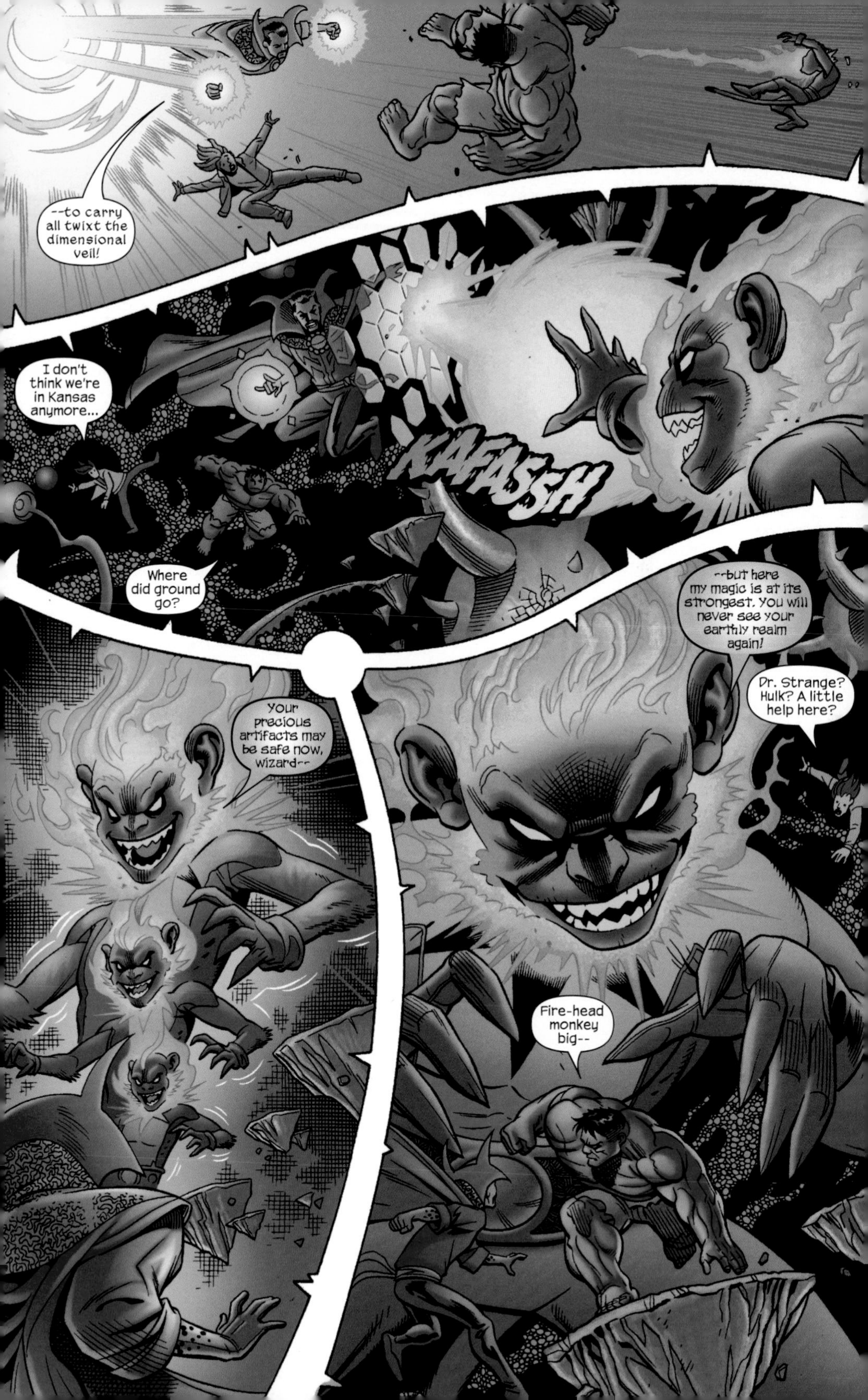
--to carry all twixt the dimensional veil!
I don't think we're in Kansas anymore...
KAFASH
Where did ground go?
--but here my magic is at its strongest. You will never see your earthly realm again!
Dr. Strange? Hulk? A little help here?
Your precious artifacts may be safe now, wizard--
Fire-head monkey big--

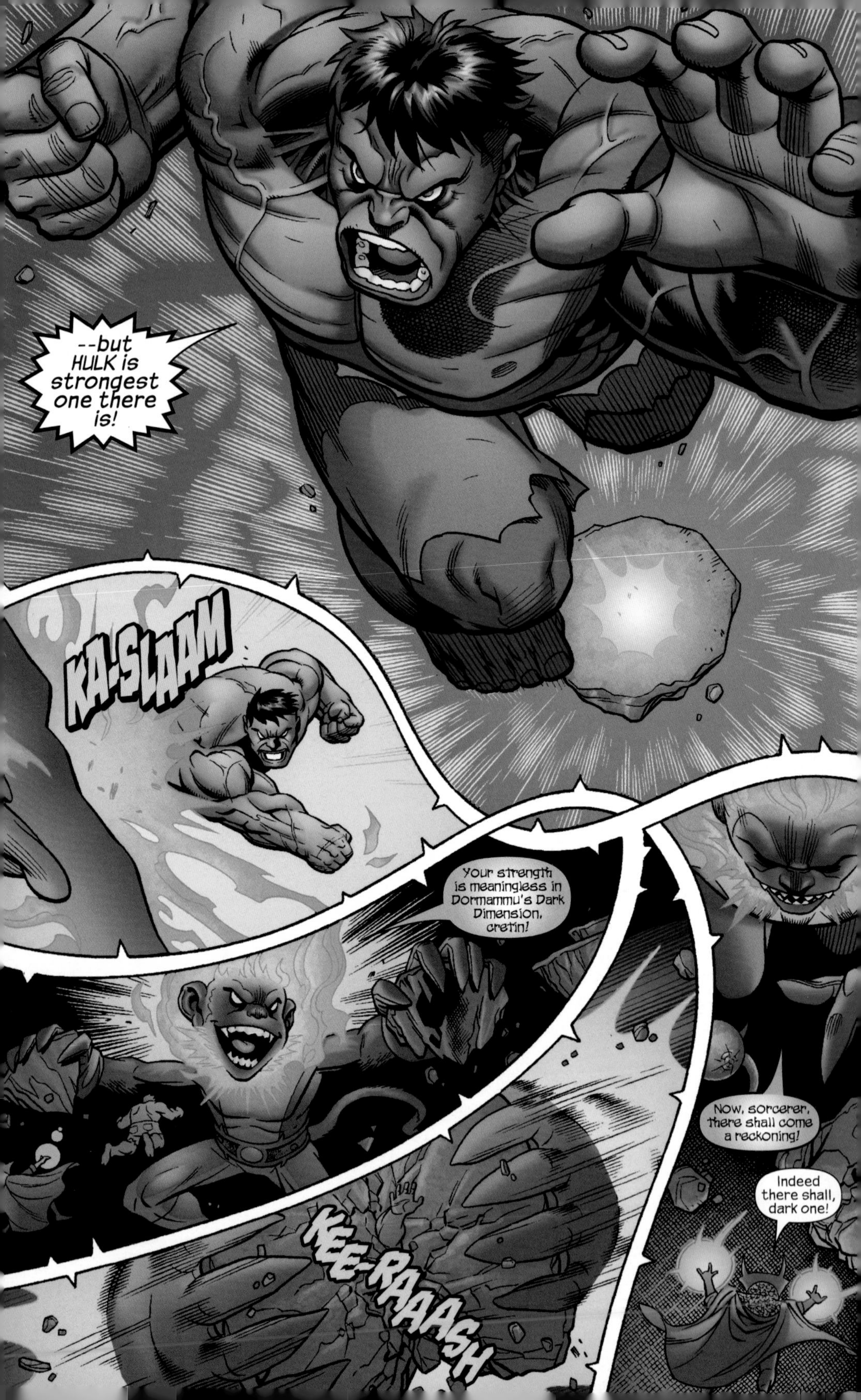
--but HULK is strongest one there is!
KA-SLAAM
Your strength is meaningless in Dormammu's Dark Dimension, cretin!
KEE-RAAASH
Now, sorcerer, there shall come a reckoning!
Indeed there shall, dark one!

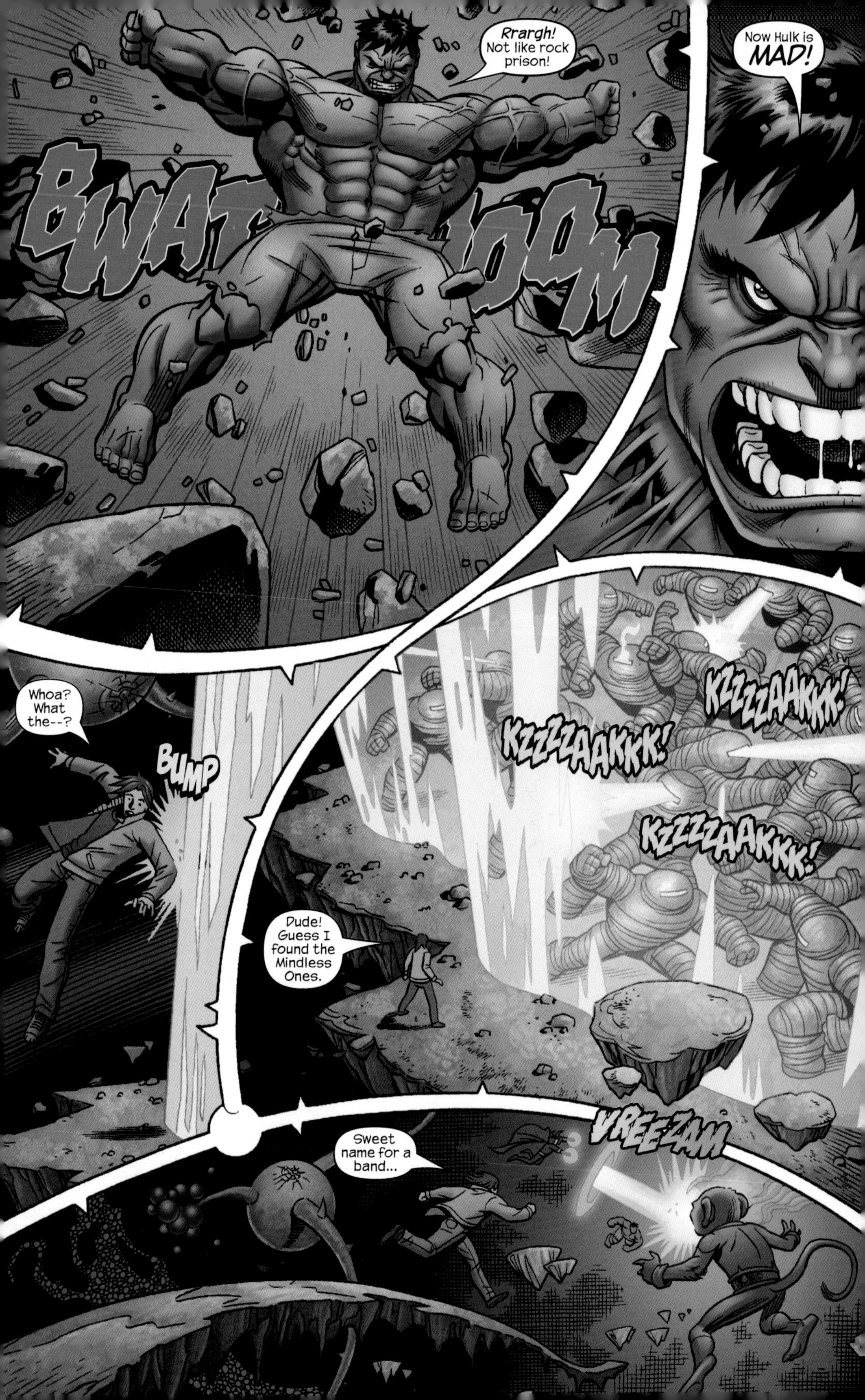
Rrargh! Not like rock prison!
BWA...OOM
Now Hulk is MAD!
Whoa? What the--?
BUMP
KZZZZAAKKK!
KZZZZAAKKK!
KZZZZAAKKK!
Dude! Guess I found the Mindless Ones.
Sweet name for a band...
VREEZAM

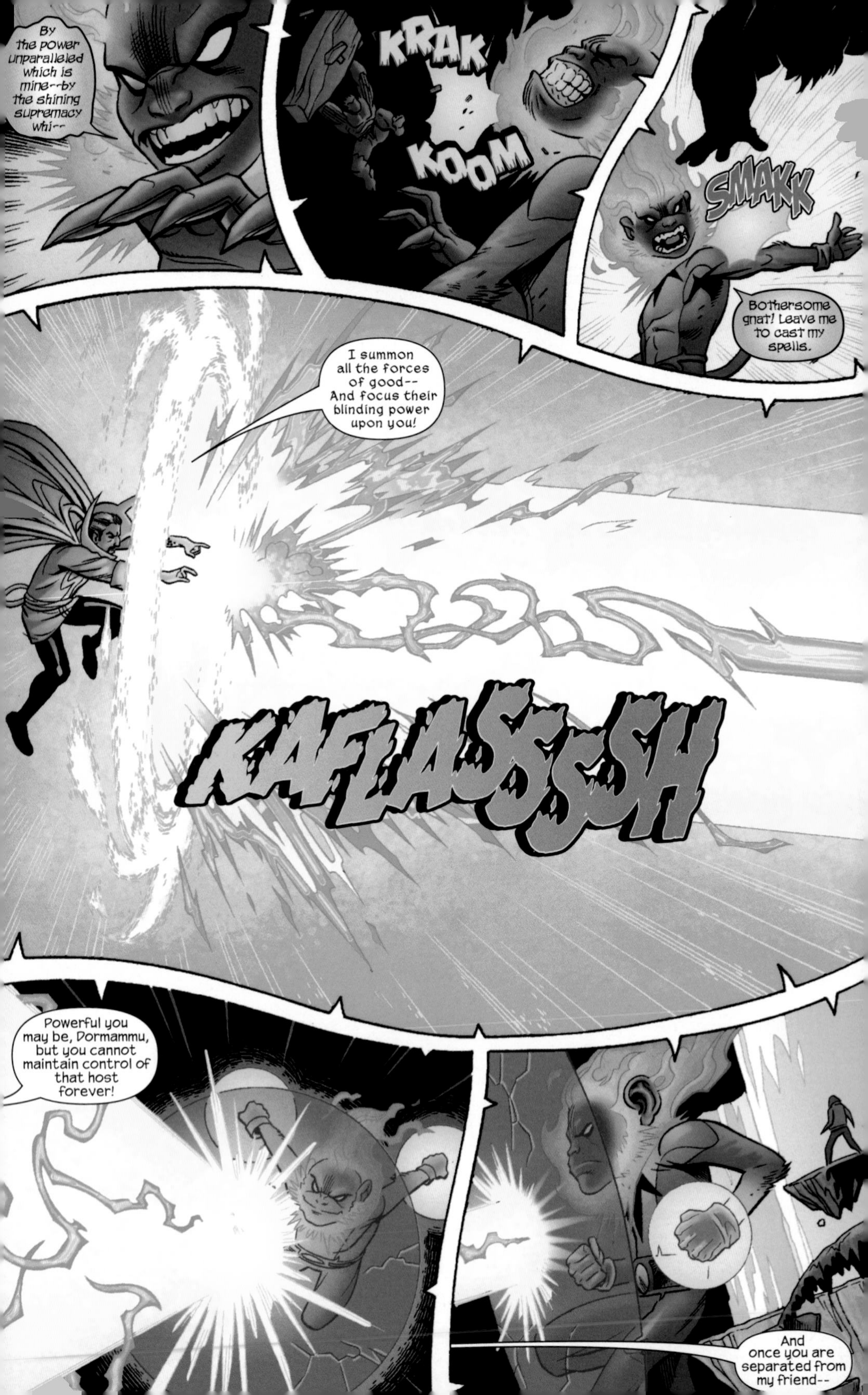
By the power unparalleled which is mine--by the shining supremacy whi--
KRAK
KOOM
SMAKK
Bothersome gnat! Leave me to cast my spells.
I summon all the forces of good-- And focus their blinding power upon you!
KAFLASSSH
Powerful you may be, Dormammu, but you cannot maintain control of that host forever!
And once you are separated from my friend--

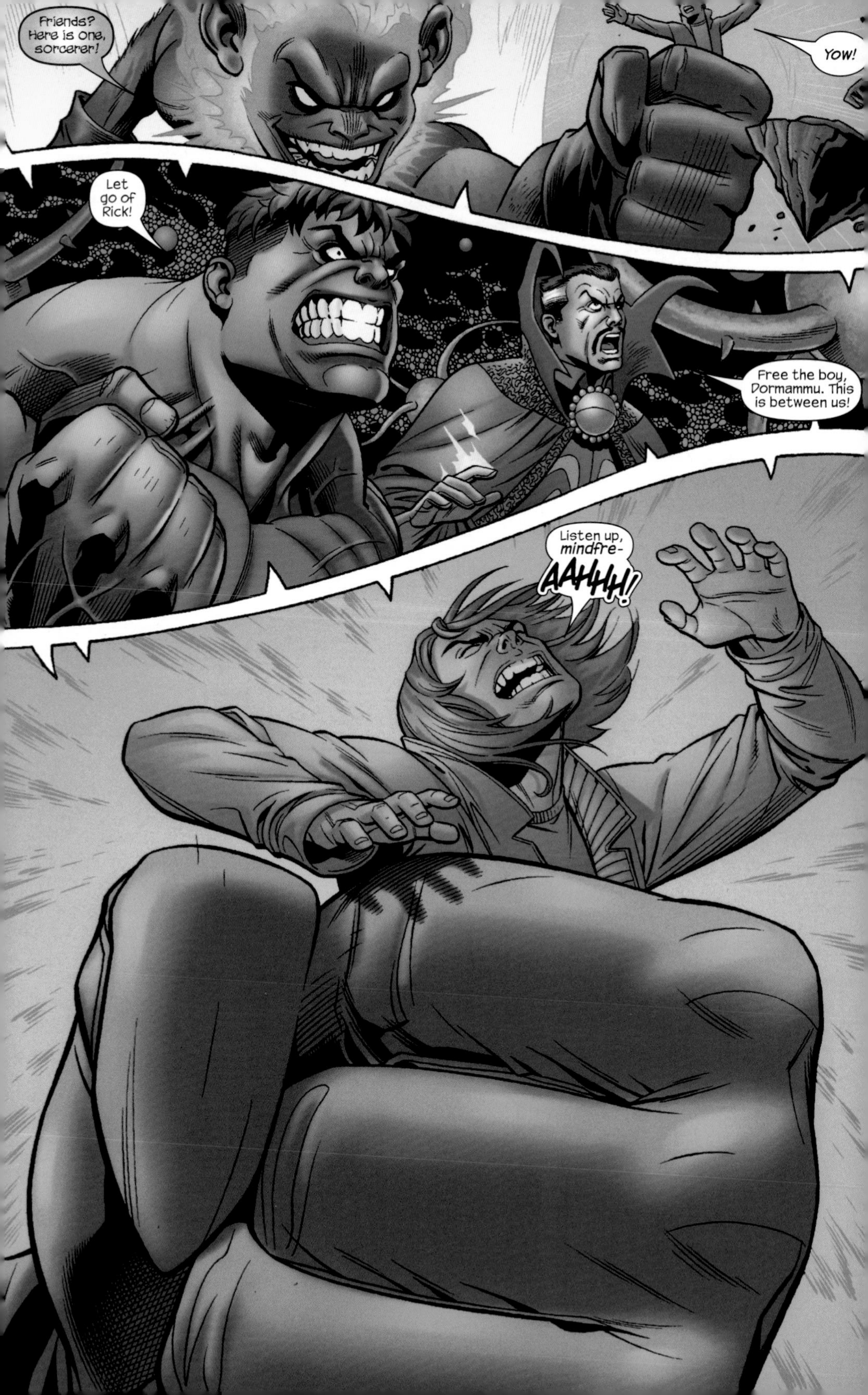
Friends? Here is one, sorcerer!
YOW!
Let go of Rick!
Free the boy, Dormammu. This is between us!
Listen up, mindfre-
AAHHH!

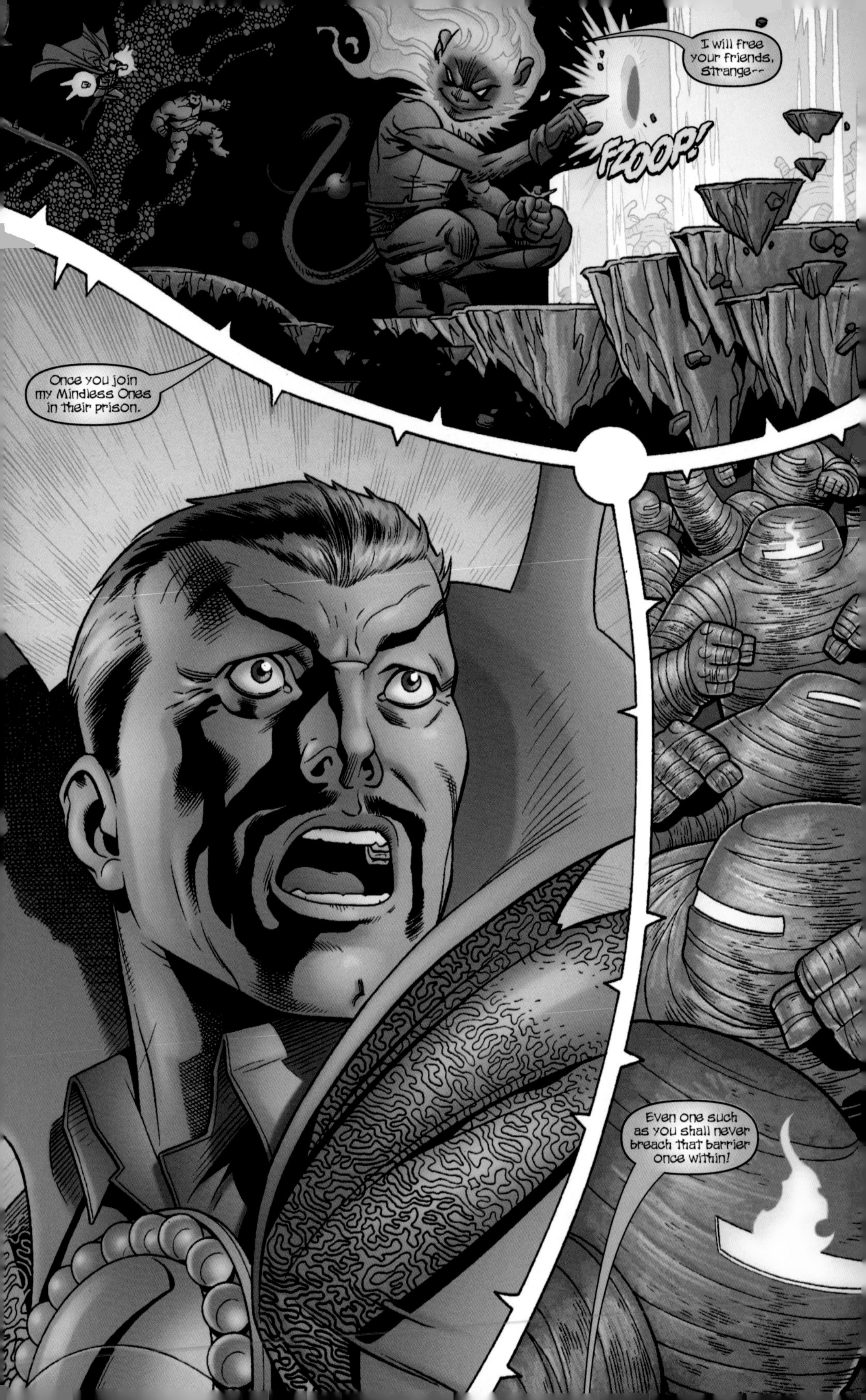
I will free your friends, Strange--
FZOOP!
Once you join my Mindless Ones in their prison.
Even one such as you shall never breach that barrier once within!

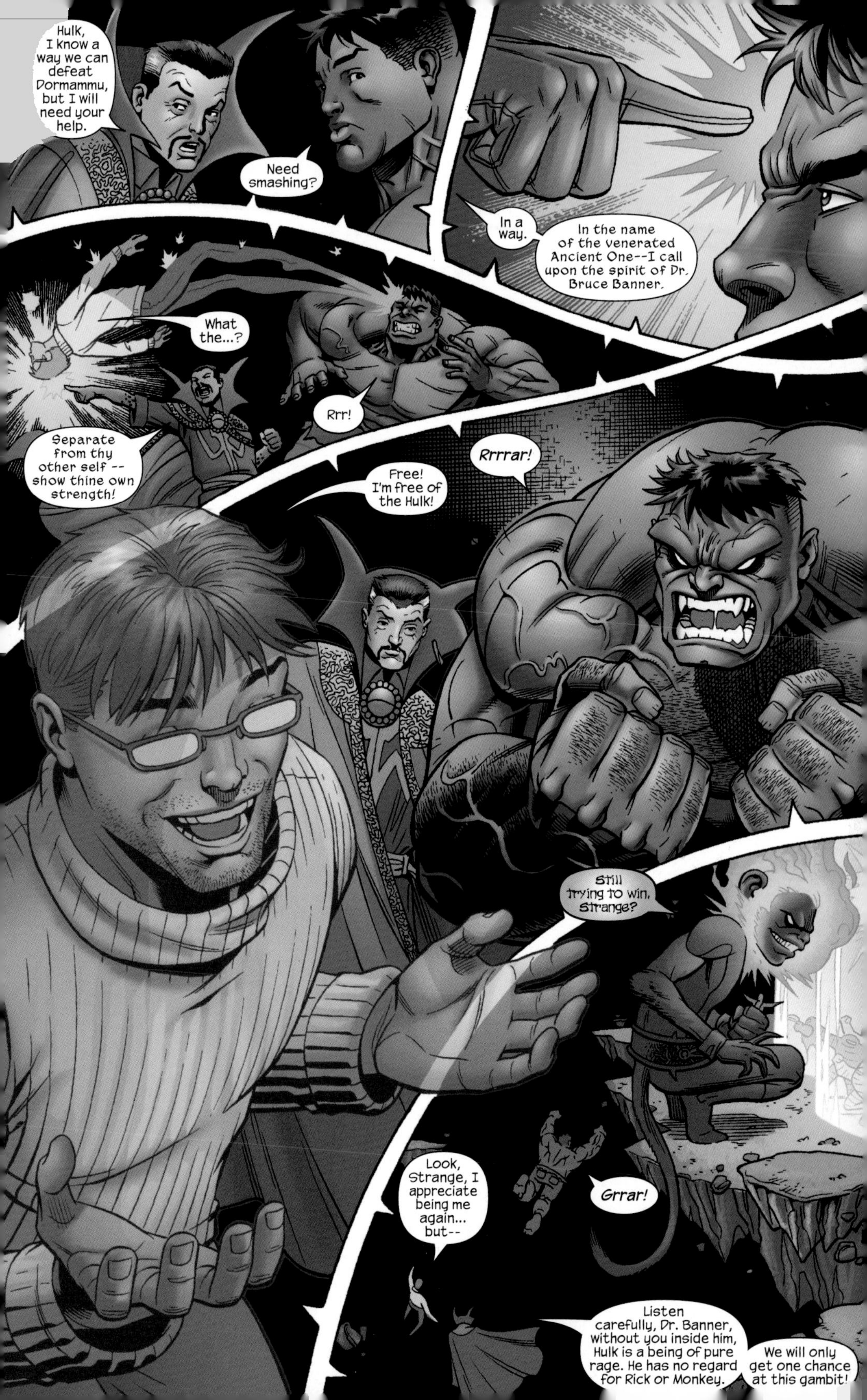
Hulk, I know a way we can defeat Dormammu, but I will need your help.
Need smashing?
In a way.
In the name of the venerated Ancient One--I call upon the spirit of Dr. Bruce Banner.
What the...?
Rrr!
Separate from thy other self -- show thine own strength!
Free! I'm free of the Hulk!
Rrrrar!
Still trying to win, Strange?
Look, Strange, I appreciate being me again... but--
Grrar!
Listen carefully, Dr. Banner, without you inside him, Hulk is a being of pure rage. He has no regard for Rick or Monkey.
We will only get one chance at this gambit!

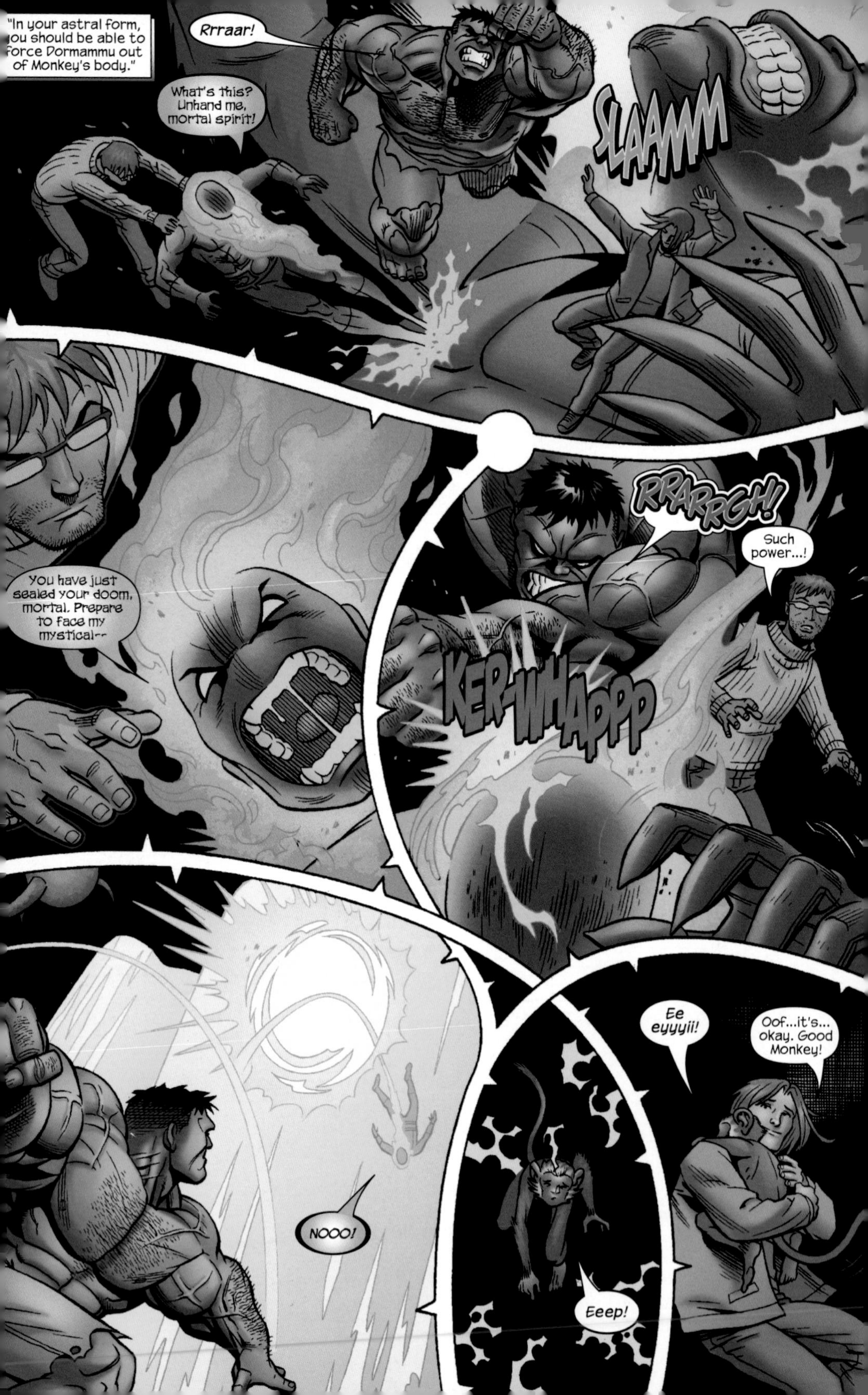
"In your astral form, you should be able to force Dormammu out of Monkey's body."
Rrraar!
What's this? Unhand me, mortal spirit!
SLAAMM
You have just sealed your doom, mortal. Prepare to face my mystical--
RRARRGH!
Such power...!
KER-WHAPPP
NOOO!
Ee eyyyii!
Oof...it's... okay. Good Monkey!
Eeep!

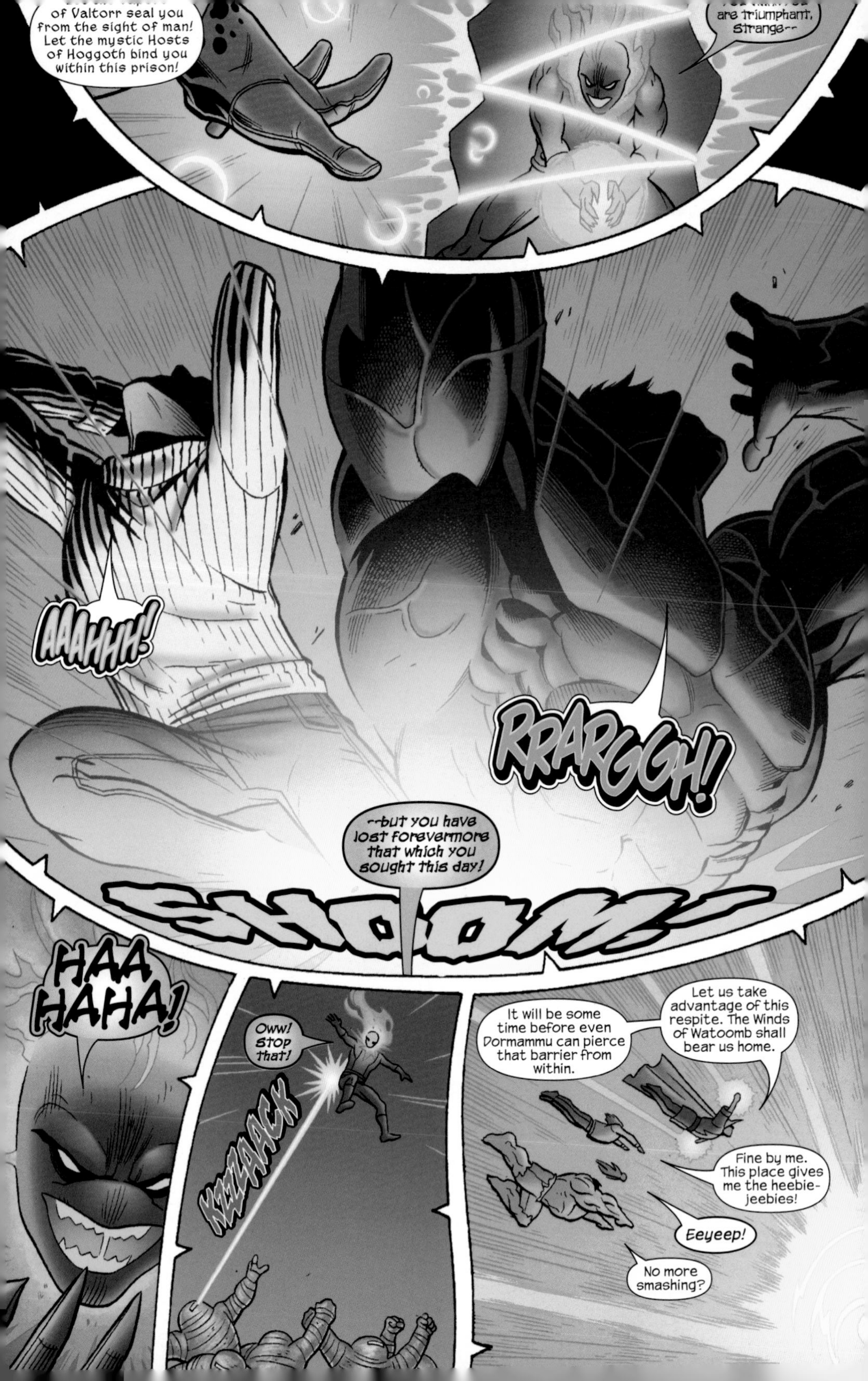

of Valtorr seal you from the sight of man! Let the mystic Hosts of Hoggoth bind you within this prison!
are triumphant, Strange--
AAAHHH!
RRARGGH!
--but you have lost forevermore that which you sought this day!
SHOOM!
HAA HAHA!
Oww! Stop that!
KZZAACK
It will be some time before even Dormammu can pierce that barrier from within.
Let us take advantage of this respite. The Winds of Watoomb shall bear us home.
Fine by me. This place gives me the heebie-jeebies!
Eeyeep!
No more smashing?

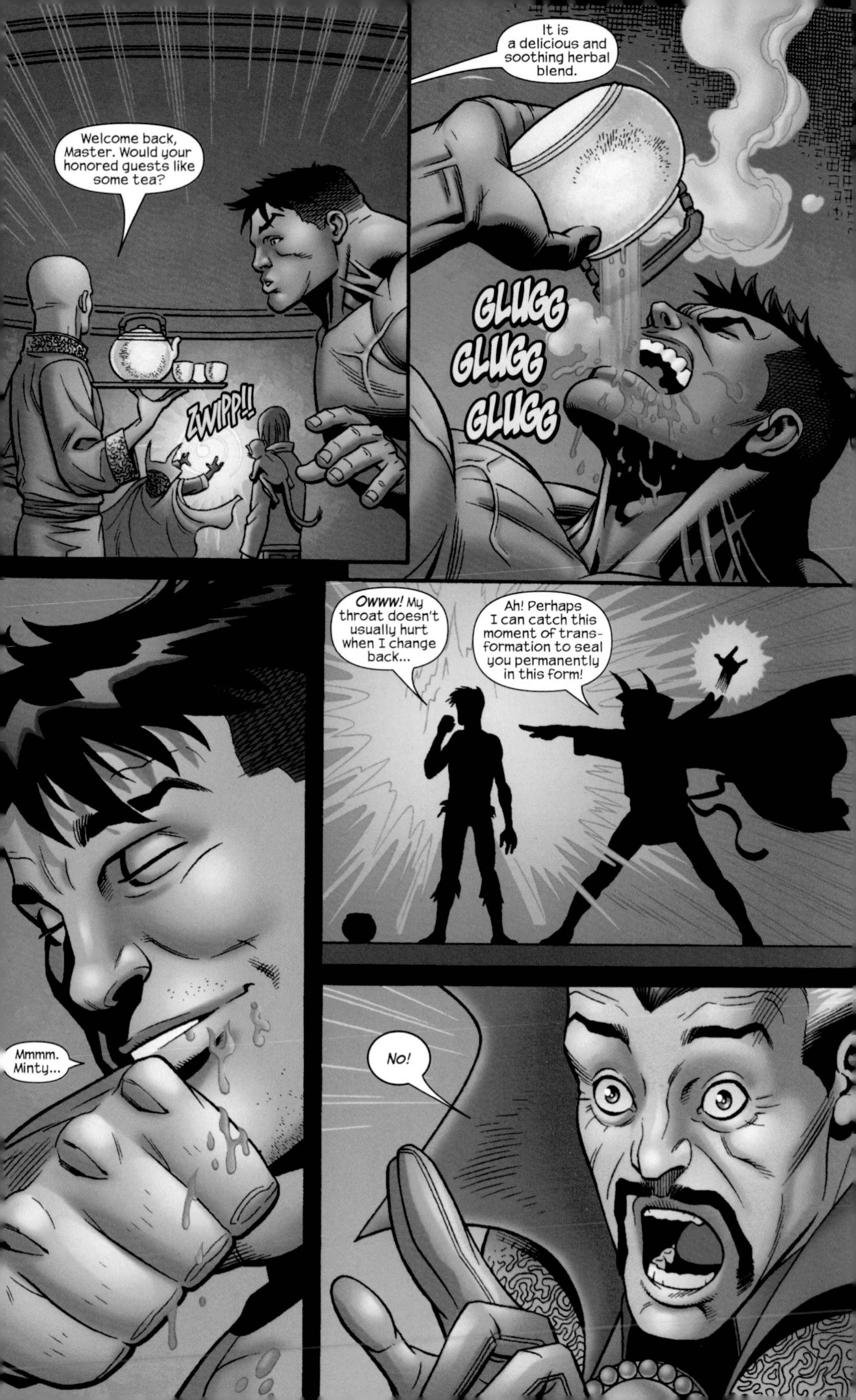
Welcome back, Master. Would your honored guests like some tea?
ZWIPP!!
It is a delicious and soothing herbal blend.
GLUGG GLUGG GLUGG
Mmmm. Minty...
Owww! My throat doesn't usually hurt when I change back...
Ah! Perhaps I can catch this moment of transformation to seal you permanently in this form!
No!

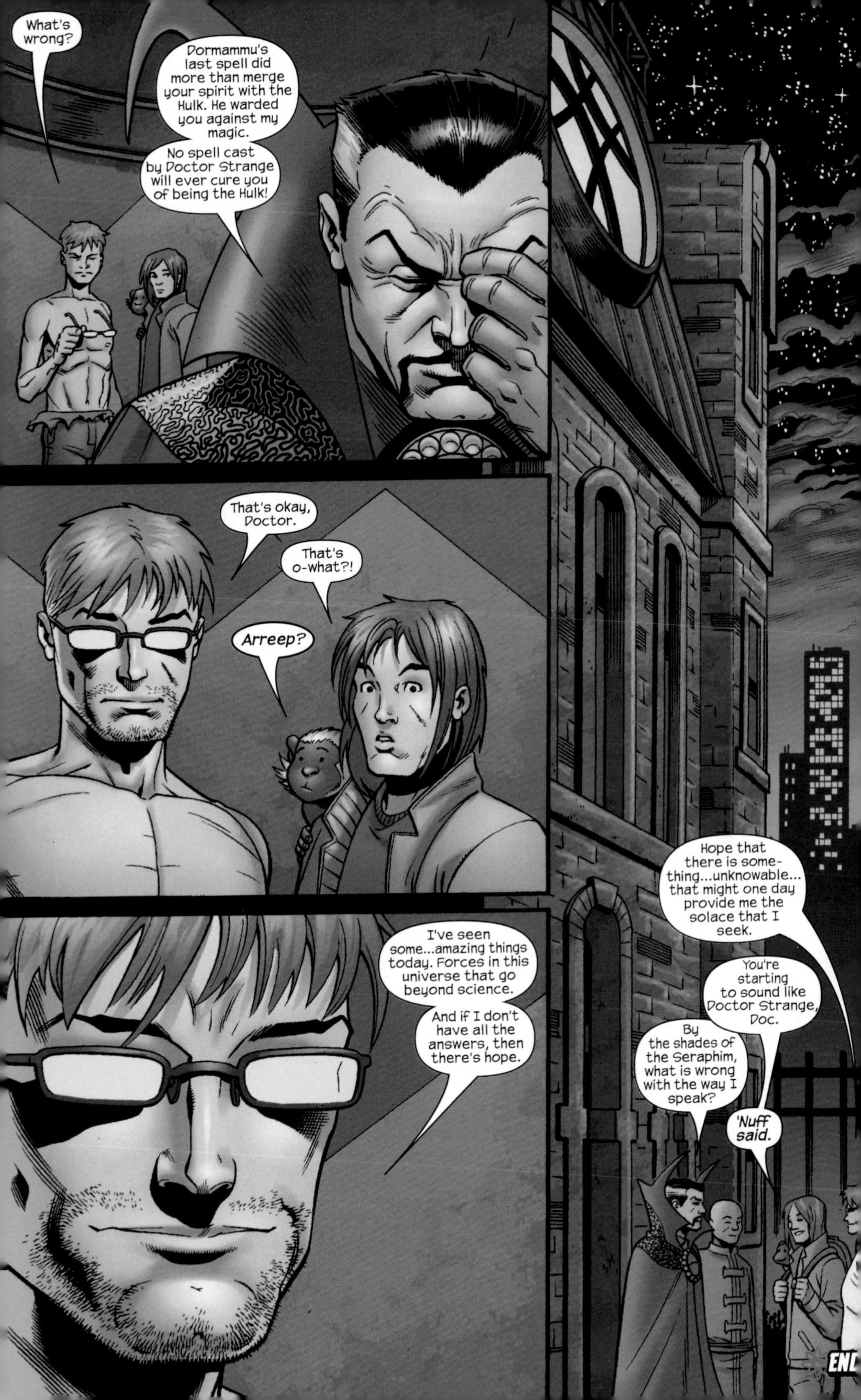
What's wrong?
Dormammu's last spell did more than merge your spirit with the Hulk. He warded you against my magic.
No spell cast by Doctor Strange will ever cure you of being the Hulk!
That's okay, Doctor.
That's o-what?!
Arreep?
I've seen some...amazing things today. Forces in this universe that go beyond science.
And if I don't have all the answers, then there's hope.
Hope that there is some-thing...unknowable... that might one day provide me the solace that I seek.
You're starting to sound like Doctor Strange, Doc.
By the shades of the Seraphim, what is wrong with the way I speak?
'Nuff said.

MARVEL ADVENTURES SUPER HEROES #5

THE CREATURE ZAKIMIYA HAS BEEN LETTING ITS CHILDREN FEED ON THE VERY FABRIC OF REALITY! CAN DOCTOR STRANGE AND SPIDER-MAN WEB SHUT THE HOLES IN REALITY AND DEFEAT ZAKIMIYA?

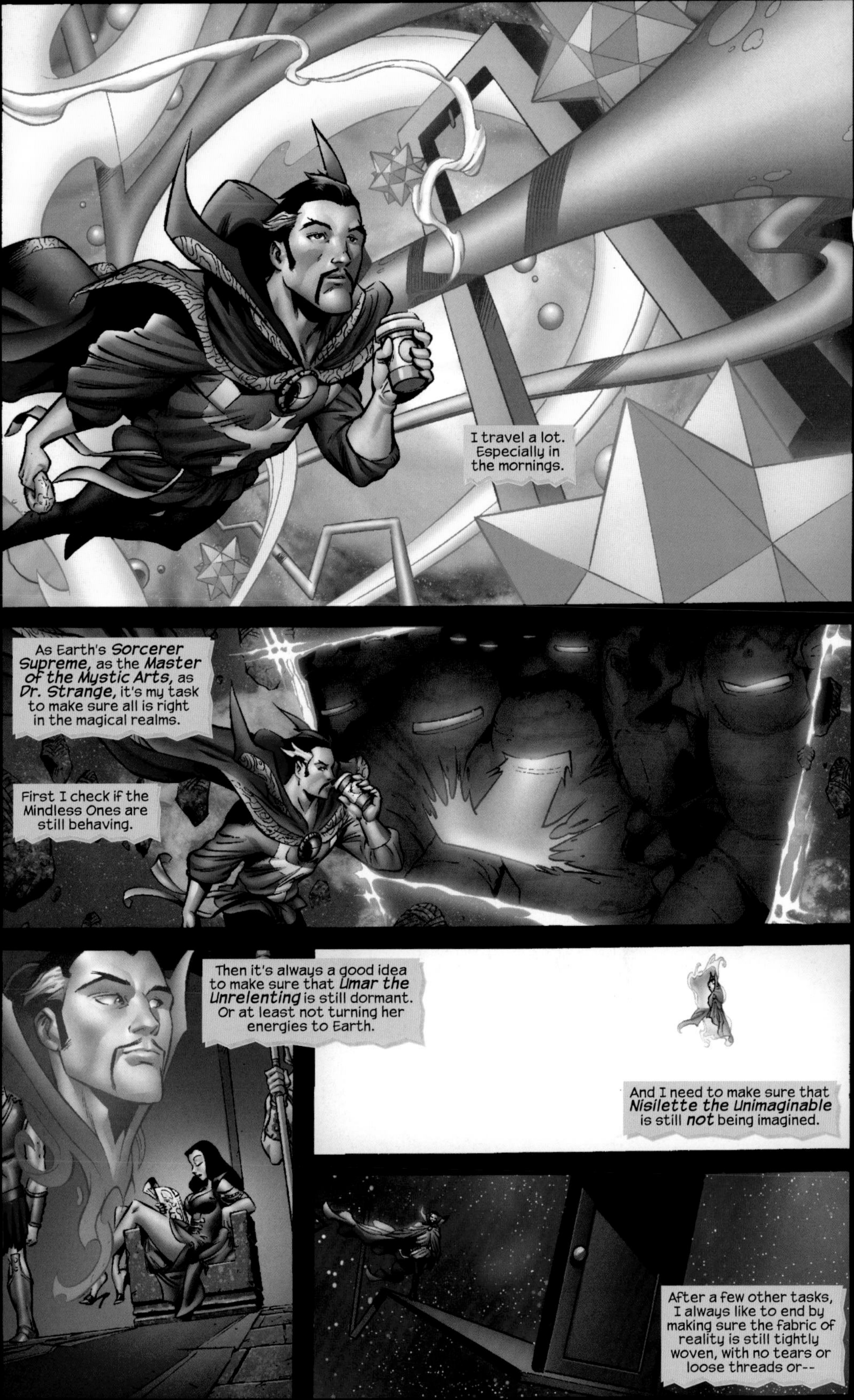
I travel a lot. Especially in the mornings.
As Earth's *Sorcerer Supreme*, as the *Master of the Mystic Arts*, as *Dr. Strange*, it's my task to make sure all is right in the magical realms.
First I check if the Mindless Ones are still behaving.
Then it's always a good idea to make sure that *Umar the Unrelenting* is still dormant. Or at least not turning her energies to Earth.
And I need to make sure that *Nisilette the Unimaginable* is still ***not*** being imagined.
After a few other tasks, I always like to end by making sure the fabric of reality is still tightly woven, with no tears or loose threads or--

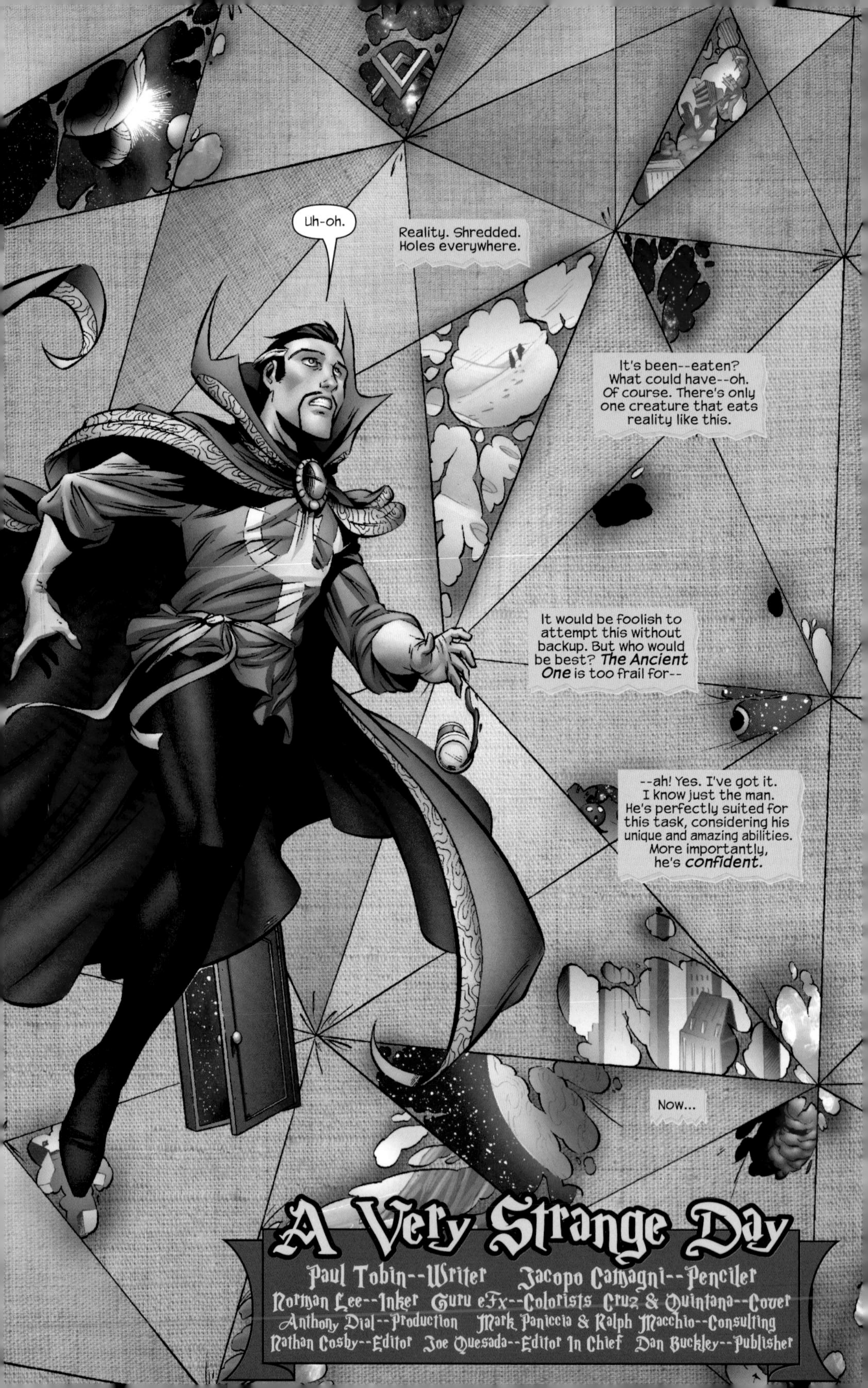

Uh-oh.
Reality. Shredded. Holes everywhere.
It's been--eaten? What could have--oh. Of course. There's only one creature that eats reality like this.
It would be foolish to attempt this without backup. But who would be best? *The Ancient One* is too frail for--
--ah! Yes. I've got it. I know just the man. He's perfectly suited for this task, considering his unique and amazing abilities. More importantly, he's *confident.*
Now...
A Very Strange Day
Paul Tobin--Writer Jacopo Camagni--Penciler
Norman Lee--Inker Guru eFx--Colorists Cruz & Quintana--Cover
Anthony Dial--Production Mark Paniccia & Ralph Macchio--Consulting
Nathan Cosby--Editor Joe Quesada--Editor In Chief Dan Buckley--Publisher

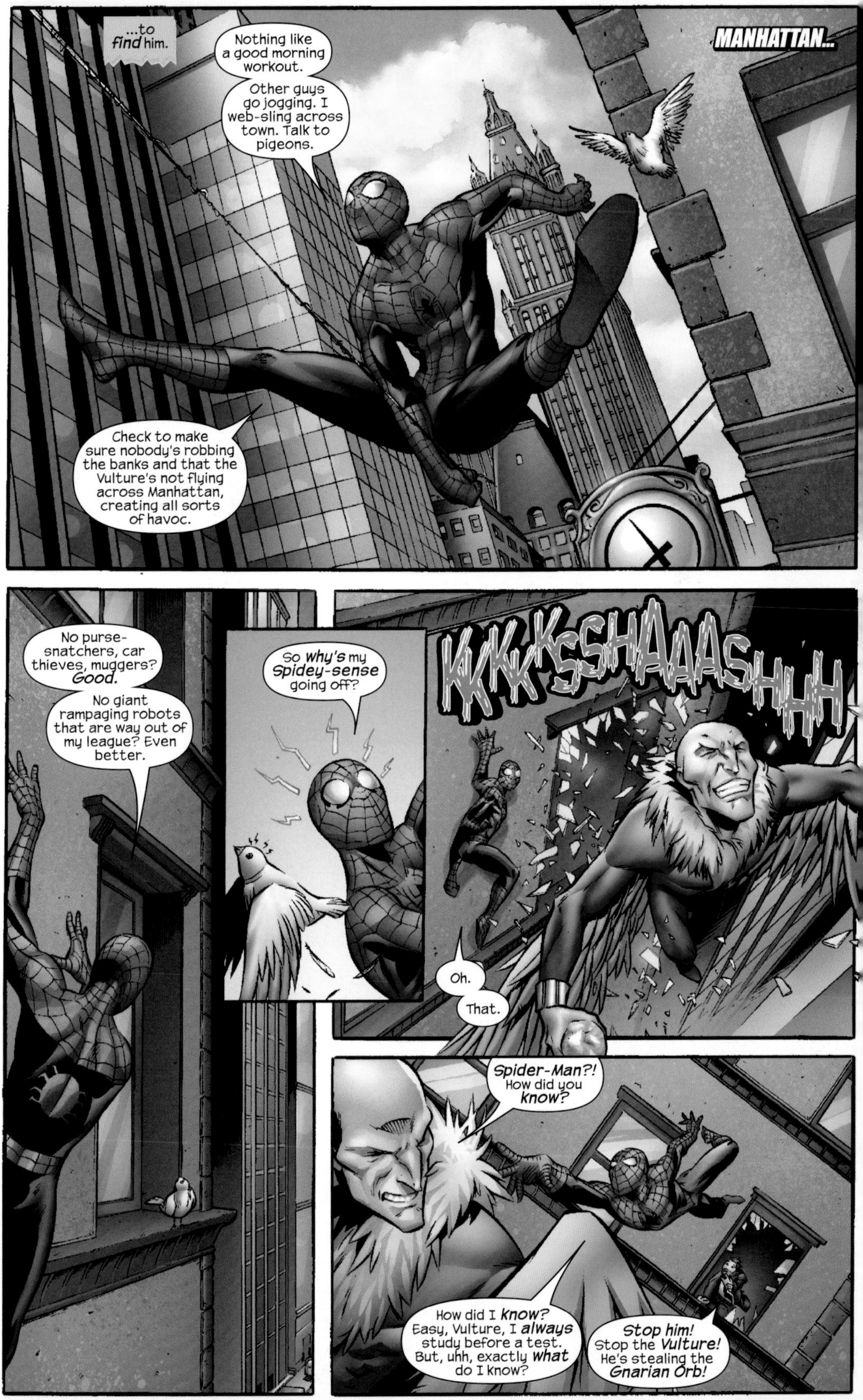
MANHATTAN...
...to find him.
Nothing like a good morning workout.
Other guys go jogging. I web-sling across town. Talk to pigeons.
Check to make sure nobody's robbing the banks and that the Vulture's not flying across Manhattan, creating all sorts of havoc.
No purse-snatchers, car thieves, muggers? Good.
No giant rampaging robots that are way out of my league? Even better.
So why's my Spidey-sense going off?
KKKKSSHAAAASHHH
Oh.
That.
Spider-Man?! How did you know?
How did I know? Easy, Vulture, I always study before a test. But, uhh, exactly what do I know?
Stop him! Stop the Vulture! He's stealing the Gnarian Orb!

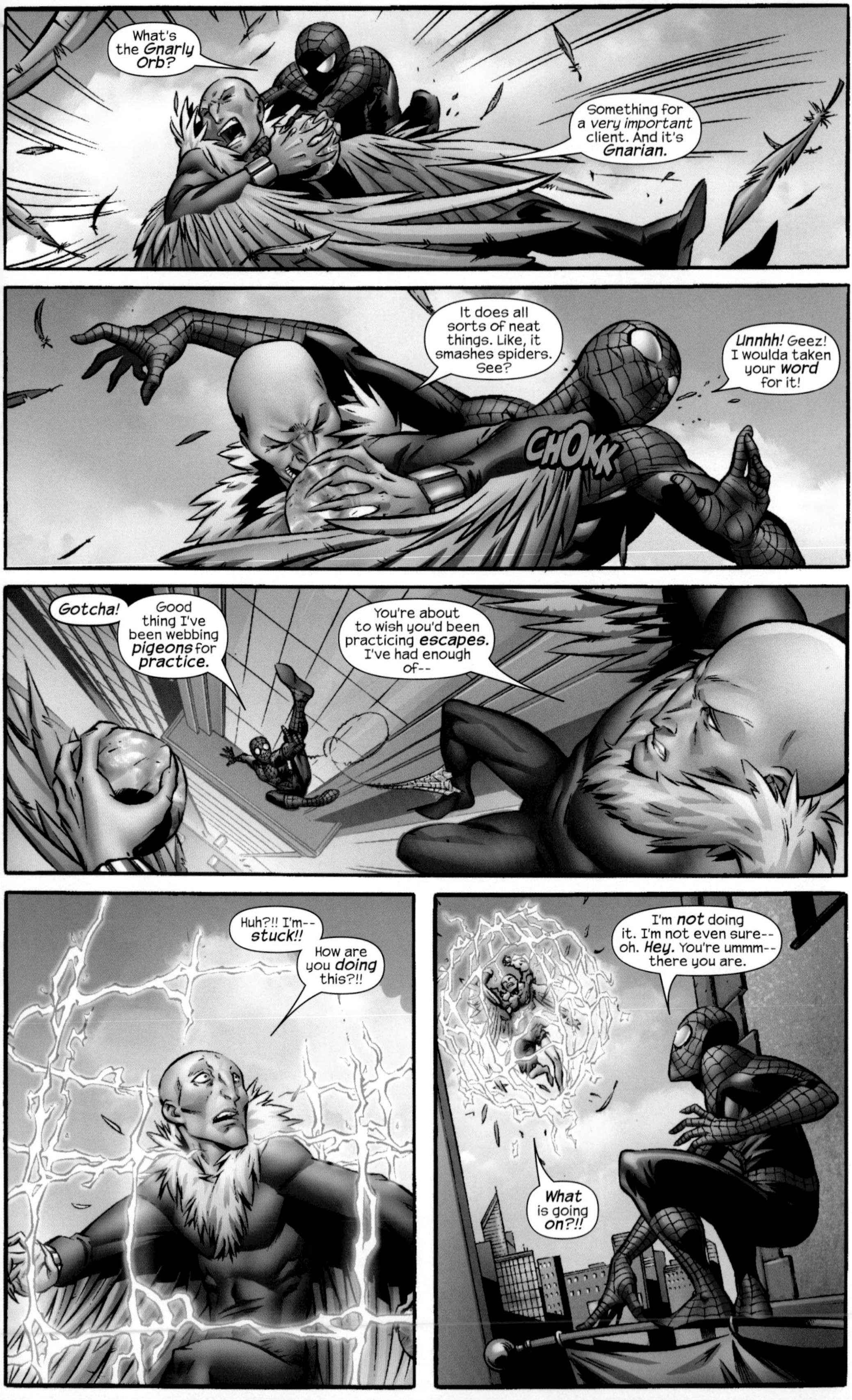
What's the Gnarly Orb?
Something for a very important client. And it's Gnarian.
It does all sorts of neat things. Like, it smashes spiders. See?
CHOKK
Unnhh! Geez! I woulda taken your word for it!
Gotcha!
Good thing I've been webbing pigeons for practice.
You're about to wish you'd been practicing escapes. I've had enough of--
Huh?!! I'm--stuck!!
How are you doing this?!!
I'm not doing it. I'm not even sure--oh. Hey. You're ummm--there you are.
What is going on?!!

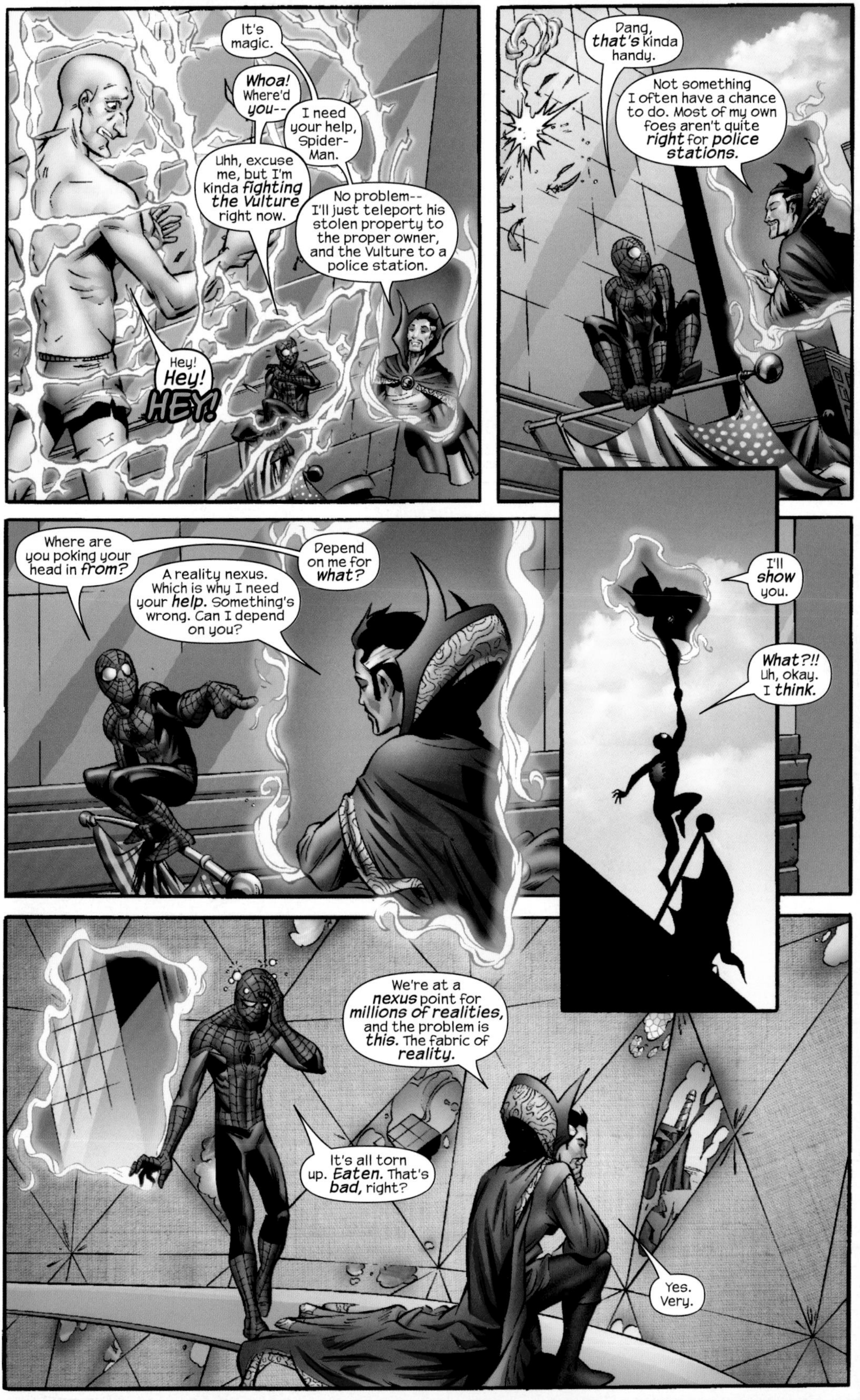
It's magic.
Whoa! Where'd you--
I need your help, Spider-Man.
Uhh, excuse me, but I'm kinda fighting the Vulture right now.
No problem-- I'll just teleport his stolen property to the proper owner, and the Vulture to a police station.
Hey! Hey! HEY!
Dang, that's kinda handy.
Not something I often have a chance to do. Most of my own foes aren't quite right for police stations.
Where are you poking your head in from?
A reality nexus. Which is why I need your help. Something's wrong. Can I depend on you?
Depend on me for what?
I'll show you.
What?!! Uh, okay. I think.
We're at a nexus point for millions of realities, and the problem is this. The fabric of reality.
It's all torn up. Eaten. That's bad, right?
Yes. Very.

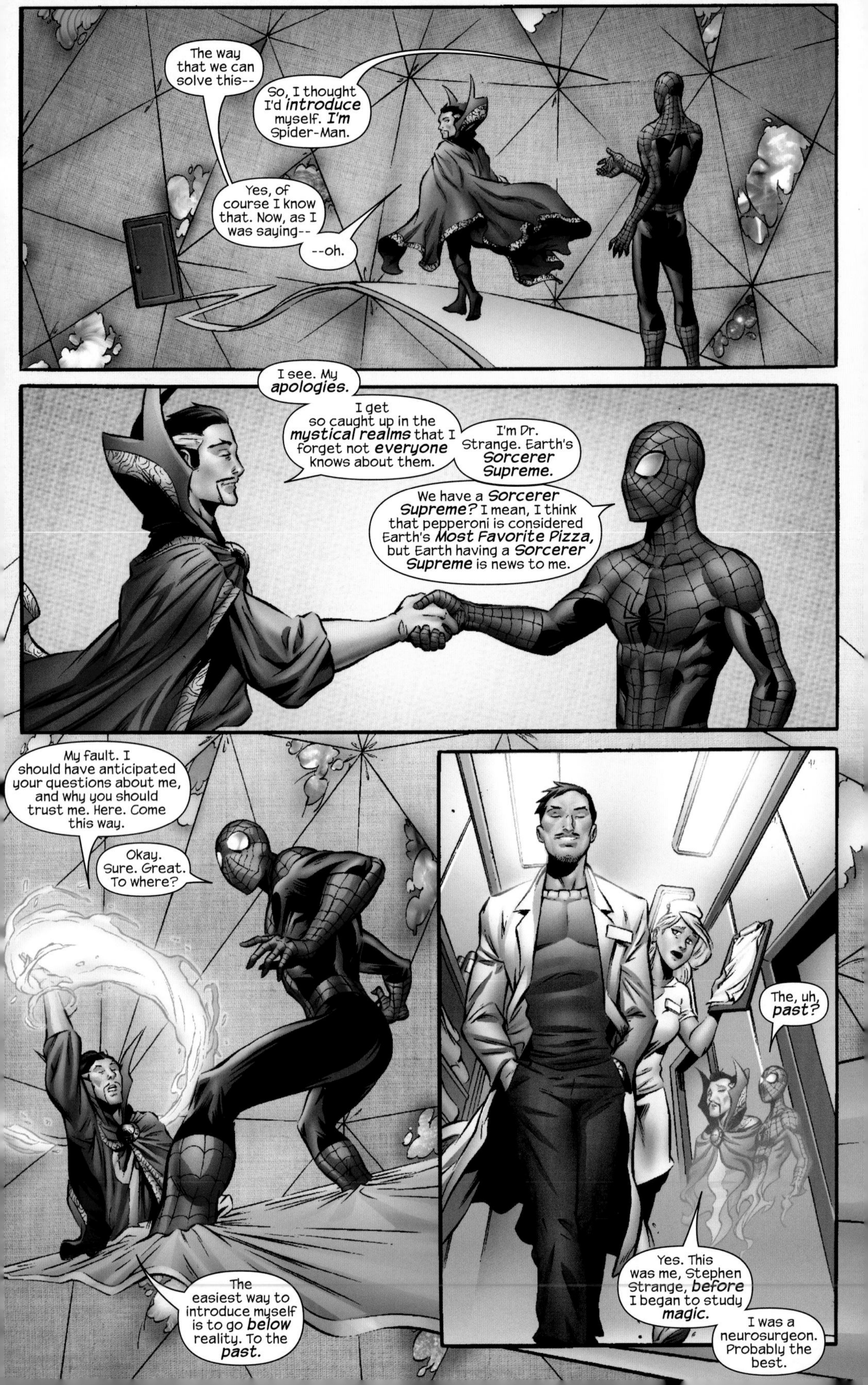
The way that we can solve this--
So, I thought I'd introduce myself. I'm Spider-Man.
Yes, of course I know that. Now, as I was saying--
--oh.
I see. My apologies.
I get so caught up in the mystical realms that I forget not everyone knows about them.
I'm Dr. Strange. Earth's Sorcerer Supreme.
We have a Sorcerer Supreme? I mean, I think that pepperoni is considered Earth's Most Favorite Pizza, but Earth having a Sorcerer Supreme is news to me.
My fault. I should have anticipated your questions about me, and why you should trust me. Here. Come this way.
Okay. Sure. Great. To where?
The easiest way to introduce myself is to go below reality. To the past.
The, uh, past?
Yes. This was me, Stephen Strange, before I began to study magic.
I was a neurosurgeon. Probably the best.

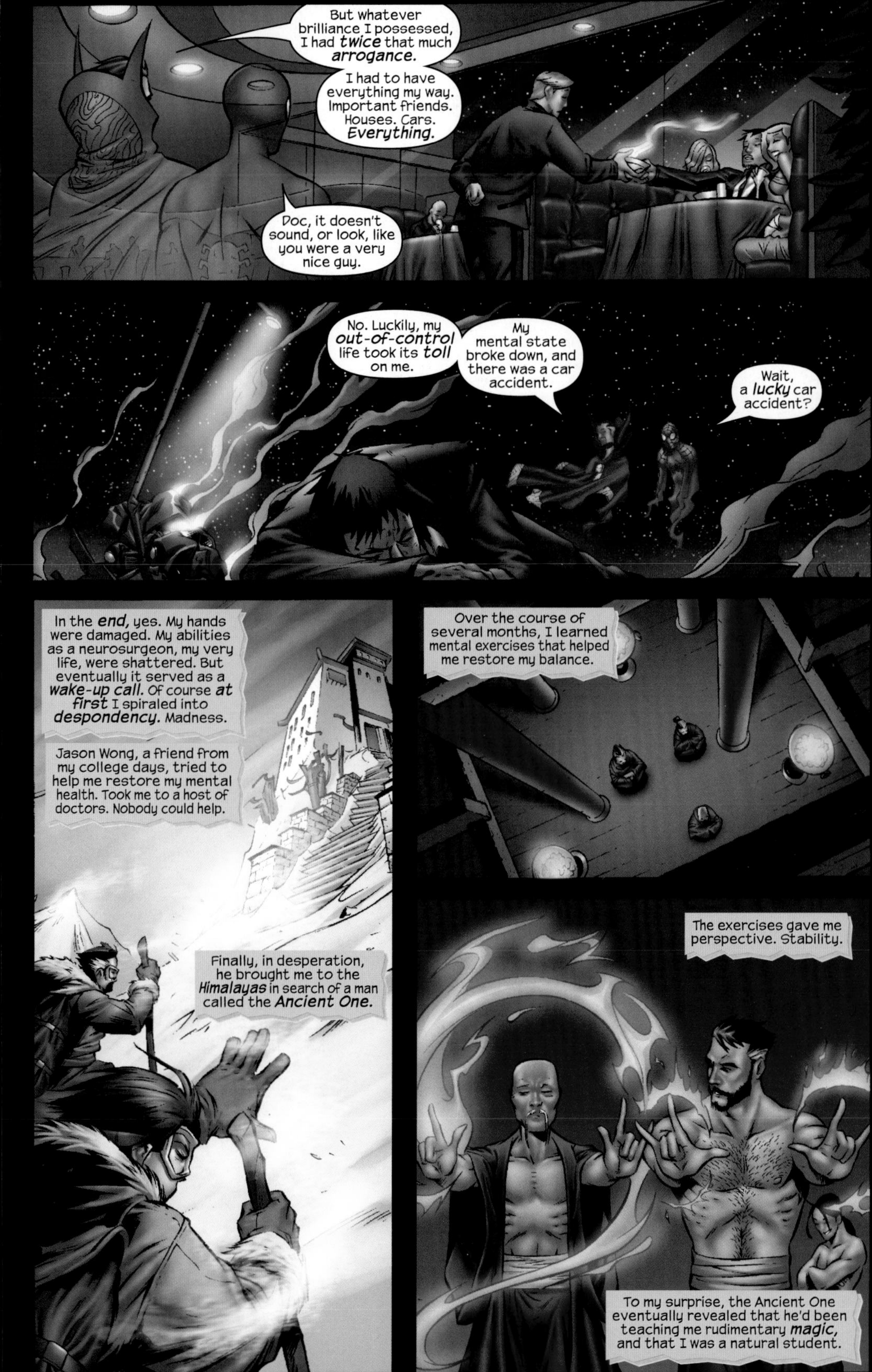
But whatever brilliance I possessed, I had twice that much arrogance.
I had to have everything my way. Important friends. Houses. Cars. Everything.
Doc, it doesn't sound, or look, like you were a very nice guy.
No. Luckily, my out-of-control life took its toll on me.
My mental state broke down, and there was a car accident.
Wait, a lucky car accident?
In the end, yes. My hands were damaged. My abilities as a neurosurgeon, my very life, were shattered. But eventually it served as a wake-up call. Of course at first I spiraled into despondency. Madness.
Jason Wong, a friend from my college days, tried to help me restore my mental health. Took me to a host of doctors. Nobody could help.
Finally, in desperation, he brought me to the Himalayas in search of a man called the Ancient One.
Over the course of several months, I learned mental exercises that helped me restore my balance.
The exercises gave me perspective. Stability.
To my surprise, the Ancient One eventually revealed that he'd been teaching me rudimentary magic, and that I was a natural student.

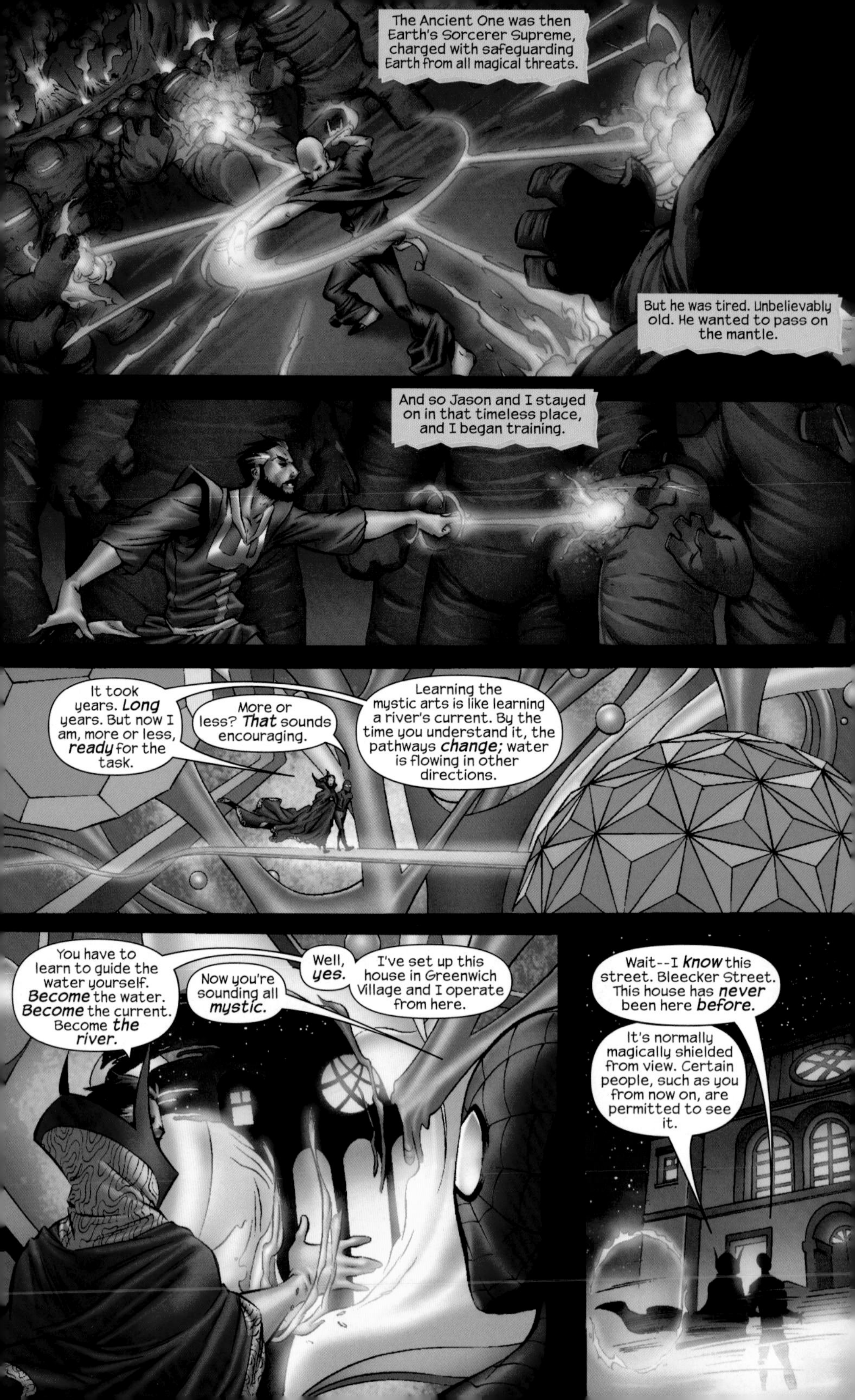
The Ancient One was then Earth's Sorcerer Supreme, charged with safeguarding Earth from all magical threats.
But he was tired. Unbelievably old. He wanted to pass on the mantle.
And so Jason and I stayed on in that timeless place, and I began training.
It took years. *Long* years. But now I am, more or less, *ready* for the task.
More or less? *That* sounds encouraging.
Learning the mystic arts is like learning a river's current. By the time you understand it, the pathways *change;* water is flowing in other directions.
You have to learn to guide the water yourself. *Become* the water. *Become* the current. Become *the river.*
Now you're sounding all *mystic.*
Well, *yes.*
I've set up this house in Greenwich Village and I operate from here.
Wait--I *know* this street. Bleecker Street. This house has *never* been here *before.*
It's normally magically shielded from view. Certain people, such as you from now on, are permitted to see it.

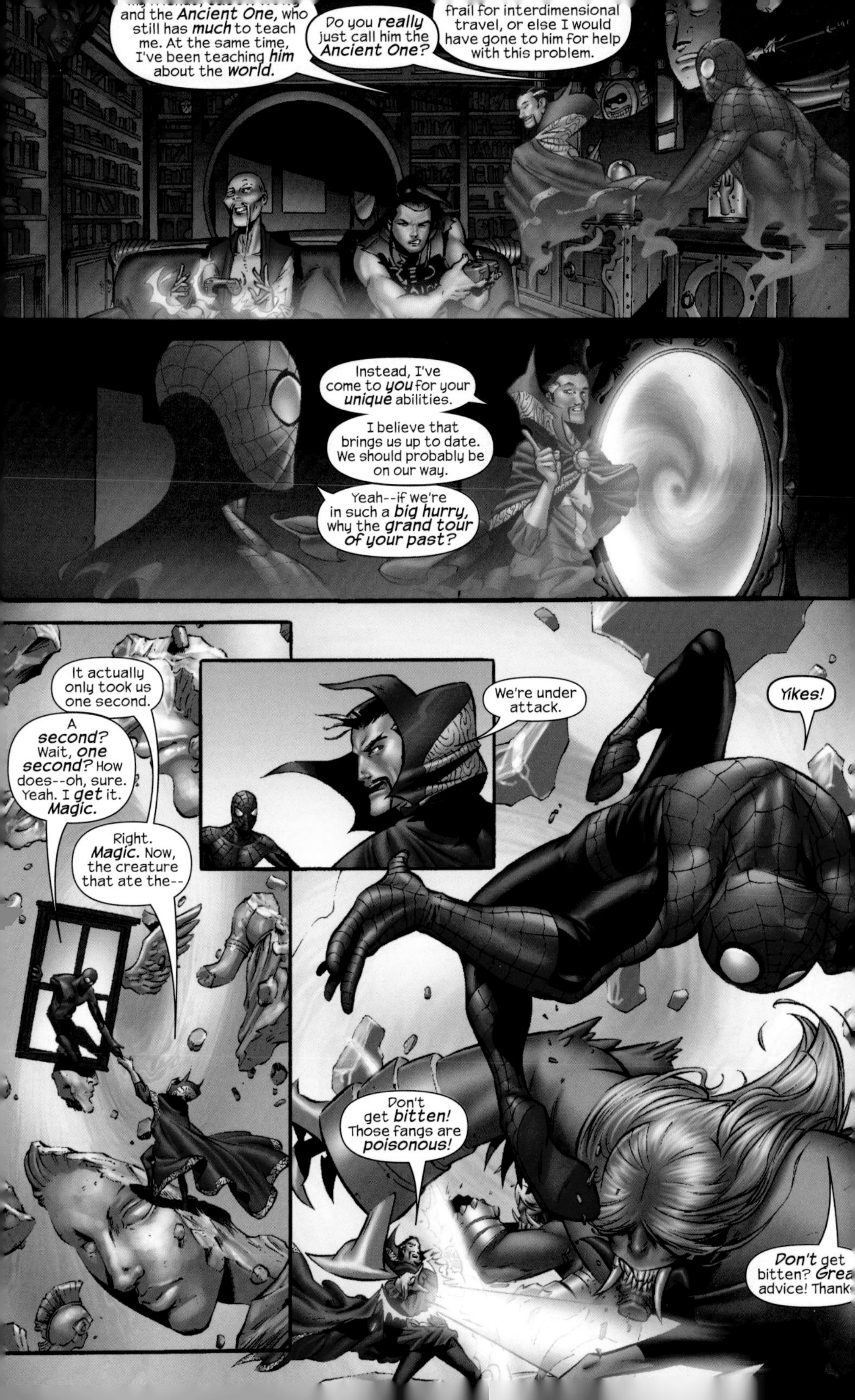

and the Ancient One, who still has much to teach me. At the same time, I've been teaching him about the world.
Do you really just call him the Ancient One?
frail for interdimensional travel, or else I would have gone to him for help with this problem.
Instead, I've come to you for your unique abilities.
I believe that brings us up to date. We should probably be on our way.
Yeah--if we're in such a big hurry, why the grand tour of your past?
It actually only took us one second.
A second? Wait, one second? How does--oh, sure. Yeah. I get it. Magic.
Right. Magic. Now, the creature that ate the--
We're under attack.
Yikes!
Don't get bitten! Those fangs are poisonous!
Don't get bitten? Grea advice! Thank

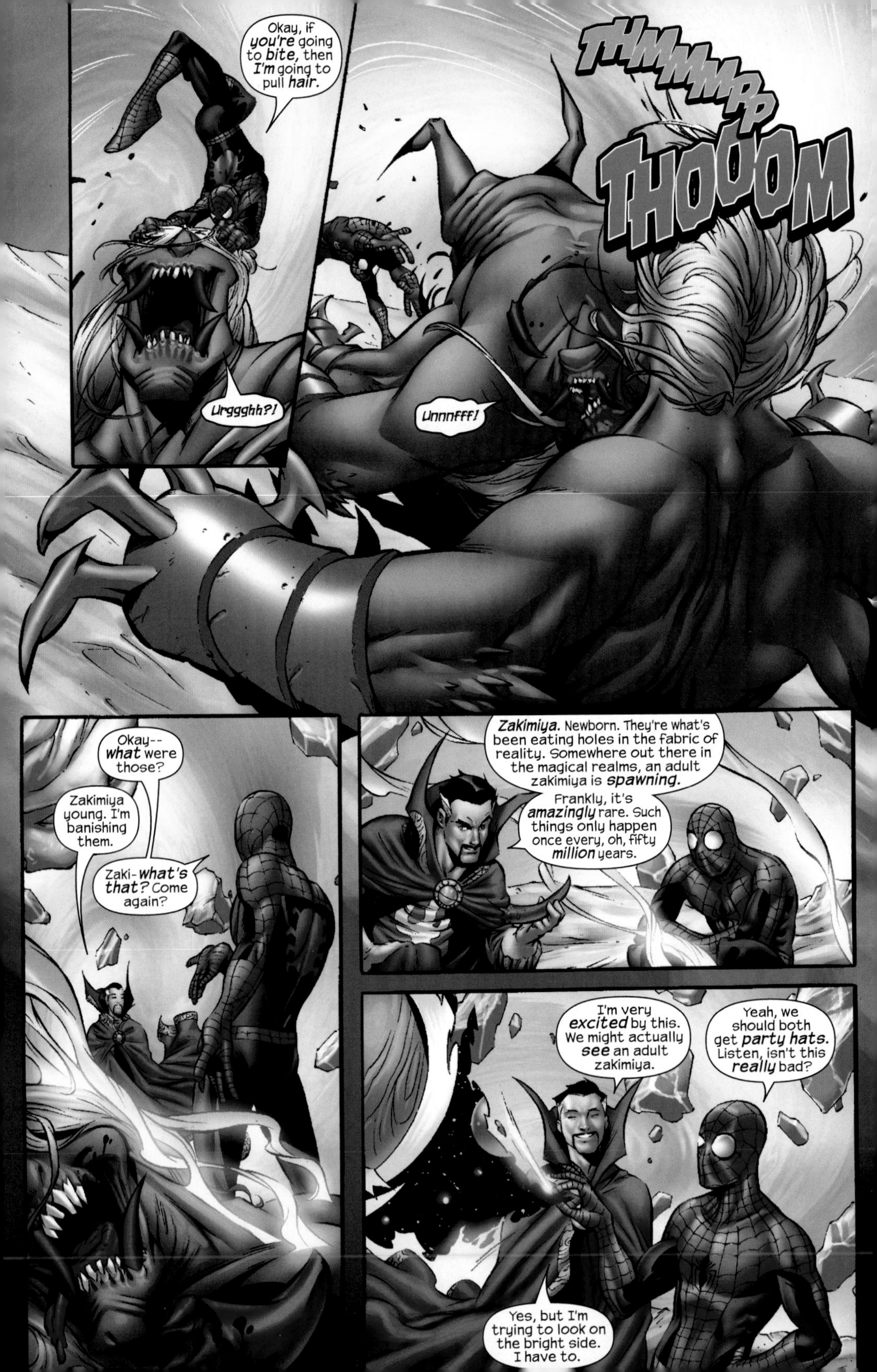
Okay, if you're going to bite, then I'm going to pull hair.
THMMMRP
THOOOM
Urggghh?!
Unnnfff!
Okay-- what were those?
Zakimiya young. I'm banishing them.
Zaki-what's that? Come again?
Zakimiya. Newborn. They're what's been eating holes in the fabric of reality. Somewhere out there in the magical realms, an adult zakimiya is spawning.
Frankly, it's amazingly rare. Such things only happen once every, oh, fifty million years.
I'm very excited by this. We might actually see an adult zakimiya.
Yeah, we should both get party hats. Listen, isn't this really bad?
Yes, but I'm trying to look on the bright side. I have to.

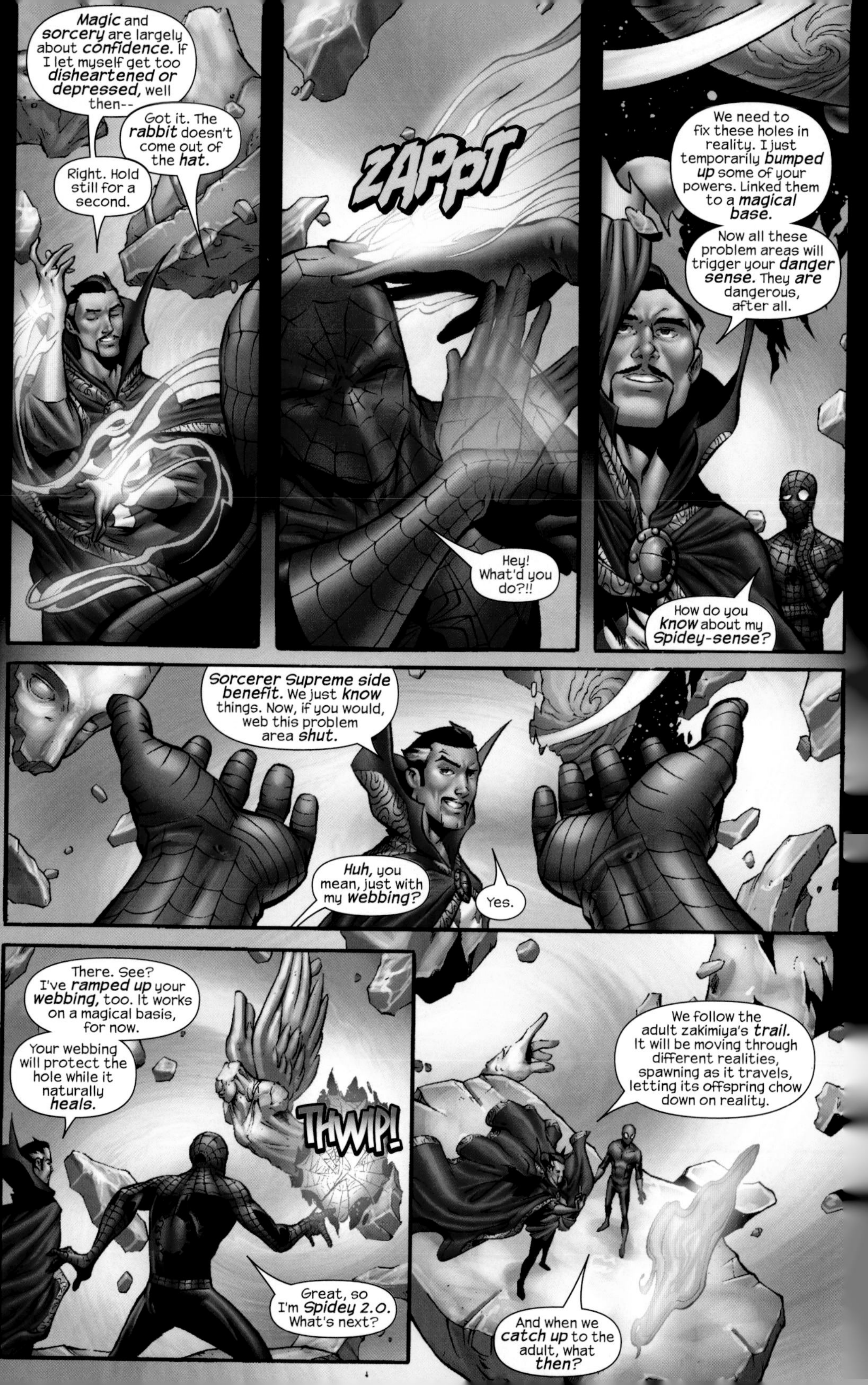

Magic and sorcery are largely about confidence. If I let myself get too disheartened or depressed, well then--
Got it. The rabbit doesn't come out of the hat.
Right. Hold still for a second.
ZAPPT
Hey! What'd you do?!!
We need to fix these holes in reality. I just temporarily bumped up some of your powers. Linked them to a magical base.
Now all these problem areas will trigger your danger sense. They are dangerous, after all.
How do you know about my Spidey-sense?
Sorcerer Supreme side benefit. We just know things. Now, if you would, web this problem area shut.
Huh, you mean, just with my webbing?
Yes.
There. See? I've ramped up your webbing, too. It works on a magical basis, for now.
Your webbing will protect the hole while it naturally heals.
THWIP!
Great, so I'm Spidey 2.0. What's next?
We follow the adult zakimiya's trail. It will be moving through different realities, spawning as it travels, letting its offspring chow down on reality.
And when we catch up to the adult, what then?

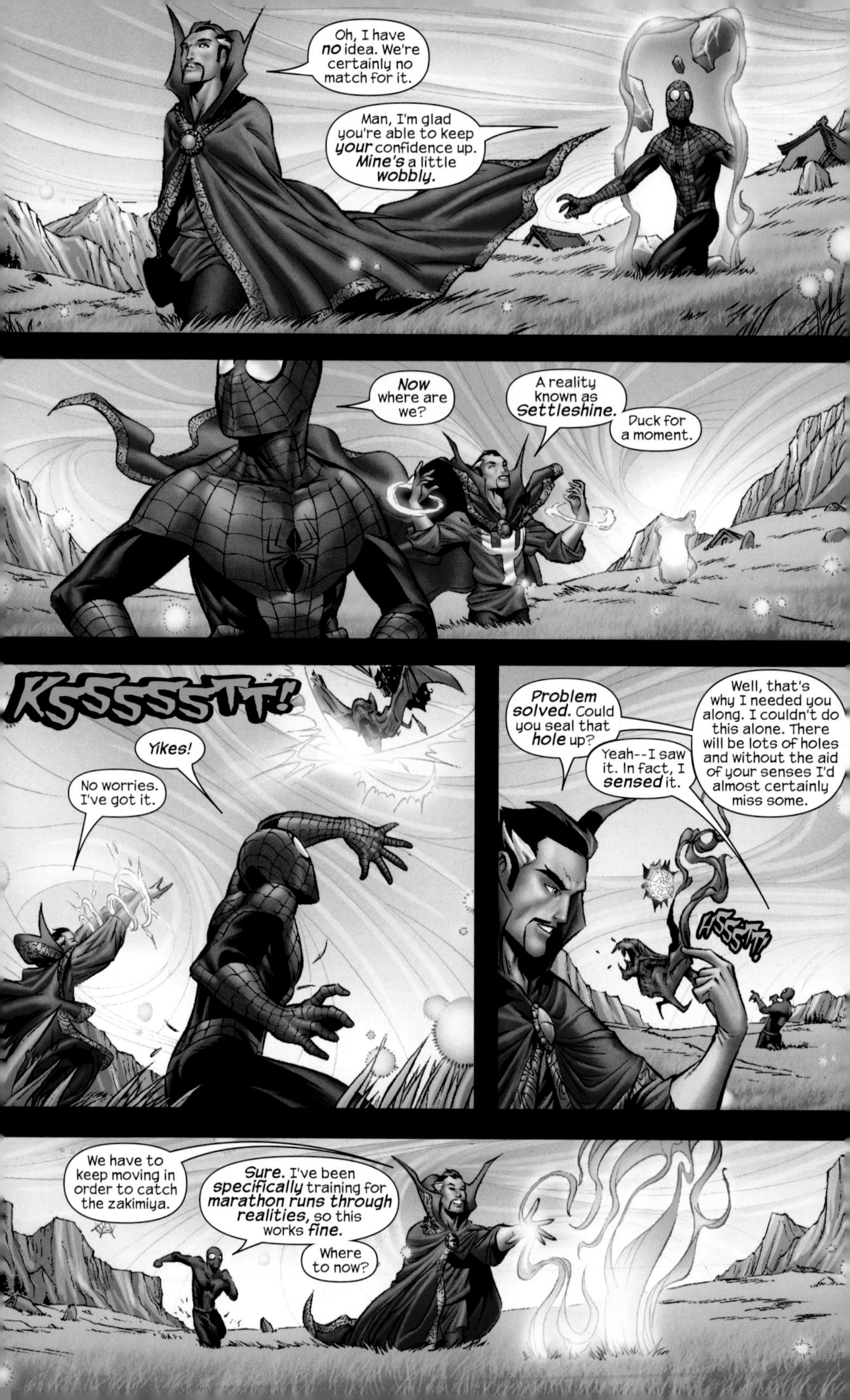
Oh, I have no idea. We're certainly no match for it.
Man, I'm glad you're able to keep your confidence up. Mine's a little wobbly.
Now where are we?
A reality known as Settleshine.
Duck for a moment.
KSSSSSTT!
Yikes!
No worries. I've got it.
Problem solved. Could you seal that hole up?
Yeah--I saw it. In fact, I sensed it.
Well, that's why I needed you along. I couldn't do this alone. There will be lots of holes and without the aid of your senses I'd almost certainly miss some.
HSSSTT!
We have to keep moving in order to catch the zakimiya.
Sure. I've been specifically training for marathon runs through realities, so this works fine.
Where to now?

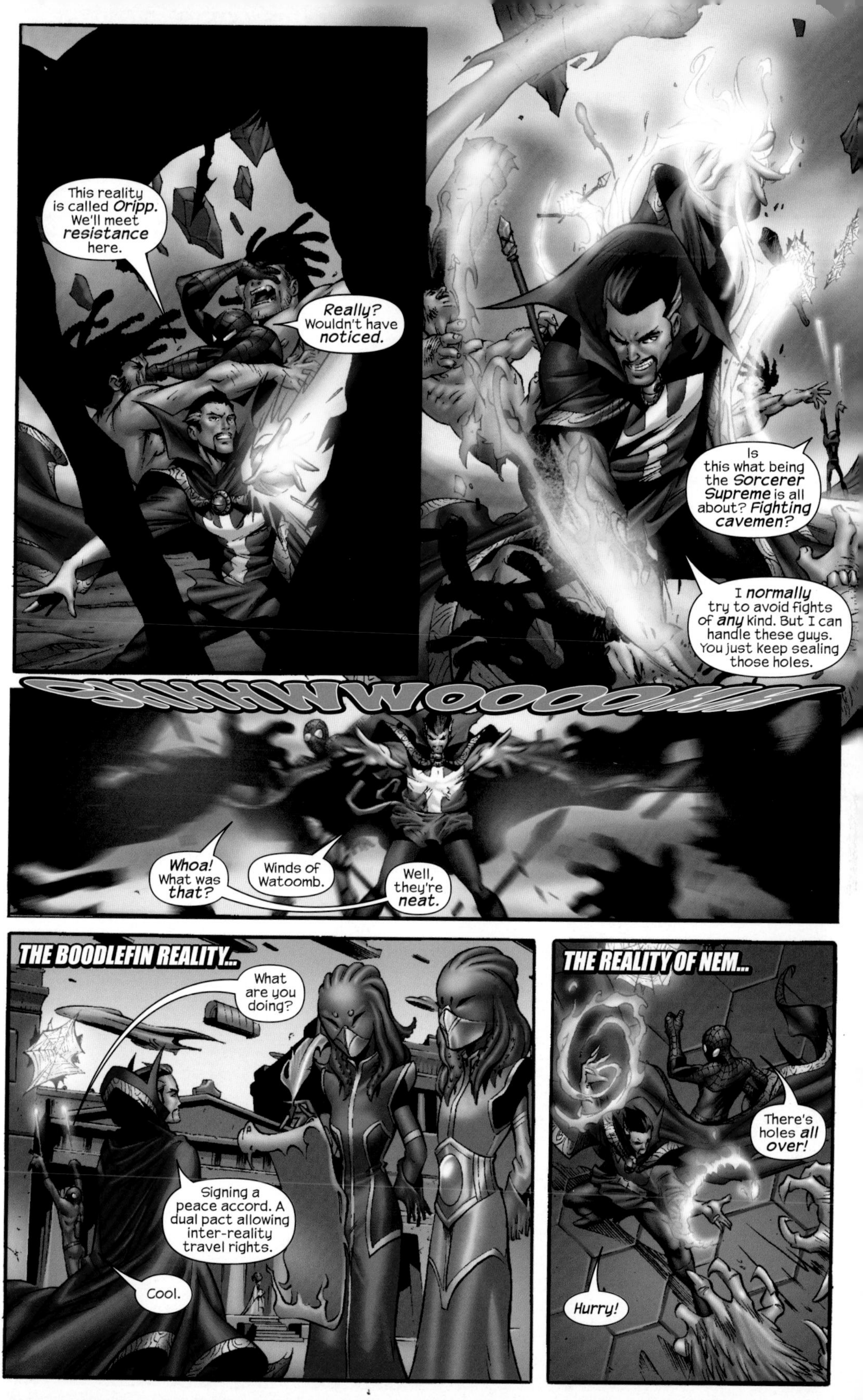

This reality is called Oripp. We'll meet resistance here.
Really? Wouldn't have noticed.
Is this what being the Sorcerer Supreme is all about? Fighting cavemen?
I normally try to avoid fights of any kind. But I can handle these guys. You just keep sealing those holes.
SHHHWOOOOMM!
Whoa! What was that?
Winds of Watoomb.
Well, they're neat.
THE BOODLEFIN REALITY...
What are you doing?
Signing a peace accord. A dual pact allowing inter-reality travel rights.
Cool.
THE REALITY OF NEM...
There's holes all over!
Hurry!

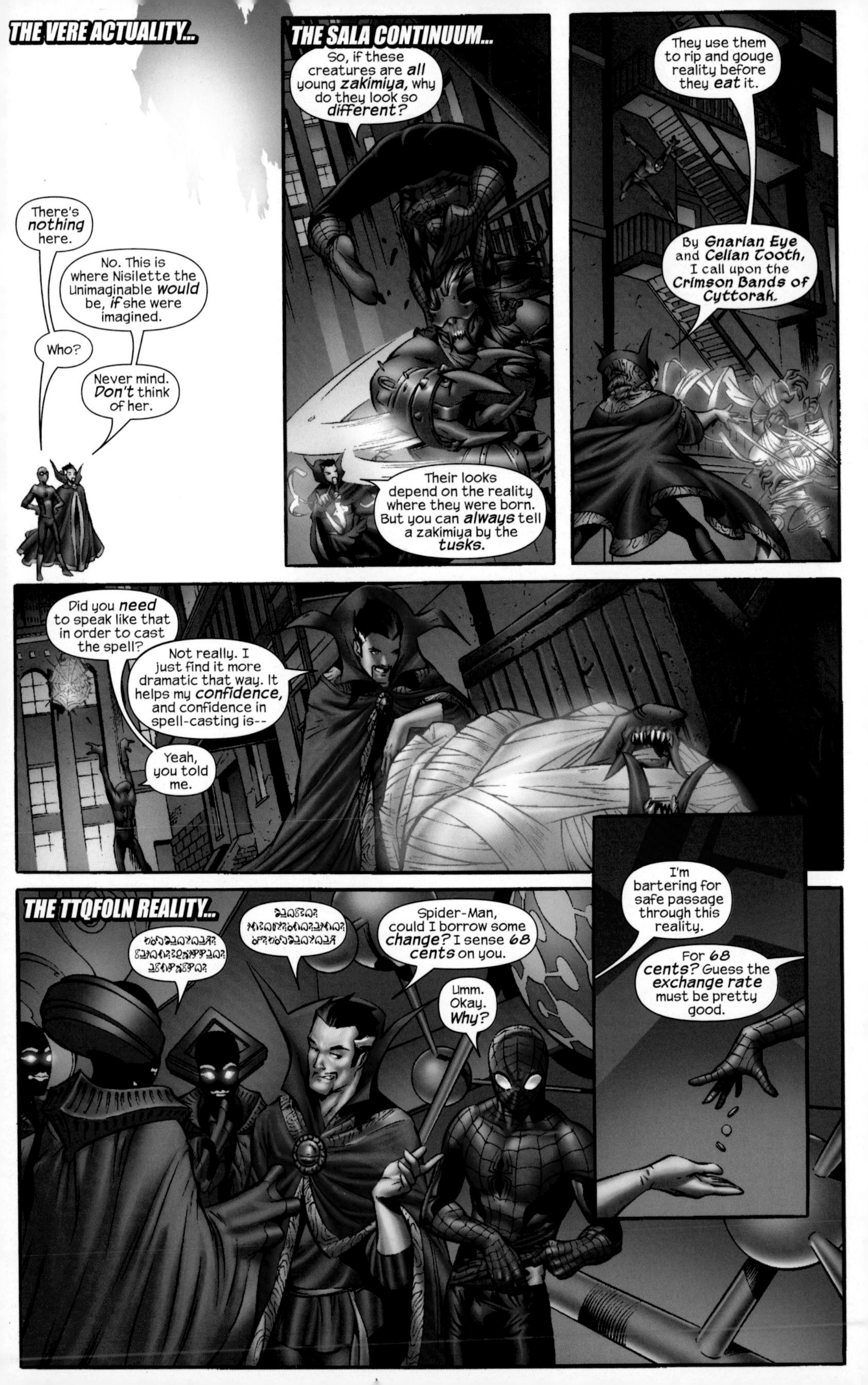

THE VERE ACTUALITY...
There's nothing here.
No. This is where Nisilette the Unimaginable would be, if she were imagined.
Who?
Never mind. Don't think of her.
THE SALA CONTINUUM...
So, if these creatures are all young zakimiya, why do they look so different?
Their looks depend on the reality where they were born. But you can always tell a zakimiya by the tusks.
They use them to rip and gouge reality before they eat it.
By Gnarian Eye and Celian Tooth, I call upon the Crimson Bands of Cyttorak.
Did you need to speak like that in order to cast the spell?
Not really. I just find it more dramatic that way. It helps my confidence, and confidence in spell-casting is--
Yeah, you told me.
THE TTQFOLN REALITY...
Spider-Man, could I borrow some change? I sense 68 cents on you.
Umm. Okay. Why?
I'm bartering for safe passage through this reality.
For 68 cents? Guess the exchange rate must be pretty good.

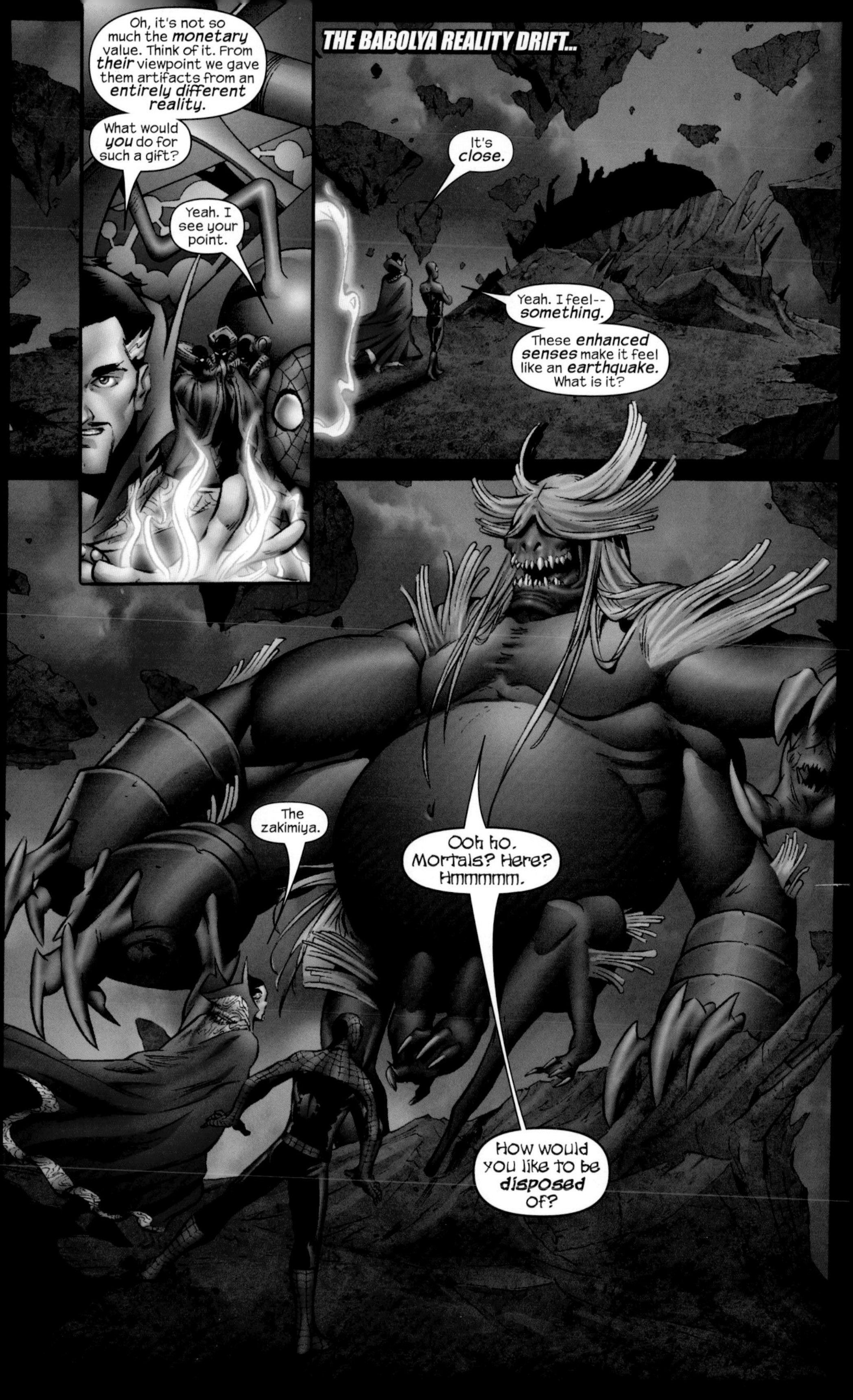
Oh, it's not so much the monetary value. Think of it. From their viewpoint we gave them artifacts from an entirely different reality.
What would you do for such a gift?
Yeah. I see your point.
THE BABOLYA REALITY DRIFT...
It's close.
Yeah. I feel-- something.
These enhanced senses make it feel like an earthquake. What is it?
The zakimiya.
Ooh ho. Mortals? Here? Hmmmmm.
How would you like to be disposed of?

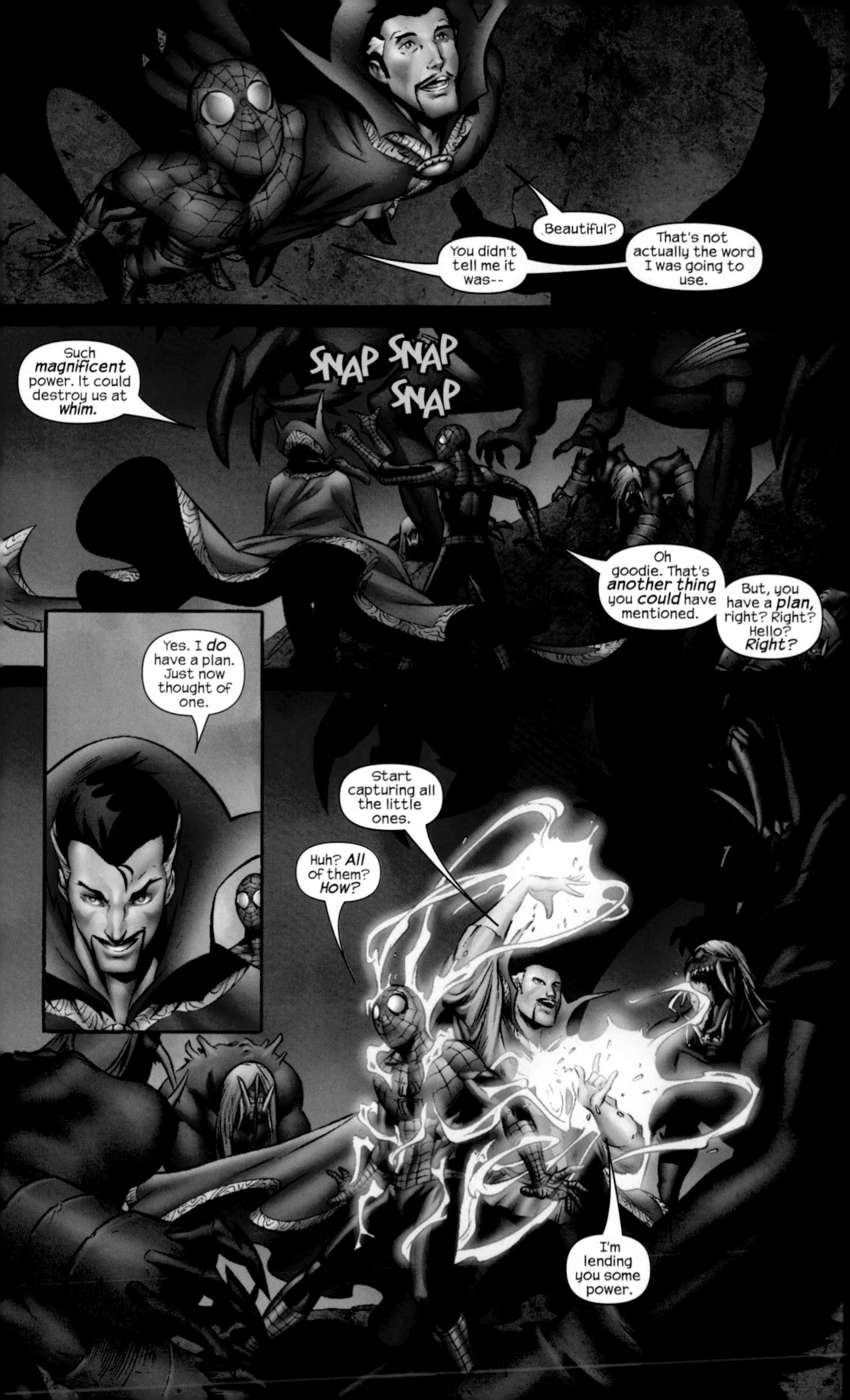
Beautiful?
You didn't tell me it was--
That's not actually the word I was going to use.
Such *magnificent* power. It could destroy us at *whim.*
SNAP SNAP SNAP
Oh goodie. That's *another thing* you *could* have mentioned.
But, you have a *plan,* right? Right? Hello? *Right?*
Yes. I *do* have a plan. Just now thought of one.
Start capturing all the little ones.
Huh? *All* of them? *HOW?*
I'm lending you some power.

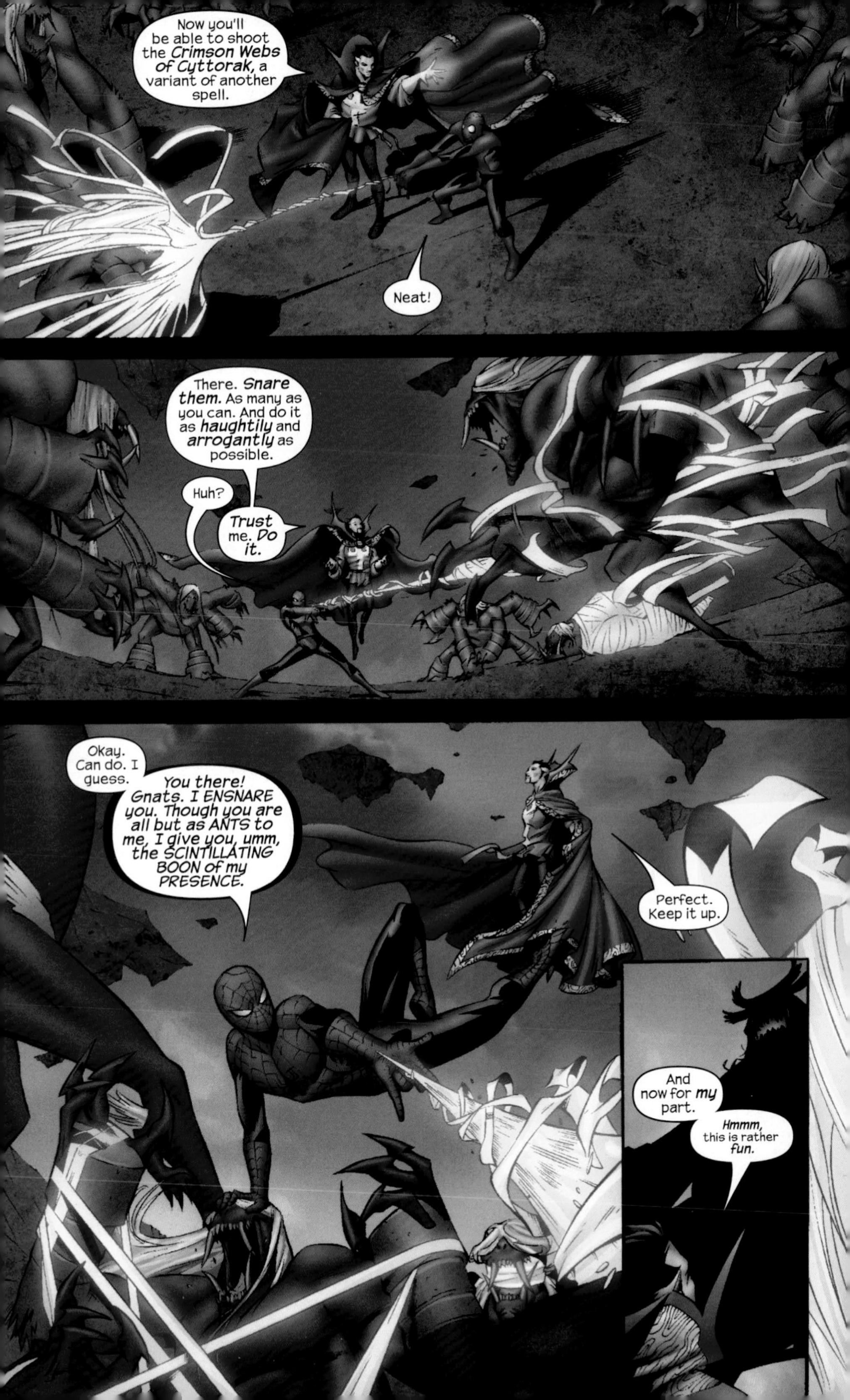
Now you'll be able to shoot the *Crimson Webs of Cyttorak,* a variant of another spell.
Neat!
There. *Snare them.* As many as you can. And do it as *haughtily* and *arrogantly* as possible.
Huh?
Trust me. Do it.
Okay. Can do. I guess.
You there! Gnats. I ENSNARE you. Though you are all but as ANTS to me, I give you, umm, the SCINTILLATING BOON of my PRESENCE.
Perfect. Keep it up.
And now for *my* part.
Hmmm, this is rather *fun.*

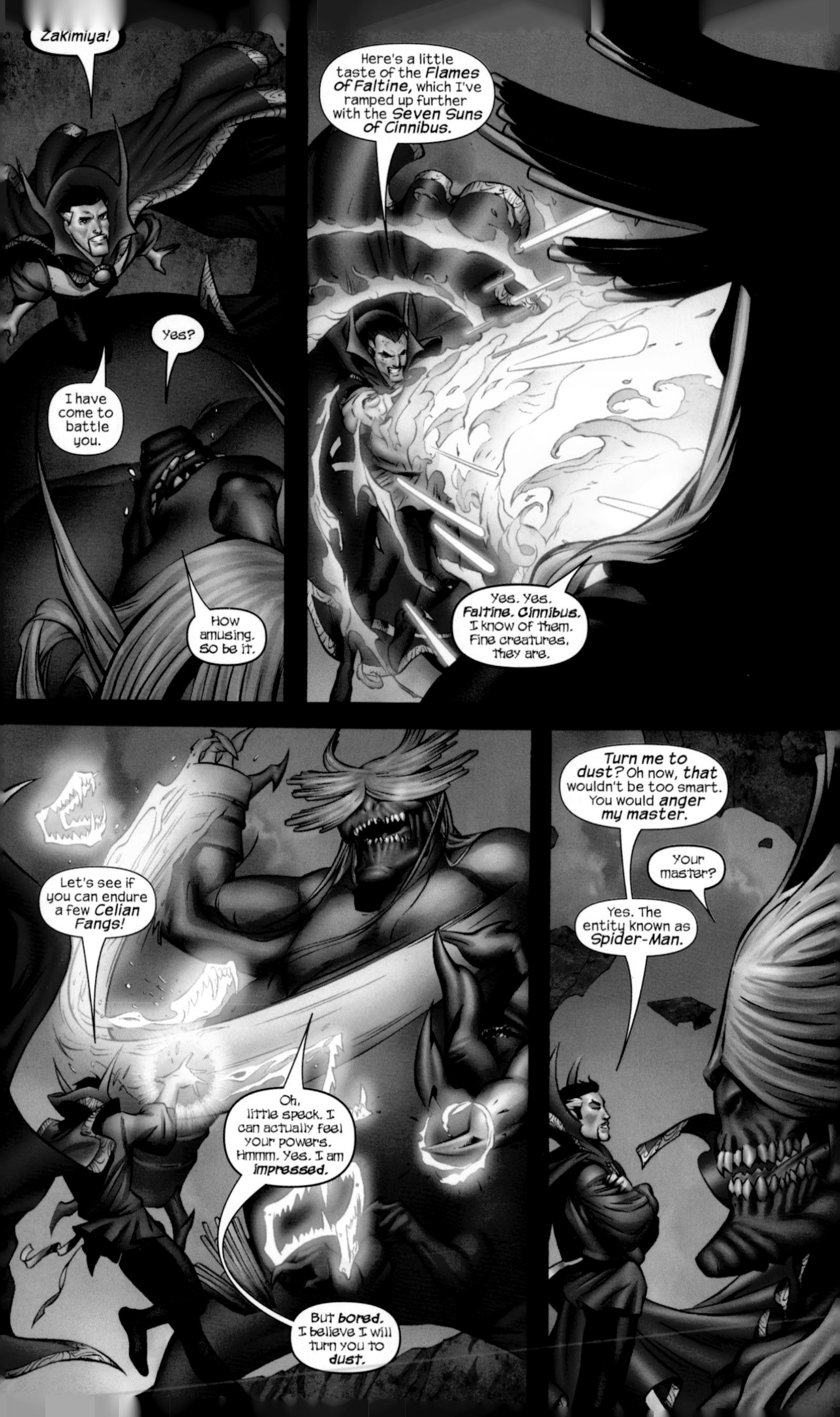
Zakimiya!
Yes?
I have come to battle you.
How amusing. So be it.
Here's a little taste of the Flames of Faltine, which I've ramped up further with the Seven Suns of Cinnibus.
Yes. Yes. Faltine. Cinnibus. I know of them. Fine creatures, they are.
Let's see if you can endure a few Celian Fangs!
Oh, little speck. I can actually feel your powers. Hmmm. Yes. I am impressed.
But bored. I believe I will turn you to dust.
Turn me to dust? Oh now, that wouldn't be too smart. You would anger my master.
Your master?
Yes. The entity known as Spider-Man.

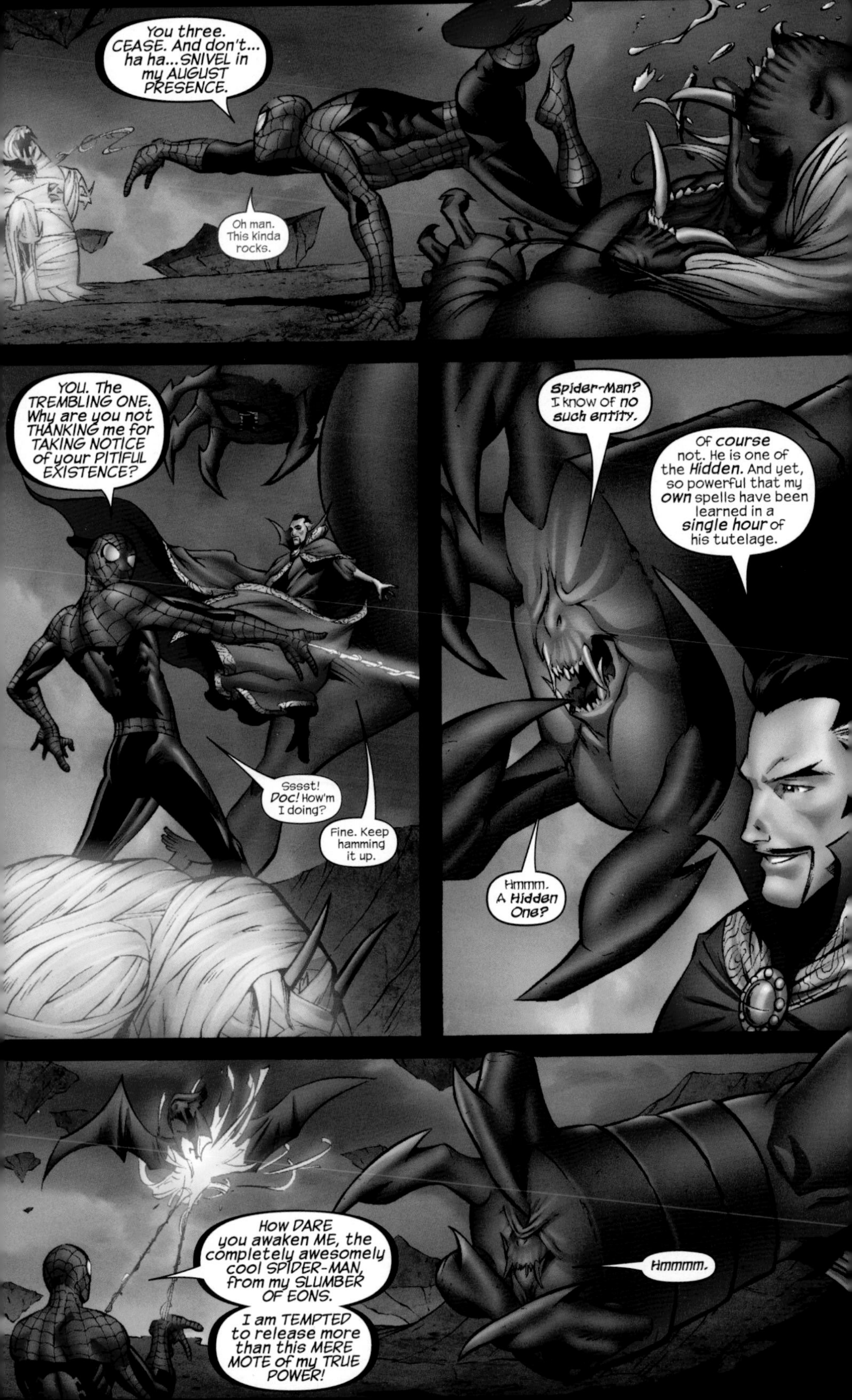
You three. CEASE. And don't... ha ha...SNIVEL in my AUGUST PRESENCE.
Oh man. This kinda rocks.
YOU. The TREMBLING ONE. Why are you not THANKING me for TAKING NOTICE of your PITIFUL EXISTENCE?
Sssst! Doc! How'm I doing?
Fine. Keep hamming it up.
Spider-Man? I know of no such entity.
Of course not. He is one of the Hidden. And yet, so powerful that my own spells have been learned in a single hour of his tutelage.
Hmmm. A Hidden One?
HOW DARE you awaken ME, the completely awesomely cool SPIDER-MAN, from my SLUMBER OF EONS.
I am TEMPTED to release more than this MERE MOTE of my TRUE POWER!
Hmmmm.

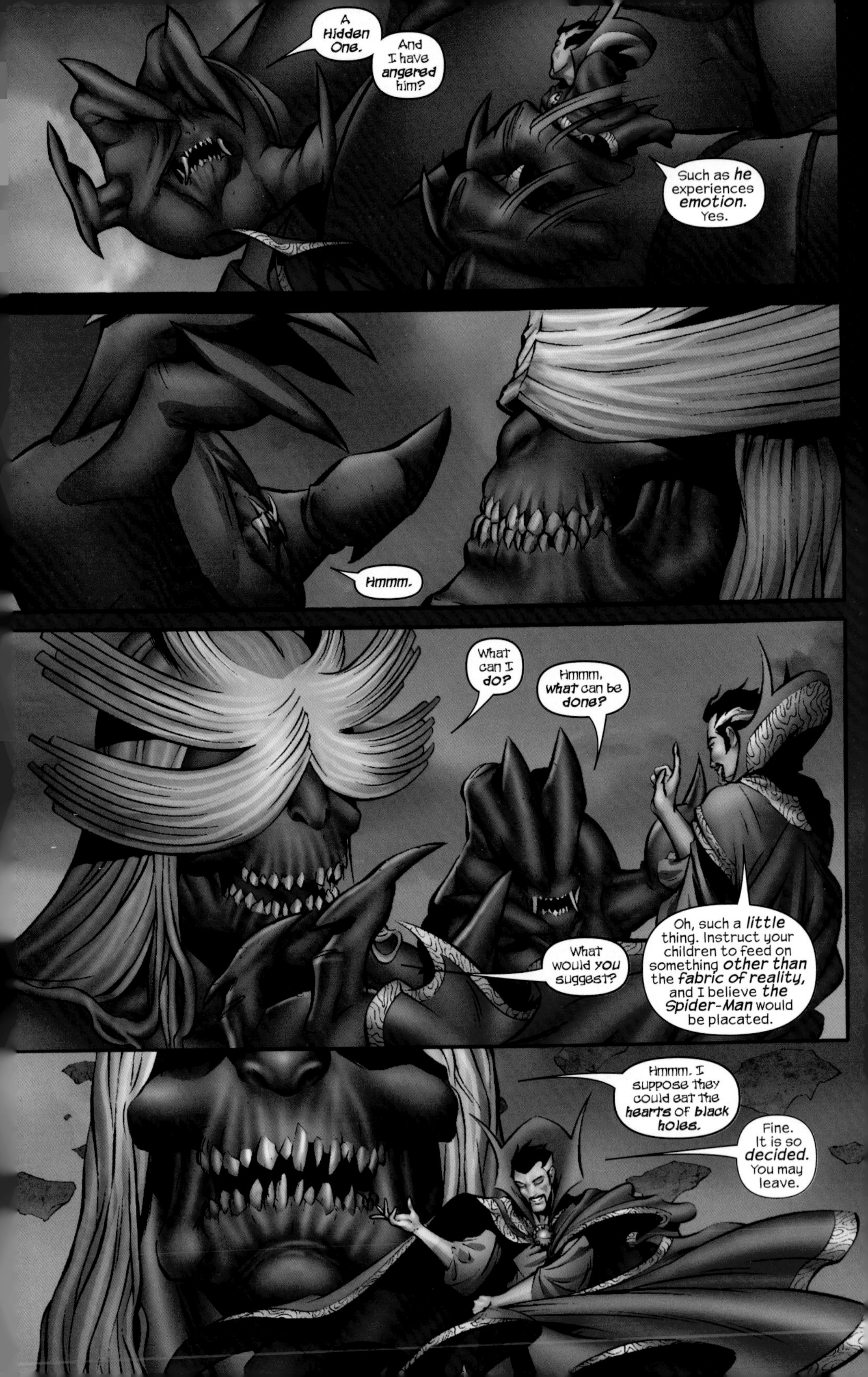
A Hidden One.
And I have angered him?
Such as he experiences emotion. Yes.
Hmmm.
What can I do?
Hmmm, what can be done?
Oh, such a little thing. Instruct your children to feed on something other than the fabric of reality, and I believe the Spider-Man would be placated.
What would you suggest?
Hmmm. I suppose they could eat the hearts of black holes.
Fine. It is so decided. You may leave.

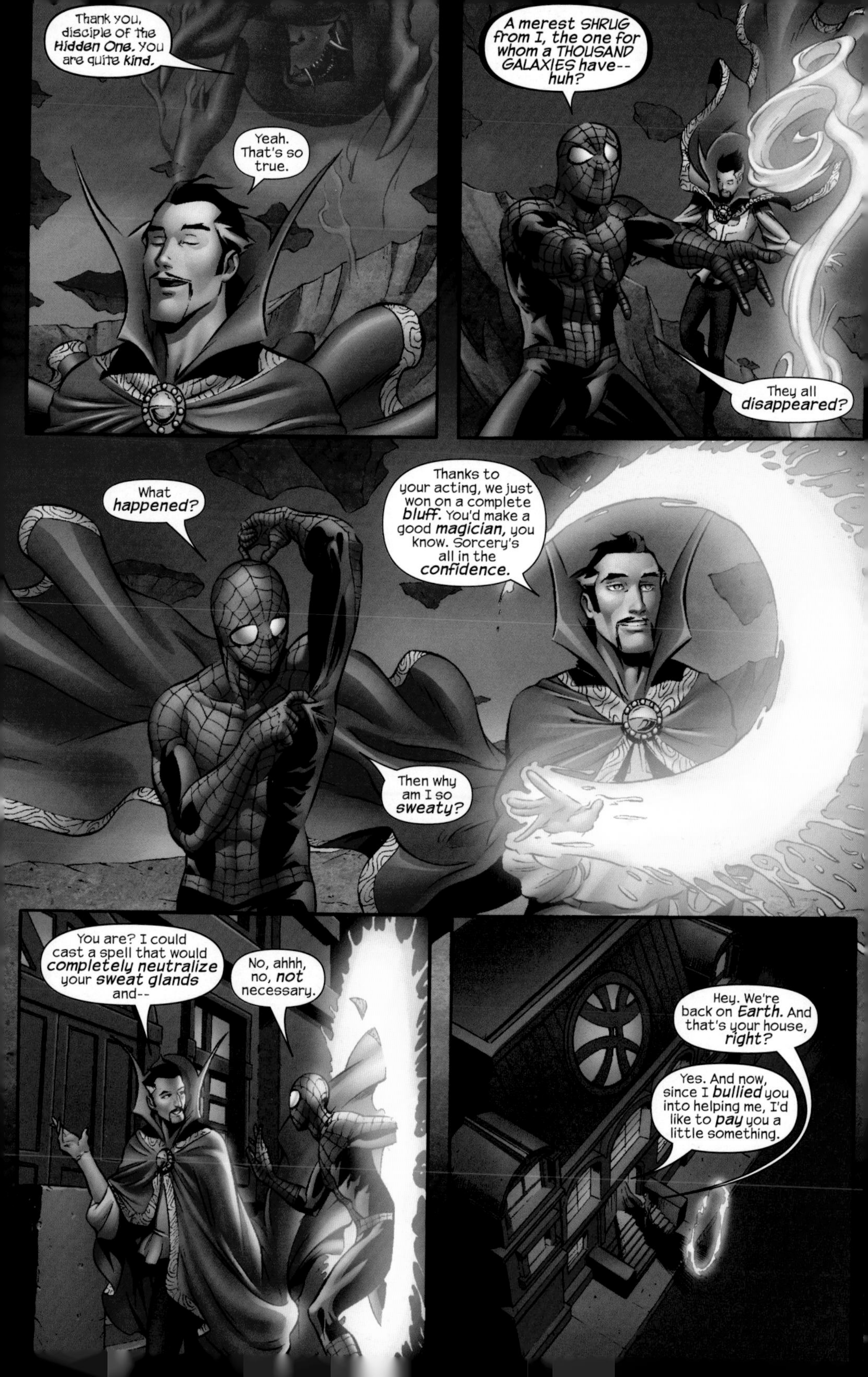
Thank you, disciple of the Hidden One. You are quite kind.
Yeah. That's so true.
A merest SHRUG from I, the one for whom a THOUSAND GALAXIES have-- huh?
They all disappeared?
What happened?
Thanks to your acting, we just won on a complete bluff. You'd make a good magician, you know. Sorcery's all in the confidence.
Then why am I so sweaty?
You are? I could cast a spell that would completely neutralize your sweat glands and--
No, ahhh, no, not necessary.
Hey. We're back on Earth. And that's your house, right?
Yes. And now, since I bullied you into helping me, I'd like to pay you a little something.

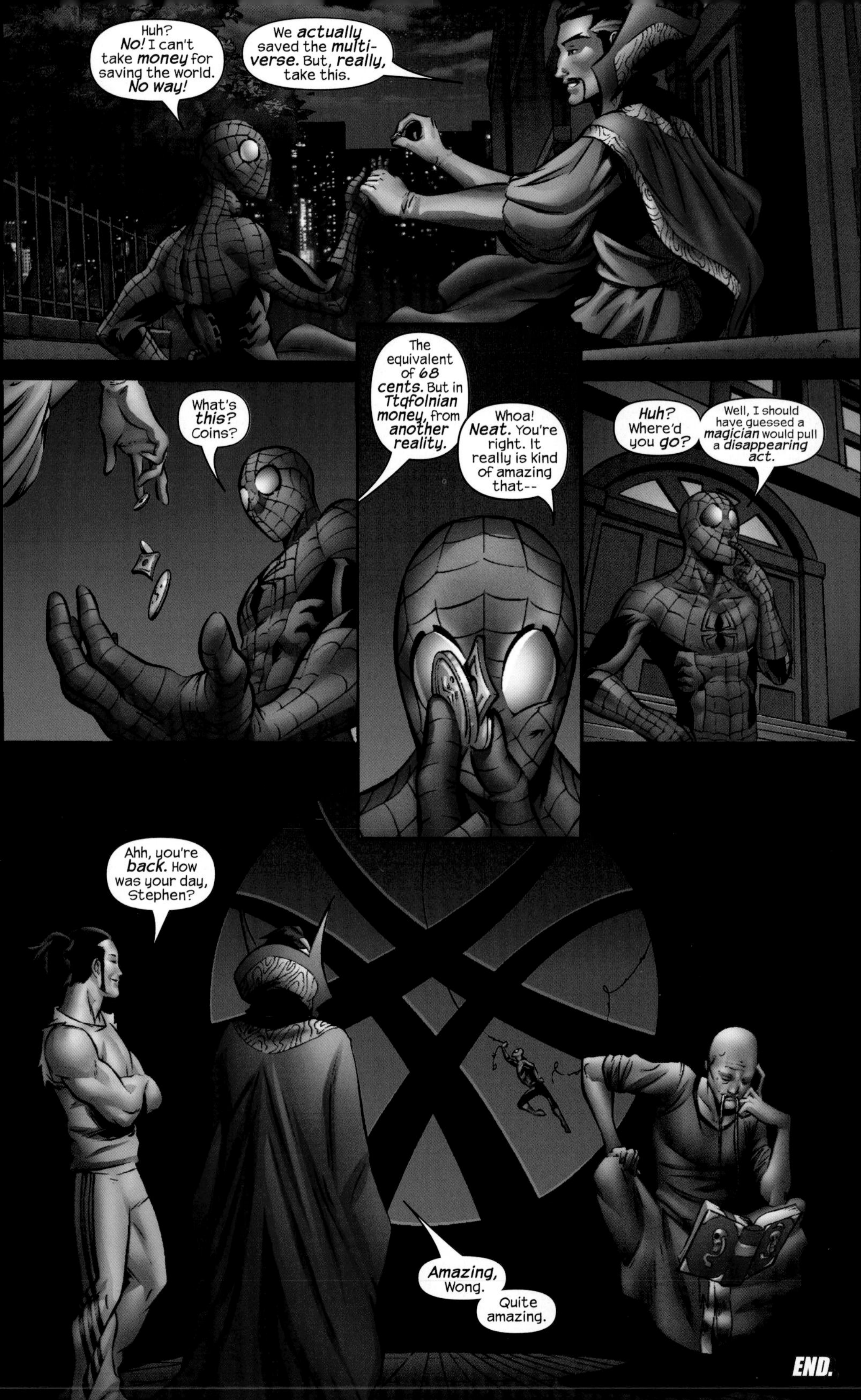
Huh? No! I can't take money for saving the world. No way!
We actually saved the multi-verse. But, really, take this.
What's this? Coins?
The equivalent of 68 cents. But in Ttqfolnian money, from another reality.
Whoa! Neat. You're right. It really is kind of amazing that--
Huh? Where'd you go?
Well, I should have guessed a magician would pull a disappearing act.
Ahh, you're back. How was your day, Stephen?
Amazing, Wong.
Quite amazing.
END.

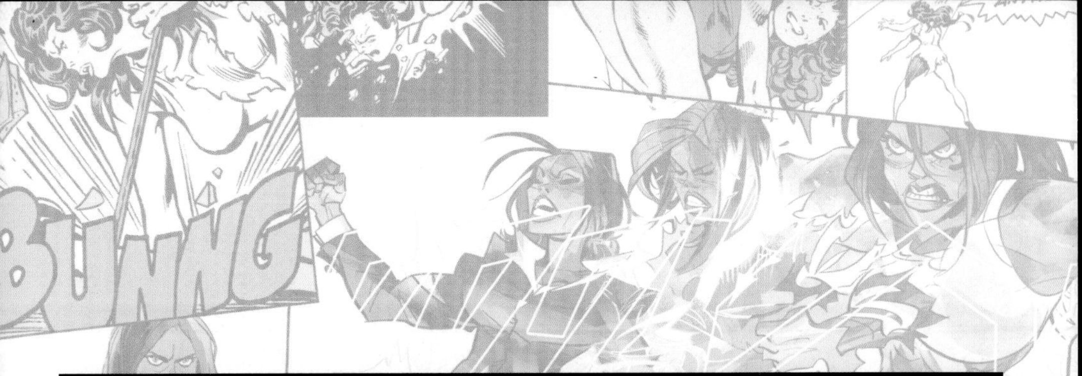
BUNNG

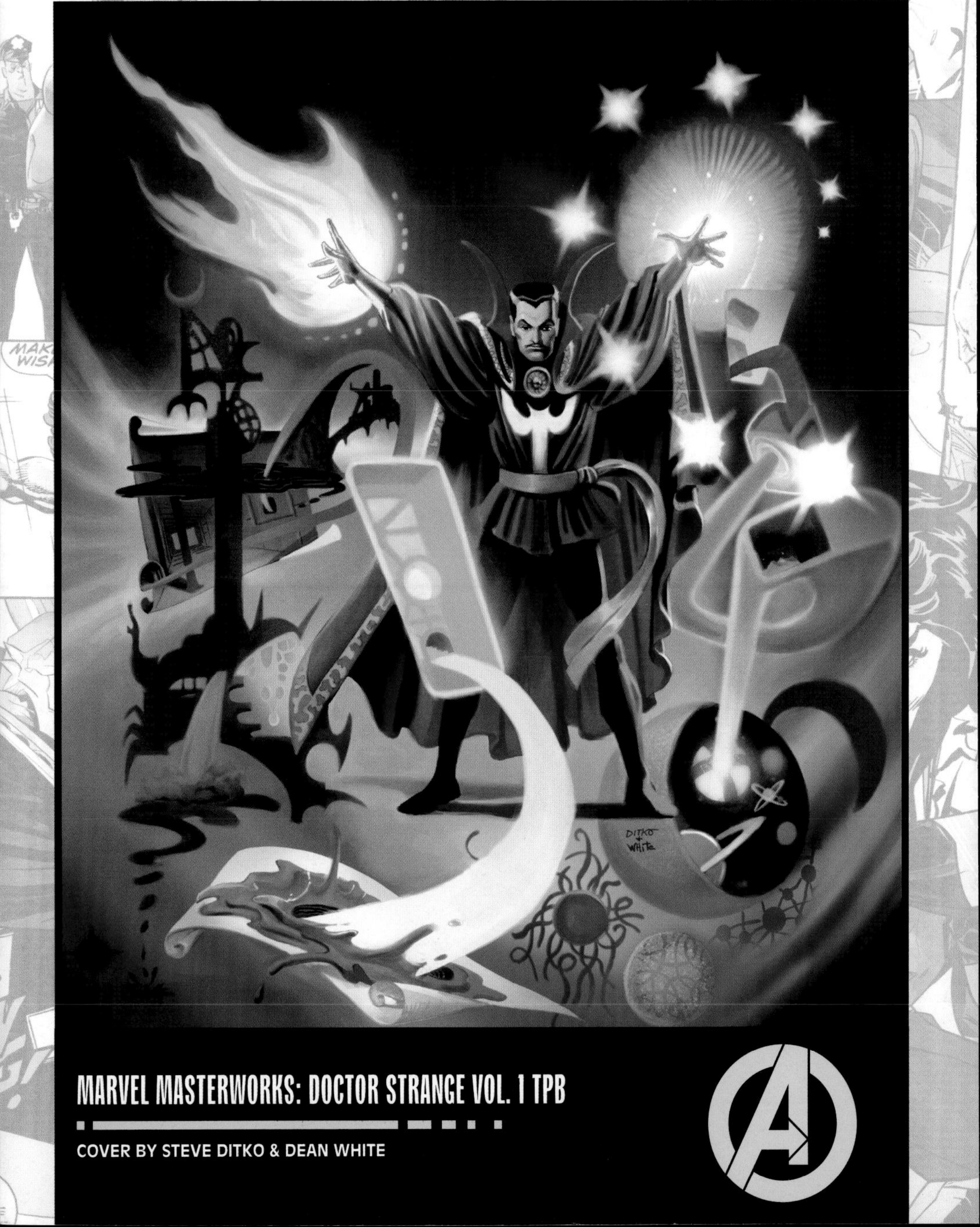
DITKO + WHITE

MARVEL MASTERWORKS: DOCTOR STRANGE VOL. 1 TPB

COVER BY STEVE DITKO & DEAN WHITE

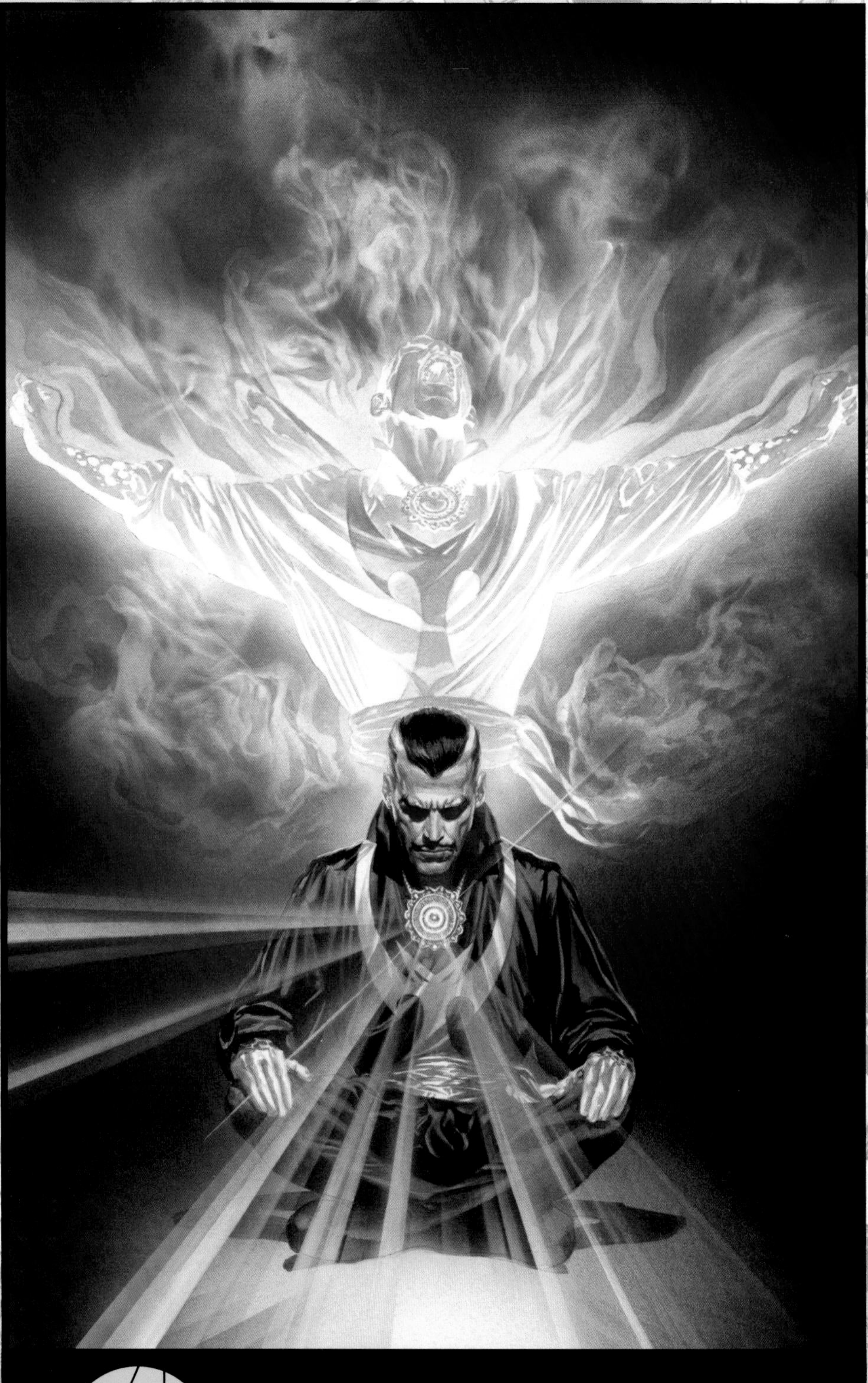

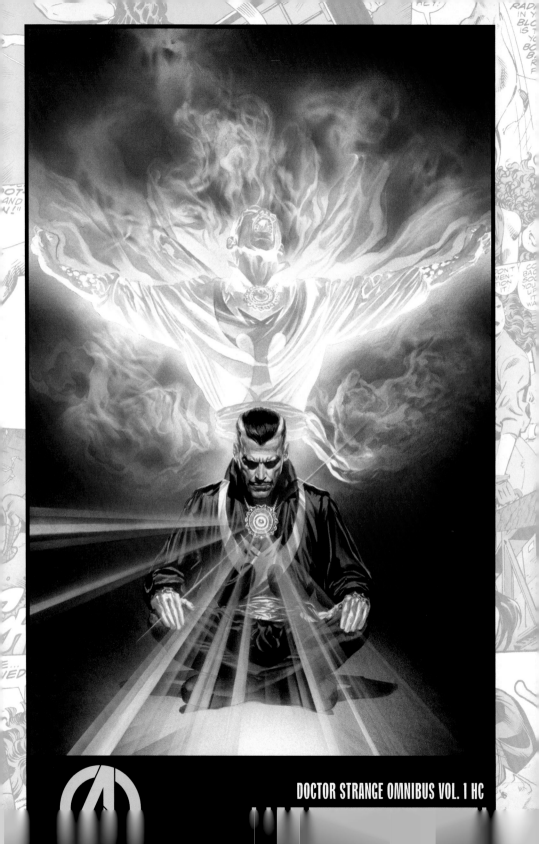

DOCTOR STRANGE OMNIBUS VOL. 1 HC

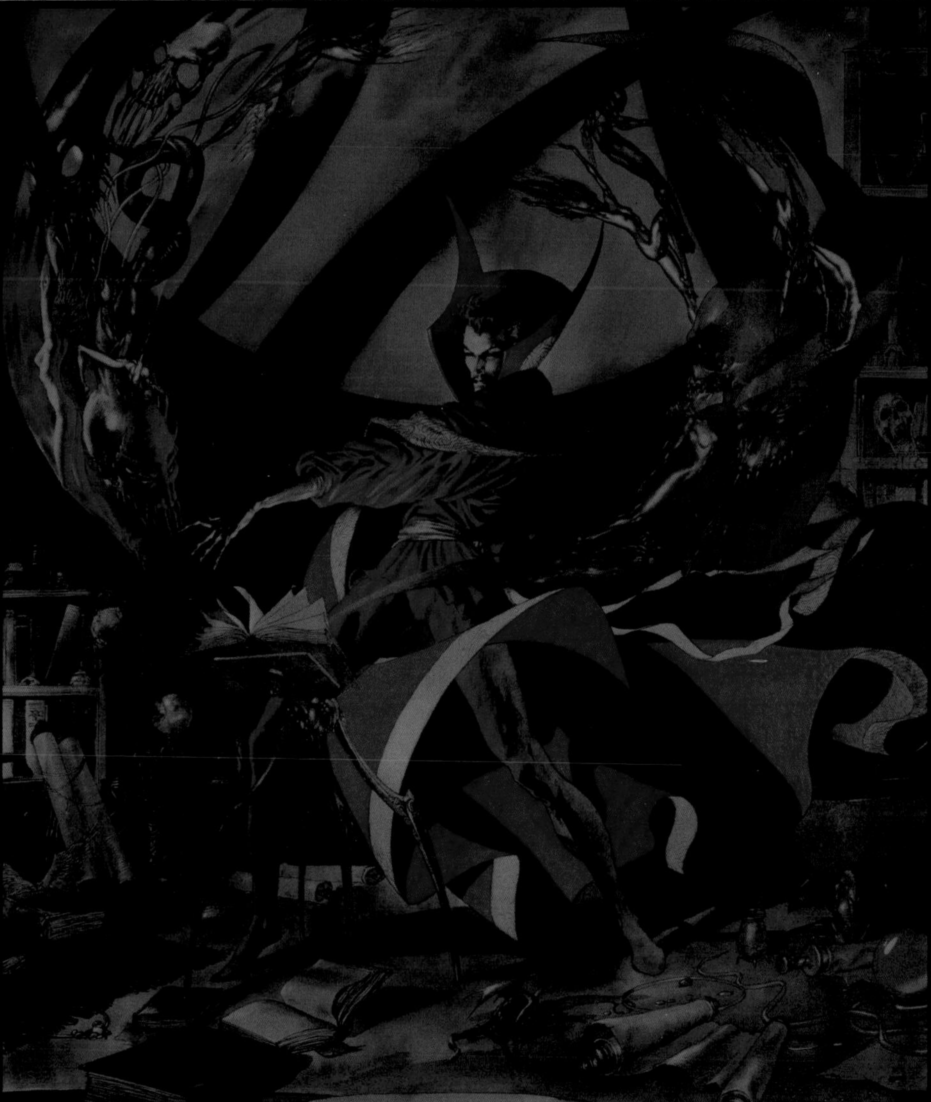

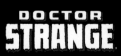

DOCTOR STRANGE

1983 DOCTOR STRANGE POSTER

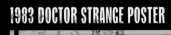

BY KEVIN NOWLAN